Crooked Hearts

Patricia Gaffney

Crooked Hearts

WHEELER
PUBLISHING, INC.
ROCKLAND, MA

★ AN AMERICAN COMPANY ★

Published in large print by arrangement with Signet, an imprint of New American Library, a division of Penguin Putnam Inc., in the United States and Canada.

Wheeler Large Print Book Series.

Set in 16 pt Plantin.

Library of Congress Cataloging-in-Publication Data

Gaffney, Patricia.
   Crooked hearts / Patricia Gaffney.
      p. (large print) cm.(Wheeler large print book series)
   ISBN 1-58724-198-6 (hardcover)
   1. San Francisco (Calif.)—Fiction. 2. Impostors and imposture—
Fiction. 3. Large type books. I. Title. II. Series.

[PS3557.A296 C76 2002]
813'.54—dc21
                                               2002016718
                                                   CIP

For Jon, who still makes me laugh.
Sometimes intentionally.

1

Don't steal; thou'lt never thus compete
Successfully in business. Cheat.
                              —Ambrose Bierce

Sister Mary Augustine's little silver derringer was cutting into her thigh.

And it was hot, hot, hot in the airless stagecoach, which needed new springs. The cowboy
sprawled unconscious on the opposite seat
smelled like an old drunk rolled up in an
alley. How could the blind man sitting next
to him stand the stench? They said blindness sharpened the other four senses; if that
was true, the poor man must be half dead
from the fumes.

A cold beer and a pillow for her behind, that's
what Sister Augustine needed. Stirring furtively
on the leather seat, she tried to shift the derringer without fidgeting; it must've slid to
the back of her garter, because it felt like she
was sitting on it. "Be careful with that thing,"
Henry had warned her; "don't shoot off anything important." If she could just get her hand
under her thigh for two unobserved seconds,
she could move the damn gun. The blind
man sure wouldn't see her, and neither would

the smelly cowboy. She slanted a glance at the fourth passenger, seated next to her. He'd been dozing a few minutes ago.

But now he was lying in wait to catch her eye. "Sister," he greeted her, with a big, friendly smile. "Mighty hot for early June, wouldn't you say?"

After three weeks on the road, Sister Augustine recognized his type, because there was one on every stage, train, or ferry boat she'd taken since leaving Santa Rosa: he was the one who wanted to talk. A whole hour of silence had gone by since the stage had left Monterey, so this one must've decided he'd waited long enough.

"Indeed I would, sir," she answered smartly. "But remember the psalm: 'With the Lord as thy keeper, the sun shall not smite thee by day, nor the moon by night.' " Sometimes, she'd found, you could head a talker off at the pass by going straight at him with the Bible.

"So true. And don't forget Matthew: 'He maketh the sun rise on the evil and the good, and sendeth rain on the just and the unjust.' "

She nodded in devout agreement, stumped.

"George Sweeney's my name," he said, sticking out his hand.

She gave it her nun's shake, limp but fervent, and murmured, "Sister Mary Augustine," while inside she rejoiced. Sweeney—Irish—*Catholic*!

"A real pleasure, Sister. What's your order?" He eyed her plain black habit curiously.

"The Blessed Sisters of Hope. We're a

2

small community; our mother house is in Humboldt County."

"You're a long way from home, then." He leaned toward her and jerked his head sideways at the snoring cowboy. "Is it safe for you to be traveling all by yourself?"

"I don't, normally," she confided. "But my companion, Sister Sebastian, fell ill in Santa Barbara and wasn't able to go on. After we determined that she would recover without assistance, we decided that I should continue our work alone. We believe it's God's will, and we have absolute faith that He'll protect me."

He sat back admiringly. "Well, I don't doubt it for a second." He'd taken off his derby hat in her honor, a generous gesture since it had been hiding his bald spot. He was short and plump, and his little feet in their shiny patent-leather shoes barely touched the floor. She'd pegged him earlier as a traveling salesman because of all the luggage he was carrying, stacked over their heads on top of the Wells Fargo stagecoach. Now, studying him more closely, she decided he looked too flush for a drummer, and too clean. All the better. And praise the Lord, his name was Sweeney, which automatically doubled her estimate of his donation potential.

"What is your work, Sister, if you don't mind my asking?"

Easier and easier. She clasped her hands to her breast with subdued fervor. "I'm on a fund-raising mission for our order, sir. We desperately need money for one of our hospitals

3

in Africa, because it's in danger of having to close—which would be a catastrophe. We've been collecting donations from the dioceses throughout the state for several weeks now. I'll be going home after one last effort in San Francisco. After that, I hope to be sent to Africa myself, where my true skills can be put to better use."

"Your true skills?"

"As a hospice nurse. But, of course, our sacred mandate is to accept God's will without question, and for now it seems His will is for me to toil for the little children in this humble way."

"It's a children's hospital?"

"Orphaned children. With incurable diseases."

Mr. Sweeney's pudgy cheeks pinkened with emotion; she thought there might even be a gleam of moisture in his pale blue eyes. She glanced away, but in her peripheral vision she saw him fumbling for his purse. "I only wish this was more," he whispered discreetly, pressing a bill into her hand.

"Bless you. Oh, bless you, Mr. Sweeney!" she whispered back. A tenner, she noted with satisfaction; exactly what she'd bet herself he would give. God, she was getting good at this. She slid the greenback into her black leather pocketbook to join the other bills and gold pieces she'd collected in the past three weeks: a little over four thousand dollars. Henry wouldn't tell her exactly how much they needed, but she was pretty sure it was more than that. Still, four thousand dollars was a hell of a start.

She glanced hopefully across the aisle at the blind man, wishing he'd feel a similar charitable tug on his own purse strings. She guessed he was awake, but it was hard to tell; his round, cobalt-blue spectacles were opaque and his eyes behind them were invisible. She'd been staring at him off and on for the past hour, feeling guilty about it but unable to stop, because his tragic good looks fascinated her. Had he always been blind, she wondered, or only since some terrible accident? How did he make his living? His black broadcloth suit was very fine, his gray silk necktie sedate and expensive. That was all to the good, but a man's shoes were the surest clue to the health of his finances, and in this case they gave Sister Augustine cause for concern. Run down at the heels and cracked across the insteps, they were the shoes of someone who was either rather poor or rather careless about his appearance, and neither trait seemed to characterize the handsome blind man. Or—distressing thought—they could be the shoes of a man who couldn't *see* his shoes. The idea made her sit back, ashamed of her rude, sneaky staring. The poor man! So young, so vital and strong. So good-looking.

He had beautiful hands, too. She'd noticed them right away, clasped around the carved handle of the walking stick that jutted upright between his knees. Long, clean, sensitive fingers, artistically bony, and short white nails.

No rings. A priest's hands, or a sculptor's. She heartily wished one of them would start reaching for his wallet.

Nuns didn't initiate conversations with male strangers, so she was relieved when Mr. Sweeney, who had been darting secret looks at the blind man with almost as much vulgar curiosity as she had, said straight out, "How do you do, sir?" He took care to aim his voice precisely, so there wouldn't be any doubt as to which man he was addressing—not that the reeking cowboy was in any condition to misunderstand.

"How do you do," the blind man replied readily. He had an English accent—the last thing she'd have expected. "It's Mr. Sweeney, isn't it? I'm Edward Cordoba." He held his hand out toward Sweeney, and they shook. "Sister," he murmured, with a small, respectful bow in her direction.

"Mr. Cordoba," she murmured back. He was *Spanish*?

You could count on Sweeney not to beat around the bush. "Do you come from Monterey, sir?" he asked directly.

"A little south of there. My father owns a ranchero in the valley."

Sweeney made a knowing, impressed sound.

"One of the smaller ones," Mr. Cordoba added with a deprecating half-smile. "Only a few hundred thousand acres."

His voice was low-pitched and intimate, like a cello playing a slow waltz. It took her a few seconds to register the last sentence. When

6

she did, she had to remind herself to close her mouth, which had fallen open.

"Cordoba," Mr. Sweeney said slowly. "That's a Spanish name, isn't it? And yet I could swear your accent's British."

Mr. Cordoba smiled. He had extremely white teeth. "You've got a good ear, sir. My mother is English. I studied in that country for a number of years."

"Aha—Oxford?"

"Cambridge."

"Well, well! You're a scholar, then?"

His smile withered. He turned his face toward the window. "I was once."

She and Mr. Sweeney exchanged looks of chagrin. There was an awkward pause.

"What takes you to San Francisco, sir?" Sweeney asked, rallying. "If you don't mind my asking."

"Not at all. I've enrolled in a school there to learn to read Braille."

"Is that so? How does that work, now? I've heard of it, but never really understood how they do it."

"It's a system of raised dots, each representing a letter of the alphabet; one feels them with one's fingertips." He dropped his chin, as if he were contemplating his long, elegant hands. Sister Augustine contemplated them with him. They looked capable of reading raised dots to her.

"Then you haven't been blind for long, I take it?"

She stared at Sweeney, confounded by the

bluntness of his prying—although he hadn't asked anything she wasn't dying to know herself.

"Long?" Edward Cordoba repeated, very low. A minute passed; she thought that was all the answer he was going to give, and began trying to decipher it. But then he said, "No, I don't suppose you'd call it long. To me, though, it seems...a lifetime."

The painful pause lasted much longer this time. She wanted to comfort him somehow, but she couldn't think how; touching him was out of the question and, under the circumstances, a sympathetic facial expression wouldn't accomplish anything. So she only said quietly, "I'm so terribly sorry, Mr. Cordoba."

He made a graceful gesture with his hands, at once dismissing her concern and thanking her for it. "And now, sir," he said with strained heartiness, "it's your turn—tell us your traveling story. Where are you from and what takes you to San Francisco?"

"Ah!" Clearly Mr. Sweeney had been hoping somebody would ask him that question. "Well, you might say I'm on a mission too, like Sister Mary Augustine, although mine's a much more secular mission. I'm the assistant curator for Chinese antiquities at the Museum of East Asian Art in St. Louis. For the past six weeks, I've been touring your fine state with a small collection of objets d'art." He turned to Sister, politely including her in his answer. "It's a cultural swap, you might say, a reciprocal traveling art exchange between our museum and the Museum of Art in San Francisco."

She murmured politely.

"Do you mean you're traveling with the exhibit now?" Mr. Cordoba asked. "It's actually on board the coach?"

"Yes, indeed. I'm on the last leg of the trip—I'm *not* sorry to say, delightful though it's been—and starting the day after tomorrow, San Francisco will host the final display."

"It must be a very *small* exhibit."

"Select," he corrected dryly. "And if I may say so, very, very special."

"I imagine the pieces must be quite valuable," Sister Augustine mused.

"Priceless. Beyond price."

She touched a thoughtful finger to her chin. "What sort of pieces are they?" she asked, and Mr. Sweeney began to talk about Ming funerary sculpture and Tang jade, screen paintings and water colors and enameled ceramics. "How fascinating," she exclaimed when he finally wound down. "Would you happen to have a catalog?"

"In my trunk, yes. I'll dig one out for you when we stop for the night, shall I?"

"That's very kind of you." She happened to glance over at Mr. Cordoba just then. He had a thoughtful finger on his chin, too.

Talk grew more general. The unconscious cowboy snored himself awake and glared around at them blearily. A few minutes later the coach rocked to a stop, and they heard the driver jump down into the road.

"Sorry, folks," he called up, "but there's going to be a little delay."

"What's the trouble, Mr. Willis?" Sweeney asked, opening his door.

"Half a split pine tree up ahead, blocking the road. Looks like lightning hit it. Can't go around, on account of a gully on one side and rocks on the other." He pushed his hat back to scratch his head. "It ain't a big pine, I think two-three of us could heft it outa the way pretty easy."

"I'd be glad to assist," the curator offered immediately. Sister Augustine eyed his pudgy frame with misgivings; something about him, maybe his short arms, reminded her of a frog.

Everybody looked at the cowboy. His hangover was palpable, drifting through the air of the hot, motionless coach like a low-lying fog. At the end of a long minute, Mr. Cordoba said gravely, "I'd be happy to lend any assistance I could, but I'm afraid I might be more of a hindrance than a help." More silence. "Still, if you think—"

The cowboy cut him off with a word that started out as "Shhhhh," and tapered off to bitter muttering. "Come on," he snarled, and stepped gingerly out of the coach.

"Won't be a minute," chirped Mr. Sweeney, with more confidence than Sister Augustine thought the circumstances warranted, and jumped out after him.

Alone with Mr. Cordoba, she took the opportunity to unbutton the front of her heavy linen habit, inside of which she was

10

sweating like a stevedore, and fan herself between her breasts. It was impossible not to stare at him while she did so, even though she could see nothing in his bright blue spectacles except her own black-robed, pale-faced reflection. She liked his scholar's forehead and his long beak of a nose, his romantic mouth. She was dying to know what color his eyes were. Brown, probably, because his hair was nearly black. A Spanish father and an English mother, he'd said. And all those acres of ranchero down in Monterey. The very thought caused even more honest Christian charity to flower in Sister Augustine's bosom.

"Warm day," he mentioned.

"It certainly is," she agreed, fanning away.

He turned his head, showing her his hawkish profile, and inhaled a deep breath. "Poppies?"

She looked out the window, following his blind gaze. "Yes, there's a bank of them just beyond a grove of oak trees, about thirty feet away."

His mouth curved in a wistful smile. She guessed that behind the glasses his eyes were closed, and that he was seeing the bright flowers in his memory. She tried to think of something consoling to say, but nothing came to mind. How *awful* to be blind. If she couldn't see, and someone told her it was God's will, she'd probably curse them.

"I'd like to make a donation to your orphans' hospital, Sister. A sizable one."

"God bless you, Mr. Cordoba," she intoned

sedately. With a silent whoop, she lifted her arms and shook both fists in the air like a victorious prizefighter.

He coughed behind his hand. "Do you have a card, a pledge form or something I could fill out?"

"I think I do. I believe I could find one." She opened her pocketbook and thumbed through the pledge cards in her stack. She had about eighty left.

"Perhaps you could give one to me when we stop for the night."

"Certainly."

"I might have to ask you to assist me, Sister, in filling in the amount and so forth."

Holy Mother of God. She squeezed her eyes shut tight and forced her voice down a whole octave from where it wanted to be. "It would be my pleasure, Mr. Cordoba."

When the euphoria abated, she remembered that the gun was still chafing her thigh. She cocked her head out the window to make sure the coast was clear. Moving slowly to lessen the sound of rustling cloth, she hitched up her bulky skirts and pulled up the right leg of her drawers. The derringer had slid to the back of her garter; she shifted it to the side where it belonged, wishing she could peel off her thick, hot, ugly black stockings. There was a reddening, gun barrel-shaped indentation on the back of her thigh that hurt; she massaged it with both hands, smiling happily at Mr. Cordoba all the while.

Gravel crunched outside. She barely got

her habit down and her face in order before Sweeney and the cowboy pulled open the doors on either side of the coach and climbed in. The driver cracked his whip, and they were off.

She liked the Saratoga Hotel. It was small, clean, and a cut above what she was used to lately. Everybody let her register first, out of respect for her station. She was glad, because all she could think about was getting naked, cool, and clean, in that order. Even so, she made herself hang back at the clerk's desk after she signed in, pretending to admire a photograph of the proprietor's children, while she waited to hear the clerk tell Mr. Sweeney his room number. Seventeen. About four doors down from hers, then. How convenient.

Her small second-floor room had all the basics, plus unstained wallpaper and a clean rug that reached to all four walls. She threw her suitcase on the wide bed, not bothering to unpack first. "God is great, God is good," she muttered as she shucked off habit and veil, rosary and crucifix, shoes, stockings, chemise and drawers. At least nuns didn't wear corsets, praise the Lord and pass the butter. She'd have a real bath later, in the communal bathroom at the end of the hall, but for now the pitcher and basin on the washstand would be heavenly.

She shook her hair down, letting it fall over her shoulders, because it didn't matter if it got wet—she'd just stuff it all up again in the headpiece when she got dressed for dinner. She pressed the cool, dripping towel to her face and neck, letting water run over her shoulders and down her breasts in rivulets. "Yes, Lord. Glory be and hallelujah." She caught her eye in the mirror over the washstand. "No offense," she muttered superstitiously, then smiled. How could God take offense at that face? *An angel,* Henry called her. *They'll turn their pockets inside out for that face.*

A dull scraping noise outside in the hall made her pause, thoughtfully rubbing the wet washcloth under one arm. The sound was coming closer, starting and stopping, scraping and tapping. Outside the door now. While she was trying to remember if she'd locked it, the handle turned and the door swung wide open.

"Mr. Cordoba!" She yelped it, but somehow managed not to scream.

"Oh, I say—I do beg your pardon. Is that you, Sister?" Urbane, unperturbed, he stood in the doorway, gently sweeping a three-foot arc of air in front of him with his cane. "I could've sworn I counted the doors correctly. The clerk said the third on the right, I thought, but perhaps I missed one. I wonder—would you mind helping me?"

She felt like Eve immediately after the Fall, huddled in a frantic crouch, one forearm and one spread palm inadequately covering the vital places. "I, um, I'm not quite dressed."

Finally he began to look embarrassed. Instead of leaving, though, he turned around and closed the gaping door with his foot—his arms were burdened with two bulky suitcases as well as his cane. "I'm terribly sorry," he said again with his wonderful English accent. "This must be frightfully awkward for you."

She made an ambiguous whimpering noise.

"But of course, you must know—there's no need for you to be embarrassed." He said this with such wistfulness, such sad, terrible bravery, that Sister Augustine's heart twisted.

And she saw his point. Feeling extremely foolish, she let her hands fall and stood up straight. "You're quite right," she agreed, trying to sound brisk. "I wasn't thinking." She stopped just short of apologizing for being insensitive.

He couldn't see her, she knew that—but it was a disconcerting feeling all the same, standing buck naked in front of a strange man. For once she felt glad of his opaque glasses, because looking into his eyes right now, blind or not, would've unnerved her completely. She took a few mincing steps toward the bed. "Excuse me..."

"Oh. Beg pardon." He backed out of the way, and she passed within a foot of him, as goose bumps erupted everywhere.

"Didn't they call a porter for you?" she said over her shoulder, rooting around in her clothes for her dressing gown.

"I told them I could manage on my own. Sometimes..." He trailed off ruefully.

Where the hell was her damn robe? "Sometimes?" she prompted, giving up and emptying everything out on the bed.

"Sometimes I'm afraid I let my pride get in the way of my good judgment," he confessed with quiet dignity.

She made a half turn toward him as she struggled into her pink chenille dressing gown. "Humility is a virtue," she said primly. "Perhaps I shouldn't say so, but I've always thought it one of the lesser ones."

He had a very rakish smile for a scholar. "It's kind of you to say so, Sister. Especially under the circumstances."

She yanked the belt tight at her waist and faced him. "Here, let me take one of those." He gave her his smaller bag, which he'd wedged under his right arm. "What room did the clerk say?"

"Fourteen." They moved out into the hall. She started to take his elbow, but he said, "This way is a little easier for me," shrugging off her hand and instead taking hold of her upper arm in a firm clasp.

"Oh, I see." They negotiated the narrow hall without incident, he moving along smoothly half a step behind her. "Here we are. Fourteen's two up from mine; you miscounted, that's all."

"I must apologize again."

"Not at all. Have you got the key? Here, let me help—"

"You're very kind, but I prefer to do it myself."

The slight edge to his voice made her stand back and watch in helpless sympathy while he set his suitcase on the floor, hooked his cane over his left arm, fumbled the room key out of his pocket and into the lock, and finally got the door open.

His room was identical to hers, she saw at a glance. "I'm putting your bag on this chair, is that all right?" He nodded, but didn't move from the doorway. She suspected he was waiting for her to leave, so he could grope his way around without a witness.

She went to him, took his hand, and squeezed it around her elbow again. "From here, the bed is straight ahead and one"—she gave his arm a gentle tug to get him going—"two, three, four—four and a half steps away. This is a little bedside table." She pressed his palm down on the wooden top. "There's an oil lamp right... here. Although"—she felt her face getting warm—"I guess you probably won't be needing it. Then, if you turn around in a half-circle and walk along the side of the bed—one, two, three, four, five, *stop*—this is the bureau."

They walked off the steps to the window, the wardrobe, and the wash stand, and then she suggested they go out into the hall and locate the bathroom.

"I'll find that on my own, thanks."

"I don't mind, really, and while we're—"

"Sister," he said in his cello voice. "You're very kind; you're an angel of mercy. But I'm aware that you're wearing a rather thin garment, a dressing gown of some sort, I suppose. If we were observed, it might be...a bit awkward for you."

With an odd but distinct feeling of regret,

17

she released Mr. Cordoba's arm and stepped away. "Of course. Thank you, I didn't think of that." She wandered toward the door. "I'll leave you, then, if you're sure you're all right?"

"Quite."

"Good. Well, then." She opened the door.

"Sister?"

"Yes?"

"I wonder—would it be against convent rules for you to join me for dinner this evening?"

She felt her smile blossoming into a big, wide grin. After a thoughtful pause, she said slowly, "Noo-o-o, I can't think of any rule that would break. Actually, we're quite a forward-thinking order, Mr. Cordoba."

She'd forgotten that he had a devastating grin of his own. "I'm delighted to hear that about the Blessed Sisters of Misery."

"Hope," she corrected gently.

"Hope. Shall I knock on your door in about an hour, then?"

"I look forward to it."

He made her a low, formal bow, which she found utterly charming, and she danced out of his room on silent bare feet.

"It happened exactly thirteen months ago. I was on a ship sailing from Liverpool to San Francisco. I'd finally finished my studies, and I was on my way home. My wedding was three weeks away."

"Your wedding?" She laid her fork down and

reached for her wineglass. Château Ducru-Beaucaillou, 1879, Mr. Cordoba had told her. The dining room at the Saratoga served only domestic Chablis; when he'd heard that, he'd gone back to his room and gotten a bottle of his own. He was a connoisseur.

"Isabella and I had been engaged for four years. She was waiting for me."

"What happened?" she asked when he paused.

"A fire broke out belowdecks on the last night. Everyone panicked. I tried to help, first with putting out the fire, then leading frightened passengers out of their smoky cabins to safety. It went on for hours. I shouldn't have done it— it was foolhardy, not brave—but I went back down for one last try, even though I knew I was exhausted. I remember hearing a terrible cracking sound over my head. And then..." He grimaced, and passed a hand across his brow. "A burning beam split, fell, and struck me on the back of the head."

"Merciful heavens!"

"The ship landed safely, thank God. Eventually I recovered from the blow, but my sight was gone. Every doctor I've been to since the accident says my condition is permanent." His hollow voice prompted her to throw caution away and take his hand, which was lying open on the tablecloth. He stroked his thumb across her knuckles and managed a wan smile. "Isabella was so brave, so plucky— she insisted we go ahead with the wedding. But of course I couldn't allow that. Couldn't let her tie herself to a hopeless cripple for the rest of her life."

"Oh, but if you loved her—"

"All the more reason. And it was the right thing to do. A few weeks ago, I received word that—that she'd married another."

She blinked rapidly. "Oh, Mr. Cordoba—"

"Edward."

"Edward. I'm so terribly sorry."

"Thank you." They shared a soft, deeply sympathetic moment. Then, "But enough about me," he said gruffly, releasing her hand. "Tell me about yourself, Sister. When did you first think you might have a religious vocation? Or—I beg your pardon, is that too personal a question?"

"No, of course not. I was twelve."

"Ah, so young. Your family must have been very devout."

"Not really. As a matter of fact, they were opposed to my taking the veil. But once I'd seen the miracle, there was nothing anyone could do to stop me."

"The miracle?"

She regarded him speculatively. "Are you a Catholic, Mr. Cordoba?"

"Edward."

"Edward."

"I used to be," he said, with suppressed bitterness. She started to say something sad and shocked, but he cut her off with Spanish imperiousness. "Tell me about the miracle, Sister."

"All right." She took a bracing sip of wine.

"I grew up near Santa Barbara. Like you, we lived on a big ranchero, and there were few neighbors nearby. None, in fact. And so my best friend was Maria Elena, the little daughter of one of our ranch hands. We were closer than sisters, completely inseparable. That is, until she developed the stigmata."

"The what?"

Her eyebrows went up. "I thought you were Catholic."

"Oh, the *stigmata*—I didn't hear you."

"It happened the first time during Mass in our little private chapel on the ranch. Right after communion, Maria's spotless white dress was suddenly covered with blood."

"Good Lord. What was wrong with her?"

She frowned at him. "I'm telling you, she had the *stigmata*. There were holes in her hands and feet, and one in her side, and little marks on her forehead from the thorns."

He set his glass down carefully. "And this was a *miracle*?"

"But of course! All the marks went away and the bleeding disappeared by the end of Mass. It *was* a miracle, a sign from our Lord of His eternal presence, and a reminder of how much He suffered for our sins."

He nodded slowly. "And that's why you became a nun?"

"Indirectly."

"I suppose Maria Elena became one, too."

She heaved a tragic sigh. "No. Not long after that she fell gravely ill—an ague of the lungs, the doctor said. Her suffering was terrible, but she never complained. Already she was a saint."

"Ah."

"The night she died, she asked me with her last gasping breath to take the veil in her stead. Of course, I said yes. She'd been in great pain and emotional turmoil before that, and my promise set her free; she died at peace. I've never regretted my decision."

Visibly moved, Mr. Cordoba reached for the wine bottle. His knuckles struck the neck; she had to grab it before it toppled over. "Sorry," he muttered. "I'm still so clumsy."

"You're not," she chided, refilling his glass. "I think you're remarkably graceful."

"It's very charitable of you to say so." He cocked his head, listening. "Aren't you pouring any for yourself?"

"I really shouldn't."

"You're not allowed to have wine?" He sounded shocked.

"We are, but only in moderation."

"Well, then. What could be more moderate than two glasses?"

She allowed a thoughtful pause before giving in. "Well, all right. But just a little." Tilting her glass to inhibit the glug-glug sound, she filled it to the top.

She told him more about her lonely childhood on the ranchero, and discovered that his had been remarkably similar. Time flew.

"It's been wonderful for me, speaking about these things," he said when dinner was over. "You're an exceptionally easy person to talk to, Sister "Thank you. I could say the same of you—Edward."

"I hope you don't mind if I tell you this." He paused uncertainly. "You have a very soothing voice."

She rested her chin on her hand. "I do?"

"I've become a bit of an expert on voices. And yours is most intriguing."

"It is?"

"Very. It's rather low-pitched for a woman, and the tone has a certain...how shall I say..." He touched his beautiful fingertips together thoughtfully. "A certain confidential quality. Soft, and yet cool and clear. At the same time, there's something innocent, almost childlike about the s's. And, rather incongruously, an unexpected gruffness that creeps into every seventh or eighth vowel."

She stared at him, utterly spellbound, wondering again what color his poor blind eyes were. His thick, dark hair gleamed bronze in the candlelight, curling ever so slightly on the ends. He'd shaved before dinner, she could tell, not only by the smoothness of his lean cheeks but also by the subtle odor of...bay rum? She leaned a little closer to identify the scent. Something about the set of his lips told her he knew how near she was. And what nice lips they were, wide and hard-looking and on the thin side, a shade paler than his tanned skin. Did he open them when he kissed? Some men did, she knew for a fact. Or did he start out closed and then open them, nudging yours apart at the same time...?

23

"Here you are!" Mr. Sweeney loomed over them suddenly like a hunter's moon. "What luck! I stretched out for a little nap, and woke up in the pitch-dark two hours later. Thought I'd have to eat supper all by myself. You don't mind if I join you, do you?"

Oh, not at all, they assured him—and if she wasn't imagining it, Mr. Cordoba's heartiness sounded just as false as hers. But she should be glad of the interruption, she realized after a sober moment's reflection, because it was Mr. Sweeney she was supposed to be cozying up to, not Mr. Cordoba. Mr. Sweeney was the one touring with a fortune in priceless art objects.

Sometimes she amazed herself. With what casualness, what brilliant, seamless tact did she bring the conversation around to security precautions for his traveling art exhibit. Did he entrust it at night—she was finally able to ask outright, having laid the groundwork so skillfully—to whatever Wells Fargo relay station he'd reached at day's end? Or did he feel it was more secure under each individual hotel's safekeeping?

"Neither," he scoffed, beaming smugly. "My own theft-prevention measures are far superior to any of theirs."

"Really?"

"Oh, yes. For one thing, the collection is hardly ever out of my sight, and I'm a firm believer in the superiority of one's own surveillance over the less self-interested vigilance of others."

"But aren't you afraid of being burgled in the middle of the night?"

He laughed indulgently, showing a mouthful of gold-filled molars. "I'd like to see somebody try."

"You're armed," she guessed. Well, then, that was that.

"Better—I travel with a suitcase full of special door and window locks, all custom-made. They're stronger and much more foolproof than anything Wells Fargo's got, not to mention a hotel safe. My room's virtually impregnable, Sister."

"Custom-made?" she probed, looking suitably amazed.

"That's right, by a master locksmith. They cost the museum a fortune, but it's worth it for the peace of mind."

That's all he would say, and for the life of her she couldn't think of a way to ask him what kind of locks they were; unless it came from a locksmith, no amount of tact could make that question sound natural.

Too bad. Henry called her an amateur because she wouldn't practice, but she *might* have had a go at Mr. Sweeney's special door locks if she'd known what kind they were. She could pick a rim cylinder in her sleep, but the newer pin tumblers still gave her trouble.

Oh, well. In truth, she felt more relieved than disappointed. As much as she needed the money, outright theft wasn't really in her line. Too crude. Did Henry even know a fence? He'd never mentioned it. And as far as she knew, he'd never actually burgled anything. The circumstances might be dire, but she expected he'd advise her now, if he were here, to find the money they needed in the old-fashioned way: by swindling it.

After dinner, Mr. Sweeney said he wanted to go outside and stretch his legs for a bit, so they said good night to him in the lobby, and Mr. Cordoba—Edward—walked her to her room. Outside the door, they both hesitated, and she wondered if he might be feeling as reluctant as she was to end the evening so early. Inviting him in was out of the question, of course. But...what if she weren't wearing a nun's habit? Hmm? What if they were just two anonymous travelers, alone and free, marooned for the night in a Saratoga hotel? The possibilities made her heart race; she felt her cheeks flush, and made a face at herself—which, fortunately, he couldn't see. Rule number one, Henry had decreed years ago, was never to let personal feelings muck things up when you were on a job. Until now, it had been an easy rule to follow. The fact that she was even *tempted* to break it must mean she'd drunk one glass too many of Château whatchamacallit.

After a long, interesting pause, Edward turned his face away from her slightly and said with the grave, tentative courtesy she found so endearing, "May I tell you something? It's of a rather personal nature. I wouldn't wish to offend you."

"I'm sure you couldn't."

"It's only that you have a very distinctive...

bouquet. For me, it's as fascinating as the fragrance of a fine wine. Now that I've savored it, I'm quite sure I'll never forget it."

She was leaning back against the wall, and Edward, half a head taller, had one arm braced across the low door frame above her. She wasn't surprised that he could smell her *distinctive bouquet*; she could smell his, too. Definitely bay rum. "And what would you say is its essence?" she asked lightly, but secretly beguiled.

He put his thumb and forefinger together in a gesture that was somehow aesthetic, saintly, and sexy at the same time. "Its essence is not the same as its odor. It smells of good clean soap, scented with apricot or orange. Apricot, I think. But the essence of it...ah."

She waited, hardly breathing.

"The essence of it...is grace."

She inhaled sharply.

He slanted his chin toward her, listening intently; his black brows drew together. "What is it?"

"Grace," she breathed, on a long, unavoidable sigh. "That's—that was my name. Before I took my vows."

"Was it? How extraordinary."

His head was so close, she could see the faint pulse beating in his neck, under his left ear. She had an urge to run her fingertip down one of the long, intriguing clefts that bracketed his mouth on either side of his delicious-looking lips. She saw her own parted lips in the reflection of his blue glasses, and the calf-eyed look on her face finally restored her senses.

"Good night," she croaked. Even she could hear the unexpected gruffness in the vowels.

"Good night." But he didn't move, so she didn't either. "It's been a memorable evening. I thank you for sharing it with me."

"My pleasure." She'd become fixated on the shapes his mouth made when he spoke; she didn't realize he was holding out his hand. Until he lifted it a little, evidently thinking he'd aimed it off-center, and his fingertips grazed the underside of her left breast. She jumped.

A bewildered look crossed his features, quickly changing to worry. By now she'd have done anything to avoid embarrassing him. Squeezing back against the wall, so he wouldn't realize how little space he'd left between them, she got her hand up and slipped it into his. His long, strong fingers clasped hers for a second, then let go.

"Good night," they said again, in unison.

It wasn't until much later, waiting to fall asleep, that Sister Augustine thought of the pledge card for the dying orphans' hospital. She'd forgotten to give it to him. Much less help him fill in the amount.

2

Everything is funny, as long as
it's happening to somebody else.
                    —Will Rogers

It was all the baggage piled on top of the Wells
Fargo stagecoach that made Reuben decide,
in the half-block between Whitey's Why Not
Saloon and the Monterey stage depot, to go
blind.

The details of the game were foggy; at that
early stage all he saw was an opportunity.
Why blindness? Because he'd never tried it
before. When he was eight or nine, he'd faked
a club foot on the corner of Fourth Street and
Second Avenue for a lucrative two weeks,
but he hadn't run a distressing physical afflic-
tion since, and he figured he was overdue. Then
too, he already had the props on his person,
so to speak: the heavy malacca walking stick
he'd taken off Bridie McCall in the stud game
the night before, and the blue-tinted "readers"
he used when he went gambling, for spot-
ting phosphorescent ink on the backs of
marked cards.

And he'd been in a mellow, expansive frame
of mind, the kind that encouraged innovative
thinking, due to the fact that he was leaving
Monterey two thousand dollars richer than
when he'd arrived three days ago. True, he was

still a bit shy of the forty-five hundred he owed the Croakers, but at least now they wouldn't kill him. At least not immediately. He felt good and he wanted a challenge.

Besides, San Francisco was a long, dusty, two-day stage ride; what else did he have to do to amuse himself? Spontaneous buncos succeeded about as often as planned ones, he'd found. And if there was one thing in the wicked world Reuben Jones trusted, it was his own instincts.

But the lure had turned out to be a bust: the boxes and bags on top of the stage held Chinese art museum pieces, not the personal effects of some rich pigeon he could pluck somehow by faking a handicap. And the art objects might well be "priceless," as Mr. Sweeney claimed, but one of the things Reuben prided himself on was that he was no thief. He was a confidence artist.

Still, he couldn't say he regretted going blind. Not while he could gaze across the rocking stagecoach and speculate on the interesting question of which thigh Sister Augustine had her little .22 strapped to this morning.

It tickled him to think that that was one of the few things he *didn't* know about her, relatively speaking—relative to what Sweeney and the cowboy knew about her, anyway. Reuben knew, for instance, that she was at least five years younger than she looked in her nun's outfit; having seen her without it, he didn't figure her for a day over twenty-two or -three. He knew she had a veritable fountain of long, curly hair the color of old gold piled up under her wimple, or whatever that veil thing was called. He knew her coarse black stockings hid the prettiest legs he'd seen on any female except for Charing Cross, the filly who'd won the triple stake at Breezeway last year. And he knew what else was under her bulky, shapeless bag of a black habit: slim, womanly hips, a minute waist he could probably get his hands around, and breasts—big palmfuls at odds with the smallness of the rest of her, as proud and perky as a couple of high-nosed thoroughbreds in the winner's circle. He even knew what beat behind the luscious breasts: a larcenous heart.

But this morning he much preferred to reflect on Sister's outside, not her inside. She had a dimple on the cheek of her right buttock, he recalled fondly, a perfect round dent, like the imprint of a playful finger. The muscles in her mile-long thighs came and went in an extremely stimulating way when she leaned forward, and her pert little behind flexed like...like...

His agreeably lascivious thoughts tapered off. She was staring at him. No—she was staring at his hands. That wasn't good. Because he'd taken off his eyeglasses and was absentmindedly polishing the smudged lenses with his handkerchief. The look on her angel's face—sharp and arrested, the pretty blue eyes narrowing in speculation—told him the significance hadn't escaped her.

He dropped his chin and made his hands go

limp; a weary, twisted smile flickered at his lips. "Look what I'm doing," he murmured, as if to himself.

"What?" asked the little curator, who hadn't noticed anything.

"The uselessness of this habit—cleaning my spectacles. Catching myself at this would've been enough to cast me down in former days, when I was so close to—well." He stopped, too discreet to mention those sordid struggles with self-destruction. "Thank God I'm past that now, that...dreadful time. Sometimes I'm even able to laugh at myself." He laughed now, bitterly, as a demonstration, and put his glasses back on. Behind them, he rolled a hidden glance toward Sister Gus. Her face had gone soft with pity; there might even be a tear in her eye. He turned his head to gaze, apparently without seeing, at the Sierra snow peaks gliding by on the far horizon.

Last night, just for a minute, he'd thought of suggesting a partnership to Sister Gus. His better judgment had scotched the idea before it could grow, but he could feel it germinating again now at the corner of his mind. He'd worked with a woman once, years ago; Hazel Mayne, she'd called herself. Before it was over, she'd stolen everything he owned, including his clothes. Never again.

Too bad, in a way, because he liked Gus's style. He didn't hold it against her that she hadn't seen through his disguise; he was an expert, after all, a master, and far better sharps than she had been taken in by his flimflams. He thought of the way she'd led him around his room last night, counting off the steps to the window and the washstand. And just now she'd almost wept because she thought he was despondent. That's what he liked about her: the combination of bunco artist and bleeding heart. You didn't find that very often, especially in a woman.

The cowboy, whose name was Blalock and who seemed to have a drinking problem, nudged him in the ribs, startling him. "Snort?" he offered, waving a pint bottle under Reuben's nose.

"No, thank you," he declined fastidiously. Edward Cordoba's tastes were more refined, and in this case so were Reuben's. In fact, he'd been thinking of celebrating his windfall in Monterey when he got home by opening the 1880 Haut-Brion Graves. He might even share it with Mrs. Finney, his landlady, who would definitely feel like celebrating when she got her hands on the back rent he owed her. He smiled in mild anticipation, letting his eyes wander across the soothing spectacle of broad hills covered with blackberry vines and wild clematis, an old adobe ruin crumbling into black clay, clumps of poppy and lupine dotting the open spaces in a grove of low-branching oaks. The first gunshots seemed to go off in his ear, so loud and unexpected that his head smacked the ceiling when he jumped.

A hooded rider flashed past the window on horseback. Reuben pitched forward, meaning to flatten himself to the stagecoach floor for safety, but Sister's bony shoulder caught him a sharp one on the chin and she got there first. He sprawled on top of her, and flung his arms around her black-robed bottom, which was still perched on the edge of her seat. Beside them, Blalock spewed curses and Sweeney whimpered, "Oh, oh, oh," like an old lady discovering a copulating couple in a church pew.

More gunshots. The coach swerved; Reuben and the nun careened leftward, ramming their companions. The driver called out, "Whoa!" and with a neck-snapping jerk the coach halted, then rocked gently on its springs. Nobody moved.

A man's harsh voice ordered Willis, the driver, to get down with his hands in the air. There were scuffling sounds overhead, followed by a heavy thump on the ground as Willis obeyed. And then a smacking sound, a pained cry, and another thump, not as loud. Reuben didn't like the way things were going.

Somebody yanked open the door on his side. "Get down! All down, now!" A short, stocky man with a grain sack over his head waved a .38 in Reuben's face. He got down.

Sister Gus followed, then Sweeney. Blalock was last, and he had a mulish look on his coarse, whisker-stubbled face. "Go to blazes," he growled, hunched in the doorway, and Reuben's respect for him rose a notch. But it plummeted when Blalock flexed his knees and sprang at the man with the .38, who

34

pulled the trigger and plugged him in the shoulder. Blalock collapsed in the dirt.

Somebody screamed, and Reuben turned to the nun to console her. She looked pale but composed, and he realized Sweeney was the screamer. Let him console himself.

He counted three bandits, two on the ground and one still on his horse, all wearing sacks with eyeholes and all holding pistols. "Move," said the one with the .38, the short, squat one who resembled a fireplug. He waved his gun sideways, away from the stagecoach and toward a shallow gully flanking the road.

Sister Gus took Reuben's hand and squeezed it around her forearm; he looked at her in perplexity, then remembered. "Stay with me, Edward," she said in a voice that quivered only a little, and began to lead him in the direction Fireplug was indicating. Behind them, one of the other robbers climbed up on top of the stage and began to throw bags and boxes down to his cohort. When Sweeney saw that, he started whimpering again.

"Money, all your money, give now. Give!"

Fireplug started with Sister Gus, who was clutching her leather pocketbook to her bosom like a suckling infant. When she shook her head, he brought his gun up until the barrel touched the tip of her nose. Her fingers loosened on the case; she handed it over, whispering a few words that didn't sound to Reuben like the Hail Mary.

"Now you."

Sweeney was already reaching for his purse;

he shoved it at the bandit like a bomb that might go off any second.

"You!"

Reuben glared at the pint-sized robber. He had eight or nine inches on him, he reckoned, and maybe twenty pounds. What he lacked was a weapon. He hadn't forgotten that Blalock lay bleeding, possibly to death, about forty feet away. And something about the glitter of bright black eyes behind the feed sack cast doubts in his mind on Fireplug's emotional stability. Moving very slowly, he drew his wallet out of his breast pocket. So long to nineteen hundred dollars, he mourned, and to his immediate prospects of staying healthy in San Francisco.

"Aiya!"

Fireplug whirled, the wallet dangling from his fingers. The tallest bandit was bearing down on them, stiff-legged with indignation, waving his gun in the air. And what a gun: a twelve-inch knife-revolver with a bayonet mounted under the barrel. Reuben, who had an aversion to knives, felt sweat bead on his forehead.

It was a relief to see that the wielder of the vicious gun, who seemed to be the leader of the group, was madder at Fireplug than he was at his captives. What was the jerky language he was cussing at him in, Chinese? He seemed to be finding fault with Fireplug for having robbed them. Reuben felt a kinship with him on that account, and hope soared when the leader grabbed all the booty Fireplug had

36

just stolen—but flew away when he shoved everything inside his own loose black shirt instead of giving it back. He barked some guttural order, and Fireplug, crestfallen, trudged back to the stagecoach and began helping the third robber riffle the contents of Mr. Sweeney's carefully packaged antiquities.

"What's happening?" Reuben asked Sister Gus. She was holding his arm now.

"Don't move. There's another one now and he's got—you wouldn't believe the gun he's aiming at us."

"And the others?"

"Two of them. They're going through the stuff on the coach, screens and sculptures and ceramics. They look like they're searching for something."

He thought so, too. They would open up a crate of paintings, toss it aside, and start on another one. Beside him, Sweeney was pale and sweating, making little squealing noises.

"Are you all right?" Reuben asked. When she nodded, he repeated himself.

"Yes," she answered hastily, remembering he couldn't see. "They won't hurt us, I'm sure. They just want to rob us."

"It's only money," he agreed. "The Lord will provide."

Her top lip curled in an irreligious sneer.

Just then Fireplug shouted out something from the stagecoach, no doubt the Chinese equivalent of "Eureka!" The leader started backing up, glancing over his shoulder. He gave another order, and the two men changed places again.

Reuben didn't care for the switch. Fireplug had something evil on his mind; he could see it in his eyes, and the way he gestured with his gun that the three of them should walk backward until they were behind a thicket of eucalyptus trees, out of sight of the stagecoach. Reuben got a hint of what the evil thing was when the bandit hissed, "Sit!" to him and Sweeney, jabbing Reuben in the chest with the gun for good measure, while he grabbed Sister by the neck and jerked her toward him. "Sit!" he screamed in an eerie whisper when Reuben didn't move. "Or I shoot," he explained helpfully, pressing the gun barrel into Reuben's Adam's apple. He sat.

"Be naked," Fireplug told Sister. She gaped at him. Reuben got a better grip on his cane, but at that moment Fireplug stuck his .38 in his belt, reached into a long side pocket, and pulled out a push dagger with a nine-inch blade. Reuben put his head between his knees.

"I say take off clothes!"

"Go to hell, you sawed-off little—Ow!"

"What's happening?" Reuben asked miserably.

"He's got the knife under her chin," Sweeney whimpered. "She's doing it, she's unbuttoning her habit. Oh my God, I can't watch."

"He just wants a look. He won't do anything." Reuben said it confidently, talking himself into it. A quick glance up made his stomach roll.

The dagger had nicked her; a tiny line of blood trickled down her throat.

"Hurry, hurry," commanded Fireplug.

"Keep your shirt on, you ugly bastard," she quavered. "It took me a half hour to get into this rig."

"I say hurry—eeyii!" Reuben looked up to see the bandit jumping up and down on one foot, clutching his shin. "White devil, I kill you!" Springing at her, he grabbed her by her veil. It fell away in his hand and she almost pivoted out of reach, but he snatched her back before she could go two steps. He brought the knife up in her face, and Reuben froze, watching sunlight glint on the long, evil blade. The whites of her eyes glimmered as she threw a panicked, hopeless glance at him and Sweeney.

"Do something!" Reuben yelled at the curator, who was holding his knees and rocking. Reuben couldn't look and he couldn't look away; a humming, grayish fog in his head censored the worst. But then—then he saw Fireplug pocket the dagger, so he could get both hands on the gaping halves of the nun's habit and tear them apart to her waist.

"Well, shit fire," Reuben muttered, and leapt to his feet. Taking a mighty swing, he whacked Fireplug on the back of the head with his cane, and the robber dropped like a sack of sand. "Did I get him?" He flailed at the air a few more times, for effect. "Did I hit him?"

A gun fired, and the whining bullet ricocheted somewhere behind them. "Get down!" cried

Sister. Reuben dove, hitting the ground near Fireplug's inert body. The nun landed next to him. He started to grab for the pistol in Fireplug's belt, but she beat him to it. Teeth clenched, eyes squinted, Sister Mary Augustine fanned a spray of bullets out of the revolver like Wild Bill Hickok, using the bandit's belly for cover. The tall robber advancing on them from the stagecoach dodged and fired back, then whirled and fled. Seconds later they heard the sound of horses' hooves galloping away.

"They're gone," Sweeney said wonderingly, crawling toward Reuben and the nun on his hands and knees. They were sprawled on their backs on opposite sides of Fireplug's body, staring numbly up at the sky. Gunsmoke drifted on the air, stinging their nostrils. "Do you think he's dead?" asked Sweeney, gesturing toward the motionless thug.

"God, I hope so," breathed Sister.

Reuben sat up on one elbow and looked at her, interested.

"For the sake of his immortal soul," she said quickly.

Sweeney stared at her, too.

"Well—if he's alive, he'll probably just commit more sins, but if he's dead, at least there's a chance he hasn't had time to damn himself for eternity. His soul might spend some time in purgatory, but then—"

Fireplug groaned.

"The Lord works in mysterious ways," Reuben said thoughtfully.

Sweeney stood up. "I'd better go and check on Mr. Willis and Mr. Blalock," he said, and trotted off.

Reuben had lost his eyeglasses. He could see them on the ground about four feet from Fireplug's outflung hand, bent but not broken. He didn't feel like pretending to grope around for them just now. He and Sister Gus surveyed each other across the body, and after a few seconds she thought to pull the torn halves of her habit together across her bosom. "That was a lucky blow you struck with your cane, Mr. Cordoba," she said slowly.

"Wasn't it? God was with us today, no question about it."

"A miracle?" she suggested, narrow-eyed.

"Exactly—a miracle. Well, let's see what he looks like." She went very still. "Figure of speech," he explained after a pregnant pause. "Sweeney said they all had on hoods." She eyed him for another two seconds, then reached down to peel Fireplug's burlap bag away from his face. Without surprise, Reuben took note that he was Chinese, and about twenty years old. "Well?"

"Old guy," she said without inflection. "Red hair, balding."

He stroked his chin. "See what he's got on him."

"What?"

"Identification."

"Why?"

"Because his friends have my money," he explained patiently.

41

"But the police—" She stopped, obviously seeing his point. With visible distaste, she started to rummage around in Fireplug's pockets. She paused with her hand inside his coat, and slowly withdrew a small clay object. A statue, about four inches high. They stared at it for a full half minute, neither speaking. Reuben thought it looked like the body of a man with the head of a cat.

"Anything?" he asked.

"Nothing yet." Deliberately holding his gaze, Sister Gus slipped the statue down the front of her lacy white chemise.

She went back to her search. From the robber's trouser pocket, she extracted a folded piece of paper. Reuben caught a glimpse of long columns of Chinese characters before she glanced up at him. "Laundry ticket," she said blandly, and slipped it down her front as well.

Willis hobbled toward them, supported by Sweeney. The driver's face was ash-gray and there was a swollen bruise on his temple, but his eyes were fairly clear and his voice was steady. "Anybody hurt?" he asked. They said they were fine and asked him how Blalock was doing. "He'll be okay if we get him to a doctor pretty soon. How's this one?" He tapped Fireplug's elbow with the toe of his boot.

"Out cold," said Sister.

"There's a Wells Fargo relay station about twelve miles back. I can send a wire from there to the sheriff in San Mateo. Sorry to delay your trip, folks, but the sheriff'll be wanting to talk to all of us about this terrible business."

Out of the question, thought Reuben. He saw the same lack of enthusiasm for speaking to the sheriff flicker across the nun's face, too.

"I must go and see to poor Mr. Blalock," she murmured, rising to her feet. The pious note in her voice put him on guard. He muttered something to Willis and Sweeney about helping her, and followed.

The bandits had left Fireplug's horse behind and it was still standing by the stagecoach, grazing. When Sister Gus neared it, the animal shied and trotted a little way down the road, spooked by her flowing black robes. She glanced back then and saw Reuben, and immediately changed direction for Blalock, who had collapsed against the stagecoach's rear wheel. She knelt down beside him and touched his face, but he didn't open his eyes.

Sweeney and the driver staggered up, lugging Fireplug between them. "Mr. Cordoba, we've got the outlaw here," panted Sweeney, "right over here to your left. Do you think you could help us get him into the stage? He's heavier than he looks, but I think if you grabbed his feet we could hoist him in there. Right over here. Got him?"

Reuben took hold of the bandit's ankles and helped sling him inside the stagecoach. Sweeney clambered up after him, pulling and shoving at Fireplug's dead weight until he had him slumped on the floor with his back propped against the far door. Willis, meanwhile, tied his feet together with a rope.

When Reuben turned around, Sister Gus was gone.

"Excuse me," he muttered to Willis, "I, um, I'm not feeling well." Cutting a swath with his cane, he shambled down the lane after her.

He saw her beyond the first bend in the road. She had one foot in the stirrup, one on the ground, hopping frantically after the horse while it pivoted away from her. When she saw him, she forgot about escaping. "I knew it!" she cried, dropping the reins and starting toward him, fists clenched, mad as a hive of wasps.

"Sister?" he tried, waving his arms. "Is that you?"

His mistake was letting her under his guard; she darted in and landed a solid right before he could duck. "It's me," she said grimly.

He clutched his stinging jaw with both hands, momentarily seeing stars. "What the hell did you do that for?" he sputtered.

"Because you're a sidewinder and a pervert."

"Hold it, now, let's—"

"Degenerate!" She squared off to punch him again. "You'd've let that Chinaman rape me!"

"How can you say that? I saved you."

"Fiend. Coward!"

He jumped back, dodging a deft left hook. "Let's have this conversation later," he suggested, grabbing for the horse's mane before the animal could shy away.

"That horse is mine, I saw him first. Stop! Damn you—"

He leapt onto the animal's back, out of the way of Sister's flying fists. The stirrup leathers were way too short; he had to bend his knees like a cricket. He leaned over, offering her a helping hand, but she slapped it away with a sacrilegious curse. He backed the horse up and kicked it into a walk.

"Hey! Wait! Damn it, you wait up!"

"Well, hurry the hell up, Gus, before they figure out we're gone." This time she took his outstretched hand with alacrity, and he hoisted her up behind him. When he spurred the horse, she had to fling her arms around his waist to stay aboard.

Nobody appeared, nobody shouted after them from the direction of the stagecoach. After half a mile of tense, bumpy silence, Reuben was ready to believe they'd gotten clean away.

"We did it!" he exulted, slowing the horse to a canter. "They won't come after us in the stage because they've got to go south to telegraph the sheriff." Behind him, Sister Gus was already fidgeting; he guessed she wasn't used to bouncing bareback on a horse's rear end.

"Where are we going?"

He could tell by the tone of her voice that she was still irritated with him. "I thought I'd go home," he said mildly.

"Which is where?"

"Fourteen Yancy Street, San Francisco." Now, why had he told her that? "Where do you live?"

"None of your business."

45

There you were: it never paid to trust a woman. "I've got about four dollars and some change," he mentioned as they trotted up out of a pine-filled canyon. "And you?"

"Nothing," she snapped. "Not one thin dime."

He grunted. "That makes it harder. We'll have to keep riding, then, at least as far as Woodside. With four bucks, we can probably get third-class seats on a train from there to San Francisco."

She said nothing.

He decided it was time they introduced themselves. "My name's Reuben Jones." He twisted around, holding out his hand. She ignored it. "And you are Miss…?"

"Mrs.," she corrected testily. "Mrs. Henri Rousselot."

He whistled. "Well, that's kind of a mouthful. Why don't I just call you Grace, and you can call me Reuben."

"How do you know my—" The beautiful blue eyes widened. He could tell the second she figured it out. He didn't know her name because she'd told it to him after dinner last night. He knew it because he'd read it on her dressing gown, embroidered in white thread. Right after he'd walked into her room and seen her naked as a straight pin.

Sister Gus shoved back on the horse's rump as far as she could go without falling off, and didn't speak another word for twenty miles.

46

3

What is commonly called friendship is
only a little more honor among rogues.
                    —Henry David Thoreau

The ghostly, soothing hoot of a foghorn intruded on the tail end of Reuben's dream, just when it was getting good. He was standing behind a lectern, delivering a sermon to a churchful of nuns. Seated in orderly rows, they all suddenly crossed their legs and hiked up their skirts, like a chorus of cancan dancers. Some had pistols tucked into their garters, and some had little floral bouquets. Smiling, swinging their crossed legs back and forth in a leisurely rhythm, they hung on Reuben's every word, and nodded in unison when he suggested that many of them might benefit from some private spiritual instruction.

The foghorn's steady, muffled bray couldn't be ignored, though; half awake, he finally gave up trying to force the dream to its happy conclusion. His conscious fantasies were never as satisfying as his unconscious ones anyway, plus they had a way of turning comical the harder he concentrated on them.

He shifted, trying to uncramp his knees; a spring pierced him in the ribs. He came fully awake and remembered where he was: on his sitting-room sofa, huddled in his underwear under a scratchy blanket that reeked of mothballs. It took a little longer to remember why: because Grace was upstairs in his bed.

Grace Rousselot. An unlikely name if he'd ever heard one. He'd used logic in arguing with her last night about the sleeping arrangements, pointing out that since they'd ridden in close physical proximity on the back of a horse for half the day and then sat side by side on a train for the other half, in nearly as intimate circumstances—well, why not just lie down together in his big, soft bed at day's end? Why let abstract concepts like horizontal and vertical complicate the simple fact that they were two weary adults in need of a good night's sleep? But he'd lost the argument. She was a woman, so logic was lost on her.

She'd gotten over her speechlessness around Portola Valley, and harangued him from there all the way to Woodside on the theme of his pervertedness, cowardice, and corruption. The inhibiting presence of other passengers on the train they'd caught at Hillsborough had finally, mercifully, shut her up, and they'd traveled the rest of the way in comparative peace. She still wouldn't say where she came from. He assumed it wasn't San Francisco; otherwise she wouldn't have accepted, with a conspicuous absence of gratitude, his offer of a free night's lodging. He thought her lack of appreciation showed a certain churlishness of character, and her continued pique over the trick he'd played on her didn't say much for her sense of humor.

He couldn't help liking her, though, in spite of her defects. She had a temper and a sharp tongue, but they didn't wound very deeply; he thought they were more entertaining than biting. And she had guts, first when she'd stood up to Fireplug and then when she'd fired back at his bandit comrade, blasting away like Annie Oakley. For Reuben, who didn't even own a gun, that had been a defining moment.

He sat up, groaning with stiffness, wondering what time it was. Early, he judged from the heaviness of the wet fog drifting past the window. He stretched painfully and pulled on his trousers, then his socks. Last night he'd forgotten to close the window that looked out over the alley, so his apartment was chilly this morning. He got up to close the window, noticing that the monkey flowers were in full bloom along the fence. The sea-stained cottages across the way gleamed like ghosts in the summer fog, and the shouts of children sounded hollow and deceptively far away. His neighborhood was old, and more colorful than respectable, which, for Reuben, helped make up for its other shortcomings. He lived in a once-grand carriage house behind a once-grand house a few blocks south of Telegraph Hill. He was a month behind in his rent, which wasn't much; but then his apartment had only two rooms, one over the other, and a tiny second-floor bathroom. He'd lived in worse and he'd lived in better. Mrs. Finney was an asset; she tolerated his eccentricities, asked no questions, and had an endearing habit of overlooking the significance of the first of the month.

He got a fire going in the coal stove and put the coffeepot on to heat. Coffee was the limit of his home-cooking accomplishments, though; he took his meals in restaurants or, if Mrs. Finney was in a charitable mood, in the big house with her other boarders. But he still referred to the corner of his living room that contained the stove and the small cabinet full of cups and glasses as the kitchen.

A sleepy groan sounded from overhead, followed by the creak of bedsprings. He took two mugs from the cabinet and filled them with steaming coffee. "Rise and shine," he called out on his way upstairs. He heard the fast rustle of covers as, presumably, his houseguest made herself decent.

"Morning, Gus," he greeted her, sticking his head in the doorway. "Hope you like your coffee black." She extended a bare arm from the blankets and made a muffled sound, which he decided was meant to express thanks. Handing her a mug, he sat down on the bed's edge, blowing steam over the rim of his own mug and watching her. She looked good. Her hair was a cloud of sexy blonde tangles, and her sleepy eyes gave him ideas. If he wasn't mistaken, she didn't have any clothes on. "How are we feeling this morning?" he inquired politely. "I trust you found the bed comfortable?"

She made another monosyllabic reply and sipped her coffee, eyeing him back. He guessed she wasn't a morning person.

"It's a beautiful day, or it will be when the fog blows away. Did the horns bother you last night? I've gotten so used to the sound, I don't even hear it anymore. How long do you think you'll be staying, Sister? Not that I'm trying to rush you; farthest thing from my mind. You're as welcome as the day is long, and I mean that sincerely. You could even move in, if you—"

"As long as it takes me to pull a stake together and find some real clothes," she broke in grumpily.

He must be physically deprived: he even found her hoarse morning croak sexy. "Clothes and a stake. Yes indeed, those are things to consider." He stroked his chin. "I imagine your husband will be able to help you out there, hmm?"

"Hmm." She ran her thumb across the place on the mug where her lips had been. "I'll need to send him a telegram as soon as possible."

Which didn't, he noticed, quite answer the question. "There's a Western Union office about six blocks from here." She hummed again and blew on her coffee. "Where exactly is your husband?" he asked offhandedly.

Equally casual, she flapped her hand in the air. "North of here."

"Aha. Canada?"

She scowled. "South of Canada."

"Well, that narrows it down. What's he do for a living?"

"Henri is..." She thought for a second.

51

"He's self-employed. You might call him an entrepreneur."

Reuben grinned appreciatively. "Is that a fact."

Unexpectedly, she smiled back. She had a hell of a smile, wide and full of sly humor. He felt the wariness between them receding; the possibility of joining forces with her tantalized him again. Not because it would be smart, but because it would be fun.

He glanced around the room. She'd draped her black habit across the back of his wardrobe; her shoes were lined up neatly on the floor, black stockings tucked modestly inside. She was an orderly ex-nun. He pulled on his earlobe. "Where'd you put the statue?"

When she leaned back against the pillow, the blanket slipped down, and he saw with deep disappointment that she wasn't naked; she had on the frilly white shift he'd gotten a glimpse of yesterday. He eyed it now, wondering if the statue could possibly still be in there.

She had her eyebrows raised innocently; he waited for her to say, "What statue?" But after a long minute, during which she appeared to be taking his measure, she set her mug down, reached behind her, and pulled the statue out from under the pillow.

She kept it on her lap, not inviting him to touch it, but they bent their heads over it together. "Priceless?" muttered Reuben. "Sweeney calls this priceless? Look at it."

"I know, but it's supposed to be old."

"What is it, a cat or a man?" He squinted

at the faded blue figure; some of its surfaces were worn smooth, and the material underneath looked like ordinary red clay.

"Both. It's a tiger-headed human figure, one of the twelve earthly branches of the Chinese calendrical cycle."

He gaped at her. "How do you know that?"

"I know lots of things," she said smugly. "I'm very well read, extremely well educated—"

"You read it in Sweeney's catalog." He laughed, remembering.

She grinned, admitting it. Her left eyetooth was slightly crooked and overlapped the neighboring incisor, a defect that gave a rakish twist to her sly smiles. "Too bad we don't still have that catalog. I just glanced at it that night in the hotel, and all I can remember about this is that it's the tiger. The others are the dragon, the goat, the horse, the monkey... I forget the rest. The dog, I think. One for every year of the zodiac, and they all mean something. I think it said they put them in tombs."

"In tombs?"

"Had them buried in their graves with them, the rich people. To take with them to the afterlife." She shook her head. "But that's all I can remember."

"Let's see the piece of paper Fireplug had on him."

"Fireplug? Oh, you mean *Cannonball*."

They chortled over that, and Reuben was beginning to admire her sane, commendably masculine reaction to an event most women would've moaned and carried on about for weeks. Then he noticed her mirthful grin had faded and she was glaring at him.

"How come you just sat there while that sawed-off little pig mauled me?" she demanded.

"Let's not start this argument all over again."

"How far were you going to let him go? What kind of a man are you, anyway?"

"Now, hold on a damn minute. Did I or did I not save you? At great personal risk to life and limb."

"You could've smacked him on the head with that cane of yours about twelve times before you finally got up the nerve to do it. But no, you and Sweeney just sat there on your hands, like a couple of sheep."

"I *saved* you," he insisted.

"Why did it take you so long?"

"Because he had a knife!"

"So? You had a cane, and you're bigger, heavier, taller—"

"I happen not to like knives. All right? I don't like 'em, that's all. As soon as he put it away, I jumped up and conked him, didn't I? For that matter, why didn't you whip out your little peashooter and blast him? How about that?"

She stared at him thoughtfully, ignoring the question. "So you're afraid of knives. Why didn't you just say so in the first place?"

"I'm not afraid of them."

"That's what it sounds like to me."

"I don't relish them, I don't cotton to them, I prefer to be absent when they're present."

"That's how I feel about snakes," she said, nodding. "But unlike you, I've got the guts to come right out and say it: I'm scared of them."

"Well, I'm *not*—"

"Oh, forget it." She distracted him from the argument by reaching down inside the neckline of her chemise and pulling out a folded piece of paper. "Here's Fireplug's laundry list." She spread it out on her blanketed knee. "Which it might be, for all I know; it's all in Chinese."

They pored over the paper briefly; the only interesting thing about it was a pen-and-ink drawing of a flower at the top, almost like a letterhead. "A lily?" Reuben guessed.

"No, the stalk's too short. A camellia?" They stared at it some more, then gave up.

While she refolded the paper and returned it to its intriguing hiding place, he reached for the blue statue and turned it over in his hands. "I know somebody who might be able to tell us more about this. A friend of mine, owns a curio shop." He stood up casually. "Knows all about art and antiques and things like that. Used to be a—"

"No, you don't." She made a fast-handed dive and snatched the statue back, just as he was sliding it into his pocket. "Nice try, Jones," she smirked, tucking it under her crossed arms.

He spread innocent hands. "I was only trying to help. Anyway, how do you figure it's yours and not ours?"

"I saw it first."

"Not true. We saw it at the same instant."

"Impossible—you were blind."

"I own half of that statue, Sister," he said menacingly. "If it weren't for me, you'd never have gotten away."

"I was doing fine until you stole my horse."

"I didn't have to buy you a train ticket."

That stumped her.

"I gave you my own bed to sleep in," he pressed. "I brought you coffee."

"So you think four dollars, a bed, and a cup of coffee entitle you to half of what this statue is worth?"

"I do. Exactly."

She fingered the blue tiger-man thoughtfully, then looked up at him. "Okay."

He waited for the catch, but she just blinked back at him, blue eyes devoid of guile. "Okay," he echoed experimentally. "Okay, good. Hand it over, then, and I'll give it to—"

She snorted. "Not on your life. What do you take me for, Mr. Jones, an infant?"

"Not for a second."

"I'm not sure what we should do with this yet; we need to think it through. Maybe your friend with the curio shop is a good place to start, maybe not. That is, if there really is such a person. But until—"

"Gus, you wound me."

"But until we think it through, tiger here is staying with me."

Her distrustfulness hurt his feelings, but he couldn't help admiring her caution; it seemed so unwomanly. And God knew, impulsive

56

behavior had gotten him into trouble more often than any other failing he possessed. He also liked the way the word "we" sounded on her lips.

"Okay, Gus," he conceded handsomely, "you're the boss." For the moment, he modified in private.

"Stop calling me that."

"What should I call you? Madame Russelow?"

"It's *Rousselot*. If that's too much for you, call me Grace."

"Grace. And a lovely name it is." She wasn't immune to flattery, he knew, although she tried to pretend otherwise. "How much money did Fireplug get from you, Grace?"

She drew up her knees. "I don't think that's any of your business."

"A bundle, eh?" He clucked his tongue in sympathy. "Bad break for the terminal African orphans."

She didn't even blush. "How much did Edward Cordoba drop?" she shot back.

"Nothing he couldn't afford to lose," he lied. "Say, this is a fascinating conversation; I hate to break it up, but I've got work to do. You know where the bathroom is. Why don't you avail yourself of the facilities first, and I'll follow."

"What sort of work do you do, Mr. Jones?" she asked interestedly.

"Business, Grace. Boring man stuff you wouldn't care to worry your head about."

Her lips thinned. "That's my *pretty little* head, isn't it?"

He snapped his fingers. "Right you are. No offense. Well."

"Well?"

"Ah! You want me to leave so you can get out of bed!"

She made a gun with one hand and pulled the trigger.

"On my way." He made her his Edward Cordoba bow—two nights ago it had slayed her—and exited.

Grace took her time in the bathroom, not to spite Mr. Jones but because his tub was enormous and the water was hot, and she hadn't had a long, luxurious, totally private bath in weeks.

"Sorry I took so long," she told him as she came down the stairs to his sitting room, habit skirts raised so she wouldn't trip.

"Find everything you needed?"

"Yes, thanks."

He got up from the chair where he'd been reading the newspaper and started past her for the steps. He didn't look a bit like Edward Cordoba this morning in his rumpled tan trousers and collarless blue shirt. The thought would've pleased her, considering how thoroughly he'd suckered her, if it hadn't come attached to an auxiliary observation: that despite his uncombed hair, bare feet, and beard stubble, he looked even better.

"Is the stove still hot?" she asked shortly.

"I think so. Why, are you cold?"

"No, I'd like to dry my hair."

"Be my guest." He stopped with one foot on the bottom stair. "And glorious hair it is, Grace. Good thing you had your veil on most of the time with Sweeney and the others, wasn't it?"

"Why?"

"Why?" He widened his eyes and spread out his hands, feigning fatuous wonder at her slowness. "Because if they'd seen that hair, they'd never forget it, and you'd probably have been arrested by now."

"Don't be an idiot."

"Or else you'd've had to cut it all off—an even more horrible alternative if you ask me."

She straightened from stirring the coals and put her hands on her hips. "Anything in the paper about the robbery?" she asked frostily to discourage any more of his nonsense.

"No, not a word. Guess we'll have to wait for the afternoon editions. Will you excuse me?" He turned, and took the steps two at a time.

His apartment wasn't very prepossessing, she noted with mixed feelings, leaning over the stove and rubbing her hair with a towel, listening to the sounds of water running and Reuben whistling in the bathroom. The flim-flam business must be in a slump. His furniture looked like regulation boardinghouse issue, and the only visible item of value was his collection of vintage wines, carefully stored in a free-standing pyramid of clay pipes—the kind cities laid water and sewer lines with, she imagined. How clever of him. So he really was a connoisseur. It was marginally consoling to know that, at least about one thing, Edward Cordoba hadn't lied.

A knock came at the back door, the one that faced onto the alley behind the refurbished carriage house. Grace laid her towel aside and moved to the foot of the stairs. "Mr. Jones?" He couldn't hear her. But she could hear him, singing "Blue-eyed Lady of Caroline" over the clank of the hot-water boiler in the bathroom. She hesitated a few seconds longer, then went to the door and opened it.

Five men stepped back in surprise when they saw her. The one in front whipped off his hat, and the other four hastily copied him. "Morning, ma'am," the leader said politely, in the deepest, raspiest voice Grace had ever heard. It sounded like a piece of earth-moving equipment that needed oil.

"Good morning."

"How you doin' this morning?"

"Fine, thank you."

"Ma'am, could you tell us if Mr. Jones is home at the present time?"

"Yes, he is."

"Can we talk to him? If it ain't too much trouble, dat is."

"He's...indisposed at the moment, but I expect he'll be down shortly."

He held up both hands, palms out. "Hey, in no way would we wish to distoib him if he's *indisposed*."

"No, I'm sure he'll be down in a few minutes," she repeated. She couldn't quite make

60

out what they were. The spokesman with the sandpaper voice was a thin, sallow-faced individual, respectably dressed except for the flashy dyed-blue carnation in his buttonhole. The others she couldn't pin down at all, at least not as a group; one had on bib overalls, two wore suits, another corduroy pants and a Western shirt with a string tie.

"Is it okay wit youse if we come in an' wait?"

She hung on the door, indecisive. They looked harmless enough, and the leader was politeness itself. "Yes, come in," she finally invited, and opened the door wide.

In Reuben's sitting room, they insisted she take the only chair, while three of them squeezed onto the couch and the other two perched uncomfortably on the arms. They all put their hats in their laps. An awkward silence ensued. "I'm Mrs. Rousselot," Grace offered at last, desperate to break it.

"Pleased to meetcha. Croaker's my name, Lincoln Croaker, and dese are my brudders. All except Winkie."

The one on the left sofa arm winked at her, solving that mystery. The others bowed their heads in a sedate greeting, and she bowed back.

Out of the next silence, Lincoln grated, "We wish to extend our deepest sympathies, ma'am."

"I beg your pardon?"

"On accounta your recent bereavement."

"My—oh, yes," she fumbled, realizing belatedly that without the veil, her black habit

61

resembled mourning clothes. "Thank you, it was...very sudden." The Croakers's sad nodding prompted her to elaborate. "We'd been married such a short time, you know. Not quite a year."

Lincoln made sympathetic clucking sounds. "Terrible, ma'am, just terrible. What carried him off?"

"Cholera. At least it was over quickly; he didn't suffer." She dabbed at her eye with a dainty knuckle.

"Tsk-tsk. Here today, gone tomorrow."

"Carpe diem," she snuffled.

"O tempora, o mores," he countered.

"To everything there is a season."

He looked beaten for a second, then held up his index finger and declared, "Time is money."

Grace had no choice but to incline her head in gracious defeat.

Another lengthy pause. When she couldn't take any more polite, mutual staring, she stood up, and all four Croakers, plus Winkie, clambered to their feet in her wake. "Why don't I go and tell Mr. Jones you're here?"

"Thank you, ma'am," they said in chorus, bowing her out.

Upstairs, beyond the bathroom door, Reuben was singing the falsetto chorus to "Rally 'Round the Flag": "The Union forever, hurrah, boys, hurrah—"

"Mr. Jones?" Grace called softly, giving the wood a discreet rap. The door opened abruptly and she fell back a step. He grinned at her through a face full of shaving soap.

"Hi, Gus."

"You have visitors," she got out, breathless, unprepared for the sight of his naked chest and long, strong, hairy legs, and the intriguing strip of white towel in between.

"Who is it?"

"It's the Croaker brothers and Winkie."

His grin went from cocky to sickly; under the shaving lather she thought his cheeks paled. But all he said was, "Tell 'em I'll be down in a second, will you?"

"Okay." She studied him, not moving. "Everything all right?"

"Sure. Hunky-dory." He held up his razor, waiting for her to go. Unable to think of anything else to say, she finally did. But she rejoined the Croakers uneasily, and their bovine courtesy didn't amuse her anymore.

"Lincoln!" Reuben exclaimed a few minutes later, with every evidence of hearty pleasure, bounding down the stairs with an athletic stride and advancing on the head Croaker with his hand out. "What an unexpected pleasure."

"Likewise."

"I didn't think I'd be seeing you quite this early in the day."

"Yeah, well, you know what dey say about the oily boid an' all."

"So true, and so profound. Did you meet Mrs. Rousselot?"

"Yeah, we already had dat pleasure. An' now, we was wonderin' if we could speak wit' youse in private, like, if the widow don't mind."

"The widow?"

"Of course," Grace said quickly. "It was lovely meeting you all."

"Lovely," they echoed sincerely.

She sent Reuben a look, one he probably didn't understand because she wasn't sure what it meant herself, and took her leave.

Upstairs, she walked briskly into the bedroom, removed her shoes, and tiptoed back down the short hall to the top of the steps. But the masculine bonhomie below had suddenly grown subdued; try as she might, she couldn't make out anyone's words, although from the cadence of the voices, Reuben's and Lincoln's, she gathered they were having a rather jovial argument. Suddenly the talk broke off; she heard sounds of movement, and a second later the click-squeak-click of the door to the alley opening and closing.

She crept down the stairs, listening intently. "Mr. Jones?" No answer, and when she reached the bottom step, she saw that the house was empty. Everybody was gone.

The suspicion that Reuben had run out on her came and went speedily. He wouldn't have left without taking a single possession, and certainly not without his beloved wine collection, no matter what the inducement. He'd gone out for a while, that was all, with his peculiar friends, to do whatever men without regular jobs did together during the day. Well, fine. Leave her here all by herself, then, with no money, nothing to eat, and nothing to do. She'd find something to do.

She cracked his desk and searched it. The locks on the drawers made her laugh; she picked them with a couple of hairpins as easily as picking dandelions. What she found inside, arranged, filed, and organized with admirable neatness and attention to detail, were the records of a half-dozen bunco games and confidence schemes, operating simultaneously from seven different city post office boxes.

Among other things, Mr. Jones ran a bogus clipping service—Readiclip, Inc., was its current name, although it periodically went out of business and reappeared as something else. He sold fake lottery tickets and Irish sweepstakes chances, sometimes forged, sometimes nonexistent. He dabbled in the rightful-heirs swindle, a complicated genealogical-investigation fraud that Henry used to work years ago, she recalled. But Henry had given it up because it had gotten too dangerous.

Here was a game she hadn't heard of: the Skytop Roof Services Company, Ltd. The handsome brochure offered amazingly inexpensive roofs to people whose only obligation, after the roof was built, was to allow potential new customers to inspect the finished product. The lucky homeowner paid for his cheap new roof up front—and never saw the salesman again.

The ad Reuben took out in newspapers from time to time was a masterpiece of small-time simplicity. It promised nothing, so it wasn't even illegal. It merely asked readers to send a dollar to a post office address, for "a little surprise in store for you. Who knows?" Grace knew: the surprise was that they lost a dollar.

But her favorite was the "International Society of Literature, Science, and Art," a combination correspondence course and talent school. Hopeful amateurs sent in their stories, pictures, and inventions, and for thirty dollars Reuben sent back advice on how to "revise" their work, to ready it for submission to a publisher or a patent office. And for a small additional fee, he offered diplomas, plaques, scrolls, certificates, and—she loved this— the privilege of using the initials A.S.L. or M.S.L. after their names.

Leafing through the Society's correspondence, she was cynically amused until she came upon Reuben's unfinished reply to the writer of one particularly bad piece of autobiographical prose, a lonely-sounding spinster from Sacramento. He was sending her money back, along with the kind and very gently worded advice that she perhaps try gardening or needlework for an artistic outlet.

In a thoughtful mood, Grace returned the contents of Reuben's desk to the proper drawers, and relocked them with her hairpins.

A few minutes later, innocently seated on the sprung couch and perusing the newspaper, she heard the door open. Pretending absorption, she didn't look up until he'd crossed the room, passed in front of her, and turned for the stairs. She only caught a glimpse of his profile, but it was enough to make her jump up, tossing the paper aside, and cry, "Holy saints, what happened to you?"

His answer was garbled; he kept moving, shuffling up the steps at an uneven gait, holding one arm across his middle. At the top of the stairs, he turned toward the bathroom, and she followed him in without hesitation.

"What happened?" she asked again. "You look like a cable car ran over you!"

He went directly to the sink and peered at himself in the mirror. "Unhhh," he groaned, and she could only echo his dismay: blood trickled from any number of places, most alarmingly from a jagged gash at the side of his mouth; one eyebrow was divided in half, possibly by a flying ring finger; if his nose wasn't broken, it had at least been grossly insulted.

"Sit down," Grace ordered, taking his arm in what she thought was a gentle clasp, but he winced and yelped, "Ow!" She jerked back, startled. "What's *wrong* with you?"

"Mph," he said, closed the lid to the w.c., and carefully lowered himself until he was sitting on it. "They hung a shanty on me."

"Who did?"

"The Croakers."

"No!" She thought of all five of them seated on the couch, like puppies in a humorous photograph. "I don't believe it."

"Believe it."

"What happened?" She found a clean towel and began to run hot water into the sink basin.

"Rough story, Grace. Not fit for delicate ears."

She muttered an indelicate word. "Why did they do it? What have they got against you?"

"Ow!" he yelled again when she held the hot cloth to his eyebrow. "Ow! Damn it!"

"Don't be such a baby. Sit still, I have to clean it." She followed his retreating head until it struck the pipe to the overhead water tank, preventing further escape. "Don't give me any trouble, Jones, or I'll use alcohol," she warned darkly.

"Alcohol!" His battered face brightened. "Gus, go into my sock drawer—top right, bureau—and bring me that pint of bourbon at the bottom."

Without a word, she dropped the towel in the sink and obeyed. In his bedroom, she unscrewed the top to the pint bottle and took a delicate swig. Well, she rationalized, smothering a cough, cleaning blood and gore from a man's face was no picnic for her either.

"Thanks," he said when she handed him the bourbon. "Care for a nip?"

"No, thank you," she said virtuously, "I never touch hard liquor."

He toasted her and drank deeply. After that, things went a little more smoothly. Reuben grew more talkative in proportion to his acquaintance with the bottle; by the time she'd cleaned his wounds and applied sticking plaster to the worst of his cuts, she knew the whole story.

It had all started about a month ago, when he'd gone to Stockton on "business," and also to locate a good poker game. Business over, he got into a high-stakes showdown with five men, four of them brothers. He'd figured out after a couple of hands of stud that somebody was cheating, but he couldn't pin down who; it wasn't until they were hours into the game that he realized it was all five of them, taking turns. By then he was practically broke.

On the last hand, he decided to bet Old Blue, a pet name for the faithful, but fake, silver mine for which he'd been carrying around phony stock certificates for years, betting or selling them as the need arose. They were allegedly worth about two thousand dollars. The Croakers beat him again—three aces and a pair of queens to four miserable treys. He handed over his stock certificates and got the hell out of town.

So who did he run into at McDougal's Card Palace on Kearny Street not two weeks later? All five of them. They'd lied about being Stockton boys for the same reason he had, so their deeds couldn't follow them home. Not surprisingly, they were annoyed with him. Using his natural charm, however, he'd placated them and bought a two-week extension on his debt. It had come due this morning.

Grace shuddered, remembering the leader's gravel-voiced solicitousness. "And I thought he was nice. Now I just think he's spooky."

"Yes, there is that about Lincoln," Reuben agreed, rubbing light fingers over his ribs. "But I'm feeling rather fond of him at the moment."

"What on earth for?"

"He's the only one who didn't hit me."

She shivered again.

"Then too, he was kind enough to grant another extension on the two grand—one more week."

"That's not kindness," she scoffed, "that's good business. If they kill you, you'll never pay them back."

"That was mentioned." He stood up slowly. "I have to lie down now."

She followed him into the bedroom, and didn't protest when he lay down on his own bed, even though she'd begun to think of it as hers. "Aren't you going to take off your shoes?" she asked, reaching for the folded blanket at the foot of the bed.

"Can't. Too stiff. Would you do it for me? Ah, Sister Augustine, you're an angel of mercy."

She remembered the last time he'd called her an angel of mercy, and yanked off his shoes with unnecessary force. "What am I supposed to do while you're lying here recovering?" she asked crossly. "From wounds you brought on yourself, I might add. Why don't you have any food in your house? Were you hoping to starve me out?"

He grinned, then groaned when the movement tore at the sticking plaster on his lip. "Around the corner on Sansome," he said carefully, "there's a restaurant called Belle's. Great corned beef, lousy stew, pretty good pie. They know me there. Say my name and they'll fix you up."

Her mouth had begun to water. "Thanks. What do I use for money?"

He made a magnanimous gesture with one hand. "Tell 'em to put it on my tab."

"Okay." She stood still, reluctant to leave. "Well." She quit fidgeting with the blanket edge, jerked it up and tucked it around his chest. "You'll be all right, I assume," she said brusquely. "By yourself, I mean."

The brown eye that wasn't bloodshot winked at her. "Fine. I'm going to sleep. Thanks for the first aid, Gus. You've got great hands."

"Head hurt?"

"Mm."

"It's probably the bourbon."

He stroked the bruised bridge of his nose, wincing. "It's not the bourbon. Oh, Grace," he remembered as she turned away. "Be sure to wake me up by three o'clock, will you?"

"Why?"

"Because I've still got business to take care of," he answered importantly.

She leaned against the doorpost and folded her arms. "You want to visit as many post offices as you can before they close," she guessed silkily. "To see who might've enrolled in the International Society of Literature, Science, and Art while you were out of town."

It was a deep, warming pleasure to watch his mouth drop open. He regarded her for a long time in silent speculation. "You rummied my desk," he said at last, and there was a

71

gratifying note of wonder in his voice, maybe even admiration.

She smiled modestly.

"What'd you use?"

"A pick and a little homemade tension wrench."

"Which you just happened to have on you?"

"A girl's got to be prepared. No," she chuckled, "I made them."

"You *made* them?"

"Out of hairpins."

"I don't believe it," he said flatly.

She shrugged. "I don't care."

"Three o'clock, Gus, wake me up. And then I want to see you crack that lock. I want to see it."

She shrugged again, then expanded it into a lazy stretch. "If I feel like it," she said airily. "Sleep tight." She closed the door with exaggerated gentleness and tiptoed away.

4

I don't know of anything better than a woman if you want to spend money where it'll show.

—Kin Hubbard

" 'Two travelers on the stagecoach disappeared immediately following the robbery, absconding with the captured gunman's horse. One is believed to have been posing as a Catholic nun, for purposes of illegal charitable soliciting. The other, a man calling himself Edward Cordoba, allegedly from Monterey, is suspected of feigning blindness for unknown reasons. Police are unsure of the connection between the two missing passengers and the stage holdup, if any. According—' "

"Why do they say *posing* as a Catholic nun?" Grace interrupted, scowling at a pink chunk of corned beef on the end of her fork. It was her second meal that day at Belle's. "Why do they think I wasn't a nun? They've got no evidence, none at all."

" 'According to San Mateo sheriff's deputies—' "

"They're just guessing."

" 'According to—' "

"That really galls me."

Reuben sighed and looked up at her over the top of page nine of the *Daily Examiner*.

"I take pride in my work, and I don't appreciate being slandered in the newspaper as a *poser* by some incompetent, second-guessing sheriff."

"Maybe they checked up on the Blessed Sisters of Bewilderment," he suggested mildly.

"Hope," she corrected, "the Blessed Sisters of Hope."

"You mean they really exist?"

She popped the meat into her mouth and chewed it unhurriedly, staring at him across the table. She was figuring the angles, he knew, trying to decide if there was any reason to keep lying. "No," she finally conceded.

"There you are, then."

"They probably checked," she agreed grudgingly. "That's the only way they *could* know. Because I never let it go, never, not even when that slimy son of a gun was pawing me."

"I never let it go either," Reuben pointed out, "but I never get any credit for it. I was Edward Cordoba to the end." In the jargon of flimflam, you "let it go" if you stepped out of character while running a skin game.

"That's different. Why should you get any credit for that?"

"Why shouldn't I?"

"Because Fireplug could've killed me! I might've *died* while you were being true to Edward Cordoba!"

Not that again. He drummed his knuckles on the table, annoyed because she had him and

74

she knew it. He guessed it was an advantage she planned to keep reminding him of forever.

"So, go on," she said, satisfied, leaning back against the high leather banquette in their secluded booth at Belle's. "What's it say about the robbery?"

The small piece of raw steak she'd made him stick on his swollen eyebrow came unstuck and fell in his lap. He retrieved it absently, deposited it on his plate, and went back to reading. " 'According to San Mateo sheriff's deputies, the only objects stolen from the traveling art exhibit were an undetermined number of funerary sculpture pieces, among them a jade dragon used as a tomb guardian during the Wei period, a Han earthenware unicorn, and twelve calendrical representations from the Ming dynasty.' "

"Eleven," Grace amended smugly.

" 'Priceless paintings, scrolls, and ceramics were left behind by the miscreants, for motives the police have not yet determined. The captured Chinaman has refused to speak, and at last report had not even divulged his name.' "

Reuben folded the paper and laid it aside, reaching for the mug of beer at his elbow. He took a sip, then gingerly pressed the cold glass to his eyebrow, grimacing. "So. Fireplug won't talk."

"Maybe that piece of paper has his name on it," she theorized. "If so, we did him a favor when we lifted it."

"Mm. My friend with the curio shop can find out what it says."

She looked unimpressed. "I can take it to the local laundry and find out what it says."

"I don't think that would be wise."

"Why not?"

"Because the fewer people who know about this, the better. Especially since we don't know what the paper says yet."

"What difference does it make?" She narrowed her eyes at him. "You've got something on your mind, haven't you? Something besides making sure you're not connected to the robbery."

Instead of answering, he set his elbows on the table and leaned toward her, the picture of earnest entreaty. In his best you-can-trust-me voice, he asked, "How much money did you lose in the robbery, Grace?"

"I told you, it's none of your business."

"Oh, come on," he coaxed. "I came straight with you about the Croakers, didn't I? I lost almost two thousand dollars, and I need forty-five hundred by next Tuesday. How much more forthcoming can I be?"

She played with the buttons at the wrist of her new India silk day dress, probably admiring the contrast between the dark burgundy and the white skin of her long, slender hand. She had a new cape, too, black with a cream satin lining, hanging on a hook behind her. He hoped she was remembering that neither the gown nor the cape, nor her new high-button walking shoes, had come cheap, and that he hadn't so much as batted an eye when he'd heard the price. In fact, after she'd modeled the burgundy silk for him this afternoon in Miss Jolie's Fashion Salon and Ready-to-Wear, he'd parted with his money without a peep.

His *hard-earned* money, make that. They'd traipsed around town to four different post offices before going to Miss Jolie's, and from each box he'd collected half a week's worth of pickings from his numerous business enterprises. "Slim pickings," Grace had labeled them, and he'd had to admit to her that his rackets were currently in a slump. Which, to Reuben's mind, made his generosity all the more commendable. Naturally he expected to be repaid, at a rate of interest he hadn't told her about yet, as soon as her husband wired money in response to the telegram she'd sent him earlier in the day. But still. He'd bought the clothes she was wearing, the meal she was eating—the bed she'd be sleeping in again tonight. Even on Grace Rousselot's cock-eyed scale of justice, that ought to earn him one honest answer.

"Okay," she said finally, "I'll tell you. On one condition."

"What's that?"

"That you promise not to whistle."

Reuben looked down at the unappetizing slurry of ground beef, mashed potatoes, and applesauce on his plate. "I can't even chew." The Croakers had loosened one of his molars.

She swept the half-empty restaurant with a glance, bent forward, and mouthed, "Four."

"Four?"

She sat back.

"Four what? Hundred?"

She looked disgusted.

"Four thousand? *Four thousand dollars?*"

"Shh!" She took a sip of coffee, relishing his amazement.

"And you collected all that as Sister Augustine?" he hissed.

She smiled.

"How long did it take?"

"About three weeks."

He muttered a number of oaths and curses in a language she wouldn't understand. "I've been running the wrong gyps," he marveled, shaking his head over and over. "Christ almighty, I should've been playing a priest."

"Three long, grueling weeks," she pointed out. "And don't think it's just a matter of putting on a clerical collar and waiting for people to start throwing money at you. It's an *art.*"

"Art, shmart. I watched you on the stagecoach with Sweeney, don't forget. He was going for his wallet even before you started batting your eyes at him."

"Art, shmart?" Obviously she'd never heard that expression. "Anyway," she sniffed, "I don't bat my eyes."

"The hell you don't." She also blushed, wept, pouted her lips, and stuck her chest out whenever she thought it would get her where she wanted to go.

"We're getting off the subject," she snapped. "I've told you how much the thieves got from me. Are you thinking of doing something about it?"

"How badly do you need the money back?"

"You've got a really irritating habit, you know that? Of answering a question with a question."

He folded his arms and waited.

"I'm not in debt, if that's what you're suggesting. Nobody's going to beat *me* up if I don't get it back."

"What do you need it for?"

"Medical bills," she answered too quickly.

"You look pretty healthy to me." His leer wasn't successful; he couldn't raise his bad eyebrow high enough, and he winced when he tried to smirk.

"Not that it's any of your business, but my husband..." She looked down, took a deep breath, looked up. "My husband," she got out with a catch in her voice, "has a bad heart."

Oh, she was very, very good. So good, he wasn't a hundred percent positive she was lying. "That would be Henri, the entrepreneur?" he asked neutrally.

"He's a former entrepreneur. I forgot to tell you he's retired."

"Aha."

"Aha," she mimicked, impatient. "Back to the question, Mr. Jones. What's your interest in my financial affairs? What's going on in that devious mind of yours?"

He acknowledged the compliment with a nod. "What I've got in mind is pretty simple, Mrs. Rousselot. Being such a smart lady, you're probably already there ahead of me."

"It wouldn't surprise me." She smiled to disarm him.

It worked; he lost his train of thought for a second, caught up in the sly, unexpected friendliness of that smile. It took a big gulp of beer to get his wits back. "I'm suggesting that you and I don't take the combined loss of six thousand dollars lying down," he said softly. "I'm suggesting we take steps to get it back. Together."

The quick gleam in her eye, there and gone in a second, proved his suggestion hadn't taken her by surprise. She pushed her plate to the side and rested her chin on her twined fingers. "How?"

"We start with Doc Slaughter. He's the antique dealer I was telling you about."

" 'Doc Slaughter' ?" She had a surprisingly girlish giggle. "That's the most unlikely antique dealer's name I ever heard."

"Well, that's his name. He's got a shop on Powell Street. I could go see him tomorrow, show him the tiger and the—"

"*We* could go see him, you mean."

"Slip of the tongue. Nice to know you're paying attention."

"I always pay attention."

"*We'll* show him the tiger, see if he can tell us something interesting about it. Even if it's not worth much by itself, it could be worth a great deal to whoever's got the other eleven pieces."

"Like a chess set with a missing queen."

"Exactly. As for Fireplug's letter, Doc's got contacts in Chinatown; he can pay somebody to translate it and keep his mouth shut afterward."

"Why does he have contacts in Chinatown? Tell me more about this guy."

"Let's go home, I'll tell you about him there." He raised his hand to signal for the bill. "I think we have to figure Fireplug for a thief among thieves, don't you? He took the tiger during the holdup for himself, either to hock on his own or hold out and sell back to his employer later."

"That's assuming he had an employer. Couldn't he and the other two have been acting on their own?"

"They could've been, but somehow I don't think they were."

She folded her napkin into a small, neat square, frowning. "I don't think so either."

"Good, we're agreed."

They stood up. He found her cape and helped her on with it. She was wearing her hair on top of her head tonight; a few blonde corkscrew curls had slipped their pins and were bobbing around her face in a cheerful, artless way. At least he assumed it was artless. With Grace, you could never be sure.

"I love my new dress," she sparkled, turning her head to look up at him over her shoulder. "Thank you for buying it for me."

She was trying to whittle down his interest rate, he knew, but he couldn't resist her pretty, twinkly-eyed gratitude. "Seeing how beautiful you look in it is all the thanks I need," he said fatuously. "I meant that figuratively, of course," he called after her, weaving through tables of diners toward the door, hurrying to keep up. "Not literally!"

Outside, a thin, sickle moon hung low in a fog-free, blue-black sky. From the crest of a hill, they could see the dark form of Alcatraz Island in the Bay, the winking lights of the Marin headlands beyond. The sidewalks in Reuben's neighborhood weren't paved yet. Grace stumbled, toe caught in a warped wooden crack; he took her arm and tucked it under his, and kept it there even when the going got smoother.

He kept the pace slow, and at Union Street he started to limp. At Filbert, he leaned some of his weight on her arm.

"Are you all right?" she asked, glancing up at him from under her lashes.

He sent her a tight smile and a grim nod. By now they were down to a crawl, and he'd added a little hitch to his breathing.

"Do your ribs hurt?"

"Nothing to speak of. Let's stop for a second and look at the"—deep breath—"view." He leaned back against a dusty, dwarfed maple tree, stifling a manful groan, and slipped his free hand inside his coat. The "view" was of a vacant lot adjacent to a harness repair shop. Grace peered at him in the paltry glow of the streetlamp, but didn't say anything. "Were you comfortable last night?" he asked conversationally. "Sleep well, did you?"

She blinked at him. "Yes, thanks. Like a brick. And you?"

"Ah." Good answer, stoically vague; he let it lie for a minute. "When I was younger, I could sleep anywhere." He trailed off again, then gave a hearty, forced-sounding laugh. "Thing about that couch is that it's got a loose spring, right about—well, about rib height, if you can believe that. Shoots up right about here." He patted his vest. "Isn't that the darnedest thing?"

She said, "Hm."

He allowed another minute to pass. "Well, guess we'd better get moving. We should probably turn in early, since we'll be needing all our wits tomorrow. Mm?"

"Mm."

"Not that I expect to get too much shut-eye on that couch." He smiled, pained but good-humored. With another grunt, he propelled himself off the tree and got them going again at a pitiful, shuffling pace. At Napier Street he stopped dead in his tracks. "Say! I just thought of something."

"What could it be?"

He didn't like the gimlet gleam in her eye, but there was no turning back now. "Well, just that—" He seemed to recollect himself. "Oh, no, excuse me," he muttered, sheepish.

"What?"

"No, no, don't regard it. Bad idea, don't know what I was thinking of."

"Tell me."

"I can just imagine what you'll say," he said with a little laugh.

"What?"

"Well, just a silly thought—that we might have shared the um, the um..."

"The, um, bed?"

"Ha! There, you see? Dumb idea. Erase it from your mind."

They walked along in absolute silence for half a block. Passing under the streetlamp at the entrance to his alley, he risked a downward glance to see how she was taking it. Her brow was furrowed in thought. He put a little more weight on her while he got the key to the door out of his pocket.

He got the door unlocked, but she stopped him before he could open it. "Reuben," she said softly.

His heart actually missed a beat; she'd never called him Reuben before. "Yes, Grace?"

"I..."

"Yes?"

"I can't stand to think of you being in pain." She pulled her hand out from under his arm and then, to his amazement, slipped it inside his coat. When she started to stroke his ribs with her fingertips, he stopped breathing. "I think I know you well enough by now to trust you."

"You can trust me."

"If you really want to, you can sleep with me."

"I—" He had to swallow before he could continue. "I really want to."

"Then you can. Of course, you'd be on your honor."

"Grace," he sighed with his eyes closed. "You're an angel of mercy." It sounded like a prayer.

All his breath came out in a whoosh when

the angel landed a restrained but effective right jab to the center of his most painful rib. "You can sleep with me when pigs fly," she clarified succinctly, and sailed into the house, leaving him wheezing on the doorstep.

The next day they went to the Western Union office together with high hopes. Grace had to scan Henry's short telegram while turning around in a tight circle, because Reuben kept trying to read it over her shoulder. "Anxiously awaiting details of quote mishap unquote stop. Advise trust no one, come home immediately stop. Leg is better, not that you asked stop. Love Henry."

The money he'd wired with the cable was a crushing disappointment. After Grace paid Reuben what she owed him, at the usurious interest rate she still couldn't believe he'd charged, there was hardly anything left. In a glum mood, they left Western Union and set out for Doc Slaughter's antique shop.

She'd have walked right by Old World Curios in the nondescript block of Powell Street if Reuben hadn't taken her arm and steered her toward it. The sign was virtually unreadable and the display window was small, dark, and almost opaque from dirt and dust; squinting, she could barely make out a jumble of antiques, if that was what they were, strewn at random across a rusty strip of velour. A bell jingled overhead when they opened the door. They stood in a small square of cleared space surrounded by piles of dark clutter, unidentifiable in the dim light struggling through the dirty window. "Anybody home?" called Reuben.

From beyond a black curtain in the rear wall, a low, melodious voice answered, "A moment, if you please."

"That's Doc," Reuben told Grace with a wink. "What do you think of the place? Something, isn't it?"

"Something," she agreed. But she had no idea what, because she could barely see it. She was neat and tidy by nature; the idea of attacking Old World Curios with a broom and a dust mop appealed to her strongly.

"It takes a few minutes for the eyes to adjust." He was scanning the contents of a long, laden table in the center of the room, looking for something. Grace saw piles of broken lamps, snuff boxes, old books with mildewed covers, a tortoiseshell comb-and-brush set, music boxes, a rusty pistol. "I wonder if that...ah, here it is. Take a look at this, Grace."

"What is it?" A plain wooden box, rough, unpainted, with a half-moon cut in the side that had hinges and a little door handle.

"Open it."

She did, and was enchanted when the tinny strains of "Beautiful Dreamer" floated out of the box. But her smile evaporated when she saw the carved figure inside, of a bald man sitting on a toilet with his pants around his ankles, grinning at her around a corncob pipe in his teeth. She slapped the door shut and pushed the box back into Reuben's hands. "Very funny." He was snickering with amusement, his grin as stupid-looking as the man on the toilet's. "Charming. Exactly the kind of thing I'd expect you to like," she said quellingly.

"I can't understand why nobody's bought it," he said, sincerely puzzled, shaking his head and putting the box back on the table. "It's here every time I come in."

"That really is unexplainable." A movement to her right caught her eye. "Oh, look— finches." Dozens of them, she thought at first, fluttering with ceaseless industry from perch to perch in a wicker birdcage. But after she'd studied them for a minute, she saw that there were only nine birds in the cage, pretty things, bright flashes of gray and yellow, incapable of stillness for longer than a few seconds at a time. "Aren't they sweet? I had a parakeet when I was a girl."

"On the ranchero?" Reuben inquired, standing too close behind her shoulder. The smell of bay rum teased her, made her want to turn around and inhale. "Was that before or after Maria Elena got the stigmata?"

She chuckled, hunting for a retort. Last night she'd lain awake for a long time, bombarded by pictures and images of what might've—no, what *would've* happened if she'd pretended to believe Reuben's sore-rib story and let him sleep with her in his big bed. Annoyingly, the images came flooding back now, graphic and familiar, uncomfortably stirring.

"Good day to you. May I help you with something?"

The voice was quiet, deep, soothing; it was the unexpectedness of it that made her spin around in a startled pivot, brushing Reuben's coat sleeve with her breast. A man stood behind them in the shadows. Pale, rake-thin, he was so tall that the top of Grace's head didn't reach to his bulbous Adam's apple. She could only see half of his face in the dimness, and guessed him to be somewhere on the far side of fifty. He wore a loose, long-sleeved jumper and a pair of baggy corduroy pants, both in an indeterminate shade of gray or brown, it was hard to tell which; on his feet were soft-soled Chinese slippers, which explained how he'd come up on them so quietly. His rather harsh features mellowed when he saw Reuben; his lips parted in a smile, revealing long brown teeth.

"Reuben, how are you? It's been a long time. I was beginning to wonder if you'd forgotten about your ring."

"Doc, good to see you. No, no, I just haven't had time to stop in. Business, you know. Keeps me hopping all the time."

Doc didn't seem to believe this any more than Reuben seemed to care if he did or not. Watching them shake hands and exchange small talk, Grace deduced that they liked each other, but weren't great friends. She sensed mutual respect, too, but not necessarily trust.

When Reuben got around to introducing her,

as an "old friend," Doc made her a courtly, old-fashioned bow. The smell of tobacco smoke hung around him like an invisible fog. "A great pleasure, Mrs. Rousselot," he intoned in his wonderful voice. "Any old friend of Reuben's will, I hope, become an old friend of mine."

She said something suitable back—then froze for a split second when he turned his shadowed profile toward the window. As if sensing her shock, he stepped back again, away from the dim sunshine wavering in beams of dust through the murky glass. But it was too late: she'd already seen the thick, livid scars that covered all of the left side of his face, from jawbone to brow. Pity immediately supplanted her horror. But there was no time to communicate anything to him, by a look or a word; with a murmured apology and something about Reuben's ring, Doc Slaughter turned his back on her and disappeared through the curtain in the wall.

"Mother of God," Grace breathed, rubbing her arms. "Reuben, how *awful*. Do you think he thinks I'm afraid of him now? I couldn't help it—I think I *jumped* when I saw his face. Why didn't you tell me? What happened to him?"

"An accident, years ago. I'm sorry, I should've warned you, but I just didn't think. I'm so used to it, it didn't even occur to me. Grace, don't worry. He's fine." His fingers gently squeezed her shoulder. "He's fine, really, you'll see."

And when he came back, he did seem to be

fine. He retreated behind a row of chest-high, glass-fronted shelves that doubled as a counter along the right side of the shop, and cleared a space among a collection of colored glass bottles for a display board, black velvet, about ten inches square.

"Come look at the ring," he invited, making no attempt this time to hide his disfigurement. But the gloominess of the shop served as a mask by itself, and the full, pitiful extent of his deformity remained obscure.

He opened a small box, removed the ring inside, and laid it on the square of velvet. Plain gold, with a half-dozen polished garnets inlaid around the circumference, the ring was handsome if not particularly distinctive.

But Reuben was elated. "It's perfect," he announced, fitting it to the fourth finger of his right hand. "Exactly what I wanted. Like it, Grace?"

"Yes, it's very nice."

"Know what it's for?"

"For?"

He smiled mysteriously. "Let's try it out," he told Doc, who reached under the counter and retrieved a deck of playing cards from the bottom shelf. Bemused, Grace watched Reuben shuffle the cards and deal five to her, five to himself, while Doc lit a cigarette and leaned back against the wall.

"What's the game?" she asked.

"Draw. Just one friendly hand. No ante, and the bet's to you."

She squinted at her hand. "I'll start with a thousand dollars."

"See that and raise you five. How many do you want?"

She looked back at her mess of nothing and asked for three.

"Three for the lady, and the dealer takes a pair. Bet is back to the lady."

"Mmm. Five thousand."

"Raise that five more."

"I'll see your raise because you're bluffing, Jones."

"Find out."

Grace spread her hand on the counter: a pair of jacks.

"Gotcha with trips," Reuben gloated, showing three deuces. Shuffle the cards."

"New game?"

"Nope." He took the deck back when she'd finished shuffling. "What'll you bet I can pick out those three little old deuces blind, Gus?"

She opened her mouth to say something smart, but then a hint of what he was up to hit her. She smiled a slow, foxy smile. "Pass."

He palmed the deck expertly, fanned it, and extracted one, two, three cards, laying them facedown on the black velvet square. Without surprise, Grace turned them over and saw deuces. The pinhole was tiny, and he'd made it in the red or the black, never the white, rendering the dot all but invisible unless you were looking for it. The bubble it made on the other side was only a speck, a grain, unnoticeable unless you knew it was there. Or you had extraordinarily sensitive fingers.

"May I see the ring?" she asked. With a wink for Doc, Reuben took the ring off and dropped it on her palm. At first she couldn't figure out the mechanism; she pressed on each red stone separately, but nothing happened. But when she pressed on two opposite stones at once, a tiny pin emerged from the gold filigree between two others.

She laughed out loud, delighted. "Did you make it?" Last night Reuben had told her about some of Doc's accomplishments, fencing and forgery among them, but nothing about jewelry making. Doc didn't respond to her question directly, but his pursed lips and modest wave of the hand were answer enough. "It's wonderful," she praised him, "really ingenious. You do beautiful work."

He took a drag from his cigarette and blew out a thin stream of smoke. "Thanks."

Reuben cleared his throat. "How about taking twenty on it until tomorrow."

She drifted away tactfully to give the gentlemen privacy to conduct their business arrangement. When she saw money change hands and Reuben pocket the ring, she moved back to the counter.

"Spare a few more minutes, Doc?" Reuben asked.

"Of course."

"We were wondering if you'd take a look at something for us. Grace has it."

She was already opening her new pocketbook,

a pretty tapestry bag that went well, she thought, with her new dress. She drew out the tiger, which she'd wrapped in a pillowcase, along with the piece of paper with the Chinese characters. Doc found his spectacles in his pocket and bent over the items on the velvet square. He made a humming noise Grace couldn't interpret, turning the tiger over in his hands. After a moment, he took it over to the window where the light was better. More humming sounds. She and Reuben exchanged looks.

"Glazed porcelain," he said, coming back. "Ming, unless it's a fake."

"It's no fake," Reuben assured him. "How old is Ming?"

"Fourteenth to seventeenth century."

"So this would be...?"

"Two to five hundred years old. That's all I can say; I'd have to show it to someone who knows more to nail it down better than that."

"How much is it worth?"

"It might be part of a set," Grace threw in. Reuben frowned at her, and she remembered she was supposed to let him do the talking.

"Depends on who's buying." For the first time, he looked up from the statue. "It's interesting that you'd come by with this today, Reuben. I was just reading in the paper yesterday about some Chinese art being stolen from a Wells Fargo stage by masked bandits."

"Is that a fact? Missed it; didn't read the paper yesterday. My grandmother passed away and left this to me."

Grace thought Doc's long, thin lips quirked at that. "Want to leave this with me?"

"Sure. We're kind of in a hurry, though. Can you find out something by tomorrow?"

"Try." He picked up the paper and unfolded it. "What's this?"

"That's something else we were hoping you could tell us."

Doc was scowling down at the paper; the cigarette in his mouth trailed smoke straight into his right eye, but he didn't blink. "Where'd you get this?"

Grace put her elbow on the counter, her chin in her hand, resigned to silence.

"Chinese guy gave it to me."

This time Doc didn't smile. "Do you know what this is?"

"No, that's why I'm—"

"This." He tapped a spatulate forefinger over the pen-and-ink flower at the top of the page. "It's a white lotus."

"So? What's it mean?"

"I've heard of it," Grace blurted out. "It's a religious sect in China, isn't it?"

"About five hundred years ago it was, yes," he confirmed. "It was a secret organization, mostly Buddhists, dedicated to overthrowing the Mongols. It died out eventually, but flourished again briefly in the late seventeen hundreds, only this time the object was to expel the Manchus and restore the Mings."

"Obviously it failed," observed Grace, who knew that the Manchus ruled China today.

"Yes, it was crushed. The Manchus denounced it by name in their penal code."

"So what's this?" asked Reuben, rattling the paper.

Doc blew smoke through his nose and didn't answer for several moments. "If you want to find out, it's going to cost you some money. More than you might think."

Reuben bristled. "Why? All we want is a translation—how much could that cost?"

"A great deal, if everyone I ask is afraid to look at it."

"Afraid? Why would they be?"

"Come back tomorrow and find out. Bring lots of money." The brown teeth gave him a cadaverous look when he smiled; Grace thought he was doing it on purpose. Reuben grumbled for a while longer, but eventually agreed. She was beginning to understand that he and Doc had a contingency arrangement flexible enough to cover all kinds of business situations.

"Wait, please, before you go." Doc held up a bony, tobacco-stained finger, stopping them. "Two seconds." He disappeared through the curtain, and was back in half a minute. "Reuben has a new ring," he said, placing a small jeweller's box on the counter. "Voilà. Something for the lady."

When he opened the box for her, Grace saw a silver brooch on a bed of dark blue velvet. "Oh, it's beautiful," she exclaimed politely, automatically—before her eyes registered the fact that it truly was beautiful.

"It's an angel." She picked it up in careful fingers, marveling over the delicacy of the piece. It was half an angel, from the waist up, with the pretty face in profile and the arms and wings outstretched, and long, wavy hair streaming to one side as if a heavenly wind were blowing into the angel's face. It made her think of a book of drawings she'd once seen, by the poet William Blake. "It's lovely, it truly is. Exquisite. I'm afraid I couldn't take it."

"But you must," Doc replied, his voice deep and gentle. "It's a gift."

"But—"

"Grace," chided Reuben, with a wholly mercenary glint in his eye. "It's a gift."

In the end she took it gladly, moved by the gesture because behind it she could see no motive except kindness. Even when Doc swore that he'd thought of the brooch as soon as Grace had walked into his shop, she was certain he had no intentions beyond generosity. Her nature wasn't cynical, but it was astute; if he'd been laying a groundwork of flattery for some future deceit, she believed she'd have known it.

Outside on the pavement, the sun blinded them. Reuben pulled her along with a long, purposeful stride; she had to walk fast to keep up. "Where are we going?" she asked, catching her breath while a carriage passed in front of them on Powell at Bush Street.

"Gambling, Grace."

"Where?"

"There," he said, pointing.

"The Golden Nugget," she read on the side of a long, clapboard-sided building on the far corner. "My, what an original name."

"Maybe not, but the play's reasonably square."

"What are you going to play *with*?" she inquired politely.

"Money. The blackjack dealer's a friend of mine, advances me a little credit from time to time when the owner's not looking."

"Why?"

"I told you: friendship." Taking her hand, he stepped off the curb and headed for the Golden Nugget.

5

Take all the fools out of this world, and there wouldn't be any fun or profit left in living in it.

—Josh Billings

The blackjack dealer's name was Alice, and she had the biggest bust Grace had ever seen on a woman who wasn't nursing.

She sat on a stool, her back to the wall, in the crotch of an L-shaped table, dealing cards to six or seven cheerful-looking men across the worn baize surface. She could've been twenty-five or forty, depending on your point of view. Grace put her at the high end, crediting cosmetics for her faultless complexion, and very likely her coal-black hair as well. She had on a low-cut gown of heliotrope brocade, snug as wax at the hips, and sprouting bows, feathers, and jet from the puffed shoulders. When she leaned forward to slap cards down in front of her glassy-eyed patrons, the surface area of bare powdered bosom increased by alarming exponential increments. *Talk about a diversion*, marveled Grace; Alice's bust was more dazzling than the sleight-of-hand of the most accomplished thimblerigger in the city. And if, once in a while, some jaded player was unawed by her prodigious endowments, she could rely on the life-size oil painting on the wall behind her—of a voluptuous reclining nude, shielding her most private place with one tiny, inadequate pink hand—to distract him from the occasional palmed card or double-cut deck.

The Golden Nugget, with its fat chandeliers, gilded paintings and mirrors, and countless gaming tables thronged with gamblers, reminded Grace of pictures she'd seen of casinos from the olden days, the wild fifties when gold-rush fever had first hit San Francisco. But it was a serious house, not a nostalgic tourist attraction, judging from the swarming herds of men throwing their money away at roulette, rondo, *rouge et noir*, faro, poker, keno, and twenty-one. The clientele was mixed, from businessmen in suits to Mexicans in blankets. There were even a few flashy women, and not all of them prostitutes. Besides Alice, the casino employed a pretty, respectable-looking girl who sat at a table and sold coffee and cakes, adding tone to the joint. She didn't have many paying customers, though; cigars and spirits were the primary refreshments here. Tobacco smoke hung from the ceiling like fog over the Bay, and the smell of beer and brandy was almost overwhelming.

Alice's bored but watchful face lit up with pleasure when she saw Reuben weaving toward her through the jostling crowd, Grace in his wake. The enthusiasm with which she greeted him made Grace wonder if credit was the only thing she was in the habit of advancing, out of friendship.

"Hi, honey," Alice greeted her when Reuben introduced them, and Grace returned a circumspect hello. That did it for conversation between the ladies, because after that Alice only had eyes for Reuben.

And he for her. Watching them together, half amused, half nettled, Grace had an opportunity to observe Reuben's technique up close. He was a killer of the first degree, she concluded in less than a minute. It wasn't even his good looks that caused the devastation; if anything he was too handsome, a man not to be trusted on that score alone. No, what really made him dangerous was the fatal thread of sincerity that wove through his effortless charm, smooth as snake oil. Henry had it, too, the ability to make you believe every word he said simply because you wanted to believe it. With men like that you couldn't help yourself—you wanted to please them, to keep that radiant, mesmerizing good will they flashed with their warm eyes and their ravishing smiles. Alice was nobody's fool; she looked as if she'd been around the track any number of times. But in this case she might have met her match: if it came to a showdown between Reuben and the dealer, Grace was putting her money on the gentleman.

Words were exchanged between them in low voices; Grace missed half, and the other half were in some kind of code. The bountiful Alice glanced around the hall, no doubt trying to spot the houseman. Grace followed her gaze, and by the time she looked back, Reuben was sitting at the blackjack table and pulling in a stack of chips in exchange for a bill she knew couldn't cover them. Score one for the gent.

Whether or not Alice's largesse extended to helping him beat her at her own game was another question; the dealer's hands flew too fast for Grace to spot any bottom deals, crimps, or seconds. But he did win, with steady, temperate play, enlivened by unexpectedly risky bets on doubtful-looking cards—bets that never seemed to fail. Grace scrutinized the byplay for signals between them, but couldn't detect any. After a while, she forgot about signs and countersigns and grew fixated instead on Reuben's hands. The hands of an artist, she recalled fantasizing on the stage-coach, and she hadn't been far wrong. His medium was cards instead of clay, but his long, crafty fingers looked as sensitive as a sculptor's. Did he file his fingertips with sandpaper? Some sharps did, until the skin bled. But cards were only one of Reuben Jones's games, so she thought he probably didn't. She suspected he was a natural. A born prestidigitator.

He was wearing black again today; even his shirt was black, and the natty string tie around his stiff white collar. If the idea was to look like a gambler, then he'd succeeded. And yet, somehow his face didn't fit the role. It was too…complicated. Not slick or purposeful or ruthless, like the faces of most professional gamblers she'd observed, in Henry's company, in her young life. There was too much going on behind Reuben's dark-lashed eyes and his beaked nose, his clever mouth. Too many possibilities attracted him, and he was good at all of them—blind Spanish scholar, roof salesman, correspondence-school principal, blackjack magician. She didn't trust him farther than she could throw an andiron.

It took him fifteen minutes to pay Alice back for her covert advance, and only thirty more to triple his poke. In his place, on such a streak, Grace knew she'd have kept playing, but one of his numerous virtues seemed to be knowing when to stop. He raked his winnings into his hat, planted a wet-looking kiss on the dealer's lips, stood up, and walked away to cash in his chips at the bar. The suddenness of the move took Grace by surprise; she drifted after him uncertainly. "Have fun, honey," Alice called to her with a good-natured wink.

She took a seat on a stool beside him in front of the long mahogany bar, resting her toes on the brass rail, resisting the blinding pull of his smile. She was back in his line of vision, so to speak, a player once more on the stage of his mind. She shouldn't be put out, she told herself; he'd only been doing his job, which he did extremely well. Henry had the same genius for making people believe they were the sole, fascinating center of his attention, and watching him employ it had always amused, never irritated her. Nevertheless, she returned Reuben's infectious grin with a cool stare; and when the bartender brought him a congratulatory beer, she ordered a prim lemonade.

She couldn't remain stiff forever, though, and her reserve softened when he showed her his winnings. When he offered her half, it melted away completely.

"What now?" she asked, fanning out her four crisp fifties, tapping the edges into neat, symmetrical alignment.

He signaled to a girl selling cigars and cigarettes down at the other end of the bar. "Poker's my game, Grace. What we want is something big."

"Here?"

He shook his head. "I'll take half a dozen of those," he said to the cigarette girl, pointing to an open box of cheroots. He told her she was pretty, made her blush with his killer smile, and sent her on her way with a ridiculously large tip.

Grace snickered, stirring more sugar into her lemonade.

"What's funny?"

"You are, Jones."

He didn't ask why; his self-conscious grin said he already knew. He lit a thin cigar with a bar match and stuck it between his teeth, one eye squinted against the smoke. He looked like a satisfied pirate. "Want one?" he asked, as if suddenly remembering his manners.

"A cigar? No, thanks."

"You don't smoke? Too bad. I had a kibitzing partner once who smoked great big stogies. He'd blow two smoke rings if a guy had a pair"—he demonstrated with two thick, perfect hoops of smoke—"three for three of a kind"—he blew three—"four for four of a kind"—four. "And furious puffing"—his head disappeared in a cloud of smoke—"for a flush."

Grace made the mistake of taking a sip of lemonade just before he demonstrated the signal for a flush. A helpless burst of laughter caused some of it to go down the wrong pipe, and the rest to explode from her mouth in a fine spray, wetting Reuben's shirtfront. He patted her between the shoulder blades, chuckling with delight.

When the coughing fit ended and she finished drying her eyes, she returned to the question at hand. "Why don't you want to gamble here? I thought you said the play was square." She glanced around the big, busy room, alive with the hum of male voices and the clink of money.

Reuben followed her gaze through the long mirror behind the bar. "Maybe it's too square."

She gave him a long, speculative appraisal through her lashes, which he returned with innocent, open-faced interest. They were both leaning on the bar on their crossed forearms. She moved closer; he followed suit. "Jones," she opened.

"Here."

"You've got good hands."

He looked down at his left one and wriggled his fingers. "Nice of you to say so."

"How's your nerve?"

Something danced deep in the light brown of his irises. The suave planes of his face sharpened subtly. "What makes you ask?"

"I've been thinking about a little brace game I once had occasion to observe. You wouldn't happen to be any good at seven-card stud, would you?"

His slow smile caused a curious fluttering sensation in the pit of her stomach. "Honey, I'm the best you ever saw."

"That's good," she said, trying to make her voice crisp. "But for this particular game we'll need something besides skill. Something extra. We'll need a cold deck."

His smile turned positively diabolical. He tossed back the tail of his frock coat, reached into his back pocket, and removed a plain deck of cards. Commonplace blue-speckled backs, as ordinary as water. "Razored aces," he murmured, lips close to her ear, voice intimate as a lover's. "A thirty-second of an inch. If you can pick 'em out, Grace, I'll give you everything I own."

Her laugh sounded shaky. "No, thanks, I'll take your word for it." She wanted to move back, away from his disturbing nearness, but the details of the game she had in mind required confidentiality.

Because it was complicated, it took a long time to explain it. When she finished, the awe in his face made her blush—something she never did. "Grace," he breathed, shaking his head in wonder. "Grace, Grace, Grace." Before she knew what he meant to do, he slid his arm around her and kissed her on the lips.

It didn't last long. Just long enough for the truth to sink in that this was what she'd wanted him to do ever since that first night, when they'd stood outside her hotel-room door and he'd pitched that bunkum about her "distinctive bouquet." His lips were firm, almost hard, but they were warm, too, and they fit next to hers exactly right. The malty taste of beer sweetened the kiss, personalized it somehow. It was just a brief, friendly buss— she didn't even close her eyes—but when it was over she had to stop herself from following Reuben's head back to keep the contact.

His dancing eyes made her smile. "Sweetheart," he murmured, still holding her by the waist, "I think we were made for each other."

She lifted skeptical eyebrows and didn't answer. In the back of her mind lurked the disturbing possibility that he might have a point.

No houseman, no shills, no rake—the Evergreen Hotel Saloon had it all. It was the third place they'd tried, searching for a quiet, clean establishment, where the play was modest but not stodgy, and most important, where Reuben wasn't known.

"You gentlemen need a fifth?" he'd inquired of the quartet at a back table, prosperous-looking types but not high rollers, maybe traveling salesmen, playing a desultory game of euchre and looking as if they'd welcome some fresh action. If professionals played here, he couldn't see any, but it was still early; the big sharps' games started much later and might go on for days.

He took an empty chair with its back to the wall, in case railbirds showed up later, and gave everybody a friendly smile. Grace had made him take off his tie, his vest, his collar, and his gold watch, claiming they made him look too dangerous—"like a big black coyote drooling in a sheepfold."

"What's the game?" he asked. "Euchre?" They admitted it. He looked bemused but agreeable; a moment later, as he'd hoped, one of them suggested they switch to draw poker.

106

The setup was simple at the Evergreen. There were no dealers, no house players, no floormen; just friendly games of chance among gentlemen, who bought their chips at the table from an invisible banker. The house provided the chips and the cards, and in return the drinks and cigars cost a little more than they would at a casino. Table stakes was the rule, but it was flexible, and for now there was a ten-dollar limit on first bets and raises.

He was Obman, he told them—a name he liked to use because in Russian it meant trickery and deceit. The tall, skinny, bald-headed fellow to his left was Burgess; next to him was Sharkey, hard and sullen, with thick lips and a thin cigar; then Wyatt, fat and jolly, sporting an old-fashioned Prince Albert coat and striped trousers; and finally red-haired Rusty, freckled and vacant, with an irritating habit of clearing his throat. Burgess and Wyatt were pals; they worked for the same photographic-equipment manufacturing company. Rusty knew them because his cousin's wife married Wyatt's brother's something or other—Reuben stopped listening and didn't catch it. The wild card was Sharkey; like Reuben, he'd invited himself into the game. Nobody knew him, nobody could vouch for him. He claimed he was staying at the hotel, though, and the bartender was letting him run a tab. Reuben guessed that was some kind of endorsement.

He had a bad moment when a new man,

apparently an acquaintance of Rusty's, wandered over to kibitz and bum cigarettes and—Reuben was mortally afraid—offer to sit in the game. Visions of having to start all over somewhere else filled him with gloom, for a sixth player would completely muck up the carefully arranged cooler hidden in his inside coat pocket. But his luck held; the man's cronies at another table called him back over, and he drifted away with a wave and a wink in a cloud of cigarette smoke.

About that time, Grace made her entrance. Reuben kept his eyes on his cards, pretending not to see her. Everybody else saw her, though. Conversations halted; dice fell silent; cards lay forgotten. Rusty finally kicked Reuben in the calf to get his attention. "Will you look at that?" he demanded. Wyatt said, "Mmm-mmm-mmm," as if he'd just bitten into a warm piece of pie. Burgess pretended to fan his face with his cards. Sharkey said something so explicitly vulgar even Reuben felt a jolt of revulsion. His antipathy to Sharkey, whom he'd disliked on sight, intensified, and he was glad. Sometimes he needed an edge, a personal motivation when he was about to shear a sheep. And if everything went right, Sharkey would be sheared the closest, because he was sitting in the sucker seat.

She wasn't really beautiful. That too came to Reuben with a jolt, for up to now he'd believed completely in the illusion of beauty she deliberately fostered. But it was a trick. She tossed her hair, looked deeply into your eyes, smiled her suicide smile—she *acted* beautiful, and by sheer nerve and sleight of hand she made you believe she was. You never saw the flaws because you were too caught up in the trick, the mystique; seduced by the patter, you were watching the wrong hand.

She glided up to the bar, oblivious to the interest her entrance had aroused, and asked for a drink. Her wine-colored dress fit her like a tight, tasteful glove, and Reuben congratulated himself again on his generosity in springing for it. The bartender set a tall glass in front of her; from here it looked like more lemonade. Before she could get her money out, the long-haired cowboy standing next to her shoved a quarter at the bartender, leaned in close, and said something to her out of the side of his mouth.

Looking directly at him, she said something back. The cowboy grinned, shuffled his feet, and straightened his collar to please her.

Her style wasn't to freeze a man out with an ice-cold stare and a cutting remark—although Reuben knew from experience she was capable of it. No, what she did was *warm* you to death with her huge blue eyes and the sincerity in her sly, sexy mouth, that tentative smile trembling at the corners so sweetly, so *kindly,* you wanted to take her home and spend the rest of your life trying to make her laugh. She was the most natural bunco runner he'd ever met.

She asked the bartender a question, and he

pointed at a table of gamblers across the way, then at Reuben's table. Taking her drink with her, she sauntered over to the first group. There were five of them—one too many, or Reuben might have joined their game instead of this one because they looked a shade richer. They all wanted her to sit down. She demurred, with some excuse that made them bark with laughter. They resumed their game at her insistence, but they looked self-conscious, sitting straighter in their chairs, refraining from spitting, slicking their hair back when she wasn't looking.

"Are we playing poker or not?" Reuben queried, clacking a short stack of chips on the table impatiently. Everybody but Sharkey grinned and looked sheepish and went back to the cards. Sharkey scraped his chair back from the table and walked over to talk to Grace.

He was a big, ugly, lumbering son of a bitch, and Reuben didn't like the way they looked together, her neat and fair and petite, him hulking and drooling like a gorilla. It was fine as long as he kept his hands in his back pockets and inflicted his oafish flirtation on her with nothing but his tongue. But when he wound one of his long ape's arms around her waist, Reuben's sense of humor went into a decline, and his interest in the scheme they'd set in motion started to thin.

He should've known she could take care of herself. With a little dance step that got Sharkey's hand off her, timed perfectly with

110

a dazzling smile that made sure he never even noticed, she moved him, without touching, toward his own table—and the look on his blockish face said he thought it was his idea.

"This here's Miss Wanda LaSalle, boys, and she's gonna sit down with us and play some cards. Anybody object?"

Far from it. Into the chorus of hearty "Hell, no's," Reuben threw in a querulous, "Well, personally, I don't cotton much to playing cards with women."

Sharkey removed his cigar, spat a speck of tobacco on the floor, and told him he didn't cotton much to playing cards with smart-ass needle dicks with bad attitudes, and that Reuben could shut the hell up and deal or get the hell out of the game. Feigning sullenness, Reuben tipped his hat over his eyes and slid lower in his seat.

Grace took the chair Sharkey had dragged over and wedged between his seat and Wyatt's. It was the right position, the place she had to be or the trick wouldn't work, but Reuben still didn't like it. "What's the game, gentlemen?" she asked sweetly. Rusty told her, and she said, "Oh," with just the right note of disappointment. What would she rather play? they asked anxiously. Well, she allowed, hopeful smile flickering, her real favorite was seven-card stud. Seven-card stud it was, the men declared, over Reuben's surly objection that stud was a sissy's game; next they'd be calling one-eyed jacks wild, he complained, and betting hair pins. Nobody paid any attention to him.

111

She bought two hundred dollars' worth of chips right off the bat, which had a slightly sobering effect on the boys' playful mood. They offered her the first deal, though, without cutting for it. Her hands on the cards were dainty, a trifle clumsy—but not too much; she shuffled the way most women ran: like girls. She was a real piece of work.

Betting heavily, she lost every hand.

Rusty felt terrible; Burgess and Wyatt tried to cheer her up; even Sharkey offered to switch to high-low. But she took her losses like a man, and stayed in the game to the bitter end—or until it was Reuben's turn to deal. He passed her two crimped jacks and another from the bottom of the deck, one up and two in the hole. She ran out of chips on sixth street, and only stayed in for seventh because everybody else checked. Except for the lone jack, she had garbage on the board, and Reuben couldn't help her; with this deck, the last card could be anything. Sharkey raised Burgess's twenty-dollar reraise, and the bet was to the lady. When her hand went hesitantly to the angel pin on her bosom, Reuben closed his eyes in relief. It meant she had something good, something better than three jacks. It meant she couldn't lose.

"This brooch is solid silver, gentlemen," she announced. "Lordy, my luck's *got* to change sometime." She fingered her river card hopefully. "My brooch to see your raise, plus another forty?" she offered, lacy lashes fluttering. She'd stuck the brooch close to the tip of her breast; she ran two soft fingertips back and forth across the angel's flowing hair, absently brushing her nipple with each pass. Sharkey swallowed and gaped, hypnotized. Rusty couldn't stop clearing his throat.

"Yeah." "Sure." "Forty, okay." "Fine with me."

The pot burgeoned. It took her a long time to unpin the brooch and add it to the kitty, but nobody complained.

In the showdown, her pocket card turned out to be a matching nine. "Jacks full," she announced happily. Reuben swore and threw his hand in without showing. Burgess, Wyatt, and Rusty did the same, although with better grace.

"Well, I'm damned," muttered Sharkey, staring at the cards, trying to believe it. He had king trips showing, probably drawing to a full house of his own. He stumped his cigar out hard, hawked, and spat into the cuspidor.

It was wonderful how Wanda LaSalle's luck changed after that. With her brooch on the table beside her, "for luck," her stack of chips rose higher and higher and higher. The game heated up; pot limits and table stakes went by the board. Wyatt, the jolly fat man, turned out to have deep pockets and a penchant for chasing trips or two measly pairs all the way to seventh street and losing big. Burgess was a fish, too, but not as reckless. Everybody enjoyed picking off Rusty, who bluffed like a kid with jelly on his mouth.

But Sharkey was the man Reuben longed to

stuff. He was a lout, but he wasn't stupid. Whether he was a sharp remained to be seen, but he hadn't lost his caution yet. The game had gotten very loose and very fast, but Sharkey still played it close, calling and betting in monosyllables, eyes hooded like a lizard. And his regard for the lovely Wanda was entirely too warm for Reuben's taste, manifesting itself in hot stares, crude lip-licking, and even a quick grope under the table once, the scope of which Reuben wasn't able to assess from his vantage across the way. But it rankled.

If he'd had any doubts about Grace's ability to win consistently in a relatively square game, she laid them to rest in minutes. She was shrewd, patient, unpredictable, and fearless—and lucky. She could read a bluff like a newspaper, and perpetrate one as convincingly as anybody he'd ever played with. Most important, she had a professional's attitude toward money, which meant thinking of the chips as abstractions, worthless as pebbles or pinto beans until the game was over. If you had too much respect for money, you were done for.

In between hands, she asked the boys about their lives. They were shy at first, then amazingly forthcoming. The atmosphere started to resemble a fire-hall social more than a high-stakes poker game. She spun them a fascinating tale about learning to play cards from her father, the late Mr. LaSalle, who'd dropped dead at the faro table in a Virginia City saloon last year, leaving her with nothing but his favorite dice and the few simple gambling skills she possessed. It was a difficult life sometimes, and not very respectable, she knew, but a girl on her own had to get along somehow.

The bare bones of the story were completely incredible, but not a man among them doubted it. She was just so damn good.

She had sharp timing, too. At almost precisely the same moment Reuben decided it was time to move on to stage two, she sent him the signal. "Looks like I win again," she chortled, gathering in another pot on her own deal. "I haven't had so much fun since Aunt Aggie's drawers fell down at the covered-dish supper."

"Hold it." Reuben's hand shot out and snagged her wrist. "I want to see those cards."

"What? Let go of me. Let go!" She made a grab for her discarded hand, but he beat her to it, scooping up all seven and fanning them out, squinting at the backs, then the fronts.

"Ha! I knew it! Look at that queen—see that?"

"What?" "I don't see nothing." "What the hell!"

They didn't want to believe it, but there it was, big as life: a pinhole right through the black ruff around the queen's neck. Reuben had put it there himself two hands ago with his new ring.

"She did it with her brooch," he accused, pointing at the silver pin by Grace's elbow. "It's been there on the table since she first bet it. She's marking the damn cards with it."

"That's not true! I never cheated in my life!" She glanced around the table, desperate for support. If they'd had nothing to go on but her angel's face, they'd have rendered a unanimous acquittal in three seconds flat. But there was the queen, stuck through the throat, and there was the brooch, six inches away; she'd even been fiddling with it off and on during the game.

"Look at this," Reuben said, clinching it. "She did it to the heart, spade, and club queens, too. She marked every damn queen in the deck."

"I didn't!" She pressed her hand over her heart. "I'm innocent, I swear. It must've been somebody else, or—or else they were already marked and you just noticed."

Reuben snorted.

"Please—I wouldn't do it, I couldn't. Don't you believe me?"

Burgess and Wyatt shifted in their chairs, intensely uncomfortable. Rusty's ears turned red and his freckles popped out. Sharkey stared at her hard, petting his mustache and scrolling his lips. Nobody spoke.

"Well, gentlemen." Her mouth trembled and her dainty hands shook, but her voice stayed steady and wonderfully sad. She pushed her winnings into the center of the table, brooch and all, and stood up. "Thank you for your company. And now...I'll say good evening to you."

It was the tears that did it. They glittered on her lashes, refusing to fall, turning her eyes into blue pools of poignant suffering.

Between the tears and her heartbreaking dignity, they were all goners.

"Wait," growled Sharkey. He grabbed her elbow and held her still. "Somebody else could've marked 'em."

"Oh, sure," Reuben scoffed. "Who's been winning?"

Rusty cleared his throat. "Maybe they were already like that. How do we know? Nobody checked 'em, we just started playing. Somebody could've stamped 'em before—days ago, for all we know. It's *possible*."

Burgess and Wyatt were nodding their heads, with more hope than conviction. They had the goods on her, but nobody wanted to admit it.

"Honest to God," Grace breathed, while a touching, childlike hope began to bloom in her tragic face, "I wouldn't know how to mark a deck of cards if my life depended on it."

More thoughtful nodding. Reuben let some of his scorn go and concentrated on looking doubtful.

"I say we get a new deck and let her stay in," Sharkey opined at last. "On a trial basis. We keep an eye on her—which won't be no hardship," he leered, giving her elbow a familiar squeeze. "We see anything fishy, we give her the bum's rush."

"Does she get to keep what she won?" wondered Rusty.

"Can't have it both ways," Reuben put in quickly. "Either she cheated or she didn't. If you let her stay in, you're saying she didn't."

They couldn't argue with that. Nobody liked it, but they decided to let her keep her winnings.

"No," Grace said, wrinkling her brow adorably. They looked at her in surprise. "I don't want it if you think I stole it. Take it back and we'll just start all over." Now they laughed at her, affectionately, indulgently. They had to talk her out of giving them their money back. "Well, at least take some," she argued, pouting a little. "Take a hundred each. No, I insist." And so it was that Grace gave four hundred dollars away—five, counting Reuben's—and got in return the trust and devotion of four very stupid gulls.

She took her seat again with murmured thanks to all, and a special smile of gratitude for Sharkey. He turned beet-red and fingered his collar. If he'd been about to suggest that they switch to a different game now, the smile brushed the idea out of his brain like a whisk broom.

Rusty got a new deck from the bartender, and play resumed. On schedule, Grace began to lose. The men were sorry to see it, since it tended to confirm their worst suspicions; but getting more of their losses back mitigated their disappointment. Sharkey was the biggest winner. The incident seemed to have untied a knot in him, dissolved a clot, and the quickness of the game in the aftermath had him playing just shy of reckless. But it wasn't only him; the fever spread to everybody as the game progressed, and Reuben pretended it had

118

infected him, too. He bet most of his chips on an inside straight draw, and lost to Sharkey's six-high flush. The fever got hotter. All the money was on the table now, nobody was holding out. The time had arrived.

Grace knew it too; she darted a subtle glance at him over her hole cards, which she always played from her hand instead of the board. She had about three hundred dollars in chips left, plus her brooch. Rusty gathered the cards up and shoved them to his left. It was Reuben's deal.

Between shuffles, he signaled the bartender for another beer. "Anybody else? Wanda, you need another lemonade?" She shrugged and said sure. Reuben passed the deck to Burgess to cut, then paused to light a cheroot. The bartender came over and set the drinks down from a tray. Grace picked up her old glass before he could, to finish off the last swallow in the bottom. She took a dainty swig, smiled at the bartender, and handed the empty glass up to him. He never touched it—she let the glass go a split second too soon and it slipped from her fingers. Reuben had the straight deck between his knees and the cooler on the table before all the glass shards quit rolling on the floor.

Exclamations, apologies, reassurances. He waited until the hubbub died down before he started to deal.

Two down, one up. They all liked what they saw. Sharkey had ace high and bet a hundred, the biggest lead in the game so far.

An excellent beginning, thought Reuben. Rusty, who had the worst hand in the deal, surprised him by raising thirty bucks, and the bet went around again. On fourth street, Burgess's pair of queens was high, and he led with another hundred. Nobody batted an eye.

On fifth street, Sharkey caught another ace. That made two, and one in the hole. His ugly face never changed; he checked his hole card with no visible excitement, like a mother checking a baby's diaper. But something crackled in the air. Reuben would've felt it even if he hadn't known the cards everybody had, and the cards they were all going to get. Burgess took a third queen, all up, and grinned from ear to ear. Before the betting was over, the pot had grown to eleven hundred dollars, and Wanda LaSalle was almost out of chips.

On sixth, Reuben mucked his hand in disgust. Rusty finally saw the light and followed suit. Reuben felt sorry to soak him so badly—he liked Rusty, and had wanted to leave him some change—but it was out of his hands now.

Fat, happy Wyatt, who already had a hidden pair of eights, caught his third jack. But he was looking across the table at his pal Burgess's three queens, and the view dampened his euphoria. If Burgess got a fourth lady, Wyatt's full house would crumble to dust. Reuben relished his indecision, which came out in compulsive stroking of his silk lapels.

Sharkey was still in, still gloating secretly

about his ace in the hole, and still raising on every bet. Grace was the dark horse. She had the nine and ten of clubs showing, the rest junk. The bet was back to Burgess and his three queens. He checked his hole cards with cagey-looking pleasure—a fairly subtle bluff. "See that and raise you another hundred." Sharkey complied without a murmur. Grace threw in her last chips; she was down to her angel pin now, with one more card to go. Wyatt's stack wasn't any higher. Reason came flooding back to him in a rush. He mucked his hand with an oath, stood up, and stalked over to the bar. In spite of himself, Reuben felt glad to know they'd left him walking-home money.

Burgess, Sharkey, and Wanda.

"River card down," Reuben murmured, dealing the last. Everybody got his heart's desire, and Reuben's job was over.

Burgess still looked high with his three queens. Trying not to let his jubilation show, he made a great business of betting everything he had left with apparent reluctance. Reuben sympathized: there was nothing trickier than bluffing that you were bluffing.

Sharkey called the bet and raised it five hundred, which cleaned him out, too. Burgess turned purple, but didn't move a muscle. He was betting on four queens, and they'd waived table stakes long ago.

Wyatt wandered back, a shot glass in his hand, and took up a place behind Rusty's chair. Everybody looked at Grace. For the first time since they'd called her for cheating she touched her angel pin, nudging it with her fingernail, toying with it. She still only had her nine-ten puppyfeet showing, the rest garbage. Wyatt had shown three jacks before he'd quit, so a jack-high straight flush for Wanda was possible but incredibly unlikely. What were the odds of it? Reuben wondered idly. Sharkey, he knew, was wondering too, but not so idly. It didn't matter; whatever the odds, Sharkey was going to deem them too high to beat his four beautiful aces.

"Mr. Sharkey," Grace said, in a voice so low everybody leaned forward to hear her. "Do I understand the bet to me is now five hundred?"

Sharkey inclined his bulbous mug in assent.

She picked up the brooch. It looked pretty resting in the palm of her hand, the silver stream of hair shining in the glow of the gaslights. "What would you say..." Sharkey and Burgess bent closer to catch the words. "What would you say to letting the lady stand in for me?"

Sharkey blinked, not getting it. "Huh?"

"Just for tonight," she clarified softly. "Five hundred plus what's in the pot, against me, wherever you like. Whatever you like."

A feather hitting the table would've made them all jump. Reuben wanted to laugh out loud at the identical expressions of dumb wonder on every face. To break the stunned silence, he kicked back in his chair and marveled slowly, "Well, I'll be goddamned."

Rusty giggled and cleared his throat. Wyatt closed his mouth and ran his thumbs up and down behind his suspenders, watching his friend Burgess for a reaction. Burgess had gone even purpler, but otherwise kept his composure.

Sharkey's thick lips tried to settle in a cynical, unruffled smile, but he kept rubbing his chest as if his heart hurt, or it had stopped and he was trying to restart it. "Get this straight," he mumbled, and had to clear his own throat. "You'll see my raise with...with..."

"Myself."

She crippled him then with a white, blinding smile; he blinked in its radiance and rolled over, a dead man. "Okay with me," he said on a weak puff of cigar smoke. He didn't even check his cards first.

Burgess sat erect in his chair, not moving. He'd shuffled the seventh card in with his hole cards, but he didn't look at them. Instead his eyes were glued to Sharkey's two exposed aces, and then to Sharkey's face. Red blotches on his cheeks gave away the ugly man's excitement; but Burgess's dilemma was figuring out if he was excited because he was bluffing, because he was stupid, or because he couldn't lose. Seconds passed. Minutes. Burgess sat on, motionless as a bald sphynx, weighing and measuring. Just when Reuben knew he'd have to strangle Rusty if he cleared his throat once more, Burgess flipped his board cards belly down. "Not me," he said softly, dignified in retreat.

Smart move, Reuben congratulated him. Burgess looked like a family man, but he'd never once protested Grace's unorthodox offer. So

123

either he was a randier old goat than he looked, or Wanda LaSalle had paragon-toppling powers of a magnitude not yet known. Reuben suspected the latter.

Sharkey's delight enhanced his ugliness. It was just him and Wanda now, and he could hardly wait for the big moment. He coasted the wet, disgusting mouth-end of his cigar around his fat lips, sucking in smoke and blowing it out through his nostrils.

Irrationally, stupidly, Reuben felt a snaky slither of jealousy in his gut. "A little brace game I once had occasion to observe," Grace had called it at the Golden Nugget. The skill with which she played it was all the proof he needed that she hadn't just observed it, she'd been the second lead in it. With her husband, Henri, no doubt. The retired entrepreneur with the bum ticker. Why should knowing that make Reuben jealous? He couldn't say. All he knew was that the smoky pall hanging over the table was so thick with the smell and the taste and the feel of sex, he could hardly breathe it anymore. He wanted it for himself. He wanted to be in Sharkey's shoes, and beat her cold with his four sweet aces.

It wouldn't happen, of course. Wanda raised her dark-winged eyebrows at Sharkey to ask what he had. He waited another twenty seconds, wallowing in the suspense, and then turned over his cards. "Four bullets," he said in a low, purring gloat that made Reuben's lip curl.

"Oh, dear." She faked a truly enchanting mix

of sympathy and girlish excitement. "I guess I win. Look, I've got seven, eight, nine, ten, and jack of clubs."

Sharkey couldn't move. He'd frozen with his mouth open, holding his cigar in the air at a rakish, celebratory angle. Grace's straight flush wouldn't register; he kept batting his eyelids at it, but it still wouldn't focus.

Go, Reuben commanded her in his brain—but it wasn't necessary. With the dexterity of a fan-tan raker, Grace was already scraping back her chair and scooping money, so much money, into her new pocketbook. "Gentlemen, it's been a pleasure. Thank you for everything, and good night." Her smile bedazzled them one last time, and then she was gone.

But not quite fast enough. Sharkey came out of his trance, leapt up, and grabbed for her arm. She had to stop—otherwise he'd have wrenched it out of the socket. Reuben was on his feet, moving toward them. Sharkey made a grotesque effort to smile, although anyone could see that what he really wanted to do was kill her.

"Hold on a second, Wanda," he urged with creepy joviality. "Aren't you going to give the boys a chance to get even?"

"I really can't," she answered, gaze level, looking him in the eye to calm him.

"Sure you can." He draped his heavy arm over her shoulders and pulled her closer. "Least you can do is have a drink with us. For old time's sake, huh?" He squeezed tight, tighter, flattening her upper arm against his chest.

"Maybe another old time," she murmured. Fires started to crackle in the sky-blue of her eyes.

"No, now. C'mon, least you can do. After all, you and me almost got to be real good friends tonight, didn't we?"

"Yeah, but 'almost' is the operative word. Take your hands off me or you'll regret it."

He was so surprised by the silk-to-steel shift in her tone, he almost obeyed. "Like hell," he snarled instead, and wrapped his big paw around the back of her neck.

Reuben sighed. "Lady says she can't stay," he pointed out, looming between them. Sharkey was bigger than he was, and Reuben was still sore from all those Croaker fists.

The big man responded with a vulgar but prosaic suggestion.

"That's so unimaginative," Reuben complained, maneuvering closer. "Not to mention physically impossible."

"Listen, you." The good part was that Sharkey let go of Grace. The bad part was that he grabbed Reuben by the collar and lifted him onto his toes. Over the giant's broad, hulking shoulder, Reuben widened his eyes and bared his teeth, telling her to *go, dammit, go.* She hesitated. He lost sight of her when Sharkey shook him like a dog, baring his own teeth and giving every indication of wanting to rip out Reuben's throat.

"Has anybody ever mentioned your breath?" Reuben panted, plucking at the muscular fingers Sharkey was trying to gouge into his neck. "Sometimes only a close friend will tell you the truth." On *truth*, he hauled back with one foot and slammed it into Sharkey's shin. He gave a shriek and let go, hopping up and down, spewing out more dull-witted expletives.

Twisting toward the door, Reuben caught a glimpse of Grace's pert behind sashaying through it. It was the second-to-last thing he saw. The last was Sharkey's ham of a fist streaking toward his sore chin.

6

The devil is the father of lies, but he neglected to patent the idea, and the business now suffers from competition.
—Josh Billings

"We need to work on our getaway." Grace jumped up, abandoning the bright mound of loot on the sprung couch cushions, and raced to the widening alley door. "Reuben," she cried anxiously, searching his face for fresh injuries. "Are you all right? I didn't want to leave you, but I didn't know what else to do! Did he hit you? Are you hurt?"

"Just a flesh wound," he muttered, leaning against the door and patting the side of his jaw with delicate fingers. A new bruise was blooming along the bone, but the excited twinkle in his light brown eyes told her he didn't mind it. "So you got home all right by yourself?"

"I caught a hansom," she said absently, catching his hand and leading him toward the couch. "Sit down. Oh, dear—is there enough room for you?" She stopped, mock-dismayed, as if just noticing the obstacles on the sofa cushion. His face lit up like a boy's on Christmas morning, and she clapped her hands with delight. "Look at it! Oh, Reuben, look!"

They sat down on either side of the money pile, beaming at each other. "How much?" he asked.

"One thousand, six hundred and seventy-five dollars and fifty cents," she answered slowly, relishing the syllables. "And most of it came from that *beast,* Sharkey. How did you get away? At least he didn't have a gun; then you'd—"

"He had a gun. He had a thirty-two in a shoulder holster."

"No!"

"Luckily the bartender had a forty-five. He and the bouncer convinced Sharkey to take his losses like a man, and I got out while they were disarming him."

"Did he know you were cheating, do you think?"

"No, he thought you were. What made him so mad was that he couldn't figure out how."

She sat back proudly. "It's such a good trick, and it almost never fails."

"How many times have you run it?"

"Oh—*I've* never run it. I just saw it once." He looked completely unconvinced, and she regretted her slip of the tongue. "God, I love money," she said to change the subject, stirring the gleaming pile of gold, silver, and paper with her fingers. "It's so comforting, isn't it? So soothing." He winked at her. "Do you like it, too, just for itself? Look at it, Reuben. Nothing else is this color," she gloated, fondling a twenty-dollar double eagle. "I even like the way it smells."

"I think I prefer what it can buy."

"Oh, well, that too." That was obvious; she dismissed it with a wave of the hand. But deep down, what Grace liked about money, even more than how it looked and felt and smelled, was what it stood for: security. Without it, everything and everyone you loved could be taken away from you. With it, at least you had a fighting chance.

"What was your plan if you hadn't caught that last nine, Gus, right before you bet the brooch?" He settled back, too, with his long legs outstretched, feet resting on the low coffee table. "You let your stack get too low; it was pure luck when you beat Sharkey's three kings at the last minute."

"I know," she admitted, "but I couldn't help it. They were dealing slop until you passed me the jacks. If I'd lost that hand, I was going to hit somebody up for a loan."

"Who?" he asked curiously.

"Not you. Certainly not Sharkey. Rusty, I think—he'd have been the softest."

"I thought you had 'em all pretty spongy by then."

"I did, didn't I?" She smiled fondly, recalling it. "They were nice men, except for Sharkey. I almost felt sorry for them."

"Did you?" He sent her a lopsided smile back. "I think that must be why you're so good at it."

"Do you think I'm good?" A self-serving question, but she wanted the compliment.

"I think you're the best I've ever seen."

She felt herself coloring for the second time that day. Why flattering words from Reuben Jones could make her blush like a child, she could not imagine. "I'm starving," she said quickly. "Why isn't there ever anything to eat in this house?"

"Let's go out." He jackknifed to his feet and crossed the room to his clay-pipe pyramid of wine bottles. "What do you feel like, Grace, a nice light Beaujolais? Or something a bit meatier, maybe a Merlot?"

"Mmm, you pick. Are we drinking?"

"We're celebrating. Ah, just the thing, Gevrey-Chambertin Clos St. Jacques. Carefree but still substantial. Trust me, from this vintage it won't be too heavy." He took glasses and a corkscrew from a shelf over the coal stove, came toward her, and held out his hand. "Let's go."

"Where?" He led her toward what she

thought of now as the back door, the one leading to the sloping terraced double lot behind the big house where his landlady lived. "I thought we were going out to eat."

"We are."

Outside, the night was mild, almost balmy, full dark at nine o'clock, with a smattering of stars blinking between smoke-colored clouds. They walked up a weedy flagstone path to the second tier of level grass, where a cluster of white garden furniture was barely visible in the murk. Reuben checked an Adirondack chair for dew, dried the seat with his handkerchief, and motioned for her to sit. "Wait here, I'll be right back."

"Where are you going?" she called to his dark-coated back, disappearing toward the house in the gloom.

"To get dinner. Open the wine, Grace, so it can breathe!"

She'd never opened a bottle of wine before; that was supposed to be a man's job, like carving the meat or driving the buggy. She twisted the corkscrew in easily enough, but had to wedge the bottle between her knees for enough purchase to draw out the cork. Good thing she was alone. Could it "breathe" in the bottle, or did you have to decant it? She decided to leave it alone, anticipating Reuben's epicurean horror if she guessed wrong. She set the bottle on the table in front of a wooden love seat and sat down, clasping her hands behind her head and leaning back to contemplate the stars.

"All she had was chicken and biscuits. She put mayonnaise on the biscuits and made sandwiches."

"Who?" She twisted around, watching Reuben saunter down the flagstone path with a covered basket in his arms. She liked to watch him walk; it was something about the way his hips were connected to his long, handsome legs, that and the smooth rhythm of his loose, straight shoulders moving with each step.

"Mrs. Finney. I told her we were drinking Burgundy, but she didn't care." His tone held disbelief. "Said it was chicken or nothing. Sorry, Gus—I can go out and try to find something else, maybe some roast beef or lamb—"

"This is fine," she said hastily, hearing her stomach growl.

"Sure? If I'd known, I'd have suggested the Montrachet. Got two bottles last week. It's really very nice. Fellow didn't know what he had; I picked 'em up for practically nothing."

"This is fine," she repeated, privately wishing he'd picked up a nice bottle of milk. She set out the sandwiches on linen napkins, pleased to discover two oranges and two bananas in the bottom of the basket, while Reuben poured the wine. She had reached for her glass and started to take a sip when he stopped her.

"Wait, a toast. To luck."

"To cheating," she amended, touching glasses.

"To your skill with the cards," he tacked on generously.

"And yours." Full of good will, she started again to take a sip, but stopped when she saw Reuben swirling his wine in the glass, dipping his nose into it like a heron, breathing deeply, sighing. She mimicked him, bemused, with no idea what she was doing. He even held the glass strangely, by the bottom of the stem instead of the bowl. "When do we get to drink it?" she cracked. He just smiled at her across the rim of his glass, and finally took a sip. She copied him, but drank it down too soon—he kept the wine in his mouth for a good ten seconds before he swallowed it. "Nice," she ventured. "Isn't it?" It tasted like wine to her.

He looked faintly disappointed. "Needed another year."

"Another year?"

"To establish its character. It's got plenty of fruit and charm, but not enough staying power." He went back to inhaling, nose buried deep; when he sipped it the next time, he drew it in through his teeth with a lot of air, making a liquid hissing sound. "Still, it's got courage, don't you think? Backbone in the face of adversity." Another small sip. "And resourcefulness. Do you taste that, under the tannin?"

She was pretty sure he wasn't joking. She took a taste, mulled it over, swallowed. "Yes, I see what you mean. And maybe a hint of misanthropy? Beneath the resourcefulness, I mean. And beyond that, a tendency to make snap judgments."

He stared down into his glass, arrested, actually thinking it over. His laugh when he got the joke was appreciative, but mostly surprised: it really had never occurred to him that his wine pronouncements might sound odd to a layman.

Sliced chicken on biscuits was an underrated delicacy, Grace decided, hunting in the basket for a third one. Not having eaten anything since before noon might have something to do with her judgment, but even so, the meal was delicious. She and Reuben ate with gusto, silent and purposeful during the first two sandwiches, talkative during the third, recounting the evening's highlights and dissecting poker hands. Reuben was almost as knowledgeable about seven-card stud as he was about wine, and had lots of hints and suggestions on how she could improve her play. She took them in good part, feeling mellow, and entirely too pleased with herself to take offense at the note of male superiority in his voice. "Tell me your life story," she invited, dabbing at crumbs on her lips from the last bite, and refilling their glasses herself. "Where were you born?"

He stuck his feet up on the table and stretched an arm out along the back of the love seat in her direction. He didn't touch her, but she was aware of his hand behind her shoulder, just resting there. "In Virginia," he answered readily, "on a plantation near Richmond. Sweetbriar, it was called." His voice softened nostalgically.

"Really? You're from the South?" Somehow it didn't fit.

"Yep."

"Were you born before or after the war?"

"During—1862, smack in the middle. My father had freed all his slaves years earlier, but when the war came he felt duty-bound to fight for his homeland. He rose to the rank of colonel—Colonel Beauregard Jones," he said proudly "—but he was killed in '62 at the battle of Malvern Hill."

Beauregard Jones? Hiding her skepticism, she asked in a level tone, "Then you never knew him?"

"I was conceived on a one-day leave, as he was marching his troops north from Fredericksburg to Richmond. He died four days later."

"How terrible," she hazarded, in case it was true.

"A year later, the Union army burned Sweetbriar to the ground."

She shook her head pityingly. "Your poor mother."

"Yes. She...wasn't a very strong person. When the war was over, rather than lose everything instead of almost everything, she married a Yankee carpetbagger named Cramer. I don't blame her—at least, not anymore. We were starving; he was rich. Son of a bitch owned the town bank. He took over Sweetbriar and restored it—that was something."

"But?" she prodded when he hesitated. The strain of bitterness in his voice made her narrow her eyes and stare at him.

"But..." He stopped again, and she found herself laying her hand lightly on his outstretched arm. "But I hated him. And I was scared of him. I saw him slap my mother once—I was four, maybe five years old. When I tried to stop it, he hit me, too. Broke my collarbone."

"Reuben!"

"She started staying in her room all the time. When I was about eight, I found out what she was doing in there." He looked away. "To this day, I can't stand the smell of bourbon whiskey."

She frowned, and removed her hand. "But you *drink* bourbon whiskey. You keep it in your sock drawer."

He heaved a sigh and rubbed his eyes, as if he were weary. "What made you so cynical, Grace?" he asked sadly. "Tell me your life story."

"Finish yours first. What happened next?"

"What happened? My mother lived for four more years in an alcoholic haze, then had a stroke and died. When I was thirteen, I ran away from home and never went back. I took odd jobs at first, moving west. At sixteen, I fell in with bad companions, and finally it dawned on me that hard physical labor wasn't the only way to make a living."

If it was true, it was a very sad story. Grace pitied the little boy who had never known his father, whose stepfather had frightened and abused him, and whose mother might as well have abandoned him.

On the other hand, she couldn't help recalling that this was exactly the way he had made her feel—softhearted, anxious to comfort him—the night he'd told her how Edward Cordoba had lost his sight, rescuing passengers on the burning ocean liner.

"You're saying you walked away from a life of wealth and ease on the plantation so that you could take odd jobs and work your way west? No offense, but that doesn't quite sound like you, Reuben. I think you're leaving something out."

His smile was wistful. "You're right, I am." He took a deep breath. "My mother was hardly cold in her grave before Cramer moved a woman into the house. 'Housekeeper,' he called her. Her name was Clarice, and she had the biggest..." He trailed off, but his hands had already sketched the noun. Big, indeed. "She gave me a surprise present on my thirteenth birthday."

"Oh, what could it be," Grace said sourly.

"Yes, well. When my stepfather found out, he almost killed me."

"And that's when you ran away?"

He nodded. "He'd never adopted me, so no part of Sweetbriar would ever have come to me anyway, even if I'd stayed."

Now she believed him. "Poor Reuben," she said softly, touching a fingertip to the warm inside of his wrist. "It must've been very hard."

He twisted around to face her. "It wasn't so bad," he denied bravely. "Thanks for lis-

137

tening, Grace. I don't tell that story to many people." When he reached for her hand, she didn't pull it away; she let him hold it, and he stared down at her fingers as if they fascinated him, stroking his smooth thumb over her knuckles in a slow, hypnotic rhythm. "You're a very kind woman," he murmured. His downcast lashes threw long shadows over his handsome cheekbones.

"Not really," she said, rather breathlessly.

"I think you are. Gracious and lovely, and very, very kind."

Where his thumb was stroking had become the most sensitive spot on her body. She let him lift her hand to his mouth and press a soft kiss on her fingertips. His lips were warm, faintly damp from wine. The moment stretched to the far side of friendship and a few seconds beyond; if it had gone on any longer she'd have ended it herself—surely she would have.

But if nothing else, Reuben Jones had timing. He let go of her hand and gave her a gentle smile that had a melting effect on her insides. "Tell me about you," he said intimately. "Tell me everything."

Lord, it was tempting. *He* was tempting. The unaccustomed urge to tell the truth warned her that she was in danger. She stood up, needing the distance, and made a business of pouring more wine, even though she didn't want it. "Well," she began, one hand on her hip, face turned up to the sky. "I think I'll start at the end instead of the beginning."

"Wherever you like."

"First of all, Henri is really my second husband." She darted a glance at Reuben; he looked dumbfounded. "It wasn't a love match—at least not at first. He's quite a lot older than I am, and in recent years he's become a semi-invalid. His heart, you know."

"Mm, yes, you mentioned that."

"Over the years I've grown extremely fond of him, but the real love of my life was my first husband, Giuseppe."

"Italian fellow?"

"Mm, from Venice. He was a count—that's like an earl," she put in helpfully "—but he was practically penniless. He'd come to California to make his fortune."

"How did you meet? In a gondola?"

"I was seventeen, living on my father's big cattle ranch on the Mad River in Humboldt County."

He sat up straighter. "How big?"

She sent him a look. "Not quite as big as the Cordobas's ranchero. But big enough. My mother..." She hesitated a little too long.

"Your mother—?"

"Died," she said flatly. "When I was ten." And that was as good as the truth. Her mother had dumped her with detestable strangers and vanished—wasn't that the same as dying? No, it was worse. "So then it was just Daddy and me. I met Giuseppe at a fancy dress ball in San Francisco," she fabricated, "at the Baldwin Hotel. We fell in love instantly. He exaggerated his fortune to my father, who was a wonderful, softhearted man—he spoiled me terribly—and after a lot of wheedling and persuasion, Daddy finally consented to the marriage." She hid a small, ironic smile, thinking of all the times in her wretched childhood when she'd fantasized a loving father who spoiled her. She moved toward the love seat and sat down again.

"And?" Reuben crossed his legs and turned toward her, chin propped on his palm.

"And we were married. We were wildly happy for six months. It was the loveliest time of my life." A tear welled in her eye. A *genuine* tear; it surprised her so much, she blinked it away before he could see it.

But he did see it. He reached out and touched her cheekbone, just for a moment. The look in his eyes—amazed and moved—told her that until this second, he hadn't believed a word she'd said.

"Even before we married, Giuseppe had begun to invest in the stock market. After the wedding he began to invest more heavily, only now he was using my father's money."

"So he was a crook?"

"Oh, no, not at all. But he was determined to make good. He desperately wanted me, and my father as well, to be proud of him. Then..." She let a hand rise and fall in her lap. "Then it happened. The stock market crashed— this was in 1883—and Giuseppe lost everything. The ranch, the cattle, the house—he'd put them all up as collateral, and in one day everything was gone. He couldn't face us." Her voice faltered. "He killed himself. He stuck a shotgun in his mouth and pulled the trigger."

No, he hadn't. But if she let herself think about how poor, sweet Joe had really died, she might start crying again. Which would add a nice touch of realism to this story she was spinning for Reuben's benefit, but it wouldn't do a thing for her peace of mind.

His strong arm around her shoulders felt warm and natural. She kept her head bowed and didn't encourage or discourage him, just took all the pleasure she could from his comfort until his light pats on her far shoulder softened to slow strokes, and then sensuous little circles. That felt much too good.

"So," she said, stiffening her spine.

"So," he echoed, removing his arm.

"So my father and I moved to a tiny house on the edge of what used to be our land. Henri Rousselot was an old friend of Daddy's; he owned a small vineyard in the Russian Valley."

His ears perked up. "Really? A vineyard? How many acres?"

"Small," she said shortly. "Anyway, when we lost everything, Henri was one of the few people who didn't abandon us. After Daddy died—of a rattlesnake bite three years ago—Henri asked me to marry him. I'd always liked him. I said yes."

Reuben was rasping his fingers across the whisker stubble on his chin, thinking. "But I thought Henri was an entrepreneur," he reminded her. "I thought Henri was the one

141

who taught you how to cheat at cards, among other things."

"I never said that." Had she?

"Well, who did? Is Henri a confidence man or a vineyardist?"

"Both," she answered, pleased with the simplicity of the solution. Besides, it was almost true. "He's both."

He blinked at her, assessing that. "What made you decide to become Sister Mary Augustine?"

"Oh, that's a long story."

"I've got time."

She shrugged. "We need the money. Henri has to stay home because of his heart. He needs an operation, so it made sense for me to—"

Reuben cut her off with a loud bark of laughter. "He needs an *operation*?"

She scowled at him, pretending to be appalled by his insensitivity. But his laughter was too infectious; after half a minute, she gave in and joined him. "All right," she admitted, grinning, "no operation. But business is bad. The vineyard's small, and for the last two years the crop's been very disappointing. We're in danger of losing the land. We need a lot of money, and we need it soon."

He nodded, in sympathy with that. "But why a nun, Gus?"

"Why not? I went to a convent school when I was a girl"—which was *sort* of the truth—"so it was a natural disguise. Don't you think I was good at it?"

"I think you were downright beatific."

His unabashed admiration disconcerted her again. She basked too much in his praise, she couldn't think why, and she was going to have to watch it. "Why were you a blind man?" she countered. "It couldn't have been so people would give you money—you weren't poor enough. In fact, you made a point of letting us know how much of a gentleman you were."

"Truthfully, it was an impulse. Purely spontaneous. I didn't have any plan in mind except to make the trip go faster and maybe have a little fun. Didn't even know I was going to do the English accent until it came out of my mouth. I've done Spanish and Italian before, but never English. I thought it was a bit of all right, eh, what?" He gave her a nudge, laying the accent on thick.

His cockiness was irritating, especially when she thought of how completely she'd swallowed the hook—and then flapped around on the bottom of the boat like a sunfish, as Henry would say. "Right," she mumbled, and started to rise.

He detained her by taking her wrist and draping it around his neck, at the same time he slipped his arm around her waist. Their knees bumped.

"What do you think you're doing?" The last two words were muffled by the pressure of his lips on hers. She couldn't claim total surprise; when men looked at her the way Reuben had been looking at her tonight, she knew what they had in mind, and kissing was usually the least of it. She closed her mouth and sat perfectly still, waiting for him to lose interest—her favorite method of discouraging ungentlemanly advances. It rarely failed, besides being so much more dignified than a vulgar physical struggle. Her eyes were open, so she knew when he opened his; she thought she saw amusement in the light brown depths—not at her but at the situation, possibly even at himself. She found herself begrudging him a tiny smile. His eyes softened even more. He said her name, then began pressing soft, slow kisses along the closed crease of her lips. At the moment she started to enjoy it, she turned her head aside.

He rested his forehead against her temple; his slow, deep breaths on her cheek tickled her skin. "Why did you come back tonight, Grace?" he whispered. "You could've caught the late ferry and been halfway to Henri's loving arms by now, sixteen hundred bucks richer." His lips nipped at her cheekbone; she faced him again to put a stop to that.

"Don't you believe in honor among thieves?"

"I'm starting to." He tilted his head and kissed her full on the mouth.

She countered this time by drawing her hands up between them, using her forearms for a shield. The taste of wine lingered on his lips, not sweet any longer, almost tart. He sampled her taste with his tongue, and pronounced it, "Mmm, sweet," in a low, appreciative murmur that stirred her, made her breath catch. The hand he was stroking along her exposed throat dipped lower and lower until, for the space of one heart-stopping second, he caressed her breasts. Desire slammed into her with such suddenness, such violence, she caught at his wrist and dragged it away—and was instantly sorry. He had her head back against the top of the love seat, trying to coax her mouth open with his tongue. Feeling safe because she had both of his wrists now, one in each hand, she let him nibble her lips apart.

A mistake. His kiss was long, thrilling, and intimate; the fact that she was allowing it proved, if she'd wanted proof, that he was even more dangerous than she'd thought. He was sucking on her tongue, which he'd somehow coaxed into his mouth; she felt like the main dish at a hungry man's banquet. Then it switched, and it was his tongue in her mouth, soft and curious, slow and suggestive. She liked it much too much; she could feel her self-control slipping away, like water through her fingers...or like clothes, a petticoat, sliding down her hips and then down her thighs... A vision flickered behind her eyelids like the one that had kept her awake last night—of naked bodies, Reuben's and hers. And of his strong, clever hands gliding so slowly over her skin. How long had it been since anyone had touched her like this? Years. "Reuben," she said, amazed at how sweet his name sounded in a whisper, with their lips touching, their mouths tasting.

"Grace," he whispered back. He sounded similarly entranced. Then *he* made a mistake. He pulled one of his captured hands out of her laughably weak grip and slid it between her thighs.

A kiss was one thing; an uninvited feel was another.

Clamping her knees together, she pulled her mouth away and commanded, "Unhand me, Mr. Jones, I'm a married woman." She didn't say it with much ire; she was only just remembering it herself, after all. And if there was one thing Grace wasn't, it was a hypocrite. "Unhand me, I said." Hazily, she wondered why she was talking like a heroine out of Sir Walter Scott.

"I would, Gus, if you'd let go of me."

She realized she'd trapped his hand between her legs. Releasing it hastily, she shot to her feet.

She had no idea how the right shoulder of her gown had gotten pulled down halfway to her elbow. She tugged it up jerkily and swatted a loose coil of hair out of her face. "That wasn't what I came out here for," she assured him, despising the silly quaver in her voice.

"Me either. Sometimes those spur of the moment impulses work out pretty damn well." He was trying to look cocky. But he'd drawn one foot up and braced it against the edge of the seat, leaning forward, both arms wrapped around his knee. She suspected why, but averted her eyes rather than check to see for sure. It was a comfort to know that, for all his seeming negligence, his voice didn't sound very steady either.

"Is that what it was?" she inquired for no particular reason. "A spur of the moment impulse?"

A minute passed; she could almost hear him testing different answers. But in the end, he only said, "No. To tell you the truth, Gracie, I've been planning it all day."

Another trick, of course; a man like Reuben would know better than anyone that a supposedly candid confession could be more disarming than the sincerest denial. But he'd called her Gracie. She could just barely remember her mother calling her that, years and years ago; nobody else ever had, not even Henry. She felt a deep, dangerous softening inside.

To fight it, she said, "Let's get one thing straight," holding up a stern index finger. "You and I aren't really friends, Mr. Jones, and so far we're not even partners. The only thing we have in common is a mutual financial mishap and a pressing need to recover what some thugs stole from us. Maybe we can help each other, maybe we can't—we'll probably know the answer to that by tomorrow. Either way, I'd like it understood that there won't be any repetition of what happened just now. Do you agree?"

"Do I agree with what? That you understand it, or it won't happen?"

She stamped her foot. But when he stood up and started toward her, she had to force herself not to give ground. "You know exactly what

I'm talking about. No more games, Reuben. If you won't promise to keep your hands off me, I'll leave. I've got plenty of money now, I don't have to stay here."

He studied her in silence, and she imagined he was weighing his chances of eventually seducing her against the discomfort of an unknown number of future nights spent on his sprung couch instead of in his own bed. He might also be thinking that she hadn't resisted his advances with much vigor, but she hoped he'd be too chivalrous to point that out.

"Well?"

He put his hands in his pockets and said, "Okay."

She let her breath out slowly, appalled by how disappointed she felt. But really—wasn't he even going to argue? Not even a little? "Okay, what?"

"We'll play it your way, if that's what you really want. But answer one question for me, Grace."

"If I can."

"What's the game now?"

She frowned at him, perplexed.

"I thought I'd played 'em all, but this is a new one on me. And frankly, I don't see the point."

Coolness seeped inside her, into all the places where she'd been warm before. "You don't see the point of what?" she asked softly.

"You playing hard to get. I'm just trying to figure out where you think it'll take you.

We're even now as far as the money goes, so it can't be that."

She made her clenched hands relax. "No," she got out, "it can't be that. And it can't be that I'm not *accustomed* to giving myself to men I've known for a day or two if I think it'll get me where I want to go. That's what you meant, isn't it?"

He didn't deny it. He didn't say anything.

Anger made her cheeks burn. Stupid, inappropriate anger. She wanted to laugh in his face to show him how little his opinion of her mattered. But her lips felt too stiff even to smile. "Thanks for an educational evening, Mr. Jones. I'm feeling tired all of a sudden. I'll see you in the morning." She said it through her teeth, and left him standing there, looking mystified.

"Grace—wait! I'm sorry. Hold it! Grace?"

She kept going, and closed her ears to his stupid, inept apology.

7

Every crowd has a silver lining.
—P. T. Barnum

"How are your waffles?"

"Fine, thank you," said Grace. "And your eggs?"

"Good, they're very good. Really very good."

"Good."

Things must be looking up, Reuben thought grimly; that was the longest conversation they'd had all morning. He watched her take a sip of her coffee and look away, as if the scattering of diners enjoying a late breakfast at Belle's fascinated her. In profile, she had a small but definite bump in the center of her nose. She probably disliked it, but he didn't. In fact, he couldn't say which of her so-called imperfections he liked better, the bumpy nose, the crooked eyetooth, or the little mole under her left ear.

Actually, his eggs were cold and runny. He put his fork down and slouched in the corner on his side of the booth, sipping his coffee and brooding, shooting furtive glances at Grace. He'd hurt her feelings last night, and so far all his efforts to make up for it had failed. It wasn't that she'd clammed up or frozen him out; if anything she was more polite than usual, insisting he take his turn in the bathroom first, offering to make the coffee. That was it: she was *too* nice. Between that and the fact that she wouldn't laugh at his jokes, he knew she was furious.

Why, though? He'd spoken his mind last night, asked a simple question—which, in retrospect, he could see hadn't come out very tactfully. So she was sensitive. He'd remember that, do better in the future. But in his own defense, he could point out that the conclusions he'd come to about her weren't all that out of line, considering the circumstances. Were they? She was no blushing virgin, he was pretty sure of that. By her own account, she was on her second husband, and if half of what Reuben had heard about Mr. Rousselot was true, he wasn't what you'd call doting. Invalid or not, any man who'd send his wife hundreds of miles from home on a dangerous swindle, completely alone, with nothing but a nun's habit and a derringer for protection— that man sure as hell didn't have her best interests at heart. And what about a man who didn't mind his wife living in another man's house, sleeping in his bed, for a stay of unknown length? It sounded like a marriage of convenience to Reuben. At best. There was another word for it, a less attractive one that he hoped didn't apply.

Not that it was any of his business. You went along to get along, and Reuben would be the last person to make moral judgments based on appearances. Based on anything, come to that.

Still. A woman who could kiss the way Grace did had to have been around the block a few times, he figured, and not just with an old geezer with a bad heart. But then there was Giuseppe, the suicidal count. Could any of that story have been true? She'd told it well, and she'd even eked out a tear for Giuseppe. But if she was as good as Reuben thought she was, that would've been part of the act. He liked to think of himself as practical, not cynical, and right now his practical side was telling him to be careful. Believing what you wanted to believe invited disaster, and women were almost always more trouble than they were worth. Two rules to live by.

Seconds after coming to that sage conclusion, he surprised himself by blurting out, "Sorry about last night, Gus."

She turned her head to look at him. "Pardon me?"

"You know. What I said and all." Ah, what silver-tongued eloquence. She regarded him blankly for a full minute. He wanted to look away, but he knew if he did, she'd think she'd won and then say something like, "I can't imagine what you're talking about." So he held her gaze, and finally it was she who looked away.

"Never mind," she muttered. "Already forgotten."

"Really?"

"Of course." She folded her napkin and looked around for the waiter. "I guess we'd better—"

"I'm not apologizing for the kiss," he pointed

out in a lower voice. "Just for the mess I made of it afterward."

He thought he saw one corner of her mouth twitch in the beginning of a smile. "Thanks for clarifying," she said dryly. In that moment, he liked her better than he ever had.

"What I said was really stupid, Grace. I thought about it all night, wishing I could take it back."

"Why did you say it?" she asked, watching him. "I'd be interested to know what made you think I was that kind of woman."

He hadn't expected directness from her. It threw him off. "Well," he said slowly, "I guess partly because of the way we met. You being on your own and all. And, you know, you seem to...know your way around. What I mean—"

"I know what you mean."

She had that steely look again, and he knew he'd lost ground. He could've reminded her that the free, inviting way she'd let him kiss her had been the biggest clue of all, as far as keys to her worldly experience went. Instead he said contritely, "Honest, I never meant to offend you. If I made a mistake, I apologize. I can see now that you're not that kind of woman, Grace. Hell, anybody could see it. Last night I got carried away, that's all. You're a real lady, a perfect gentlewoman, and I was a complete..." He trailed off when she burst into a tickled laugh.

"Oh, Reuben, you overdid it. You should've quit while you were ahead." His deliberately baffled look made her laugh again. "I thought you had more subtlety."

"What do you mean?"

"You know exactly what I mean. I may not be what you think I am, but a *'perfect gentlewoman'* is taking it way too far. I think it's time for you to shut up."

"Oh. Okay." He felt chastened, but at the same time the good humor in her wide blue eyes cheered him enormously. "Does this mean we're friends again? Last night you said we weren't."

"What difference does it make to you if we're friends or not?" she asked alertly.

Hell's bells, there was a female for you, always wanting to pin things down, put everything into *words*. He was sorry he'd asked. "None at all," he said airily. "If we end up being partners for a while, it would make things simpler. That's all."

"Fine," she snapped, as if his answer didn't suit her. "Let's wait and see if we're going to be partners, then we'll decide if we're going to be friends."

"Fine." She definitely looked prickly again, so he stuck his hand out across the table to disarm her. "Shake on it?"

She hesitated, then shook. She wanted it short and businesslike, so he hung on. Gradually her stiff fingers relaxed; when he smiled at her, she couldn't resist smiling back. And then she looked so damn pretty, it was all he could do not to lean across the table and kiss her.

"Ready to go?" He glanced at her plate; she'd hardly touched her waffles.

"They were terrible," she confided, her eyes dancing.

He laughed for the sheer pleasure of seeing her like this again—the old Grace. He'd missed her like hell. "Eggs were inedible," he confessed.

She stood up, letting him help her with her cape. "Why do you come here?"

"Belle lets me run a tab."

"Don't tell me—out of friendship?"

The smell of his soap on her skin beguiled him; he kept his hands on her shoulders long after settling the cape over them. "Can't help it if I'm a friendly sort of fellow." She made one of her humming noises, low, sexy, and heavy with humorous skepticism. He was growing extremely fond of the sound—and used to it, since it was the one with which she greeted most of his quips. Feeling better than he had all day, he followed her out of Belle's, and together they set off for Old World Curios.

The curtained door in the rear wall of Doc Slaughter's shop led to another room, one that was just as cluttered as his store but with different things—easels, jars of oil and watercolor paints, half-finished paintings, covered lumps of clay, lacquered statuary, porcelain, pottery—all the works in progress of Doc's lucrative "reproduction" business. Here he also carried on a popular printing enterprise that specialized in altering documents or creating new ones. Reuben had known Doc for years, but he'd only been invited into the back room once, to inspect a batch of counterfeit autographs he'd commissioned him to create. Hobby collectors were the easiest people in the world to fool, and could always be relied on to pay top dollar for "authenticated" signatures of people like Benjamin Franklin, Cotton Mather, or Stonewall Jackson, on fake canceled bank checks, old letters, the fly-leaves of books, the battered family Bible. So Reuben was surprised when Doc invited Grace, whom he'd met only once and who could've been anybody, into his workroom without a second's hesitation. The old thief must be going soft. If so, he wasn't alone, Reuben thought crossly; he hadn't met a man yet who could resist her.

Doc led them to his cluttered desk and offered Grace the only chair, taking a paint-spattered stool for himself; Reuben cleared off a corner of the desk and leaned against it. Fireplug's letter lay on top of the scattered piles of paper. "Did you find out what this is?" Reuben asked, tapping the white lotus drawing with his finger.

"I did."

"And how much is it going to cost us to find out?"

Doc smiled his slow, somewhat unnerving smile. He was so pale he always looked half dead, or recently dug up. "Ah, Reuben, ever the mercenary. Let's discuss petty fiduciary matters later, shall we? But you were wise to come to me and advise discretion, my friend, because it's as I thought."

"What's as you thought?"

"This." He lifted the paper and let it flutter back to the desk. "A dangerous document, this. It contains the terms of allegiance for new recruits into the Bo Kong. Which," he explained for Grace's benefit, "is one of the most vicious tongs in Chinatown. And now I really must ask you to be more candid with me about where you found it. The name of the initiate on the document is Loke Ho, a brand-new Salaried Soldier, or hatchet man, for the Bo Kong. Forgive my skepticism, but I doubt that Mr. Loke Ho gave this to you."

Grace was looking at Reuben expectantly; obviously she'd decided to trust Doc as completely as Doc had decided to trust her. Reuben sighed. What the hell—Doc had been straight with him in the dealings they'd had so far. Besides, if the scheme went any further, they'd need his help, and they wouldn't get it without leveling with him.

"Loke Ho is a fellow Grace and I met, in a manner of speaking, while we were traveling from Monterey to San Francisco."

Doc registered no surprise. "That wouldn't have been on a Wells Fargo stagecoach, would it?"

"Always ahead of me, Doc. Amazing, isn't he?" He winked at Grace. "We've been calling this Loke Ho character 'Fireplug'; it's like an endearment, since we're so fond of the guy. He's cooling his heels at the California Street Station, where I hear he's not saying a word."

"Ah," Doc said in the low, tuneful intonation that sounded as much like a musical instrument as a voice. "This is most unusual." As always, he'd seated himself so that the scarred side of his face stayed in the shadows. "Corruption and violence are routine among gang members in Chinatown, but it's extremely rare for tong-backed crimes to be perpetrated outside the ghetto on white people. Extremely rare."

He stooped to open the bottom drawer of his desk, bringing out the pillowcase-wrapped statue of the tiger. "That's one odd aspect of the Wells Fargo robbery. Another is that the thieves made off with only a small part of the booty on board the stagecoach, and they seemed to know exactly what they were looking for. They stole exclusively funerary sculpture, even though there were older and more valuable pieces there for the taking."

"We noticed that ourselves."

"According to the newspapers, the police are baffled. But I have a theory." He shot them a shrewd glance from beneath his heavy eyelids.

"What?" Grace asked obligingly.

"That if the authorities could make your friend Fireplug reveal his connection with the Bo Kong tong, they wouldn't be baffled anymore."

"Why not?"

"Because the leader of the Bo Kong is a very unusual man. A cultured eccentric in some ways—a scholar, a poet, a calligrapher—and an old-fashioned thug in others. His name is Mark Wing. He was implicated in the seventies in a plot to murder the regent to the Chinese throne, and fled to this country about twelve years ago. Now he's an exile. Here he's known as Kai Yee, or the Godfather."

"Mark Wing," Reuben repeated thoughtfully. "I've never heard of him."

"That's not surprising. Secrecy surrounds him, as it does all the tongs. Outside Chinatown, very little is known of these people, and inside, fear keeps most of my informants' mouths closed. But not all."

He pulled a cigarette from the pocket of his jumper and lit it with long, bony fingers, stained yellow from nicotine. "The Bo Kong began in China as a secret anti-Manchu movement. In this country, it's become corrupt, like so many of the tongs. Here it's a gang of hoodlums with no principles except devotion to vice and violence. Because of the secrecy and the fear, it's often hard to separate fact from fiction, but it's well known that Mark Wing is involved in the gambling and opium trades, as well as the importation of slave girls from China for prostitution."

Grace made a disgusted sound.

"A few years ago, he tried to enter wealthy white society by frequenting places like the Palace Hotel and the opera house, escorting beautiful Caucasian women. He cut a strange figure, dressed in Western clothes but always surrounded by his sword-wielding body-guards. He's very rich, and outwardly quite smooth and cultured, so he was never denied admittance or thrown out of any of the fancy establishments he tried. But he never got anywhere in white high society—an experience he must have found humiliating, because after a short time he retreated back into the bowels of Chinatown, and now he never leaves his residence on Jackson Street."

"Never?" marveled Grace.

"I exaggerate. The exception is on Friday nights, when he invariably dines at the Placid Sea restaurant, buys a lottery ticket from a street vendor, and then goes to the Chinese theater, always surrounded by his cadre of *boo how doy*—hatchet sons—for protection. On the way home, he checks on his gambling dens in Waverly Place, of which he's reputed to own at least half a dozen, and most of the opium parlors on Dupont Street as well. He owns the brothel next door to his own house, which must be very convenient. It's called the House of Celestial Peace and Fulfillment."

Grace was wide-eyed with fascination. "Is he married?"

"Not currently. He's had innumerable con-cubines and at least two wives, whom he divorced when they failed to bear him children." Doc dragged deeply on his cigarette, lifted his head, and blew smoke at the ceiling. "He's reputed to be an art collector, although I don't know of anyone who's actually seen the collection. It's said to be as eccentric as he is, and consists mainly of—Can you guess?"

"Yeah," said Reuben, "but go ahead and tell us."

Doc nodded. "It consists mainly of statuary taken from ancient tombs, and icons of various Chinese gods and goddesses of immortality." He smiled, uncovering his long brown teeth. "It seems the Godfather has a fascination with death."

Grace was jubilant. "That's him, Reuben, that's our man! It has to be. Can you get a message to him?" she asked Doc.

"Probably." He rolled his eyes back to Reuben. "For a price."

"Always a price," he grumbled, doubly irked because of the suspicion that if he weren't here, Doc would've done it for Grace for nothing.

"What message would you like me to convey?"

Grace started to answer, but Reuben cut her off. "Tell him we have something he needs. Tell him the price will be very high, but he'll find it worth his while because it completes a collection he recently acquired."

"Very good. And if he asks who sent the message?"

Reuben thought for a second, then smiled. "Tell him the owners of the tiger."

"Let's go to Chinatown."

"Now?"

"Why not?" Grace slipped her arm through Reuben's and got him moving east, toward Stockton Street. "It's this way, isn't it?"

He nodded. "Haven't you ever been there before?"

"No, and I've always wanted to go. When Henri and I were here two years ago, he wouldn't take me. He said it was too dangerous."

"Two years ago? You live in the Russian Valley, and you haven't been to the city in two years?"

"About that."

"Why so long, Gus?" He pulled her out of the way of a turning ice wagon, and they stepped back up on the curb at Clay Street. "Life at the vineyard's so idyllic, you can't bring yourself to leave?"

Grace thought about what her life was like at Willow Pond. Despite her miserable adolescence, she'd always loved the farm. But it wasn't the old white house or the increasingly barren fields that had kept her and Henry from visiting San Francisco for the last two years. It was hard to remember now exactly what she'd told Reuben about Henry; she had an idea she'd told him conflicting stories, which wasn't at all like her. She gave a mental shrug and decided to tell the truth for once. "Henri's not allowed in San Francisco anymore. Or..." Better rephrase that. "He's been asked not to return."

Reuben halted in the middle of the sidewalk and stared at her. "Who asked him not to return?"

"Some men. Respectable men. City fathers, you might say."

"Why?"

"Because. He embarrassed them."

Understanding made him break into a grin. "You mean he swindled 'em! Right? But they can't admit it because it was an illegal racket to begin with. Am I right?"

The grin was so engaging it tempted her to say yes. She resisted. "He embarrassed them," she repeated. "Anyway, now he can't go into the city." She pressed her lips together to make it clear that that was all he was going to get out of her.

They started walking again. "Is that why Sister Augustine had to collect charitable donations on her own?" he asked.

"Partly. That and Henri's heart," she remembered to say.

"Oh, yeah. That bum ticker."

"So," she resumed, "will you take me to Chinatown?"

"Sure, if you really want to go."

"You mean—it isn't dangerous?" If not, she wasn't sure she wanted to go after all.

"Not particularly. Not for Caucasians in the daytime, and probably not much at night either."

"No?"

"Most Chinese are scared to death of us," he explained, taking her hand to negotiate through the foot traffic at Joice Street. "We're *fan kwei*—foreign devils. Besides, the hoodlums and hatchet men in Chinatown can rob and assault each other, kill each other in broad daylight, and the cops will almost always look the other way. But let a Chinese guy lift his pinkie finger against a white man, and the law's all over him."

"But that's not fair."

"No, it isn't. Haven't you heard the saying about a Chinaman's chance?" He stopped walking. "Here's Stockton Street, Gus; this is where it starts. What do you want to see?"

"Everything," she decided. It was raw and windy, a typical wretched San Francisco summer day. She drew her cape tighter around her shoulders and started off north on Stockton, her wrist tucked under Reuben's arm, intrigued already by the novelty of everything around her. The streets and sidewalks were packed with pedestrians, and every shop looked full of customers; everyplace she looked was animate with moving or lounging humanity.

"It's all so quaint," she marveled, eyeing a string of whole fish, heads and all, hung out on a wash line in the alley between two narrow buildings. They were walking past a cobbler's shop, next door to an herbalist's, and the odors of leather and spices and musk combined in an indescribable mixture that embodied, in her impressionable mind, the essence of this alien neighborhood. "The newspapers always print lurid stories about evil characters slinking through dark alleys bent on foul deeds—but it's just people, isn't it? Trying to make a living." Reuben made an ambivalent sound. "No, but what's sinister about it? Look, a shrine."

"It's a joss house," he told her; they stopped in front of a queer-looking building, painted red and gold, and through the carved door they could see statues and images made of wood and tinsel. The odor of burning sandalwood wafted toward them; deep in the black recesses of the shrine, a dark-robed woman was lighting what looked like sparking firecrackers. "They're everywhere, these temples," said Reuben. "This one's to the goddess of walkers, actors, sailors, and whores." Grace sent him a look. "It is," he insisted. "Her name's T'ien Hou, and she protects travelers."

"And prostitutes classify as travelers?"

"Sure. They're streetwalkers, aren't they?"

They moved on, and within half a block of the joss house she spied a woman who looked as if the goddess of streetwalkers might very well be looking out for her. "Was that a prostitute?" she whispered, turning to stare over her shoulder at the young girl they'd just passed in a doorway.

"Probably."

"How can you tell?"

"Mathematics, for one thing. The ratio of men to women in Chinatown is about thirty to one. And not many of the girls here are wives."

"Oh."

"Besides, she was wearing the cheongsam, the slit-skirted dress most of the whores wear. They call them singsong girls. Most of them are here illegally, sold into slavery by their families in Canton or Hong Kong."

Shocked, she glanced over her shoulder again, but the woman in the doorway had disappeared. "Why don't the police stop it? If that girl's a slave, why doesn't she run away?"

"Sometimes they do run away, but they're usually caught, and then punished for it in ways you don't want to know about. The Methodists run a mission here, and sometimes a girl will escape and take refuge there. But as often as not, the *boo how doy* send the police after her with an arrest warrant, claiming she stole her own clothes or the jewelry she's wearing, some bauble a customer gave her. Honest Chinese people never interfere in the slave trade because they're terrified of the tongs. Girls can bring as much as two or three thousand dollars on the block, which means the hatchet sons take a dim view of anybody who tries to crimp the trade."

"You mean nobody tries to stop it?" She'd read about the slave trade, but the stories were so detestable she'd shrugged them off as exaggerated and sensationalized. "The police don't do anything? That's appalling. Disgusting." She looked around at the tiny flats and blank-faced alleys they were passing; no singsong girls were in sight at the moment, but she imagined them inside their squalid cribs, plying their unsavory trade. Mark Wing, she remembered, owned the brothel next door to his own house. The thought sharpened her aversion to him. Good: it was easier to gouge somebody, she'd found, if you could work up a strong, healthy dislike for him beforehand.

They stopped in front of a goldsmith's shop to watch the owner making jewelry at a work table in the window. Grace kept waiting for him to look up, maybe smile at them—they were potential customers, after all—but he never did. He knew they were there, though, she could tell. They drifted on past the sweetmeats dealer and the dried-fish seller. At the corner, a huddle of men were sitting on the sidewalk in front of a hockshop, placidly playing checkers. They had on the same loose-fitting, dark blue blouses and baggy trousers that all Chinese men seemed to wear, with black felt fedoras or skullcaps, and long, skinny pigtails. One of the men looked up, and quickly away again when Grace caught his eye. She had the impression that she and Reuben were safe here, but not particularly welcome. She thought of Ah You, Henry's houseboy, whom she'd known for as long as she'd known Henry—six years. She tried to imagine him here in Chinatown, hustling to make some kind of living on the mean, dirty streets. It was impossible; she could only think of him at Willow Pond, spouting his pseudo-Confucian sayings and puncturing Henry's self-esteem with exaggerated obsequiousness.

Reuben caught her hand and swung it between them in his big one. She smiled up at him, thinking how funny it felt to be strolling through Chinatown hand in hand, like a couple of out-of-town sightseers. Honeymooners, maybe. The funny part wasn't how odd it felt, though, but how natural.

The street they were on narrowed to an alley and finally ended in a vile-smelling courtyard. They turned around and retraced their steps, passing countless smaller alleys and side streets, all dark and dismal-looking even though it was just past noon. How easy it would be to get lost in this labyrinth of dirty, identical-looking narrow lanes. A sign on the brick building they were passing said "St. Louis Alley" in English, under Chinese characters, and Grace pulled on Reuben's arm to stop him. "Look," she said, pointing, "it's another joss house." She started toward it, but Reuben pulled her back. She looked at him in surprise.

"I've heard of this place," he said shortly, his face grim. "St. Louis Alley. You know what's under this temple?" She shook her head. "The barracoon. It's a detention house—the Queen's Room, they call it. It's where the highbinders bring slave girls after their ships dock at the Embarcadero. They sell them here."

"No."

"Yes. Strip them first, so the buyers can see what they're bidding on. Sometimes they've been beaten, sometimes branded with hot irons. They hardly ever kill them, though, because they're too valuable."

Grace pivoted and walked away, arms wrapped tightly around herself. Reuben caught up to her before she got far, steering her away from the dead end she was blindly heading for. On Dupont Street, he took her arm and slowed their pace; they walked for a time without speaking.

"How do you know things like that?" she burst out accusingly. It was easier to turn the horror into anger than to keep it inside. "How do you hear about such awful things?"

"I'm a man," he said lightly. "It's my job to know things like that."

She snorted with scorn, yanking her hand out of his. "It's your job as a man to know about depravity and vice and cruelty?"

"Those things are part of the world, Grace. I'm a man of the world."

She wasn't going to get a serious answer out of him, that was clear. She felt her temper cooling anyway. Getting angry at Reuben because evil existed didn't make very much sense.

"I used to wish I were a man," she said in calmer tones, slipping her hand back under his arm. "When I was little. Sometimes I still do."

He looked amused. "Why?"

"Because you have it so much easier. Maybe not easier," she amended, "but at least for you life is more interesting."

"Is it?"

"I loved being Sister Augustine because I

was on my own. Fooling people, having power over them. That's close to being a man, isn't it?" He only smiled at her. "And men left me alone and didn't bother me. *Most* men," she added pointedly. "Would you have believed I was a nun if you hadn't seen my gun?"

"Probably. But I'd still have asked you to have dinner with me."

"You would? Why?"

He stopped, peering down at her as if she were slow in the head. "Because, Gus, you were so damn *pretty.*"

She looked away and made another snorting noise. Her face felt warm, and she knew she was blushing. *Blushing,* for God's sake. "Let's go in here," she suggested abruptly, pulling him toward a doorway. Through it she could see a short corridor that led to a room with a long gaming table in the center, surrounded by eager-looking gamblers. Even from here she could hear the click of dice and dominoes.

"Hold it, Grace—you can't go in there."

"Why not?"

"They won't let you."

"Why won't they?"

"Well, for one thing, gambling's illegal in Chinatown, and for all they know we might be cops. And even if we aren't, we're white devils, so we'll bring them bad luck."

"Don't be silly, they'll let us in. Everybody gambles in Chinatown."

He shrugged. "Okay, you go ahead, then." She looked at him doubtfully. "Go ahead, go on in."

"Aren't you coming with me?" She glanced back at the door. A man sat on a stool beside it, guarding the entrance. He looked harmless enough, gray-bearded and stoop-shouldered, blinking dreamily and gumming an unlit cigar.

"No, you go ahead. It's all right, you'll be fine."

She knew he was daring her. Fleetingly she wondered how he could know that a dare was the one thing she could never resist. "All right, I will." She wheeled around and strode toward the door.

Quick as a snake, the elderly man reached up and grabbed a rope she hadn't noticed before, suspended from a hook above his head. She heard a loud bang, and jumped in fright when the inner door, the one at the far end of the dark corridor, slammed shut on a fast spring lock. A muffled roar went up from the room beyond the door. Spinning around, she raced back to Reuben, hauled on his arm, and dragged him away from the gambling den at a fast trot. Her heart was pounding, but when she threw a panicky glance over her shoulder, she saw that no one was coming after them. She felt like an idiot. And she had to listen to Reuben's infuriating chuckling for half a block.

"Wait, I can't go any farther," he panted, pulling her up short, pretending he was winded.

She glared at him. "Why didn't you just tell me?"

"This was more fun. Wait!" He grabbed her

before she could flounce away again. "If you really want to go gambling in Chinatown, Grace, I can think of one place where they might let us in."

"Where?" she asked suspiciously.

"Come on and I'll show you."

The place where he took her had no sign, no window. It was literally a hole in the wall; the door looked like a fissure in the side of a stone cave. From the entrance no lights were visible. "Wait here and don't move," he cautioned her—needlessly; where did he think she would go? Leaving her at the entrance, which was unguarded as far as she could tell, he disappeared inside the fissure.

Immediately she remembered every story she'd ever read about kidnapped Caucasian women, sold into slavery and forced into lives of harlotry and degradation. What was Reuben thinking of, to leave her out here on the street by herself? Everybody on the sidewalk looked sinister all of a sudden. A man in a long wool overcoat and Western shoes walked straight toward her, bare white ankles showing. His forehead was shaved, and his long black queue hung down over one shoulder. He had mild brown eyes. Deceptively mild? They caught hers and held them. The closer he came, the harder Grace pressed back against the rough wall. At the moment the man drew level with her, someone clamped a hand on her shoulder from behind. She let out a squawk and jumped half a foot in the air. Whirling, fists clenched, she confronted Reuben.

"Damn it, Grace, you scared the hell out of me!"

Her racing heart wouldn't let her speak for a few seconds. When she got her breath, she said deliberately, "Don't—ever—do that to me—again."

"Do what? Come on, let's go, you shouldn't be standing out here by yourself." She mumbled inarticulate curses, which he ignored. "The look-see man says we can come in, but we can't play. I had to give him some cumshaw. Don't forget, you owe me two bucks."

He was pulling on her hand, leading her through the crack in the wall. "What's cumshaw?" she asked shakily.

"A tip, a bribe. The specials earn a pretty good living that way, in payoffs to look the other way. A special is an auxiliary cop," he said before she could ask.

Except for the low ceiling, the roomy, well-lit gambling den bore no resemblance to a cave whatsoever. It was fairly clean, not too crowded, and it even had a band—two men playing strange music on odd-shaped instruments in the corner. Along the sides of the room were tables for cards, dice, dominoes, and white-pigeon ticket—a form of lottery, Reuben explained. But the primary game here was the one going on around a square table covered with matting in the middle of the room.

"It's fan-tan, isn't it?" she asked in a whisper, standing as close to Reuben as she could without stepping on his feet. She was acutely aware that they were the center of suspicious attention and that every gambler in the room was sneaking dark, baleful glances at them when their heads were turned.

Reuben nodded. "Do you know how it's played?"

"Not really." It looked simple, but she couldn't figure out the object. A man with a long wand, like a conductor's baton, was sliding small porcelain buttons in groups of four out of a larger pile of buttons. The gamblers standing around the table stared intently at this operation, mesmerized. When the man with the stick—the banker, she assumed—stopped counting because the pile of buttons was depleted, several of the watchers were paid off in bank notes from a purse the banker wore around his waist. They'd won, obviously, but how or why, Grace couldn't fathom.

"How does it work?" she asked out of the side of her mouth.

"The guy with the purse is called the *tan kun*, which means the 'ruler of the spreading out.' Watch what he does now. See? He takes a bunch of buttons out of that bowl, and now he hides them."

"Why?" He'd put a lid over the pile of buttons immediately after placing them on the table.

"So the players can't try to count them until after they bet. Now they're betting."

The gamblers were putting money down on the four numbered sides of a square painted in the middle of the table—she hadn't noticed it until now. "What are they betting on?"

"They're guessing how many buttons will

be left after the last spreading out—one, two, three, or none."

"That's it?"

"That's all there is to it."

The banker began the "spreading out" with his wand, sorting the buttons in fours with lightning quickness, never faltering or making a clumsy pass. Within seconds he was paying off new winners—this time, the men who had put their money on the number three—and reaching into the bowl for another handful of buttons. "I like it," decided Grace. "How much do you get if you win?"

"Four times your bet, minus a small cut for the house."

She had another question. She should wait, ask it outside, but she was dying to know. Under her breath she murmured, "How do you cheat?"

"You can't."

She looked at him in disbelief. "Nobody can?"

Now he was whispering too. "Sometimes the dealer uses a wider stick and hides a button in it to foil the heaviest bettors. But a player can't cheat, not unless he's connected to the house."

"Amazing." She'd never heard of a game you couldn't rig somehow. She was impressed.

"We should go," Reuben said.

"Oh, no—so soon? Are you sure we can't play? I'd love to try it."

"No, and the sooner we get out of here, the better they'll like it." He made a gesture with his chin toward the players.

"Why? We're not bothering anybody."

"We're bad luck, I told you. White is the color of mourning and death, and we're white. They associate us with losing."

"The house ought to pay us to stay, then," she muttered, letting Reuben guide her toward the door. Hostile stares followed them all the way; she felt them on the back of her neck. When they reached the street, she couldn't help feeling relieved.

A man in a bamboo basket hat was selling spiced pork on the corner, and the enticing smell reminded her she was hungry. They found an eating house on China Street. Grace balked at first, put off by the pigs' heads hanging from the rafters and the chicken gizzards and livers proudly displayed in bloody wooden bins at the entrance. But Reuben insisted, and when the meal came she had to admit it was delicious. She didn't ask what was in the bowl of rice they were sharing, though, and she noticed he didn't, either.

It was getting dark by the time they finished dinner. Grace said they should go north and see if they could find Mark Wing's house, but Reuben said Jackson Street was too far away. She argued with him, more from habit than conviction, but gave in when he pointed out that they wouldn't know Wing's house if they saw it, and it wasn't likely he'd have his name on the door.

They were walking through a particularly unsavory neighborhood near St. Mary's Square; in the gathering twilight, the character of the streets and narrow houses changed, seemed to grow subtly more menacing. In a dark doorway, a woman's form materialized; Grace caught a quick glimpse of her young, pretty face before she faded back into the shadows and disappeared. A lady of the evening, no doubt. Reuben had told her St. Mary's Alley was one of the places where whores congregated after dark. Just then they passed a ramshackle building, with one brightly lit window on the ground floor. Behind the window—Grace blinked hard and looked again, to make sure—a woman sat, naked to the waist, smiling woodenly at passersby. Reuben was looking the other way; he went three steps by himself before noticing Grace wasn't beside him. She'd stopped in her tracks to gape.

"Did you see that? Did you see it?" she sputtered, letting him take her arm and drag her away. "That girl—did you see her?"

"I saw her."

"She was just *sitting* there—naked as a jaybird!"

"Come on, Gus."

She craned her neck for one last glimpse. "What did the sign say? Did you see the sign under the window?"

"I saw it."

"What did it say?"

"How would I know? It was in Chinese."

Something in his voice convinced her he knew exactly what the sign said. "But the money was in English," she insisted. "Three amounts—one dollar, two dollars, and ten dollars. What was it?" He kept shaking his head until she pulled on his arm. "Come on, Reuben, tell me. You know, I can tell. What were the amounts for?"

"Why do you want to know so much?"

"I just do. I'm curious. Come on, tell me."

He looked up at the sky and heaved a put-upon sigh. "I *think*—and I'm only guessing, of course—that for a dollar, the customer gets to fondle one of the lady's...charms."

"In the *window*?"

He nodded; his face was grim because he was trying not to smile. "And for—"

"Never mind, I can work the rest out for myself." For two dollars, the customer could fondle both "charms," no doubt, and for ten, he got the most intimate favor of all. She wondered how exactly the sign expressed the latter, but at the same time she was glad Reuben couldn't tell her. Or could he? Maybe he knew everything about it because he visited girls like that all the time. A little fire, hot and unpleasant, flared up in her at the thought. It almost felt like jealousy—but, of course, it couldn't be.

Besides, she couldn't imagine Reuben having to pay a woman to have sex with him—even though some men, she'd heard, liked it better that way. But Reuben...well, he was too good-looking, for one thing; and for another, he was such an accomplished confidence man, she wouldn't put it past him to figure out some way to make women pay to sleep with *him*.

"Let's go home, Grace."

"I'm not ready to go yet," she said perversely. "I want to go to an opium den."

"You *what*?"

"I want to see one."

"What the hell for?"

"Because I never have before. I've read about them, and now I want to see one, and this is probably my only chance. Have you ever seen one?" He gave a reluctant nod. "Why did you go?"

He shrugged. "Curiosity."

"There you are. Take me to one, Reuben."

"Out of the question."

"Why? You said it wasn't dangerous, not even at night." She argued with him until he gave in. Jubilant, she clutched his arm and started walking. "I wish we had a gun, just in case. You don't have one with you, do you?"

"Of course not, don't be an idiot."

"Don't you ever carry a weapon?"

"Certainly not. Why would I? I'm not a criminal."

She shook her head at him, mystified. "Do you know where a den is?" she asked, keeping her voice low, scaring herself on purpose.

"They're everywhere. We won't have to go far."

He was right; they hadn't gone a block before he guided her into a rubbish-strewn alley—Fish Alley, he told her; in single file because the passage was so narrow, they squeezed between two foul, sweating stone walls and came out into a fetid courtyard, as dirty

as the alley had been. The door to the den—
she knew it was a den because of the sweet
fumes of the drug, strong even at this distance—
stood partly closed, and a young man with only
one arm stood guard in the half-light. "You
smoke?" he asked, grinning and gesturing
with a long pipe. His eyes were glazed; his
expression was imbecilic. "We got Turkey
drug, Persia drug, good smokee. You come
inside?"

Not far away, a man in rough work clothes
was passing heavy wooden chests from a
loaded cart to another man, visible only from
the shoulders up because he was standing in
a hole in the pavement—on steps or a ladder,
presumably, leading to the den's cellar. "Is that
chests of opium?" Grace whispered to Reuben
in amazement.

"No, green tea," he whispered back sar-
castically. "They're called piculs. That's what
the drug comes in from India or Turkey or wherever." He took money from his pocket and
handed it to the smiling doorman, conveying
something to him under his breath. "Okay,
boss," the guard responded, grinning wider.

"Come on," Reuben said to Grace, taking
her arm. "Let's get it over with."

At first she couldn't see anything except half
a dozen dim lights scattered at random around
a small black room. As her eyes adjusted,
she made out mats on the floor, then benches,
then bunks in stacks as high as the low ceiling.
The stench was stupefying, the heavy air
nearly opaque from smoke. Now she could see

people reclining on the makeshift beds, women as well as men, in various stages of narcotism, from dreamy languor to unconsciousness. Everything was absolutely quiet, like a tomb.

The lamps dotting the room were for lighting the pipes, she realized. She watched a thin, frail old man with no hair reach for his pipe, which was about eighteen inches long, with a curved stem. He dipped the end of a long wire into a metal container, like a snuffbox, and extracted a lump of something dark and gummy-looking. Holding the wire to the flame of his lamp, he waited until the lump began to sputter and bubble. With practiced fingers, he stuffed the stewing opium pellet into the bowl of the pipe and began to puff, exhaling through his nostrils. The gurgling sound of the cooking drug, like fat in a frying pan, was revolting; Grace shivered involuntarily. Presently the man's eyelids drifted shut; the pipe slid from his fingers. He lay without moving in an opium trance, as pale and still as a dead man.

"My God," she murmured. "It's horrible." Beside her, Reuben nodded. Nothing but his solid, reassuring presence kept her from bolting. She took his hand and made herself look at the smoke-blackened walls and ceiling, the filthiness, the cloudy, reeking air, and most of all the hopeless lassitude of the addicts. They seemed more dead than alive, zombies dreaming narcotic dreams while their bodies decayed and their souls sank into depravity.

Reuben's arm came up around her shoulders. "Let's go home, Grace," he said softly.

His gentleness had the baffling effect of making her want to hold him tight in her arms and feel his arms around her. She let him lead her out of the murky den and into the marginally more wholesome air of the courtyard. They found their way to Dupont Street without saying much, and hailed a hansom cab heading north. It wasn't until Reuben unlocked the door to his house in Yancy Street and held it open for her that her deadened spirits began to lift. She guessed it was because she was home.

8

Absinthe makes the heart grow fonder.
                              —Addison Mizner

"Anybody home? Hey, Gus, you up there?" No answer. She couldn't be asleep yet, it was too early, only eight or so. "Grace?" Reuben shouted louder. He wanted to tell her the good news—that he'd just won two hundred and forty dollars and a ruby stick pin at blackjack, completely on the square.

He thought he heard a mumbled reply, and then the sound of water running in the bathroom. Good; then she'd be down soon. His news would go a long way toward smoothing over the awkwardness they'd been dancing around since this morning.

There was still a corked half-bottle of Sauvignon de Touraine on the table, left over from last night's celebration of the three hundred bucks they'd won in a seven-up game at the Paradise Hotel. Not quite on the square, but close enough; a crimped ace or two and a couple of double discards didn't count. They hadn't come close to duplicating their windfall at the Evergreen, but that was all right. They weren't losing. Besides, the secret to sustaining a brilliant brace trick was not to use it too often.

Reuben poured himself a glass of the Sauvignon and sat down, swirling the wine to test its second-day legs, then just staring into it moodily, not drinking. He'd been sitting here this morning when the mail came. From this spot he'd watched Grace, across the room on the sofa, open a letter from her husband. The letter had come with a big box of clothes, which she'd already opened, exclaiming over every skirt, shoe, shirtwaist, and unmentionable inside. You'd've thought hubby had sent her bags of gold nuggets instead of a bunch of old clothes. But that was understandable; most women were a little crazy when it came to clothes, and a smart man just sat back and enjoyed the spectacle. That wasn't what had ticked Reuben off. Sitting here observing the amusement and pleasure on her face while she read her husband's letter—

that's what had made him feel like tearing the letter into little pieces and sprinkling them over her head.

"How's the old man?" he'd inquired irritably.

She'd waved her hand to shush him, not even looking up.

"Did you tell him we sleep together?" That made her look up. "In the same house," he clarified with a big smile.

"Henri is very understanding," she'd said calmly, and gone back to reading. Something in the letter made her smile, then chuckle, then laugh heartily. Reuben stood up and sauntered over to her, taking a seat on the wide upholstered arm of the sofa. A corkscrew curl dangling in front of her ear needed pulling back; he did it, gently, while she pretended to keep reading. She wasn't, though, he could tell because her eyes weren't moving across the page. He craned his neck to try for a peek at the letter, and she sighed irritably, folded it, and tucked it down the front of her dress.

He moved his hand to the back of her bare neck, so she had to look up at him. "Do you tell your husband everything, Gus?"

"Of course. We have no secrets."

"None at all?"

"None."

His fingers slid into her hair, caressing her scalp. "Then you must've told him about the night I kissed you. Hmm? And you kissed me back. Did you tell him about that night, Gracie?"

Her face didn't change, but her pupils

dilated, wide black circles almost eclipsing the clear blue irises. "I forgot," she said, trying to sound matter-of-fact. "It completely slipped my mind."

"Did it?" He brushed his thumb across her lips, daring her. "Let me refresh your recollection." He kissed her before she could turn away, and once their lips met she held perfectly still. But he knew from experience that Grace's first line of defense was a show of indifference. Determined to get under her guard this time, he kept the kiss gentle while he held her face between his hands, stroking her cheek and tracing the arch of her eyebrow. He nuzzled her, pressing soft little sipping kisses to her lips, until her eyelids fluttered closed and her pretty mouth began to soften. "Is it coming back to you now?" he whispered. To keep her from thinking about the answer, he slipped his tongue under her top lip and ran it along the smooth, slick surface of her teeth. She reached out and gripped his shoulder. She was trembling, head pressed against the high sofa back. He put his palm on her chest to feel the pounding of her heart. Vivid images of her naked body kept tantalizing him; he saw her the way she'd looked that first night, wet from her bath and pink from embarrassment, trying to cover herself with her hands. But her lush breasts had been too generous to hide— and now they were straining against the soft material of her dress, inviting him to touch. Whispering love words, he sleeked his hand inside her gown.

185

Soft. Springy and warm. What a luscious curve. Grace held her breath and let him touch her. "Hey, honey," he mumbled against her lips, finding her cool, silky nipple, playing with it until it peaked. Wanting more, he moved to her other breast. Something rustled; the unexpected feel of a sharp edge startled him. Henri's letter.

He didn't know if it was the rustling sound or the sharp edge pricking her soft skin, but one or the other definitely took all the romance out of the moment. In two seconds, Grace went from soft and pliant to mad and betrayed, and he knew before he opened his mouth that she wasn't going to buy his explanation.

He tried anyway. "I forgot about the letter, Grace. I swear, I didn't even remember it was there. All I wanted—"

"Oh, shut up." She shoved him away and stood up, all wounded pride and shaky dignity, pulling at the top of her dress. "You're a snake, Reuben Jones. It's a good thing I don't even like you."

He said, "Aw, Gus," feeling terrible.

"I'm going for a walk," she announced in a high voice, spun around, and escaped through the door to the alley.

She'd stayed away for twenty minutes. When she'd come back, she'd acted as if nothing had happened. He'd tried another apology, which she'd accepted without a second's hesitation, and for the rest of the day she'd treated him with horrible, nerve-wracking politeness. But when he'd asked if she wanted to go gambling with him tonight, she'd declined. "I'm not really feeling up to it. I think I'd like to be by myself."

He took a morose sip of warm white wine, regretting the whole damn thing. All he'd wanted to do was seduce her. Was that a crime? He hated hurting Grace's feelings, but every time he touched her, that's what he ended up doing. She wasn't like any other female he'd ever met—not even Hazel Mayne, and she'd been crooked as a pretzel. But Hazel didn't have Grace's sense of humor, or her brains, or her sly sweetness. The women he customarily associated with in his line of work—prostitutes, hangers-on, flimflam-mers—were hard. The few who were nice weren't very smart, and the smart ones were mean. But Grace was wise to the life, and yet she was soft inside. He wasn't used to that. A clever girl who still had a heart—that was a rarity to him. Every day he liked her better, and he was actually starting to think he'd miss her when she went away.

Something white on the newel post caught his eye. From here it looked like an enve-lope. Henri's? He put his glass down and went to investigate.

It was an envelope, but it wasn't from Henri. The seal was already broken; there was no stamp. "Mr. Jones, Mrs. Rousselot," it read in semi-legible script, and Reuben recognized Doc Slaughter's careless scrawl. He must've delivered it by hand, maybe slid it under the door while Grace was out. The one-page letter inside had no salutation, just got right down to business.

"A meeting has been arranged between you and the gentleman whose acquaintance you seek. You are to go to his house tomorrow, at four o'clock in the afternoon. No. 722—the street you already know."

"Balls," muttered Reuben. Why did they have to meet Wing in his own house? Why not a restaurant, or a park bench? But they'd run out of time to argue over the arrangements; tomorrow was Sunday, and the Croakers wanted their money by Tuesday morning. That left only one extra day to negotiate.

The letter continued. "If you missed this afternoon's papers, there's an item of interest concerning the gentleman arrested after the incident near Saratoga. He won't be providing the authorities with any information, you may be sure. The unfortunate fellow was found dead in his jail cell this morning; his jugular had been slashed, so deeply—the *Daily Alta* relates, with obvious relish—his head was barely left attached to his torso."

Reuben lifted a hand to his throat in reflex. Poor Fireplug. He was a mean son of a bitch, but he probably didn't deserve that. Who had killed him? Tong thugs, so he couldn't betray the Godfather?

"My fee for contriving this arrangement, whose potential for you is so very lucrative, is a paltry two hundred dollars. I'd like it in gold. My advice, however, is free: Be careful."

"Grace?" Reuben shouted up the stairs.

"Where the hell are you?" A muffled reply. He took the steps two at a time and strode down the short hallway to the closed bathroom door. "Gus?" No answer. "You okay in there?"

"Go away," he heard finally, in a watery-sounding whimper.

He put his hand on the knob, alarmed. "Grace? Are you sick?"

"Sick?" she repeated, as if considering it. "Not exactly. Not precisely."

He opened the door a crack and peeked inside. She was lying in the bathtub; all he could see over the rim was her head and the tops of her bent knees. "Gus?" She turned to look at him, bleary-eyed, trying to smile. She'd been crying. He started toward her—and stopped when he saw the tall green bottle resting on her stomach, submerged in an inch of soapy water. Château les Pradines Saint-Estephe, he managed to notice, although the bulk of his attention was elsewhere. Sister Augustine was drunk as a skunk.

"You're probably pretty clean by now," he said, taking a gentle hold of her shoulders. "Let's get you out of there, honey, before you drown."

But she pushed his helping hands away. "Reuben, you shouldn't be looking at me, I haven't got a stitch on."

"I noticed that." He handed her a towel. She used it to wipe her eyes, then dropped it over the side of the tub. "Are you sure you're not ready to come out of there now?"

"No, I'm not finished." She flapped her

hand, and he assumed she was dismissing him. "Wait—don't go."

"You want me to stay?"

She shrugged. "Don't you want to talk to me?"

"Sure. You bet." She was definitely *shikker,* but at least she wasn't slurring her words. He retreated to the w.c., lowered the lid, and sat down. From here he could see only head and knees again. "What are we celebrating?" he asked genially.

"It's the twelfth of June."

He nodded sagely, waiting.

"Six years ago today, I lost my Joe."

He pondered that for a time. Was Joe a person? Maybe "joe" was some female expression he wasn't familiar with, a girlish euphemism for virginity. "How'd you lose your...Joe?" he ventured.

"We were going to get married." Her face turned pink, and fat tears welled in her eyes.

"Who?"

"Me and Joe. We—"

"Wait now. Is this before or after Giuseppe?"

She frowned. "Who? Oh—Giuseppe." When she giggled, he saw that the wine had stained her teeth purple. "Joe *is* Giuseppe. Was, rather." The tears spilled over. "He wasn't really a count," she confessed, smearing her cheeks with the back of a wet hand. "He was just a summer hand on my stepfather's farm."

Stepfather? Farm? "I thought it was a vineyard."

"No, a farm. It's called Willow Pond. It *used*

to be a vineyard," she sniffled, "but now it's a farm, and a no-good one at that. Henry's the worst farmer in the world, and I'm the second worst."

"Tell me about Joe," he urged, fearing more tears.

"Ah. Joe." She heaved a huge sigh and wiped her eyes with the washcloth. "He had black hair and blue, blue eyes, and muscles *everywhere*. He was the handsomest boy I ever knew."

"What happened to him?" he asked coolly, beginning to conceive a dislike for brawny, blue-eyed Joe.

"It's a long story." She sat up to tell it, and Reuben stopped breathing. She held the wine bottle up to the light, squinting to see how much was left. Only a swallow. She finished it off, then emitted a ladylike belch. "Excuse me," she apologized, facing him, bare-breasted and oblivious. To keep from laughing, he propped his elbows on his knees and covered his mouth with his knuckles.

"By the way," she said, peering across at him blearily. "This wine?" She held up the dead soldier and wagged it at him. "I found it on the callow side. But under its awkward, child-like surface, I sensed a real willingness to please." She pounded her fist in the bath-water, sending a wave over the side of the tub. The joke doubled her up, snorting and snickering, convulsed with mirth. "Aha," she sighed at last, in an exhausted falsetto. "What was I saying?"

"Joe," he said helpfully.

"Joe." She wiped her eyes, sobering. "It was a long time ago. He came to help out on the farm in the spring. My stepmother didn't trust him, wouldn't even let him in the house. Poor Joe had to eat his meals by himself, sitting out on the back porch. I fell in love with him right away."

"Naturally."

"He did, too. We used to meet down by the creek whenever I could get away from the house and he could get away from his chores." She gazed, dreamy-eyed, at her big toe, which she'd stuck in the faucet nozzle. "I was so happy. That was the happiest time of my life." Her nostalgic smile faded slowly. "Then..."

"Then?"

"One day my stepfather caught us. Just *talking*," she pointed out, disgusted, "not even *doing* anything."

"That time."

"That time," she agreed. "He told Joe to clear out, be gone by the next morning, or else he'd take the bullwhip to him. This is my pious *Christian* stepfather, mind you."

"How old were you?"

"Sixteen and a half. So that night Joe climbed up the rose trellis and knocked on my window. He said to come away with him and we'd get married. Of course I said yes. We kissed. For the last time," she said dramatically, one hand on her heart. "He started down the trellis, and I heard a crack. Like wood snapping? Then he let out this surprised yell—I'll never forget the sound—just before his head disappeared below the sill. I heard an *awful* noise then," she mumbled through her fingers, and started to sob in earnest.

Reuben got up and went to her. When he sat on the edge of the tub, she reached for him with both hands.

"I thought it was the trellis, but later I knew—it was his neck! Joe broke his neck!"

"Shh," he comforted, drenched. She was half in the water, half in his lap. The feel of her warm, wet, slippery skin under his hands helped him beat down a horrible impulse to laugh.

Finally she stopped crying, distracted. "I told you not to look at me, Reuben. I'm *naked.*"

He reached for the towel on the floor and tucked it around her. "There, now you're all covered up."

She snuggled closer, until she was in his lap and nothing was left in the water except her feet. "You're being awfully nice to me," she said affectionately. "I like you much more than I thought I was going to."

"Such a flatterer. Do you want to brush your teeth or anything?"

She shook her head. "I think I'll just get in bed now."

"Good idea. Careful, there—"

"I can do it." She swung her legs over his knees, bare bottom swiveling on his thighs, and managed to stand up. "Whoo," she breathed, laughing, arms outstretched like a tightrope walker's. The towel slipped. She clutched it to her chest, unaware that her backside was bare. Spellbound, he watched her wobble into the bedroom.

Perched warily on the edge of the bed, he tucked her in. She had a nightgown now—he remembered her pulling it out of the box from Henri—Henry, rather—this morning. But he didn't feel up to helping her put it on right at the moment. He stroked the damp blonde hair back from her cheek and smiled at her. "You go to sleep now, honey."

"Reuben, I feel *wonnnderful*."

"That's good." He didn't have the heart to tell her that this was the best she was going to feel for a long time.

"You can kiss me if you want to," she offered magnanimously, blinding him with a purple-toothed smile.

"Well, that's a mighty generous offer. How about if I take a rain check?"

"Oh." She stuck her bottom lip out, disappointed. "Not even a little one? Teeny-tiny?" She held up her thumb and index finger, a millimeter apart. "Eensy-weensy?"

He had to laugh. Against his better judgment, he bent over and pressed a chaste kiss to her lips. He meant to draw away immediately, but the light, tentative touch of her hand on the back of his neck kept him motionless a little longer. Even drunk, she was the *sweetest* girl he'd ever met. "Night, Gracie," he murmured against her soft mouth, and straightened.

"Night." But she'd pinched a piece of his shirtsleeve in the same thumb and forefinger, and she was holding him still. "I've been thinking about your hands," she said in a confiding whisper.

"My hands?"

"I've been thinking what it would be like. You know. To be touched by hands that can find the shaved aces in a deck of cards."

He simply couldn't help himself—he covered her cheek with his palm, watching her dreamy blue eyes close, feeling her softness and her warmth.

"Not there," she admonished, yawning.

He swallowed with difficulty. "Where?"

Her answer was a soft snore.

Grace woke up four hours later. She couldn't be sure what had awakened her: the pounding headache, the ravenous thirst, or the vivid, crystal-clear memory of how she'd disgraced herself. The room spun when she sat up; it slowed after a minute or two, but realizing she was naked made her want to lie back down and pull the covers over her head. The need to use the bathroom was too strong, though. She got up, pulled her nightgown over her head, and padded down the hall to the lavatory.

She brushed her teeth while she was there, and dried her tangled hair, which was still wet from her bath. "Moron," she muttered to her sickly, pale-faced reflection in the mirror over the sink. "Damn blockhead." Her skin was pasty, her eyes watery; she looked like somebody who hadn't yet recovered from a near-fatal disease. It was a miracle she wasn't sick to her stomach. In fact, she was *hungry*. This afternoon Mrs. Finney, Reuben's landlady, had brought over a bowl of soup and a ham sandwich for her supper. She'd eaten the soup, but the sandwich was still sitting on a plate downstairs in the kitchen. The thought of it made her mouth water. But the thought of waking Reuben up and having to speak to him dried it up again.

Her stomach growled. Hunger won out. She found her dressing gown and tiptoed downstairs.

The sandwich was still there, but Reuben wasn't. The door to his backyard was standing half open, and through it she caught a faint whiff of cigar smoke. Leaning against the door frame, pensively chewing a bite of sandwich, she peered out at the misty darkness. Behind her, a foghorn bayed. The lonely sound made her shiver a little in her bathrobe. She liked the feel of the cool, damp air on her skin, though, because she was burning up. When the mist thinned, she saw a pinprick of orange light in the distance. Reuben's cheroot. She watched it come and go through the fog, moving and disappearing, appearing again. Swallowing the last of her sandwich, she slapped crumbs from her hands and squared her shoulders. Might as well get it over with.

He was in the tiered garden, sitting in the same love seat where they'd had their first tête-à-tête. She stopped twelve feet shy of him, tongue-tied. He didn't speak, but she thought he might be smiling at her. From here, she couldn't tell what kind of smile it was.

"I didn't think you'd be home so early," she opened, outwardly cool, inwardly mortified. "I thought I'd have my annual wake for Joe over with before you got back. Sorry you had to see me like that, Reuben. It must've been...very tiresome for you."

Whatever kind of smile it was, it got broader. "Tiresome isn't the word I'd use," he said in a soft, rumbling voice. "For seeing you like that."

She folded her arms and hugged herself, stuck for a response.

"How are you feeling?"

"Dreadful."

"Want some water?" He gestured, and she noticed a glass on the table in front of him.

"No, thanks."

"Shot of whiskey?"

She shuddered.

"Come over here and sit," he invited, patting the space beside him. She hesitated. "Come on, I'm harmless."

It would've been a mercy if the whole evening was one long blank in her mind; but unfortunately, she remembered everything. In particular she remembered sitting on Reuben's lap stark naked, snuggling in and telling him how much she liked him. And later, asking him to kiss her. And touch her. Oh, he was harmless, all right, but she wasn't. She was a danger to herself and others.

After a long minute, she accepted his invitation and sat down beside him, drawing her cold bare feet up on the seat and tucking her robe around them. To make conversation, she asked, "What time is it?"

"Around midnight, I think."

"What are you doing still up?"

"Couldn't sleep." He took a last puff on his cigar and flicked it into the grass. When he settled back in the seat, their shoulders brushed. She stiffened for a second, then relaxed, feeling silly. The touching of clothed shoulders was the least of her worries. Besides, his warmth felt good. Comforting. The silence between them seemed remarkably easy, all things considered. Even when Reuben broke it, his question didn't take her by surprise. "Did you really love Joe?"

She nodded. "I did. As much as I could at sixteen years old. I was lonely, and he really was a nice boy. I know I loved him partly to spite my stepparents, and I know if we'd really gotten married it probably wouldn't have worked out very well. But I did love him. And every year on the anniversary of his death I...remember him."

To her surprise, Reuben put his arm around her and pulled her close to his side. She shouldn't be surprised, though—he'd been nothing but kind and comforting all night. She laid her head on his hard shoulder, ruminating on the odd circumstance that even after all that had happened, sitting here beside him in the damp gray haze she felt closer to him than she ever had before. And even though she missed Henry every day, and Ah You, and Willow Pond, not once since she'd come to San Francisco had she been lonely. Not once.

"If Mark Wing really gives us a lot of money for the tiger tomorrow, what will you do with your share?" she asked after a long time. "Once you pay off the Croakers, I mean."

"Move farther west."

"Farther west? But there isn't anyth—"

"Keep going, all the way around the world. Just keep going. Keep on moving."

She felt a sinking in her stomach, a hopeless, dismayed kind of emptiness whose meaning she had absolutely no desire to examine. "What would you do when you got all the way around? When you got home, I mean, back to Sweetbriar."

"Sweetbriar?" He said it as if he'd never heard the word before. Then he put his head back against the bench and laughed, without a bit of humor. "Then I'll start all over again. And when I get tired of moving, I'll stop and buy myself a big spread somewhere. A cattle ranch like Edward Cordoba's. And I'll sit out on the veranda drinking iced champagne all day, watching other people work. For me, of course."

"Really?" She didn't quite believe it. She peered at him in the dimness, trying to read his face. "Don't you want to make something of yourself?"

"Sure. I want to make myself rich and idle." He smiled down at her. "What about you? What do you want out of life, Grace?"

"I don't know," she answered, honest for once. "Something, but I'm not sure what."

"A husband and children?"

"I have a husband," she reminded him softly.

"Kids?"

She shrugged, murmured something vague, and looked away. The old sadness reared up like a hand from a grave, but she pushed it back down.

"Don't you want to be rich and idle?" he pursued.

"Rich and idle," she repeated slowly, thinking about it. "Rich would be nice. But idle... I don't think so. Wouldn't that be boring?"

He looked at her as if the possibility had never occurred to him before. For the longest time he didn't say anything. When he finally spoke, it wasn't to answer the question at all. "You're staying home tomorrow night, Grace. I don't want you going with me to Wing's house."

She pulled away, sitting up straight. "Why not?"

"Because. It's too dangerous."

"Don't be silly. Of course I'm going with you!"

"No, you're not, and that's final. There's no sense in arguing about it, the subject's closed."

9

Man was created a little lower than the angels, and has been getting a little lower ever since.

—Josh Billings

"You just keep your mouth shut and look pretty. I'm doing the talking, Gus, and that's final. The subject's closed."

She drew herself up, clicked her heels together, and saluted.

Reuben turned away in disgust, muttering under his breath. The door knocker on No. 722 was an upside-down dragon. He lifted the snout and hammered it against the bronze plate underneath twice. Before he could bring it back for a third whack, the heavy door swung open and a Chinese manservant in baggy blue pajamas appeared. "Yes, I can help you?"

"We're here to see Mr. Wing."

"Yes, you are named?"

"Smith. We're the Smiths."

"Oh, say, that's brilliant," Grace said out of the side of her mouth.

"You are known to be coming?"

"We've got a four o'clock appointment," Reuben assured him.

"Yes, in re?"

"What?"

The servant looked baffled, as if he'd been

201

challenged to a duel. "In re?" he repeated hopefully.

"With regard to," Grace translated, as if speaking to children.

"Ah!" said Reuben, in unison with the enlightened manservant. Apparently a password was expected. "In re a tiger," he said meaningfully, wriggling his eyebrows.

The servant's bland-featured face turned crafty. "Follow me," he said in a conspirator's voice, turned his back on them, and walked away.

It was a surprise to find they weren't in the house yet. The front door turned out be set in a thick stone wall, a false front; and instead of leading to the house, it led to an outdoor courtyard, grassless and treeless, cement-covered, resembling an army parade ground more than somebody's front yard. Three stories of brick and stone encircled it, with numerous windows, balconies, and catwalks covering the walls. In Re didn't dawdle; he marched straight across the courtyard to another door, this one heavier than the first and studded with big iron nails. "No moat?" asked Reuben. "No sharks?"

Inside the house, they stood in an ante-room the size of his entire apartment, with whitewashed stone walls decorated with weapons and medieval armor. "Now this is cozy," Grace murmured, standing under an eight-foot pikestaff with a gleaming silver blade. "I like a house with its weapons on display. You know where you stand."

"Good afternoon."

They both jumped. Behind them loomed a gaunt-faced man in a long black robe, an unsheathed sword stuck in a sash around his waist. In Re said something to him in Chinese, bowed, and vanished through the door to the courtyard.

"Mr. Wing?" Reuben inquired, careful to keep his eyes off the glittering sword blade.

The black-robed man lifted his top lip in disdain. A thin scar from his forehead to the end of his nose adorned a face already ugly from smallpox. "I am Chief Swordsman to Kai Yee. My name is Tom Fun."

"Well, that doesn't surprise me a bit. Does that surprise you, Gus? Doesn't he look like the kind of guy who'd always be up to some wacky shenanigan or other?"

Tom Fun sneered again, showing his teeth, and this time he fingered the ivory and silver handle of his naked sword. "Come with me."

Making faces at each other—for courage—they followed him down a long, plain, white-walled corridor and into a small, bare, white-walled chamber: another anteroom. This one preceded a spacious hall where, from the sound of chanting inside, some sort of ceremony seemed to be in progress. Tom Fun stationed himself at the arched doorway between the two rooms, but to the side so that they could clearly see the festivities going on behind him. "Is it a birthday party?" Reuben inquired politely. The Chief Swordsman ignored him. Being blade-shy, Reuben would've been content to view the celebration from a distance, but Grace took his arm and moved him closer to the door. "I want to *see*," she whispered when he hung back. Tom Fun had no objection; he stared straight ahead, arms akimbo, not deigning to look at them. Reuben had a suspicion they were *supposed* to watch the ceremony—that their arrival had been timed, in fact, on purpose to coincide with it.

The principal player was a man with long, straight, snow-white hair, reclining on a high throne chair. The Godfather, no doubt. Surrounding him were about twelve other men, all wearing the same long black robes as Tom Fun. And all, Reuben couldn't help noticing, armed with one or more sharp objects— swords, knives, hatchets, machetes, sickles, cleavers. His mouth dried up; he felt a prickle of revulsion sidle up the skin of his neck to his scalp. Concentrating on the Godfather, he took note that he too wore a long, flowing robe, but his sported every color in the rainbow. When he held up his hand, the chanting abruptly stopped. A young man Reuben hadn't noticed before, wearing only a pair of baggy saffron trousers, walked slowly around to the back of the throne. The white-haired man—he had to be Kai Yee—clapped his hands once; the young man dropped to his knees and, to Reuben's astonishment, crawled underneath the throne chair and disappeared behind its gilded brocade draperies. Then the chanting started up again.

"Did he drop something?" Reuben asked

Tom Fun, who slanted him an evil look and said nothing.

The Godfather clapped his hands again, the chanting ceased, and the man in yellow pajamas crawled back out from under the chair. Some of the black-robed hatchet men lit incense and pieces of gilded paper and tossed them into a brazier in front of the statue of some ferocious-looking idol in a sort of temple affair in the corner. Somebody dragged a wooden box in front of the Godfather's throne, reached inside, and lifted a live rooster out by the neck. Kai Yee rose from his chair, pulling a curved saber from the bright orange sash around his waist. Even knowing what was going to happen, Reuben didn't look away in time. The Godfather's arm rose and fell in time with a barbaric, hair-raising yell. The rooster's head hit the floor with a rubbery-sounding *slap,* and blood spurted like a fountain.

Grace bit off a disgusted curse and put her face against Reuben's chest. He held her in a firm, manly grip, swallowing repeatedly to control his nausea.

More chanting and shouting. Finally the initiate—the man in yellow drawers—donned one of the long black robes everybody else was wearing. The Godfather handed him a sword, made a short speech, and the ceremony was over. All the hatchet men, including the new recruit, filed out through a rear door. Tom Fun went inside, spoke a few words to the Godfather, and followed.

"Now, *that's* entertainment," Reuben said

in Grace's ear. She still looked pale, but her breathy, nervous chuckle told him she was all right. Taking her elbow, he guided her into the throne room, careful not to step in any rooster blood. Out of the corner of his eye he could see the bird's torso, tossed on the floor near the shrine, still twitching. Kai Yee remained beside his chair, tall and unmoving, the ruddy, dripping sword dangling from his fingers. The silence stretched longer, tighter; to Reuben it began to seem intentionally dramatic. "Hi," he said to break it. "Hope we didn't interrupt anything. Some kind of party, huh? Looks like a good time was had by all."

Mark Wing didn't move or speak, just continued to stare at them. No, not at them—at Grace. Reuben might as well have been invisible, or nonexistent, for all the notice Wing took of him. The sensation was eerie; from the tense grip she had on Reuben's forearm, he knew she felt it, too.

In the queer new silence, he saw that Wing was much younger than he'd thought at first; the stick-straight, unbound, silvery-white hair was deceptive, for his unlined face was that of a man only in his forties. He was slender, austere, perversely handsome, with dark brows and intense black eyes, a flat nose, and thin, feminine lips. And he couldn't take his eyes off Grace.

"What was that," she asked, "some sort of initiation ritual?" Her manner was courteous, but Reuben knew her motive in speaking was the same as his—to break the weird silence.

She had better luck. Wing's soft lips curved in a smile as he laid his sword down and began to untie the sash around his waist. "Yesss," he answered in a spooky whisper, "a rite of passage. You found it quaint?"

"Quaint," she repeated, with a pretense of thoughtfulness. "That's not exactly the word I'd use."

He shrugged out of his parti-colored kimono, under which he was wearing—surprise—striped trousers and a sober gray morning coat. The Western clothes transformed him: except for the hair, he now looked like a banker. He tossed the robe aside and strode toward them, smiling broadly. His hand was pale and bony, but he gave Reuben's a strong California shake and said, "How do you do, Mr.—Smith?"

"Algernon Smith. This is my sister, Augustine."

Wing took Grace's hand and bowed over it, holding it in both of his. His hair hung down on either side of his head from a perfect center part, hiding from view whatever he was doing to her hand with his mouth. When he finally straightened, his black eyes snapped with a peculiar kind of fire, and Grace's cheeks flamed pink. "Yesss, an initiation ritual, as you say. I am leader of a group of bissness and community leaders; we are called the Society of the Perfect Harmony of Heaven. Today we inducted a new member. No doubt it seemed quite pagan to you. But the old ways are still strong among many of us in the Dai Fow—Chi-

207

natown," he explained with a bow, "and keeping up the ancient traditions encourages loyalty and morale."

"I doubt the chicken would agree," murmured Grace.

Wing smiled, delighted. "A symbol only."
"Of what?"

He held her gaze without blinking. "Of the fate of one who betrays the Ssociety," he hissed, back to the creepy whisper. "In a figurative sense, of course."

"Of course." She swallowed. "And the crawling under the chair?"

"Ah, that. Another symbol, this one of rebirth. As head of the Society, I am sometimes called Ah Mah, or Mother. The novitiate is reborn, so to speak, as a member of the company, or hong."

"Don't you mean *tong*?" Reuben put in.

Wing finally looked at him. "We are not a tong, Mr. Ssmith," he said evenly, "we are a benevolent society. A brotherhood."

"I get it. And you're the mother *and* the god-father."

His feminine smile thinned. Instead of responding, he took Grace by the arm and abruptly led her out of the room. Reuben followed on their heels.

They went back along the white corridor, past a number of closed doors, and into a large, dark-paneled room with English hunting prints on the walls and venetian blinds over the windows. A huge oak desk covered with books and papers confirmed that this was

Wing's office; but it could've been Henry Frick's office or J. P. Morgan's, so determinedly Western were the room's style and furnishings.

"Since you have come today to discuss bissness, perhaps we will be more comfortable here," Wing said courteously, escorting Grace to a leather armchair and waving Reuben into an identical one next to it. He said something in Chinese then, and Reuben turned in surprise to see a girl hovering in the doorway. Where had she come from? She wore a green satin robe tied at the waist with a gold sash, and high, cork-soled shoes on her tiny feet. She was barely five feet tall, and probably not yet twenty years old, and she had the face of a tragic doll. After listening with care to Wing's instructions, she bowed deeply and shuffled backward out of sight.

In minutes she returned with a heavy tea tray; she set it on a table and began passing out cups, saucers, and plates with cookies and little sandwiches—an English tea. Reuben would have preferred a glass of bourbon. He didn't mention it, though, because there was something about the way Wing issued orders to the tiny doll-servant that set his teeth on edge.

"And now," their genial host began, after dismissing the girl with a flick of his long, pale hand, "plees tell me how I may be of service to you. The message I received was pussling; it spoke of a recovered object, an article of funeral sculpture, if I recall correctly. But I confess I am at a loss as to how this concerns me, or how I might be able to help you."

Reuben draped his ankle over his knee. He decided to light a cigar, not because he wanted one, but because he figured it would annoy Wing. "Maybe you're confused because you've got it backwards. See, Mr. Wing, we're the ones who can help you."

"Indeed." He had to hurry over with a priceless-looking jade bowl before Reuben flicked a hot match onto the expensive carpet. He left the bowl on Reuben's chair arm and went back to his own seat. "How can that be, Mr. Ssmith?"

Reuben had about a third of Wing's attention; the rest was still riveted on Grace, to whom he seemed to have taken a shine. She did look spectacular today, no denying it, in a cream silk suit with an Eton jacket and a little vest, cream-colored high-heeled shoes, and black silk stockings. She had her hair up in one of those heavy, two-tiered affairs popular with the ladies these days, an engineering marvel Reuben could never figure out, even though he'd watched carefully in more than one lady friend's boudoir while it was performed. On Grace it was particularly stunning, because her hair was such a pretty color. Old gold, he'd called it once, and lately he'd refined it to yellow topaz. Exactly the color of a ring, long since hocked, that he'd stolen from his shrewish stepmother about twenty years ago. If he'd kept it, he could've given it to Grace and said flowery things about it and her hair. It might've worked; you never could tell.

From experience, he could see that the

Godfather was prepared to be polite and inscrutable all afternoon, until his cunning and courtesy finally wore them down and they laid their cards on the table. Why waste time? And why give him the satisfaction? Flicking a fat ash in the general direction of the jade bowl, Reuben came to the point.

"Mr. Wing, we've got the tiger. You've got the dog and the monkey, the goat and the rat—you've got all the rest, but they're no good to you without the tiger. My sister and I are prepared to sell it to you for ten thousand dollars."

That got his attention. He raised a porcelain cup to his lips and took a silent sip, dark eyes hooded. Reuben liked the idea that good old American directness had thrown him off his subtle Oriental stride. Of course, if he now said, "I have no idea what you're talking about, Mr. Ssssmith," they'd be back where they started. After a long, intense moment, during which Wing kept his flat black eyes fastened on Grace, he set his cup down and rose, his movements languid and, to Reuben, offensively graceful. A tall glass-and-teakwood case stood in the corner by the window; he went to it, opened the door, and took out a small object. Then he crossed back to Grace's chair and made her a low bow. "Miss Smith, a gift for you."

Reuben slid down farther in his chair. First Doc, now the Godfather—what was it that compelled sensible men, within minutes of meeting her, to shower Grace with presents? This one was a miniature bronze statue of a woman, he noted sourly, about the size of his little finger. Even from here, he could see that it was lovely. He hoped it was worth a fortune.

"Oh, she's *beautiful*," Grace gushed, cradling the statue in her palms. "Thank you very much—I couldn't possibly accept it." She didn't hand it back, though.

"But I insisst. You must have her—I knew it as soon as I saw you. She is a bodhissattva—an earthly guide to Nirvana in the Buddhist faith; to you, a kind of guardian angel."

Reuben groaned and sank lower.

"She is very old, from the Tang dynasty. Much older than this tiger of which you speak, Mr. Smith, and—forgive me for being crasss," he apologized to Grace with another bow, "much more valuable. I am a wealthy man, it's no secret. My art collection is, permit me to say, extremely fine. The piece you claim to have is only a Ming bauble, and so I am at a losss. Why would I pay the ridiculous amount you suggest, even if I were in possession of the rest of the collection?"

Reuben blew a smoke ring at the ceiling. "Well, I don't know, Mark, it's your obsession, not mine. The only reason I can think of is because some rich Ming guy got himself buried with this bauble, and that warms your peculiar little heart."

The only sign of rage was the flush on his sallow cheeks and the fleet, serpentine dart of his tongue over his thin lips. He stayed motionless for ten seconds, then pivoted with the grace of a dancer and moved leisurely back to the window. There he took up a pose, hands in his trouser pockets, one ankle crossed negligently over the other, head back against the wall. The confident San Francisco businessman—except that he had white hair down to his elbows, and all the warmth of a rattlesnake in his dead black eyes.

Deliberately, Reuben waited. Just as Wing opened his mouth to speak, he cut him off. "My sister and I didn't come here to haggle or negotiate. The price is ten thousand, period. Take it or leave it, and don't waste our time." He took out his watch and flipped it open. "It's up to you. We've got an appointment in thirty minutes with another potential customer." He snapped the watch closed and drummed his fingers on the chair arm.

Through stiff lips, Wing managed to say, "Do you have the tiger with you now?"

Reuben laughed rudely. "That's a joke, right?"

"How do I even know you have it?"

"You don't."

His cheeks were mottled, his hands balled into bony fists in his pockets. He was too angry to speak, and Reuben decided he'd pushed him far enough.

"As you say, you're a wealthy man," he said placatingly; "ten thousand's nothing to you. Then too, what good is your zodiacal calendar if it's got a year missing? Think what a shame it would be if you botched up your one chance to complete the set, Mark, just because you and I can't stand each other."

Wing had himself under control again, the reptilian smile back in place. "What you say is sensible, Mr. Ssmith. I find that, on second thought, I am agreeable to your terms."

"The statue for ten thousand?"

"Just so."

"When?"

"Tomorrow."

"Good." Hiding his jubilation, Reuben put his hands on his knees and started to get up.

"I attach a condition, however. A small one. Of no importance to you, but absolutely essential to me."

Reuben sank back in his chair, steepling his fingers against his chin. "I'm listening," he said warily. Wing's smile got weirder by the minute, and it was getting on his nerves.

"Miss Smith must bring the tiger. And she must come alone."

"No." He was on his feet, shaking his head, before Wing finished the first sentence. "Out of the question. Absolutely not, no way in—"

"Then we have no bargain."

"Fine, then we have no bargain. It's been nice—"

"Don't be silly, Algernon, of course we accept Mr. Wing's condition."

"The hell we do. I'm telling you, Gus—"

She rose and went past him toward Wing, who was still lounging against the wall. When she stopped in front of him, a look of wonder erased the subtle antagonism in his face. She held out both hands, but he was too stunned to react; when his wits came back, he reached out as if she were handing him the keys to heaven. Or Nirvana. "It's a deal, Mr. Wing," she said in a low voice, holding his penetrating gaze.

"Tomorrow evening at nine?" he whispered.

"Yess."

Was she mimicking him? Reuben felt torn between amusement and outrage. "Hold it. Hold on one damn minute. She's not coming by herself. Not at night, not at any time, and that's—"

"Until tomorrow," Grace murmured, sultry and oblivious. Wing hadn't heard a word he'd said either. Reuben watched, open-mouthed, as they squeezed each other's hands and drifted apart. "Coming, Algernon?" She glided by him into the white corridor. The tiny servant must have been lurking by the door; she bowed to Grace and walked away. Grace followed, calling, "Algie?" over her shoulder.

Stymied, he glared at Wing. The Godfather hadn't recovered yet; he was still grinning a big, stupid grin, like a man realizing his river card gave him a belly-buster straight. "Forget it, she's not coming," Reuben threw at him, and stalked out of the room. The last thing he noticed was the bronze bodhisattva on the table by Grace's chair. Priceless, for all he knew. She hadn't taken it, and he was glad.

Glad? *Glad?* He hurried after her, primed for a fight.

10

That there is a devil is a thing doubted by none but such as are under the influence of the devil.
—Cotton Mather

"Are you starting up again? Reuben, my throat's sore from arguing with you. I'm going in, by myself, right now."

Although he was close enough to touch her, he could barely see her through the fog. Across the street from where they were standing, nothing but a wavering pool of yellow light marked the door to No. 722. The sidewalk was muffled in damp silence. Occasionally a cloudy human form loomed out of the wet mist and disappeared back into it, quiet as smoke.

"I don't want you going in there alone." His own voice sounded strange, almost disembodied. Also hoarse from arguing, which they'd been doing for the better part of the last twenty-eight hours.

Grace stamped her foot on the wet pavement. "You told me yourself they only hurt each other. You said no matter how vicious the tongs are, they never do anything to white people, they keep the violence inside their own quarter and never—"

"I said *usually*." The urge to stuff his handkerchief in her mouth had never been stronger.

ANOKA COUNTY LIBRARY

Title: Crooked hearts
Item ID: 32085020694397
Date due: 7/20/2015,23:59

Access "My Account"
through:
Web: anoka.lib.mn.us
Phone: 763-717-3261
Facebook:
/anokacountylibrary

"This tong's already broken the rules by holding up a Wells Fargo stage and terrorizing the passengers. Wing isn't playing with a full deck, Gus, so we can't predict what he'll do."

"He wants the statue," she countered stubbornly. "That's one thing we can predict."

"Not as much as he wants you." They always came back to that. For the life of him, Reuben couldn't understand why that didn't end the argument, with him the hands-down winner. But she treated his best, most salient debate point as if it was some whiny, childish irrelevancy.

"Oh, for Pete's sake, Reuben. Wing might be a little unhinged, and I'll admit he does seem to have a yen for me—" She broke off to nudge him in the ribs, trying to make him laugh. He didn't. She sighed. "I'm a big girl, I can take care of myself. Wing doesn't frighten me—I've handled plenty of men much scarier than the Godfather."

"Oh, I'll bet you have," he snapped before he could stop himself. She went stiff as a poker. "Damn it, Grace, is that supposed to make me feel better?"

"I couldn't care less how it makes you feel," she said icily. "I'm going in, and you can't stop me."

"The hell I can't." They glared at each other through the mist. As usual, they weren't getting anywhere.

"Look," she said after a minute, stiff-lipped but trying to sound placating, "we've been through this a hundred times. He won't give us the money unless I go in by myself and get it. Nothing will happen to me. He'll flirt a little, I'll be nice to him, he'll hand over the money, I'll leave. Give me one hour—"

"Half an hour." He couldn't stand the thought of Grace being nice to Wing for a whole hour.

"No, an *hour*," she insisted. "It's not likely that I'll need it, but I want the extra time just in case. Along with everything else, I don't want to have to worry about you charging in at the wrong minute to rescue me."

He hated it, but he finally said, "All right," through his teeth.

She sighed, and lost a little of her combative posture. "Good." She looked over her shoulder at Wing's house. "Do you have the gun?"

He patted his coat pocket.

"You won't need it, of course. But just in case, remember—it only fires two shots, and it's no good beyond about six feet."

"I'll remember," he said grimly. "And you've got the tiger?"

She patted the purse under her arm. "Okay."

"Okay. Well. Guess I'd better go."

"Yeah."

But she didn't move. Did she want him to touch her? He wanted to—but he was afraid if he did, he wouldn't let go. He'd drag her all the way home and kiss ten thousand dollars good-bye.

At the last second, he reached for her anyway. She was in the act of turning away; his hand brushed her shoulder blade clumsily, as if he were patting her on the back. She muttered something and kept going. In seconds the fog swallowed her.

She reappeared in the pool of light across the street. He saw her lift the dragon knocker and let it fall, but the thick mist pillowed the sound; he could barely hear it. The heavy door swung open.

"This is crazy."

He said it out loud, and the truth of it had him moving toward the house at a jog, stumbling once over some invisible obstruction in the road. He was stepping up on the opposite curb when Grace vanished through the door. It closed behind her with a muted, final-sounding thud, and Reuben pounded to a halt. Even from here, the entrance to the house was hardly discernible, swaddled in the chilly, dripping, shifting mist. Yesterday he'd joked to Wing's servant about a moat, and now the fog made one; the illusion of impregnability was persuasive, and it kept him planted where he was. Kept him from storming the castle.

He streaked his hands through his wet hair. Maybe he was acting like the worried old maid Grace had been calling him all afternoon. He moved toward the street lamp on the near side of the Beckett Street corner; taking a position against the damp wall of an anonymous, unlit building, a foot or two beyond the

219

weak circle of light the street lamp cast, he waited.

And waited. It was too dark here to read his watch. How the hell was he supposed to know when an hour was up? The hell with that anyway, he'd knock on Wing's door any damn time he felt like it. Like now, for instance. The fog and the quiet were stretching his nerves. He decided to reconnoiter.

An alley ran between Beckett and Kearny streets; the back of Wing's fortress of a house must face on it. He wished he'd worn shoes instead of boots, so he wouldn't make so damn much noise when he walked. Beckett Street was deserted, but in the alley a rat party was in progress. The lure must be the rotting garbage he could smell all around him.

Moving east, he stopped when he calculated he was looking up at the mesh of windows and fire escapes at the back of Wing's building. Where would the Godfather entertain Miss Smith? He peered hard at the lighted windows, but most of them were curtained, and the ones that weren't were empty.

To his left was another three-story building, and every one of its windows was lit up, although most were covered with thin, discreet shades. With a start, Reuben realized it was Wing's brothel. The House of Celestial Peace and Fulfillment.

While he watched, the figure of a woman passed a third-floor window of the whore-house, reappearing an instant later in an adjacent window of Wing's house. It took him a second to register the significance. They connected! "Very convenient," Doc had labeled the proximity of the two buildings. Wait until Reuben told him *how* convenient. He was shaking his head in amused disgust when a noise behind him made him freeze. A rat, probably, or maybe a cat, since it was louder than—

Sparks ignited in front of his eyes, in time with a resounding *fwack* and an excruciating thud against his left temple. The ground coming up didn't hurt; a black pillow cushioned his fall. Nothing. Zero.

"Careful, these stairs are sometimes a trifle sslippery."

Not half as sslipery as you, thought Grace, avoiding Wing's helping hand by pretending not to see it. How the hell had she gotten herself into this predicament? The deal was done: he had the tiger and she had the money, all ten thousand of it, safely tucked away in her pocketbook. It was time to go home, not take a tour of the catacombs.

But Wing had been so insistent, so persuasive. He'd offered a toast with sam shu—Chinese brandy—to the successful conclusion of their "bissness affair," and invited her to have a look at his art collection. Right around then he'd started calling her "thee" and "thou," speaking of "thy gracious goodness," and how she couldn't deny him the pleasure of showing off a few trifles from his humble little museum. It would give him so much pleasure, especially since he rarely had an opportunity to show the collection to anyone, "for reasons I'm certain I don't have to explain to you, Miss Ssmith." Meaning he'd stolen it, she assumed. The honor of being taken into the Godfather's confidence was a dubious one, particularly when all she could think about was getting out of here, flying home with Reuben, and celebrating their incredible windfall. But she had to admit she was curious about Wing's art collection. "Then too, surely you are anxious to see the tiger sculpture back among its fellows at lasst? Come, it will take but a moment, and I promise you shall be amply rewarded for your time." An intriguing invitation, but he'd left out one little detail: the collection was in his basement.

So here she was in the damp, drafty, not very clean cellar, moving down a narrow stone corridor, trying not to touch the sooty wall on her right or the swinging arm of her peculiar host on her left. At a turn in the corridor, a door stood half open. She caught a glimpse of two men laboring inside, pushing wooden casks around and stacking them against the walls. Wing's firm hand on her elbow got her moving again, at the same instant she remembered when and where she'd seen wooden chests just like those: three nights ago, on the sidewalk outside the opium parlor, being loaded through a trapdoor into the cellar. Did that mean Wing stored the drug for his own dens right here? Right in his own basement?

They came to a closed door, illuminated by a shuttered lantern hanging from the ceiling. Wing withdrew a key from the pocket of his conservative black frock coat, unlocked the door, and threw it open.

"Oh, my," Grace breathed, a reaction that seemed to please him immensely.

He spread out his arms. "Thiss—thiss is my gallery," he said, his creepy whisper echoing strangely in the enormous room. "Welcome, Miss Ssmith." His voice went even lower; he clasped his hands and screwed up his face, like a hungry beggar. "Or...Augustine? May I call thee Augustine?"

"Sure," she said, distracted.

He crossed his wrists over his heart and bowed low. "My thanks," he whispered fervently.

"Don't mention it." She turned away from his unnerving ardor to gaze around the room. It really was a gallery, as high, wide, and opulently furnished as any of the exhibition rooms she'd seen in the San Francisco Museum of Art. The walls were of dark oak paneling, not damp stone; the carpet on the floor was a thick, breathtaking Oriental; discreet gas lights on the walls and ceiling created the illusion of natural light. Even the air was sweeter here than in the musty basement corridor they'd just left. Watercolor paintings, scrolls, and silk screens covered three of the paneled walls, and long glass cases full of sculpture and ceramics lined the fourth. A sound like plucked harp strings was coming from behind a tall painted screen. Grace sent Wing a questioning glance. "For thy enjoyment," he simpered, with another theatrical hand wave. Stepping sideways, she saw that behind the screen sat a young girl in a red satin gown, playing a pear-shaped instrument vaguely resembling a lute. If this was a seduction, it was having the opposite effect on Grace, who had an almost overwhelming urge to giggle. Wouldn't Reuben love this when she told him?

"Ah, you are drawn to the paintings, I see." He sidled closer, and she realized she was staring at a watercolor drawing of a robed man with a long goatee and a topknot. "As works of art, paintings satisfy the Western aesthetic more readily than sculpture or ceramics, do you agree? That is a portrait of Li Po, our greatest poet. It's not very old, only five hundred years or so. Liang K'ai is believed to be the artist."

"One of my favorites."

"Indeed?" He looked charmed. "Thiss, Augustine." He moved to a bust on a pedestal in the middle of the room. "She is also a bod-hisattva—an angel, if you will, of mercy and kindness. The phissical resemblance is not as marked as with the small statue I offered thee yessterday," he said with gentle reproach, "but the spirit of selflessness and generossity is the same. Dost thou not see it?"

"You bet." What was this "Dost thou not" business?

He pulled something from his pocket. "Take this."

She reached out automatically. "What is it?"

"A simple piece of jade. Touch it, Augustine. The purity of the form, its cool smoothness, the extreme simplissity—they lift the soul in a kind of ecstasy, beyond the world of appearances. Do you feel it? Do you know that you and I are the same?"

"Beg pardon?"

"The universal essence, the oneness, the unity of all things. Within the One, differences are only illusions of the senses. Thou, Augustine, and I: we are one and the same."

She dropped the lump of jade back into his palm. "That's an interesting philosophy, Mr. Wing. I'll give it some thought, but right now I think I'd better be running along."

He hung his head. Heavy white hair slithered over his shoulders, curtaining the sides of his face. The plunking music stopped; Grace heard rustling behind the screen, and a moment later the girl in the red dress came toward them, bearing an ebony tray. Two lotus-shaped bowls full of some dark red liquid rested on the tray. Wing took one of the bowls and handed it to Grace—"Oh, no, one's my limit," she tried to say, but he pressed it into her hands firmly—and took the other for himself. The servant bowed and retreated behind the screen.

"Thiss is my final oblation," Wing hissed sorrowfully. "I fear thou and I shall never meet again." He raised his cup to her, a sad, beseeching look in his eyes.

I'll drink to that, thought Grace, and downed hers in three swallows. The cool, sweet liquid was delicious, and tasted more like fruit than alcohol—which she guessed meant Wing had given up on seducing her. He had his peculiarities, no doubt about that, but he also had some undeniable good points. Generosity, for example. And let's not forget urbanity. He wasn't all that bad to look at, either. She smiled to herself, thinking he was starting to sound like one of Reuben's wines—"Suave and attractive, with a big heart."

"Hm?" Wing intoned, moving in closer.

Good Lord, had she said that *out loud*? "This," she clarified hastily, waving her lotus leaf at him. "What is it?"

"Rice wine."

"Really?"

"In China we have an expression—to drink rice wine together. It means to become friends. Companions."

"Sweet." She looked around for a place to set the empty bowl, but couldn't see one. "Well, guess I better be going now. My brother'll be wondering what's keeping me."

Wing's thin lips compressed. "He is very devoted to thee."

"Who, Algernon? Oh, yeah, very." Still carrying her bowl, she let him take her arm and escort her out of the gallery and into the damp, drafty corridor.

They turned right where she could've sworn

they were supposed to turn left, and a few feet later they stopped in front of a door she knew she hadn't seen before. Wing pointed to painted Chinese writing above the door, then translated it for her with his lips close to her ear: "The Realm of Eternal Life."

"Sounds nice. Gotta go."

His flat hand between her shoulder blades prevented her from backing up. "A moment only. So important."

"No, really."

"Plees."

"I'm already—"

He reached past her and pushed open the door. The fact that there were lights and people inside lessened her trepidation. When Wing motioned her over the threshold, she shrugged and stepped inside.

Two men in rough work clothes were kneeling at the base of a gigantic stone rectangle, hollow inside, applying gold paint to tiles inlaid around the arched entrance. More men were busy inside the rectangle, a sort of squat, windowless building, with trowels and plaster. "What are they making?" she asked.

Wing's black eyes, usually somber and flat, shone like polished coal. "They are making my tomb."

"Oh, your tomb." She stopped nodding abruptly. "Your *tomb*?"

"Come and ssee."

"No, thanks. Here—" She started to hand him the lotus-leaf bowl, and froze in amazement when she realized it was full of the ruby-red liquid again. "What the hell," she breathed, staring at the bowl, then at Wing.

"Don't be afraid, my golden one. Here thou art safe. Look, the dragon guards the entrance; no evil may disturb us here." He made one of his graceful gestures at a waist-high ceramic statue of a snarling lizard, on guard at one side of the tomb's door. "And there, the man-beast." He pointed to another ferocious image, at attention on the other side. "Now dost thou see that thou art ssafe?"

"Um—"

"Yess," he hissed, moving in. "You see, Augustine, because you have been blessed with a special wisdom."

"Right. Listen, I'd—"

"Do you know the worst sin a man can commit, Augustine?"

Letting his so-called friend go into a crackpot's house all by herself? she guessed silently. Why was it so *hot* in here all of a sudden? She sighed, and took a small sip of her fruity wine. "What?"

"To have no sons. This is the most heinous of all acts of unfilial conduct. Why? Because without sons, a man cannot enter heaven. The prayers of his sons intercede for him with the Cosmic Powers, just as the soul of his dead father intercedes for him. In its ignorance, the West calls this 'ancestor worship,' but of course it is not our ancestors whom we worship."

"Of course not." When she looked around for a place to set her wine bowl, a warm wave of dizziness washed over her. "Uh-oh." She reeled; Wing steadied her.

"Come and see what I am taking with me to heaven," he said—or she thought he said; on second hearing, it didn't sound very likely. "Thiss way, Augustine, beyond the curtain."

"Uh-oh," she said again, but that seemed to be about it as far as resistance to Wing's will went. Feeling oddly flatfooted, she let him lead her past scattered tools and paint-spattered sawhorses to a curtained alcove at the back of the big room. Inside, it looked like another gallery, but smaller than the first one, and devoted to sculpture.

"In centuries past, the wealthiest noblemen gathered about them in life all the things they would need in the afterlife, Augustine. Pets, special foods, favorite works of art. Servants."

She licked her dry lips. "Servants?"

"Representations of them." He smiled. "Behold." He gestured toward a group of sculptures on a table. "Beautiful, aren't they? Here, a dancer and an acrobat, both from the Han dynasty. Exceptional pieces. These sculptures are women servants—Wei period, fourth century. And these, musicians and singers, from the Song dynasty. Are they not graceful? Would they not be worth taking to the afterlife?"

They would. The face of one of the musicians arrested her attention, round-cheeked and sly-eyed, a jolly little drummer. It was really very, very charming. She put out her hand to touch it, but Wing caught her fingers and brought them to his lips. His cool, thin, feminine lips. She shuddered inside, but she let him nuzzle her knuckles. His tongue came out to stroke across her fingers like a little pink brush, and she didn't move a muscle.

"Farther back in time," he whispered, tickling her wet hand with his breath, "instead of sculptures of servants, slaves were sacrificed and buried with the corpses of the dead noblemen. To serve them for eternity."

Her mouth was bone-dry; she had to wet her lips again before she could speak. "What a warm tradition."

The lotus cup was still in her hand. He lifted it to her lips, and she drank thirstily, draining it. "More?" he murmured. He pressed his thumb against the bronze stem, and at once the receptacle filled again with wine.

"A false bottom," she marveled, blinking at it.

"Drink."

She obeyed.

He reached inside his coat then, and Grace waited patiently, expecting anything. But instead of a dove or a rabbit or a colorful scarf, he withdrew the tiger sculpture she'd just swapped him for ten thousand dollars half an hour ago. For the first time she noticed how small it was, and how lovely, how incredibly *kind* the tiger's face. "Ohhh," she sighed, a sad, wistful lament. The thought of trading back crossed her mind, then drifted away. Wing drew her away from the table and toward a glass shelf attached to the wall. "The others," he said simply, and she saw them—the dragon, the horse, the monkey, the snake. Ox, pig, goat, and dog. Rat, rabbit, tiger. "I shall take them all with me now. All." With careful hands, he set the tiger in its place among the others, and stepped back. He took a deep breath and emptied his lungs in a long sigh—a sound of completion.

Grace envied him for it, because she was feeling strangely incomplete. Unsatisfied. Not hungry or thirsty, but...wanting. She thought of Reuben, and then the thought drifted away.

"We must go now."

"Yes," she agreed. He had to help her, though, because her legs weren't working right; she was gliding rather than walking, and in her mind she had an image of the Godfather pulling her by a string like a child pulling a wagon. The image disintegrated when they got to the cellar steps; then it was more like a man pushing a rock up a hill. "What's going on?" she asked curiously, arms limp at her sides, letting him press against her backbone while she lifted her leaden feet up each separate step. "What's happening?"

He didn't answer, just levered her gently up step after step till they reached the top. They started down the hall toward the front door; but when they arrived at it, Wing turned left, toward another staircase.

"Wait, wait," mumbled Grace, twisting around so slowly, pointing toward the door. Wing circled her waist with his arm and started climbing, ignoring her low, repetitious, "Uh-oh's." On the landing, she planted her feet. "Reuben won't like this," she said distinctly.

"We won't speak of him again," Wing reproved her gravely.

"We won't?"

"No."

Her will was coming and going in waves, making her feel strong and purposeful one minute, weak as water the next. During one of the weak periods, Wing led her around the corner to another staircase, this one narrow and candlelit, with huge shadows dancing on the walls. Panic crept through her skin past blood and bones to her vitals. It was a peculiar, disengaged kind of panic, though, as if some woman she barely knew were being coerced up unknown steps by an insane man. The fear came and went in the same waves as her will, now a spiking arc of anxiety, now a trough of weird tranquility.

Wing was supporting her with both arms, and yet her body felt curiously agile, more flexible than usual, as if normally one-way joints like elbows and knees could twist and turn in any direction she liked. If not for the fear, and the vague, disturbing, unspecific longing for something she couldn't name, she might have called this surpassingly peculiar state of mind and body pleasurable, or at least interesting.

But the fear kept rising and falling, surging and ebbing, spoiling the peaceful periods when her strongest emotion was curiosity.

She was flowing down the shadow-strewn corridor like slow water through a tunnel, now stopping at a doorway, now moving into a room. She heard herself say "No" through numbed lips, then forgot what had frightened her. How *beautiful*—a bed as big as a river, high and wide, covered in gorgeous silk swirls like beaten eggs, yellow white orange red, pillows like plump suns and fat starbursts, gold silver bright brilliant soft, soft, and Wing whispering "Augustine," with his slow hands on her skin. Back, back, falling. Cool silk watery soft, airy whispered words against her cheek. Behind his black shoulder a girl, servant. Familiar. He spoke—she disappeared.

"Scared," Grace tried to say. "Skth" came out of her mouth. She gave up. White hair, a dove's wing brushing her throat, soothing. *"Augustine,"* in her ear, a hot heated whisper. *Call me Gus, Reuben does.* "Reuben" fell out of her mouth like marbles, like coins. *Oh, God, Reuben!*

"Lie still, my opal. Wait for the blisss, for it will come. Ahhh." Pale face looming, hair draping, teeth gleaming. "Dost thou know how often I've dreamt of thee? The golden-haired woman. I knew who you were the moment I saw you. The vision—my wife, beside me, enthroned, while at our feet our strong sons play like lion cubs."

Grace lifted a long, stern forefinger in the air to point something out. What was it, though? Oh. "Barking up the wrong tree," garbled around the limp thickness of her tongue.

Wing smiled: a wonderful joke. Kai Yee, God-father; Ah Mah, Mother. Thin lips pursed, puckered, sucked her pointing finger inside the black wet cave of his mouth. Revulsion, snakes twisting in her belly—and then a shocking liquid change. *Touch,* she thought. Said? *Touch me.* Evil knowing eyes sparkled, flicked down, aware. The suave fumble of fingers at her breast...cloth tearing so slowly... warm air on warm, shamed skin. His hands. *Touch—don't touch.* Oh, God, his hands...

The woman again, girl servant. With a pipe, a candle, metal wire. Flame crackle, burning poppy smoke—"No! Bastard, bastard—" No use. Fire in her throat, chest burning, eyes streaming—and some of the poison sneaked in, she could feel it slink, slither, curl like a worm in her skull.

The Godfather, filled with the poison, rose over her, white moon face glimmering. "Wait for me, golden one, my dahlia. I will go and prepare myself for thee. Wait for thy hus-band. Patience"—the hiss of a snake. She shuddered. But his lips opened hers, and she took the long slide of his tongue like a lover.

Stillness. Behind her closed eyelids, fires flick-ered. Her blood had become lighter than air. She dreamed that she was rising above the bed, floating through the ceiling, up through the blue air of the sky, higher and higher until every-thing in the universe spread out beneath her like a rug. With exquisite indifference, she understood it all, every detail. Everything was clear; everything was revealed. A huge philosophical work took shape in her mind, long, unfolding links of thought, a great synthesis of all knowledge that would explain everything in existence. She couldn't wait to tell everybody.

But...something was happening...something in the room with the bed... Oh, yes—Wing was coming back. Because he was her husband, and he was preparing.

She opened her eyes and lifted her head. Nobody there. *I'm safe.* Safe on the riverbed of scarlet silk, crimson silk, arms tight in the sleeves of her dress, bare-shouldered, bare-breasted—

A wash of horror suddenly prickled her skin everywhere, drenching her. She threw her body up and out of the river, and landed hard on the bank, scrabbled to her feet, lurched to the door. Locked. Walls, curtains, scrolls, hangings, drapes. "Well, goddamn it!" It rang in her throat like a bell, wonderfully clear and outraged. *Where the hell is the goddamn window?*

There, past waterfalls of dangerous silk, sly as a strangler's hands. Her fingers clutched wood; her muscles hardened, and the sash flew up, up. She staggered and caught herself on the sill, smacking her ribs. Light from the room gleamed on a metal grid outside—fire escape! "Oh, help me!" Sobbing, diving, hands grappling wood, knees flexed—

"No, my lady. No, my lady." Gentle arms pulled softly, insistent.

Grace screamed. But it wasn't Kai Yee, it was the girl, the servant.

"Help me?"

"Yes."

"*Help me.*"

"Yes, my lady. Come."

Docile, hopeless, she let the girl lead her away from the window toward the bed. Bridal bed. *Damn.* Slow tears trickled down when the girl, whose hands were gentle as birds, unfastened Grace's torn dress and eased it down to the floor. Shift next, petticoats, then shoes, stockings. *Reuben, where are you?*

"Lie," said the girl, and Grace lay.

"Help me." One last pathetic try. Cold silk on her spine warmed insidiously.

"Here is help," said the girl. "I tell you: don't fight. Understand? Best help—give up."

11

Death: to stop sinning suddenly.
                              —Elbert Hubbard

"You okay, boss? Okay now?"

"Ow, quit it. Get your—ow!"

"So sorry, boss! Okay now? You want drink? Want girl? All on house! Boss feel better now, okay?"

Snarling, cradling his head with both hands, Reuben hoisted himself to a sitting position on a squishy velvet sofa that smelled like dirty clothes and rancid perfume. Two men hovered over him, chattering to each other in worried-sounding Chinese, while a middle-aged woman in a voluminous black gown tried to press a wet, vinegary-smelling cloth to his temple. He batted her hand away and glared at all three, unappeased by the anxiety in their faces. "What happened? Who the...uhhh." He gritted his teeth against the stunning pain. "Who the hell hit me?"

Nobody raised his hand, but the taller of the worried-looking men said, "So sorry, boss, big mistake," and hung his head.

The woman rose from beside the couch and made him a low, abject bow. "Plees accept apologies for terrible error. You white gentleman, very fine sir. Sometime bad men sneak in house in back, take favors from girls, not pay. We keep watch. Dark tonight, make big mistake. You okay now—no police. Feel like glass plum wine, any girl you want? Got special very young virgin, father big prince in China. You like?"

The cotton stuffing inside his brain thinned to let a little light in, enough to get him on his feet and ask weakly, "What time is it?"

"Plenty time, early, have good—"

"*What time is it?*" He clutched at his head, fighting the return of the stuffing, swaying.

"Ten-thirty."

"Ten..." He took his hands away and stared in horror. They grabbed at him when he tried to bull his way through their solicitous semicircle to the door. "Move! Move, damn it!" They fell back, and he charged outside.

He had to halt in the grainy mist and reckon where he was. He'd come out the front door of the House of Celestial Peace and Fulfillment—so the murky yellow light forty feet to his right had to be the entrance to Wing's house. Racing toward it, he tripped and slammed his knee on the wet sidewalk. He cursed foully, but the shock helped clear his head.

The dragon knocker set up a hell of a racket. He hammered it harder, louder, wishing it was a weapon. The heavy portal finally cracked open, and In Re stuck his head out.

"Yes?"

"Grace was here—Miss Smith, she was here visiting Wing. Did she leave yet?"

"Nobody here by that name."

"You mean she left?"

"No Smith come, no lady." He started to close the door.

"Hold it! She was here—the same woman who came with me yesterday. I saw you let her in, she— Hey!" In Re got the door an inch away from the latch before Reuben could get his foot in the threshold and stop it. "Listen, you son of a bitch! Open the door, open it or I'll—"

"Yes?" With the speed and ease of a farmer scything grass, In Re brought up a nine-inch scimitar, and made a frame for Reuben's throat in its gleaming crescent.

Reuben lifted both hands in the air, palms out: an outclassed dog rolling over, telling the big one he gave up. Very gently, In Re closed the door in his face.

He made it to the sidewalk before he had to stop and grab for his knees, head dangling between his legs. From experience, he knew that if he thought about the knife, saw in his mind the silvery edge, sharp as a hair, or imagined the curved blade slicing across flesh—a fingertip, a cheek—oh, God, a *tongue*—he would either faint, vomit, or start screaming.

He took his hands off his knees in slow degrees, straightened, and gulped in a great chestful of the cool night air. With the next gulp, he shouted, "Grace!" at the top of his lungs.

Silence.

Hands cupped around his mouth: *"Grace!"*

No answer.

She wouldn't have gone home by herself, she'd have waited for him. So she was still in the house. Wing had her.

They were surprised to see him again so soon at the House of Celestial Peace and Fulfillment. "Esteemed sir," exclaimed the black-gowned madam, grinning falsely and wringing her hands, glancing behind him to see if he'd brought any cops. "You feel okay now? Sorry, sorry, many—"

"I need a girl," he panted, "any girl. That one—I want her." A small, homely thing, trying to hide behind the red sofa he'd been stretched out unconscious on ten minutes ago.

"You like Toy Gun?" simpered the madam.

"Sure, she's for you. On the house. You want whiskey, we send up—"

"Yeah, later." He advanced on Toy Gun, who was trying not to cringe, and looking as if a large, wild-eyed white devil was not her idea of a good time. She was too docile to fight him when he grabbed her hand, though, and she let him hustle her out of the parlor and up the gaslit staircase to the second floor without a chirp. Behind them, the madam and the two bouncers who'd carried him inside the house called up jovial encouragement and best wishes for his health and happiness.

Toy Gun tried to stop at a closed door midway down the hall that ran the length of the brothel, front to back. "My room," she got out, pointing, but Reuben kept going, pulling her along behind him. As he'd hoped, there was another staircase at the back of the house, servants' stairs, since they were darker and narrower than the ones in front. The girl started protesting in Chinese when he jostled her in front of him and trotted her up the steps. "Third floor," he muttered behind her, "I want the third floor, gotta have it. Hurry, hurry."

Another dim hallway, lined with closed doors, behind one of which he heard a man's loud, drunken laughter. To the right of the landing, a short, dark corridor ended at a black door with a window in the top half, covered with a bead curtain. Toy Gun balked when he drew her away from the landing and into the alcove. "Nah! Nah!" she wailed, trying to tell him he was going the wrong way. Ignoring her, he turned the doorknob. Locked. Toy Gun went white and stopped wailing when he reached in his pocket and pulled out Grace's little two-shooter. Using the barrel, he bashed a hole in the window, flinching at the noise the glass made when it shattered. Through the jagged hole, his hand found the key in the lock and twisted it. "Come on," he told his shrinking captive, and towed her through the door.

He got her about three steps down the new hall before she skidded to a stop and dug her heels in, refusing to be moved. "Nah, nah, nah!" she started up again, in a high-pitched whine.

Reuben hunkered down to bring his face to her level. "Kai Yee," he whispered menacingly. The two words reduced her to shuddering, terrified silence. "Where is he? Take me to him. Take me to Kai Yee." She rolled her eyes and shook her head, and kept shaking it until, in desperation, he brought the derringer back out and waved it at her. The poor girl's teeth were chattering; her hand trembled like a palsied old woman's, but she got it up and out, and pointed vaguely down the carpeted hall and to the right. "Where? Show me," he demanded. But she was just too scared. Giving her a frustrated pat on the shoulder, he left her standing there, frozen to the spot and—he hoped—too frightened to scream. At least for a minute or two.

Unlike the hallway in the whorehouse next door, all the doors here were open, and they were all dark. He hoped that meant they were all empty. Toy Gun had pointed to the right. Thirty feet away he could see a staircase; just beyond it, light spilled out of a doorway onto the thick Persian carpet. Crouching, booted footsteps muffled by the rug, Reuben moved toward the light.

Voices from the second floor drifted up the stairs on the odor of incense. He didn't pause, didn't even glance down as he passed. Flattening his back against the wall, he listened intently, but could hear no sound coming from the lighted room. He checked the pint-size derringer in his palm, and hoped he wouldn't shoot a finger off if he had to use it. One deep breath. Using his right foot for a pivot, he spun into the doorway.

A woman screamed. Not Grace—Grace was spread out buck naked on a huge canopied bed, propped up on her elbows and smiling at him. The other one—the one who'd shuffled in and out with tea yesterday—she was the screamer. She shut her mouth when she saw the gun, and when Reuben moved toward her, she moved back.

"Hi," said Grace.

"Gus, damn it, get up and get your clothes on!"

"Okay." She slid her legs over the side of the bed, but when she tried to stand up, her knees buckled and she sank very slowly, very gracefully, to the floor. "Uh-oh," she said worriedly, blinking down at her lap, her bent knees, her splayed fingers on the rug, as if she couldn't figure out how she'd gotten there.

Jesus Christ God Almighty. She was drunk.

When he moved toward her, swearing viciously, the little maid ran behind him and bolted out the door. He let her go, concentrating on Grace. "Where'd you put your clothes?" he said roughly, pocketing the gun and kneeling beside her. Her head lolled back, a heavy flower on a too-thin stalk, and banged the bed frame. She didn't even notice. He took her by the shoulders and gave her a shake. "Come on, Gus, where's your dress? What'd you do with your shoes?" There wasn't a stitch of clothing in the orange, opulent, overdone room that he could see, except for a yellow dressing gown that the servant girl had dropped on the floor before she ran.

He got his hands under Grace's arms and hauled her up so that her behind was perched on the edge of the bed. When he let go she lunged for him, winding her arms around his neck. "Oh, Reuben," she sighed, trying to kiss him. "I'm so glad you came." He dodged her mouth, and she settled for his cheek, planting a noisy smacker on him while she pushed her breasts against his chest.

"That's good, honey." He dragged her arms away and looked her in the eye. "Stay right here and don't move, Grace. Don't move a muscle. Got it?"

"Got it." She sent him a lopsided grin and tried to salute—and smacked herself in the forehead.

"Unbelievable," he muttered, propping her up again, then turning away to scoop up the yellow kimono. He had it in his fingers when he heard the first shout, a high, blood-curdling war whoop that made his hair stand on end. He froze for a second, staring at the open doorway. Footsteps pounding up the stairs jolted him into motion. He vaulted to the door, slammed it, fumbled for the key, and got it turned in the lock. Two seconds later, somebody's shoulder slammed against the other side, jarring the door, the wall, the whole damn room.

Grace was on her feet, swaying, her pretty yellow-corkscrew hair standing out like crooked sun rays. "Fire escape," she said clearly, and pointed to a closed curtain on the wall behind her.

He wasted precious seconds getting her uncoordinated arms into the sleeves of the silk dressing gown. A mighty crash made them both jump, then gasp when they saw an ax blade smash out a large chunk of the door. Reuben wrestled the curtain aside and wrenched the high window open. "Come on, come on," he urged, supporting Grace around the waist, trying to get her to straighten her legs so he could shoot her out the window feet-first. Blows to the door were coming fast and steady, but he didn't look back to check the hatchet's progress. Grace said "Oof" when he ducked and caught her in the stomach with his shoulder, hoisting her off her feet. Somehow he got her and himself out the window and onto the landing of the wet, slippery, swaying, rickety fire escape.

The ladder to the second floor dropped straight down—no angle, no safety railing. "Hold on to my belt," he ordered, and Grace started fumbling at his crotch. "Higher, Gus. *Belt.*" She finally found it under his coat, and wrapped her hands around it tightly. He had to keep his left arm braced across the backs of her thighs or she'd slide off, which left him with only one hand to grab the ladder. "Don't let go," he advised. "Ready?" She mumbled something nasal and upside-down-sounding, and Reuben stepped out into thin air.

The trick was holding onto the ladder without banging Grace's dangling butt against every rung. He succeeded most of the time, and when he didn't, she informed him of it by yelping. By the time they reached the second-floor landing, his right arm was shaking from the strain of holding their combined weight upright. He'd have set her on her feet if he'd thought she could climb down the last half-length of ladder on her own power; but she was hanging over his shoulder with all the tension and muscularity of a bag of wet cement, and he knew there wasn't a chance. Ignoring the increasingly alarming noises coming from above, he hefted her higher on his shoulder and began the second descent.

With both boots on the last rung, he was still ten feet above the ground. The hard ground. Various strategies for reaching the pavement without dying flitted through his mind. They narrowed to a single basic one when the metal rungs under his hands and feet vibrated violently, and outraged shouts rang out directly overhead. A gun fired. He flexed his knees, bending to grab the third-to-last rung. "Hold on," he warned, and let his feet slide out from under him. For two seconds they hung above the misty alley—all the time Reuben needed to realize how unthinkable it would be to actually drop—*drop*—to the lethal cement below. Another shot sounded. His right arm was burning out of the socket. He let go.

When his feet hit, he fell forward so Grace wouldn't land on her face, with the result that he landed on his. His arms cushioned her fall, but she still got a pretty good whack on the bum. He rolled off her and scrambled to his knees, fumbling the derringer out of his pocket. Aiming straight up, he fired once. The gun made more of a pop than a bang, but there was a satisfying screech from overhead, followed by panicky scrambling noises.

In the seconds-long interlude of safety, he got Grace up on her feet and one of her arms around his shoulders. "I can walk," she assured him in a breathless pant. He gave her a test, moving east toward Kearny Street, and found out that what she could do was shuffle. A bullet smacked into the brick wall beside them, striking sparks. Reuben fired back with his last shot, then threw the gun away. Snatching Grace up in his arms, he ran.

The fog was their best friend; before they got halfway to the corner, the fire escape was invisible. He turned left at the corner and kept close to the walls of the featureless shops and houses, pausing every few seconds to listen for sounds of pursuit. It was impossible to tell whether the dark breaks between buildings were streets or alleys or dead-end crannies in the ceaseless, convoluted labyrinth of Chinatown. After a few minutes he wasn't even sure they were still on Kearny Street, and they might've been heading east instead of north for all he knew—or west, or south. In the rank crevice of some foul-smelling edifice, he stopped to rest, setting Grace on her feet and pulling her back from the street. She said, "Reuben, I'm—"

He heard a noise and covered her mouth with his hand, pressing harder when she started to sputter. *"Shh,"* he commanded, maneuvering in front of her to block her canary-yellow robe from the street. He didn't turn to look, but he heard someone pass behind his back, swift and secretive on soft-soled shoes.

Grace shivered, and he felt like shuddering in sympathy, unnerved by the eerie stealthiness of their silent follower. Neither of them moved for a full minute. He noticed that her body in his arms felt firmer, more elastic, less like a sack of jelly. She must be sobering up. He whispered in her ear, "Think you can walk now, Gus?" and she nodded. They separated, and clasped hands. There was nothing to hear on the foggy street, but he knew better than to trust the silence. "Let's go," he said, and led her back out into the night.

Home was north and east of Chinatown, but that was no help since they could easily be moving in circles. The fog horns bleating from the Bay were the only guide, and they were deceptive, echoing and re-echoing off the cobbled streets, sounding from everywhere and nowhere. It was impossible to read a street sign in the fog unless it happened to be directly under a street lamp, and standing under street lamps was a dangerous enterprise tonight. Occasionally a walker passed by on a narrow sidewalk, or startled them at the mouth of some sinuous alley; they would freeze, and brace for the worst—and the mist-swaddled figure would walk on, harmless. But Wing's men must be everywhere by now, and their luck couldn't hold much longer.

It ran out in a short, stinking, inky-black alley they stumbled into by accident. Reuben was carrying Grace again because of the broken glass littering the dirty pavement. With no warning, fast footsteps sounded dead ahead, coming straight toward them, so quickly that all he had time to do was drop her on her feet and fall into a boxer's crouch. The figure of a man loomed out of the dark mist and halted in front of him. His eager, youthful face looked familiar. The new recruit—the one who'd crawled under Wing's chair to be reborn.

Whatever revolting, sharp-edged weapon he favored was still in his pocket or tucked in his belt—so it was now or never. A peaceable man, Reuben knew only one sucker punch. He uttered an aggressive shout and came at his opponent fast, arms stretched out wide, making himself look so undefended that the only evasive action the recruit took was to grab him around the torso and squeeze. But he wasn't as dumb as he looked—he kept his thighs locked and his hips cocked back, so it was impossible to jerk a knee up into his groin. Reuben had already huffed all his breath out to simulate defeat; now he wished he'd saved some for his second, and last, trick. His arms were still unpinned. Bringing his hands up and out, he clapped them as hard as he could on either side of the recruit's head—flathanded, so as not to break his eardrums.

"Eeeyow!"

It worked. The hatchet man dropped to his knees and doubled up in pain, clutching his ringing ears.

Reuben lacked the stomach to disable him further, although he'd seen plenty of bar fights in which the fun was just beginning at this point. "Grace?" he called softly, and she limped toward him out of the darkness. She looked stunned, as if he'd poleaxed her instead of the bad guy. "Let's get out of here," he suggested. She reached for him. He picked her up and started running.

The fog wasn't their friend anymore. It concealed the way out, and it concealed the enemy. Finally a street sign in English gave him hope. He recognized the name; it was a scabby, sordid, sin-ridden defile on the western edge of the Barbary Coast—the eastern edge of Chinatown. As vice and violence went, this neighborhood was even worse than Chinatown, but at least the whores here were white, so a barefooted blonde in a yellow bathrobe wouldn't stand out quite as much. He hoped.

Grace was flagging, though. She hadn't spoken for ages, despite his constant, soft-voiced encouragement. They were resting in the dark beside a squat, sweating building, on the edge of a weak splash of light coming from a half-window in the building's front door. The painted sign over it was too vague to read from here. He left Grace by the wall, stepped into the light long enough to read the sign, and dove back into the shadows.

"We're in luck," he exulted. "It's a hotel— the Bunyon Arms, no less. A flophouse, from the looks of it; they probably rent all the rooms by the hour. What do you think, Gus? Should we go in? We could—"

"Yes," she said instantly, a reflexive gulp of an answer that worried him.

"Okay." He touched her cheek, which was cold and wet. "How do you feel? Are you sick?"

Her eyes were black, all pupil, and as big as saucers. She shook her head, nodded, and shook her head again.

"Well, that's clear." He smiled, giving her a quick kiss to buck her up. It just made her groan, though, and his concern increased.

Checking again to make sure no one was nearby, he guided her toward the entrance. "Don't say anything," he warned in a whisper. "Just stand there, honey, and let me do the talking."

But registering at the Bunyon Arms wasn't the least bit tricky. The white-haired desk clerk was half asleep; Grace in a silk kimono and nothing else didn't so much as raise one of his eyebrows. "Two bits." He yawned, reaching behind him for a key from a board covered with hooks.

"We want the cleanest room in the house. Clean sheets, and a bathroom that connects."

His hand veered away to a different key. "Four bits, and there ain't no connecting bath. Have to go down the hall."

Reuben grunted. "We need a bottle, too."

"I ain't no liquor salesman."

Reuben laid a dollar on top of the desk.

The clerk reached under the counter and pulled out a bottle of whiskey. "Folks have a nice night." By the time they got to the stairs, he was snoring again in his chair.

12

True passion is a consuming flame, and either
it must find fruition or it will burn the
human heart to dust and ashes.
　　　　　　　　　　—William Winter

The bathroom was in the middle of the
hall on the way to their second-floor
room. Reuben stood guard at the door while
Grace made a lot of splashing sounds inside.
They went on for so long he finally tapped at
the door and called, "Say, Gus, you didn't go
for a swim, did you?"

Abruptly the door opened. "Sorry," she
said in a strained voice, not smiling.

"That's okay." She looked scrubbed and
fresh, and the floor in front of the enameled
iron lavatory was wet; he guessed she'd been
taking a stand-up bath. He took her hand to
lead her down the hall to No. 8, wondering at
her mood. She looked tense and brittle, as if
she was holding something dangerous in
check. As soon as they were inside the room,
she left him and went straight to the window.

There was a scorched oil lamp and a box of
matches on a bureau in the far corner. He set
the whiskey bottle down and lit the lamp,
then surveyed the room in its dim, flickering
light. "Lovely," he pronounced, for the sake
of something to say. It was small and ugly, with

a low ceiling and no rug on the unswept floor. The only furniture besides the bureau were a washstand and a bed. The mottled walls might've been blue once, but now they were the color of the fog outside, only dirtier. The door had a foot-shaped chunk of wood missing below the knob, and somebody had filled in the hole with plaster. The lock worked, though. And the sheets covering the thick, lumpy mattress on the iron bedstead looked clean, at least from here. All in all, he thought, things could be worse.

Grace still had her back to him. She was holding the broken paper shade away from the window so she could stare out at the shifting mist. The fog had turned her curly hair into an enormous halo. He stared at her thin, fragile shoulders and her pretty back. She'd belted the yellow robe tight around her waist, which emphasized the sexy, womanly flare of her hips. Her blue-veined white feet under the hem looked cold, and unbelievably naked. He remembered how she'd looked tonight, languid and nude in Wing's bed, and wondered how much longer he was supposed to go on like this.

"Can you see anything?" he asked.

"Fog."

"We'll stay here for a couple of hours, then find a way to get home. Wing's men can't stay out all night looking for us." He hoped.

She didn't move or speak; he wondered if she'd even heard him. After a while she dropped the shade and hugged herself, rubbing her arms hard under the wide kimono sleeves.

He said, "Grace?" She didn't turn. "What was it all about?" She didn't answer. He went closer. A shadow crossed his mind—an awful thought. "Did he hurt you? Grace, did he touch you?" Despite what he'd seen, for some crazy reason he'd made an assumption that nothing had happened yet between her and Wing. Now he feared the worst.

She still wouldn't talk. He reached out for her. "Honey, did he—"

She spun around at his touch. The look on her face startled him. "Reuben," she said indistinctly, and began to rub his arms the way she'd been rubbing hers.

"Are you okay? How do you feel?"

"I'm on fire," she whispered. She threw her head back and moaned—a long, tortured sound that shocked him. He took her in his arms and started to say something comforting. She pushed against him with her whole body, her hands clutching at his coat. "I'm on fire," she repeated, desperate, mashing her pelvis against his thigh.

He blinked at himself in the watery mirror over the washstand. "Well, now."

"Touch me," she pleaded. "No, don't. Oh, God." She buried her face in his shirt. "He gave me something."

"He—what?"

"You like me, don't you? You always— nnnh." She gritted her teeth and ground her forehead against his breastbone. "Reuben,

I'm burning up. If you don't touch me, I'm going to burst out of my skin."

He patted her on the back, trying to get it. "You're saying…"

She growled low in her throat and pulled back to look at him. "Help me," she commanded. "If you laugh at me, Reuben, I'll—I'll—" Her blue eyes welled with tears.

In wonder, he brushed her left breast with his fingertips, and she gasped. Pressing against him again, she got his thigh between hers. He couldn't believe what was happening. She pushed into him four times, hard, and then she climaxed, a rough, pained, desperate-sounding orgasm that left her panting in his arms, limp-limbed and sweating.

He laughed—he couldn't help it, it was his first stunned, uncontrollable reaction. When she went rigid, he remembered that that was the one thing he wasn't supposed to do. "Not *at* you, Gus," he muttered into her hair, "just—the situation, I couldn't help—"

"Shut up."

"Okay."

They stood still for a few minutes, breathing quietly, while Reuben studied the reflection in the mirror of himself stroking Grace's back, and the coming and going of numerous indescribable expressions on his face. Presently he felt a long tremor shudder through her. "Are you okay now?" he ventured.

"No."

"Are you cold?"

She simulated a laugh.

255

"No? You're not cold?" She was shivering all over. She still had his knee between hers, and she was starting to do that thing again with her thighs, squeezing his between them in a slow, steady rhythm that got him hard again fast. "Uh, Grace, maybe this isn't such a good—"

"It's happening again."

"What?" He still didn't get it.

"Reuben, they made me drink something!"

"You mean, it's still..." She nodded. In the mirror, he watched his hands move down to her buttocks and pull her up tight against him.

She bucked once and cried out, and slowly collapsed in his arms.

He was sweating now. "Let's lie down," he suggested weakly. She turned without a word and climbed onto the bed, struggling with the top sheet. Her robe drifted around her body, loose and open. She might as well have been naked, so he helped her take it off; but even after all that had happened, it still felt like a presumption. Not that she was in any state to take offense. That was the problem. In the spirit of evening the score, so to speak, he said, "Grace, should I, um—"

"Yes."

"Right." He sat up and took off his clothes.

Before getting back in bed, he crossed to the bureau and lowered the wick on the oil lamp, a gesture toward discretion that struck him, under the circumstances, as pretty funny. He crawled under the sheet Grace had modestly pulled up to her chin. She had one arm over her forehead, in distress or embarrassment or both. He took it away to see her eyes. They looked haunted, the pupils still dilated. "It's all right," he told her, "you're safe now, and you can have anything you want." He brushed curls back from her forehead. "Do you feel like talking?"

She hid her face again in the crook of her elbow. Drawing in a deep breath through chattering teeth, she whispered, "Please... please...would you please..." She couldn't get the verb out. He didn't want to make a mistake, so he put a very light, very tentative hand over her right breast. The nipple rose to greet him immediately, a hot, hard little pebble he wanted to spend more time with. But Grace wasn't interested in preliminaries. Capturing his hand, she dragged it down her stomach to the hot center of herself. He'd barely brushed her, hardly felt the soft wet heat, before she was gritting out another tortured groan, thighs locked around his wrist, jerking arhythmically against it.

"There now," he said in a ridiculous quaver when it was over. Gently disengaging his hand, he dried it surreptitiously on the sheet. "Better?"

She turned her head away and nodded with her eyes closed. She was trembling a little, biting her lips, pink-faced with need and confusion.

"What did he give you?" he asked, stroking neutral territory—her arm from shoulder to elbow, up and down.

"Don't know. Something red. Plum wine, he said."

"Spanish fly," he muttered to himself.

But she heard. "Probably. I should've known. Oh, Reuben," she wailed, "he took the tiger and kept the money, and it's all my fault!"

"Never mind," he said gallantly. "The important thing is that you're okay."

She didn't look consoled. "That's not all," she said after a minute, and turned her face back to the wall.

"Tell me." What else could there be?

"Opium," she whispered. "He made me smoke from a pipe. I couldn't help it, he made me."

He lay without moving, trying to believe it, then trying not to believe it. *Goddamn son of a bitch.* "I'll kill him," he said wonderingly. "By God, I'll kill him." She covered her whole face with her hands, and he realized she was scared. "Don't worry," he said as calmly as he could. "You'll be fine in a little while, just like it never happened."

"When?" she croaked.

"I don't know, an hour or so. You're not going to become a dope fiend, sweetheart, not from a couple of puffs."

"How do you know? What if I end up like one of those people in the den? What if it takes over my mind, what if—"

"It won't, that's not how it works."

"How do you know?"

"Because I know." She shuddered, still not

looking at him. He put his arms around her, and asked his next question without looking at her. "Did he touch you, Grace?"

"No. I mean, yes."

He sighed. "Which?"

"He did. And I let him. I didn't care, not *enough*. I said to myself, 'Uh-oh,' but I didn't try to make him stop. And then he went away to prepare himself, he said, and the woman came and took my clothes off, and—oh, God, I *wanted* her to—sort of, because I knew what it meant, I knew he was coming back and he could take this terrible—*feeling* away—but I knew it was wrong, too, but I—"

He stopped her by holding her face between his palms. "Let it go, Gus. You weren't responsible, you couldn't help yourself."

"I know that, I know it, but—"

"No buts. It wasn't your fault."

A little of the anxiety went out of her eyes. She turned her head, and captured two of his fingers in her mouth. He went absolutely still. But when she made a slippery sucking sound, he couldn't help himself—he draped his naked leg over her thighs. She didn't protest. Protest? She twisted around so that their bodies were flush against each other, private part to private part. Now he was the one who was groaning.

The drug had loosened her tongue along with her inhibitions. "Reuben, you can't bel...believe how that feels," she said hoarsely.

Unlike her, his voice sounded *higher* than usual. "Oh, I wouldn't say that." She blew all her breath out against his chest in what he took for a laugh.

Laughter: that was the ticket. He croaked out a chuckle. She followed with a harsh *ha ha* that made her breasts wobble against his hot skin. "Mmm," she said next, scouring her nipples against his chest in little back-and-forth motions. He set his teeth and pressed his lips to her hairline. "I grew up in a room like this," he gritted, scanning the water stains on the wall and the cracks on the ceiling. She didn't seem to hear. "Yeah, it looked a lot like this. Something like this. I was nine, eight, seven, I can't recall. Very hot in the summer. The mattress smelled like old logs."

She stopped moving. Good: he could stop talking. She made an effort to open her eyes and focus on his face. "Sw...Sweetbriar looked like this?"

"No," he said immediately. "No, Sweetbriar, of course, looked— Are you kidding? How could Sweetbriar look like this?"

He stared her down, his irate innocence no match for her at the moment. She blinked, acknowledging her error, and laid her cheek back down on his collarbone. "Mph," she said.

They shared a few minutes of blessed rest. Reuben's blood stopped pounding and his body softened to more normal contours. As soon as he felt like himself again, she let out a low, worried, rising wail, pushed him down flat on his back, and straddled him.

"Hi!" came out of his mouth before he could call it back.

"Hi." Her inflection was entirely different. He started humming when she lifted her pretty breasts, one in each hand, and offered them to him. Her knees cut in on either side of his waist, and her warm, slick sex massaged his pelvic bone until he smacked his hands on her hips and forced her to stop.

"Hold it."

"What?"

"Listen to me. I'm a strong man, I'm a regular shtarker. Women like me, always have, because I'm pretty good at this. But—"

"What?"

"But you're driving me absolutely crazy."

"Come inside me, Reuben." She hadn't been listening.

"Grace."

"Mmm?" She slid back a little way on his thighs, and he jumped when her hand closed around him. She stroked him with more enthusiasm than expertise, softly at first, then more purposefully, up and down, and on every third or fourth pass she gave his testicles a friendly little squeeze. "Guess what," she said with her eyes closed.

He got out a sound, vaguely interrogatory, while grinding his teeth.

"While I was lying there, waiting for Wing? I kept thinking I wished it was you who was coming to me. I kept thinking of you. I wanted it to be you. Oh, hurry, Reuben, let's do it."

"What about Henri?" he managed to ask.

"Who?"

He scowled at her. "Your husband."

"Oh—Henry. He's not my husband, we just live together."

While he was thinking that over, she scooted up on her knees and got the head of his penis in position to enter her. A quick jerk of her hips, and he was in. But only an inch.

"Come—*in*—Reuben," she gasped, "right now, right now, right now." She kept shuffling closer, higher.

"You're going to hate me in the morning," he tried, hanging onto her knees.

She threw her head back and said to the ceiling, "Better then than now."

She was a furnace, a long, cylindrical fireplace, a blast oven. And he was burning up, trying with all his might to hold still so he wouldn't explode. He felt her tighten and squeeze on him, and they yelled out something in concert. But by some perverse miracle, he didn't come when she did: he focused on a housefly on the sheet beside her humping thigh, and got through it by concentrating on its long, sucking proboscis.

She collapsed on top of him, whimpering. "My God, Reuben, how can you stand it? No—oh, please don't move," she begged when he shifted. He was still hard, still tilted up inside her like a tent pole. "Don't—if you could just—how long can you stay like that?"

"All night," he said confidently. *About thirty more seconds. Forty if you don't move.*

She had her arms around his head on the pillow, her face turned to his; when she spoke, her breath tickled his ear. "When do you think it's going to stop?"

His heart sank. "You mean it hasn't stopped yet?"

"For now," she said ominously. "I think it's coming back."

He shut his eyes tight, and clenched his teeth to keep from groaning. "Well, it can't last forever, it's bound to wear off soon."

"When?"

"Soon." He patted her weakly, and reached down for the sheet to cover her. The sweat on her skin was drying as she cooled off.

She was quiet for a while, then surprised him by asking suddenly, "What's a *shtarker*?"

"A shtarker? A tough guy. A hero."

"It sounds like German."

"German, right." Why not?

"How do you know German?" she asked on a yawn.

"I don't know German. That one word, I know. Learned it from an old girlfriend. Gretchen was her name. She used to—"

"Never mind."

He put his fingers in her hair, smiling. Good thing she didn't weigh much, he mused, because she'd wilted on top of him like a deflated balloon. "How'd you get this curly hair?" he asked, toying with the soft, springy ringlets.

"My mother, I guess."

"Was hers yellow, too?"

"Mm. I thought it was so pretty. She used to let me brush it for her." She yawned again, making the skin under his ear tingle. "She used a perfume that smelled like lilacs. I thought it was the sweetest smell in the world." Her voice began to slur. "She put it on whenever she was going out, or whenever one of her...gentleman friends was coming to visit. I still think of her whenever I smell lilacs. It always makes me sad."

Reuben lay motionless, not daring to breathe. If she'd fallen asleep, his faith in prayer, the Almighty, and the hereafter would be restored in one stroke. He ran a testing finger lightly along her backbone; her only response was a delicate little snort against his throat. *Thank You,* he prayed fervently.

Now the trick was to get her off his chest without waking her up. He wanted a big slug of whiskey in the worst way. She heaved a big, tremulous sigh, and he froze again until her body quivered and went still. Her hair didn't smell like lilacs; it smelled like the pine soap in his bathroom. A familiar scent, but exotic on her. He put his palms on her sides, barely grazing, just to touch her. She had incredible skin, softer than an infant's. And she didn't have any husband at all, much less two of them.

The slow, gentle in-and-out of her ribs assured him she was fast asleep. Just then the oil lamp across the room sputtered and went out. He closed his eyes in the sudden darkness, thinking how far away the bureau was, and the bottle. How chilly the floor would be on his bare feet. How nice and warm it was here in bed, even with a hundred and some pounds of Grace passed out on top of him. I'll move in a minute, he told himself, and fell asleep with his nose in her piney hair.

He woke up cold and alone. It wasn't morning—the room was still dark. Sitting up, he spied Grace in front of the window, holding the shade back to look outside. She threw a glance over her shoulder when he put his feet on the floor, but she didn't speak. Following her lead, he crossed to the bureau in silence, uncorked the whiskey, and took a small swig from the bottle—the maid service at the Bunyon Arms had forgotten to put out glasses. He studied Grace while the cheap liquor warmed in his belly, noticing that she was back to rubbing her arms again in the sleeves of her yellow dressing gown. He took another sip of whiskey and went to her.

"Have a little snort," he offered, holding out the bottle. "It'll do you good."

"No, thanks." She smiled briefly, eyes flicking nervously over his naked body, then went back to staring out the window. He set the bottle on the sill. When he put his hand on the nape of her neck, she bared her teeth and dropped her head back. "This isn't funny anymore," she said tightly.

He went behind her and began to massage her shoulders. "Well, it is, sort of. When it's all over, you'll look back and—"

"No, I won't. *You* will, but I won't."

He smiled to himself, thinking what a funny girl she was: she knew all about Spanish fly, but nothing, apparently, about touching herself. Must be the Catholic upbringing. He crossed his arms around her waist and she leaned back, warming him. Her body was beginning to feel as natural to him as his own. "Anything I can do for you?" he murmured neutrally, nuzzling her hair.

He waited patiently. A whole minute passed before she whispered, "Yes," in a voice so soft he could hardly hear it. "If you wouldn't mind."

Her robe felt like warm water on his skin. He tugged at the lapels, uncovering her breasts. "Ah, Gracie, you're so...pretty," he said inadequately, caressing her, softly squeezing.

"Reuben, you don't have to say—things."

He put his cheek next to hers. "Do you think I don't mean it?" Her pretty round breasts were so full his hands could barely cover them. He liked the way her nipples looked, sticking out between his fingers.

"I don't know," she sighed.

"I think you're the prettiest girl I ever saw." His hands trailed down to her stomach. "Look at this beautiful belly button." He tickled it gently, playing with the tiny whorls. "And look at this pretty hair." He made a comb of his fingers and separated the crisp curls with it. Grace made a sort of grinding noise and let her head fall back against his shoulder.

"Open your legs a little," he said huskily.

She sidled her feet a few inches apart, and he sleeked a finger down her soft, wet sex, opening the velvety wings. She reached out for the window rails and held tight to either side, moaning. He kept his touch gentle, even when she began to rub her cheek against the bristly whisker stubble on his jaw, deliberately abrading her skin. His name on her lips made him crazy; she said it over and over, until the syllables ran together and became meaningless. His own control was teetering, so he slipped his fingers inside her, thinking that would end it sooner for her.

But she surprised him by twisting in his arms to face him. "Take me to bed. Don't you want to? I want it to be us. Not just touching, but—you and me, Reuben." She wound her arms around his neck and stood on tiptoe to whisper in his ear. "Let's make love in bed."

It sounded good to him. He picked her up and carried her to the bed.

She wanted him facing her, both of them sitting up, their legs wrapped around each other. He came into her gently, watching a host of fascinating expressions flicker across her face. "Is it all right if we kiss?" she whispered. For some reason that made him laugh. She smiled back, and they drifted into a slow, tender mouth-caress that became, for him, as arousing as anything they'd done all night. He had her silky breasts in his hands, and she mumbled unexpectedly against his lips, "Do you *sand* your thumbs?"

"What?"

"Nothing—don't stop."

Without breaking the kiss, they started a deep, slow rocking. He didn't see how they could get any closer. He held her bottom in his palms and raised her while she hung onto his neck, gasping her pleasure into his mouth. He felt her stomach muscles harden—felt himself getting much too close to the verge. He dragged his mouth away and went still, desperate for a distraction.

"For God's sake, Reuben—"

"Honey—"

"I want you to!"

"No, but—"

"I think you could put out the fire—once and for all—"

He held her tight to make her stop. "Think, Grace," he pleaded. "You don't want us to make a baby. That's not what you want to do."

"Oh, my dear." She cupped his face in her hands, and the sudden sad tenderness in her eyes startled and confounded him. "My sweet Reuben. I promise you, we can't make a baby. It's not possible."

He was burning for her, but he made himself say doggedly, "You can't always go by what day of the month it is, sweetheart."

"I know that." She touched his lips lightly with hers, murmuring, "It won't happen. Believe me. Love me, Reuben, make love to me." Her mouth opened and she slipped her tongue between his lips, tickling the roof of his mouth.

His hold on her tightened and she fell back,

back, pulling him on top of her, twining her legs around him again. "Yes," she kept saying to everything he did. "Oh, God, Reuben. There, right there, right—yes." Then she said a couple of words a nice Catholic girl shouldn't know, and it tumbled him over the edge. He hooked his hands around her shoulders and pumped into her, his jaws grinding, body hunching, suffering the force swelling and gathering inside until he couldn't hold anymore and he exploded. He called out her name in the intense heat of the moment, pounding into her helplessly. It went on and on, and when it was over he wanted more. Impossible; there was nothing left. How could he be this empty and feel this complete? Grace had her face turned to the side; her wild hair hid her expression. By slow degrees all his muscles gave out, and he sank down onto her as gently as he could.

She wasn't moving. No idle, exhausted hand stroked his back, no grateful lips nuzzled his skin. He rested for a minute, listening to her breathing, which was soft and steady. Then he rolled to his side, taking her with him.

With their heads on the pillow, foreheads touching, he had to confess. "I, uh, sort of forgot about you at the end there, Gus. Was it okay? Did you, um…did you…" She just stared at him with her eyebrows raised, not helping. "Did you come?" he asked bluntly.

She seemed to think it over. Then she smiled a slow, lazy smile, sexy and mysterious. "Maybe. I'll let you know in a minute." She snickered at his tortured-sounding groan and burrowed deeper into the crook of his arm.

He grinned up at the ceiling, hugely relieved. He knew a satisfied woman when he felt one, and Grace had that sack-of-potatoes heft to her that meant all was well. "It was good, wasn't it?" he gloated. In fact, it had never been better, at least for him. Maybe he'd absorbed some of the Godfather's aphrodisiac, he thought whimsically. From her skin to his.

Grace caught his hairy thigh between her knees and gave it a squeeze, at the same time she pressed a kiss to his left nipple. "My shtarker," she said on a yawn.

He chuckled. Some kind of strange, exhausted energy was filling him; he felt like talking— he had a hundred things to say. But when he looked down, he saw that she'd already fallen asleep, with her head on his shoulder. He kissed her, and whispered something he'd never said to anyone before. But he was safe. Even if she heard, she wouldn't understand what he'd said, because he'd whispered it in a foreign language.

13

Nobuddy ever fergits where he buried a hatchet.

—Kin Hubbard

His first hint was the smell—a fresh, raw, grapey stab to the nose that made him afraid, at first, that a bottle of wine had burst. Maybe the Gewürztraminer from that phony Swiss vintner in Monterey he'd never trusted anyway, he had time to speculate in the second it took to pull the key out of the lock and push the door wide open. Even then, with the proof of it in front of him, around him, even behind him on the back of the door, Reuben's brain couldn't take it in.

Catastrophe.

He registered the broken, upended furniture and the ripped curtains, the crockery in pieces on the kitchen floor, the sofa spilling its cottony insides out on the slashed rug, the smoking remains of his desk—they must've burned it when they couldn't open it. Finally the significance of the plum-colored stains on every wall penetrated the barriers of confusion he'd thrown up for protection, and he knew it was gone, all gone, every bottle in his collection. His Rieslings and Chardonnays, his Hermitage Syrahs, the Rülander Auslesen—smithereens. Madeiras and sherrys and muscats, pooling in fruity puddles at the bottom of the stairs. Sauvignons, the Trentino Gewürztraminer, all the Beaujolais, the Pinot Gris, the Pinot Noirs, all the Cabernets—gone, all gone, everything smashed to fragments against the four walls of his apartment.

His knees felt weak; he'd have sat down on the floor, except there was broken glass everywhere. He stumbled forward and saw the note pinned to the newel post.

Dear Reuben,
   We are very disappointed on account of you having turned out to be a snake and a liar. I personally am deeply hurt, having thought you were on the square. My brother Jefferson says you are lower than snail slime, and I feel likewise. The boys think you don't deserve a warning, but I am a benevolent person. Here is the warning: If we see you again, we will kill you.

Sincerely yours,
Lincoln Croaker

He pulled his watch from his pocket and flicked it open. Eleven o'clock. The time they'd agreed on for the payment was ten. One thing you could say about Lincoln, he was a stickler for punctuality.

Thinking about what else would've gotten smashed if he'd been on time—his head, for instance; many of his bones—finally got Reuben moving. He took the stairs two at a time, and saw without surprise as he passed his bedroom door that they'd trashed that room, too. The bathroom was the least vandalized, probably because everything in it was nailed down; the Croakers had contented themselves with shattering the mirror over the sink and pulling the toiletries off the shelves. In fear and dread, he closed the w.c. lid and stepped up on it. The heavy enamel cover over the water tank looked undisturbed. He shoved it sideways and peeked inside. "Yes! Stupid, ignorant bastards, blockhead sons of bitches," he muttered, full of gladness and belated wrath as he reached in and pulled out his most precious possession: his bottle of Dom Perignon Premiere Cuvée, 1882. Perfect and unscathed. And taped next to it were the two twenty-dollar gold eagles he'd stashed here long ago for emergencies.

Closer inspection of the debacle of his bedroom revealed that Lincoln and the boys had exercised uncharacteristic restraint when they'd sacked it: everything Reuben owned was in shreds, while everything of Grace's was perfect. He found the traveling case Henri— *Henry*, rather; Henry the non-husband—had sent Grace with her clothes, and stuffed it with a hasty selection of skirt, shirtwaist, underwear, stockings, and shoes.

Downstairs, he found an unbroken pencil amid the wreckage, and wrote a note to Mrs. Finney on the back of an untorn envelope. He put one of the twenty-dollar gold pieces inside, and set it on top of the newel post. With a last doleful look around—brief, though; if he lingered, he was afraid he'd burst into tears—he said good-bye to the house he'd lived in for almost a year, a record for him, and walked out.

Nobody suspicious-looking was loitering around the Bunyon Arms. Nobody *Chinese* and suspicious-looking, that was; the denizens of this neighborhood looked more or less unsavory at all times, though less so at this early hour than they would later on in the day. The same white-haired clerk was manning the front desk, with the same diligence and attention to detail. Reuben walked past him without disturbing his rest, and went upstairs.

"Who is it?" called Grace when he tapped at the door.

Various corny, flirtatious answers occurred to him. Since he didn't know her mood yet— she'd been dead to the world and unwakeable when he'd left—he answered prosaically, "Reuben."

The key turned in the lock. He waited, but the door didn't open. After a few seconds, he let himself in.

She was all the way across the room already, busy at the washstand, splashing and washing, wringing and drying. She had her yellow-robed back to him, and she threw a quick "Morning" over her shoulder without turning her head enough for him to see her face.

"Morning," he hazarded, setting the traveling bag down on the bed. "Brought you some clothes."

"Oh? I was wondering mfpgwhg."

"Pardon?"

She took the wet towel away from her face. "I wondered where you went," she said to the wall, and went back to splashing.

"Ah. Well, that's where I went, all right. Home to get you some clothes." The rest was too painful to speak of yet; he'd tell her in a minute. He stood with his hands in his pockets in the center of the room, watching her repetitive-looking ablutions, pondering his next conversational sally. Nothing seemed safe enough; even "How are you feeling?" was freighted, if you thought about it, with meanings and implications and complications he didn't care to get into right now.

Maybe he'd dreamed last night. That would explain why Grace was treating him with all the warmth and friendliness of a bus conductor. He was dying to know what the night had meant to her, if anything. It had meant something to him, although he hadn't had time to figure out exactly what. The most amazing part was this extremely strange *gladness* he had inside. His world had just gone to hell: he had nowhere to live, five American and who knew how many Chinese men were trying to kill him, his possessions had shrunk to twenty dollars and a bottle of champagne—and yet he couldn't remember, drunk or sober, ever being this happy. His body and mind felt right with each other for a change, and his spirit, whatever that was, felt comfortable. He was a contented man.

Mornings after were always difficult, he reminded himself. This one went beyond difficult; but then, last night hadn't exactly been routine as far as first-time lovemaking experiences went. What had it meant to Grace? What did she think of him now? Was she ever going to let him touch her again? Was she ever going to stop washing?

They weren't the kind of people who talked much about their feelings, he supposed. Usually that was fine with him; women were much too keen, in Reuben's experience, on mulling and classifying and categorizing every little speck of information once a relationship got interesting, interesting meaning physical. Right now, though, just this once, he wouldn't have minded a quick, candid conversation in which everything got said and settled, so they could get on with being...whatever it was they were going to be to each other.

"Would you mind going out of the room while I dress?"

He stared at her. "Say that again?" He cupped his ear humorously.

Not a trace of a smile crossed her face. She put her hands on her hips, belligerent. "I'd like some privacy. Is that too much to ask?"

She was trying to pick a fight! Well, she wouldn't get one out of him. "Of course not," he said solicitously, walking to the window. "I'll stand here with my back to the room— how's that? I'm afraid it might not be safe out in the hall, Grace. Is this all right?" She made a hostile, frustrated sound, presumably of assent. While he waited, idly scanning the street below, a fantasy came into his head. In it, he spun around and grabbed her, lifted her up in the air by her narrow waist, and gave her a big, joyful, smacking kiss between her breasts. She shrieked at first, then started to laugh. He held her tight and said something perfect—affectionate but not binding—and she agreed with him. They fell on the bed in a heap and made noisy, athletic love.

That's the way it was supposed to be. So why wouldn't she talk to him? What the hell was going on in that complicated female head?

Many things. Not the least of them was the realization that her body felt as if a train had run over and pulverized it. Everything ached, including her hair. She imagined this must be how circus acrobats felt after the last show. Bad acrobats, the ones who'd let themselves go. Looking at herself in the mirror over the washstand had taken an act of personal courage, and she still cringed at the memory of barbaric hair, bloodshot eyes, pasty skin where it wasn't chapped and livid from Reuben's beard stubble, funny little bruises on her neck whose origins she remembered perfectly. The fact that he looked disgustingly fit and well-rested only darkened her mood.

Taking him at his word, she threw off the hated yellow dressing gown and began to struggle into her clothes, keeping a wary eye on his back. He hadn't forgotten anything in the unmentionables department, she noticed sourly as she pulled her white lawn chemise over her head. Which just went to show. His nonchalant posture annoyed her, she wasn't sure why. She'd been hoping he would come back and act as if nothing much had happened, and that's exactly what he was doing. Now that annoyed her, too. Did he think last night's goings-on were an ordinary occurrence for her? A bit more intense than usual, maybe, because of the circumstances, but still, the sort of thing she was pretty much used to? Well, damn him for a horse's behind if he did!

She yanked a silk stocking over her knee and anchored it with a garter. She already knew what he thought of her morals; he'd made it plain that night he'd kissed her outside in his backyard and then wondered what "game" she was playing when she wouldn't jump into bed with him. Last night's bizarre chain of events could only have reinforced his opinion.

Well, so what? What did she care? She hadn't done anything wrong, it was all because of the drug. Everything was the drug's fault. She only had one regret, really, when all was said and done, only one thing she wished that she, on her end, could take back. She wished she hadn't said, "Let's make love in bed," last night in the heat of the moment. And later, "Love me, Reuben, make love to me." *Love,* it went without saying, had nothing to do with it, not for her and certainly not for him. She just wished she'd been more precise in her choice of words. She just wished...

Oh, who was she kidding? The truth was,

she was scared to death. Last night—God, just thinking about it had her face hot and her hands trembling. All that wantonness, all that need, and the worst was knowing, deep down, that Wing's drug wasn't even responsible for it. Not all of it, anyway. Her passion for Reuben had come burning up from a much stronger, *natural* fire inside herself. She hadn't needed the Godfather's aphrodisiac except for an excuse. A scapegoat.

Even so, she wasn't ashamed of herself for wanting Reuben. By some miracle, in spite of everything her stepparents had done to teach her that sex was dirty and disgusting, the lesson had never quite sunk in. So she could admit without shame that she'd been attracted to Reuben from the moment they'd met. Sex wasn't complicated, it wasn't a sin, and it wasn't what scared her.

What scared her was the possibility that she was falling in love. Horrible, awful, perverted curse, absolutely out of the question! Hadn't she had enough of abandonment and loss and disillusionment to last a lifetime? *By God,* she wouldn't put herself on the line again, ever, for anyone, especially not for a man like Reuben Jones. Reuben Jones! Out of all the men in the whole world, why did she have to fall for one who was even crookeder than she was? Was it a joke? God's idea of a good time, something to chuckle over when things got dull up in—

"Holy shit."

She jerked her head up, fingers freezing

on a jet button at the back of the rose tulle shirt-waist he'd brought, to go with her black taffeta skirt. How had he known they went together? What kind of man knew such things? "What—?" she began, when he whirled, and the look on his face stopped her heart. He lunged for her and started to pull her toward the door. "Reuben, wait, my—"

"Tom Fun's down there with another guy, pointing at the building. Come on, Gus, they've found us!" She jerked out of his grasp and ran back for her shoes—she wasn't going to run around Chinatown barefooted a second time. "Come *on*." He grabbed her again and yanked her out the door. She let him pull her along the hall, hopping on one foot, holding her second shoe in her hand. "Not that way," he muttered when she started toward the front stairs. "Back way—this way. Hurry!"

A set of servants' stairs from the Bunyon Arms' long-dead past led down to the first floor and, more important, the door to the alley behind the building. Grace got her second shoe on and finished buttoning her blouse while Reuben scouted the alley. From the inter-section with the street to the left, he motioned to her that the coast was clear; she darted out of the building and ran toward him.

"Where are we going?" she asked as they went along, walking fast, craning their necks to look behind them every few feet. The narrow street was quiet and almost empty, except for one drunken sailor winding his way toward them.

"North, I hope. Away from Chinatown."

They reached the corner. "Then we're going the wrong way." She skidded to a halt, pointing to the street sign on the side of the building they'd just passed. It was in Chinese.

Before they could turn, a man trotted around the corner from the right, silent in cork-soled sandals. When he saw them, he stopped in his tracks, looking as startled as they did. He grinned nervously and shuffled closer. When Reuben tensed and tried to pull Grace behind him, the man threw up his hands, palms out. "Mean no harm!" he assured them, and stayed where he was. He was an unlikely-looking hatchet man, chubby and jolly-looking, bald except for a black fringe in back from ear to ear. Grace thought he looked like an Oriental Friar Tuck, only smaller.

"Anything we can do for you?" Reuben asked him, holding her hand.

He bowed without taking his eyes off them. "Have message. Mean no harm," he repeated, smiling.

"What's the message?"

"Message is, Kai Yee not want anyone to die," he said carefully, as if reciting a poem he'd memorized. "Kai Yee only want lady. Say come, treat good, nobody hurt." He grinned and bowed some more, waiting for applause.

"Well, there you have it," said Reuben. "A gracious invitation if I ever heard one. What do you say, Gus?"

"I don't think so."

He shrugged apologetically. "The lady

doesn't think so. Would you excuse us now? We're in just a bit of a—ahhha."

The hatchet man had pulled a meat cleaver out of his blue pajamas. He held it up, blade out, next to his round, grinning face.

Grace felt Reuben's suddenly sweaty grip on her hand slacken, saw all the blood drain from his face. "Ahhha," he said again, smiling sickly. "Why didn't you say so? Here—if you want her that bad, take her." She gasped, and he gave her a little push in Mean No Harm's direction.

The surprised Chinaman grabbed her wrist with the hand that wasn't holding the meat cleaver and started backing up. "Get your paw off me, you—" She jerked back, trying to fling away from him, but he held on tight while keeping an eye on Reuben—an unnecessary eye, since he was still standing in the same spot, baffled-looking, arms at his sides. "Reuben!" she shrieked at him. She couldn't believe he was going to let the jolly hatchet man kidnap her. "Reuben!"

He waved, sadly, and put his hands in his pockets.

Mean No Harm's chubby little hand was breaking her wrist. She tried a kick to his groin, but he dodged nimbly and gave her arm a painful, punishing yank. "Son of a bitch!" she called him, and clamped her teeth over his knuckles.

"Aya! Aya!" He hit her on the shoulder—with the heel of his hand, not the cleaver—but she only shut her eyes and bit down harder.

She heard a scuffling sound behind him. He heard it too, but not in time.

Crash! Glass everywhere, and bubbles, and dripping water. No, not water—wine. Reuben had the broken green neck of a wine bottle in his hand, his mouth open in an expression of excited anguish, watching the hatchet man drop to his knees and fall over on his back like a sack of rice.

"Gone," Reuben whispered, heartsick, disbelieving. "Gone."

"No, he's just unconscious," she said gently. "You didn't kill him."

He turned his tragic eyes on her. "Not him, you numbskull, the Dom Perignon. The Premiere Cuvée—a masterpiece—irreplaceable—" He choked up and couldn't go on.

The silver handle of a pistol was sticking out of the waist of Mean No Harm's baggy trousers. Grace bent and snatched it out. A cheap .38; if he'd used it instead of the meat cleaver, he wouldn't be lying on his back in the gutter. "Thank God for the hatchet tradition," she muttered, sticking the pistol in her skirt pocket. "You weren't really going to let him take me, were you?" she thought to ask. "You were just waiting for him to let down his guard, right?"

"Right," he said reflexively.

She wasn't sure he'd heard the question. He looked grief-stricken, as if his best friend had died. She had to drag him away, still mumbling disconsolately. "Come on, come on. *Hurry,* Reuben, we've got to get out of here, get home and out of sight. This street? Where is

283

everybody? Is this north?" It was too cloudy to see the sun. She looked uncertainly down a lane that wound out of sight before the first block. She didn't like the look of it, but if that was north—

"We can't go home."

"Yes, we can. If this is north and we just keep—"

"We can't go home because the Croakers trashed it."

"Oh, no!"

"Everything's gone, there's nothing left. Except a note that says they'll kill me if they find me."

"My God." They stared at each other. "Reuben, what are we going to do?" Over his shoulder, she saw a man rounding the corner. It was Tom Fun.

He saw them and started to run. Reuben grabbed her and they fled, back the way they'd come.

At the first cross street, they careened to the left. For precious seconds their pursuer couldn't see them. "Look," Grace panted, hauling on Reuben's hand to slow him down, pointing into the mouth of a damp, dark alley. "We could hide, get out of sight—" He grunted, and they ducked into the alley.

Bad idea. The alley was blind, although they didn't know it until they'd gone twenty yards and tried to follow what had looked from the street like a dogleg to the right. It was a dogleg into a brick wall, with no door, no crevice, not even a trash can to hide behind.

Running footsteps made them spin around and freeze. Tom Fun, gaunt and scar-faced, appeared in the alley's stinking angle, holding a big, ugly ax.

Reuben groaned piteously and went white again. "Shoot him. Oh, please shoot him."

She'd forgotten she had the gun. She fumbled it out of her pocket and took aim.

Tom Fun didn't even break stride. "Shoot him," Reuben begged.

She couldn't pull the trigger. Tom Fun raised the ax and kept coming.

"Shoot him!"

"I can't!"

The hatchet man lunged and swung, missing Reuben's head by a hair. Stumbling into him, Reuben grabbed him around the waist. Now she could shoot—she knew she could—but they kept turning and grappling, she was afraid she'd hit Reuben by mistake. She circled them, gun pointed, barely aware that she was shrieking, "Reuben, get out—no, the other—no—move!"

Tom Fun jerked his elbow up into Reuben's throat, and he had to let go, choking. The hatchet man hauled back with his ax. Reuben pivoted toward Grace while she skipped sideways, looking for a shot. The ax caught him on the hip with a sickening thud, and he fell. "Reuben!" she screamed. Tom Fun's body blocked her view; like a lumberjack about to split a log, he reared up again with the ax. At the height of his swing, she pulled the trigger and shot him in the buttocks.

He fell on top of Reuben, squealing like a wounded pig, while the ax skidded sideways. Reuben squirmed out from under him, cursing, bleeding. Grace let the gun slip from her fingers and clatter to the ground as she dropped to her knees beside him. With his eyes closed, there was absolutely no color in his face except for the ash-gray of his lips. "Please don't faint, Reuben. How bad is it? Can you walk?"

"Walk?" he croaked, incredulous. "I'm dying, he killed me."

Tom Fun was writhing on his side two feet away, groaning, holding his rear end. Grace picked up the gun she'd dropped and put it back in her pocket—so he wouldn't get ideas. "You're not dying," she told Reuben briskly. What she wanted to do was lie down beside him and pass out. She made herself lift her skirts, bite a hole in the side seam of her cotton petticoat, and rip a long strip of the hem off at the bottom.

Reuben cringed, watching her fold it into a bandage. "Don't touch me, it'll hurt."

"I thought you were a shtarker."

"No, I'm a *lemish*. What are you doing?"

"What does it look like?"

He tried to grin while she unbuttoned his trousers. "Gee, Gus, all you had to do was ask."

It might've been funny, except that she knew everything she did was hurting him. No time to check the wound to see how bad it was—they still had to run—but the amount of blood staining the side of his pants gave her a clue: bad. "What's a *lemish*?" she muttered, to make him talk while she slid the fat square of petticoat inside his knee-length flannel drawers as gently as she could.

His head fell back. He bared his teeth and gritted, "Not a shtarker," the cords in his neck bulging like cable wire.

"Another word your German fraulein taught you?"

"Hildegard, yah. She vas vunderbar."

"Gretchen," she corrected, rebuckling his belt. "Reuben, you're going to have to stand up and walk."

"Right. And then how about a nice polka."

"Sit up and put your arm across my shoulders. Get your left foot under—there. Ready?"

"No."

"And—*up*."

He made it, leaning against her like a drunk, swaying from dizziness. "Give Tom a kick for me, would you, Grace? I can't manage it and I want to say good-bye. Hit him a good one right in the—"

"Come on," she fretted, already stumbling under his weight.

He stopped talking to concentrate on walking, which got a little easier as he went on. But at the top of the alley, he had to lean against the wall to rest. "What's your plan?" he asked with his eyes closed.

"How much money have you got?"

"Twenty dollars or so."

"Give it to me." He handed her a gold coin. "Nothing smaller than this?" she asked in dismay. He rummaged in his other pocket and pulled out three wrinkled dollar bills and some change. "Good, this should be enough. Here, take your jacket off."

"Why?"

"And tie the sleeves around your waist—I'll do it. To hide the blood, of course. Now, stay here in the shadows and don't move. You take the gun."

"No."

"Yes! It's you they want to kill, not me." She tried to put the pistol in his hand, but he wouldn't take it. "Damn it, Reuben—"

"Where are you going?"

"I'm going to find somebody who'll—" She broke off at the sound of wheels clattering in the street behind her. "Help us," she finished, jubilant.

"A coal cart?" Reuben said querulously, but she was already striding off the curb and into the street. The high-sided wooden vehicle was almost empty, she could tell because the back flap was down. The sleepy-looking driver woke up when she stopped his mule by stepping in front of it and dragging on the harness.

"Hey! Hey, get outa the road, whaddaya think you're doing?"

She walked toward him, trailing a hand along the mule's rump as she went. The driver looked Irish and tough as nails, with a wild, gray-flecked red beard and hair to match. But his face changed from belligerent to beguiled in the time it took her to go from the mule's nose to its behind, and she knew that whatever that *thing* was she could do with men when she wanted to, she was doing it now.

"Hi."

"Hi."

"I could use a ride."

"That so?" They grinned at each other, first her, then him. They were sharing a joke they couldn't have put into words; they just knew it was hilarious and very, very sexy. From the age of seventeen, when she'd first discovered it, Grace had known that this particular method of seduction, if she chose the man correctly, could not fail. Thank God her coal-delivering Irishman was the right man. "Where you want me to take you?" he inquired, loading the question with lusty implications.

"The Clay Street wharf. I need to go right away."

He patted the splintery wooden seat beside him. "Yer chariot awaits."

She liked his style. She made him a coquettish curtsey and put her finger on her cheek. "Oh—I forgot—I have a friend. Can he go, too?" She gestured behind her, and Reuben limped out of the alley into the light, scowling.

As expected, her Irish savior wasn't pleased with this development. His rosy cheeks mottled and his bushy brows met over his nose. He was starting to say no when she played her ace. "I'll give you three dollars if you'll take us. He," she added with a careless shrug, "can ride in the cart."

She didn't know if it was the seating arrangement or the three dollars that swayed him, but the coalman agreed. She had to force herself not to hurry, not to show fear or urgency by her manner. Reuben needed assistance getting into the cart, though; no help for that. "He's swacked," she explained, hoisting him over the back, talking over his agonized groan as he settled on his good side, still glaring at her. "We had us a bit of a hullabaloo last night at O'Malley's pub. D'ye know that joint on Montgomery Street?" A wee bit of a brogue crept into her tongue, easy as pie. She reached up trustingly, and the Irishman stuck out a great paw to help her into her seat. *Hullabaloo*—that was Irish, wasn't it?

"No," he said, "I don't think I know it. Montgomery Street, y'say?"

"Oh, aye, a great black hole of a place, you ought t' go there sometime. Tell O'Malley I sent ye."

"And who might you be?"

"Faith, I'm Sheila O'Ryan. Pleased t' make yer acquaaaintance."

And so it went, all the way to the Embarcadero.

The trip home was a nightmare. As usual, the Oakland ferry was teeming with passengers, and Grace had to tell a man that Reuben was seasick just to get him a seat. The man had no trouble believing it; Reuben's gray, clammy face was all the proof anyone could need. The choppy Bay waters made the crossing torture for him, but he kept up a stream of jokes and cracks anyway. She wasn't sure who they were designed to distract, her or himself, but she was grateful to him for trying and joined in as well as she could. At Vallejo, she left him slumped on a bench in the railway station while she went to send Henry a telegram: "Urgent you meet 5:40 p.m. train Santa Rosa stop. Bring Ah You and wagon not buggy stop. Love, Grace."

The train was smoother than the ferry had been, but Reuben looked worse, and now he was too weak to bother making jokes. That scared her more than anything. His head fell on her shoulder, waking him up from a restless doze. He looked around blankly. "Where are we?"

"On the train."

"Where are we going?"

She shivered; she'd told him twice already. "We're going to my house."

He closed his eyes. "Home, sweet home," he sighed, and slept again.

She wanted to look at his wound; they were in a middle seat of a crowded parlor car, though, and she couldn't see opening his pants while half a dozen passengers looked on. No blood had seeped through his jacket yet. She took that as a good sign.

"I'm dying," he told her a little later.

Her skin prickled and sweat broke out on her palms. But she made her voice crisp and said dismissively, "I don't think so."

"I'm going to bleed to death sitting on a train."

She touched his forehead, which was hot and dry. "Don't talk."

"I think I need a doctor."

"Ah You is better than a doctor."

He didn't seem to hear that. "Last night, Gus. Last night?" He didn't look at her. She had no idea what he would say next, and she waited in a curious state of dread. His lips moved, but no more words came out, and then she didn't know if she was glad or sorry. After a long time, he startled her by saying, "Will you miss me when I'm gone, Gracie?"

He had his eyes closed; she couldn't tell from his waxy, pain-stiff face if he was joking or not. "Hush, Reuben. You're not dying, so I won't get a chance to miss you. Be quiet now and rest." He sighed again, raggedly. She waited until he was asleep. Then she reached for his hand, and held onto it tightly all the rest of the way home.

The porter hollering "Santa Rosa Station!" woke him up.

"We're here," Grace told him, peering out the window for a glimpse of Henry.

"Santa Rosa?"

"About five miles outside of town."

"I thought you lived in the Russian Valley."

She smiled, pleased to hear him so lucid. "I was lying. Look, there's Henry." She waved, trying to catch his eye, but the train slid by and he didn't see her. The sight of him, dapper and distinguished as always, his handsome black-and-silver hair glinting in the afternoon sun, warmed her to her bones. She hadn't known until this minute how much she'd missed him.

The train ground to a stop. "Come on," she told Reuben, standing up and hovering over him. He leaned forward and she got her arms around his back. But when he tried to rise, his whole body shook and beads of sweat popped out on his forehead.

He fell back, panting, hands clenching on the wooden arms of his chair. "Can't," he said through his teeth. "Can't get up."

She looked behind her in a panic. The porter was out on the platform, assisting an elderly lady down the steps. Leaving Reuben, Grace ran down the empty aisle to the door. "My husband's ill," she said quickly. "I have a friend who'll help me. There—"

The porter said, "Yes, ma'am," and tipped his cap, but she was already turning away and rushing into Henry's open arms.

"Here, now, what's all this?" His tone was brusque, but he hugged her hard, and his lips pressing against her cheek were warm.

She broke away first. "Help me get him off the train."

"Who?"

"Reuben." She pointed toward the window where his white face was framed, watching them, his eyes dark and burning. "He's hurt, I can't get him up by myself. Did you bring—"

"Ho, Missy! Welcome home!"

"Ah You!" She wanted to hug him, too, but there was no time. She clasped his tiny, birdlike hands in hers; his ageless face was wreathed in smiles, bright black eyes beaming. "Did you come in the wagon?"

"Yes, Missy."

"Bring it up as close to the platform as you can, and then come and help us."

"Okay!"

"Come on," she told Henry, and dashed back into the train. Between them, with the porter's help, they got Reuben out on the platform. Every second she thought he would faint. "Something he ate," she muttered to the worried porter. Ah You replaced him at Reuben's left side, and the porter watched the three men tack unsteadily toward the wagon, Grace twisting her hands and walking backward in front of them, until the train whistle blew and he had to reboard.

Getting Reuben into the wagon was the hardest part, everybody pushing and pulling, trying not to hurt him. He was a big man, but she'd never realized before how *heavy* he was. Ah You jumped up into the wagon bed after him, agile as a monkey. Grace sat beside Henry on the seat. Usually she drove, but she was too shaky and upset for it now, her hands trembling too hard. Henry turned the wagon inexpertly and shook the reins, setting the horses to a trot. Reuben groaned. Grace put her face in her hands. Half an hour later, they arrived at Willow Pond.

14

A good patient is one who, having found a good physician, sticks to him until he dies.
—Oliver Wendell Holmes

"Wake up. Wake up, Reuben."
The voice nudged like soothing fingers at the sides of his nightmare, softening for just a second the razor edges of the blades. Dozens of blades, shiny silver-blue, hacking and hacking. The sound they made slicing across his flesh was a high, juicy *sssst*. No blood, just excruciating numbness, like an electric shock. He couldn't scream anymore; he rolled himself up in a ball, became the center of the ball, surrounded by thick layers of stuffing. Then he was round, he could move any way he chose, crush the blades under the heavy weight of the ball. A merciful respite, but already the ball was disappearing—he could never stay in it for long in this dream— and now he was flat again and helpless, and the blades began to flay him again, *sssst, sssst, sssst—*

"Wake up, open your eyes, Reuben. Come on, wake up."

He opened his eyes. Immediately the burning pain in his hip flared like a bonfire. He didn't move, though; he knew from experience that moving made everything much, much worse.

Grace swam into his line of vision. "You were dreaming," she told him, as if he didn't know that. Her anxious face was a powerful comfort, but he made himself close his eyes. Another thing he'd learned was that she would go back to her chair if she knew he was awake and all right. But if he feigned sleep or, even more, if he groaned out loud from the pain in his hip, she would sit on the bed next to him and touch him. Hold his hand, sometimes stroke his face or softly rub his scalp. So he kept his eyes closed. And sure enough, in a little while he felt her light, cool fingers on his forehead.

"Are you awake?"

"Mmm," he answered, noncommittally.

He had only a vague memory of arriving—yesterday? the day before?—at a sprawling, two-story white clapboard house at the foot of an oak tree-covered hill. Everything since then had been pain and bad dreams. Sometimes Grace took care of him, sometimes a tiny Chinaman with a sonorous voice and gentle hands. Ah You, she called him. Ah You was the one who had sewn the endless miniature stitches in his hip, but it was Grace who had held his hand and talked to him all the while, telling him it would be over soon, telling him he was the bravest shtarker she knew.

He thought two days had passed, but he couldn't be sure. His room had white walls, plain wooden furniture, bright red curtains on the window at the foot of his bed. He could see the sky through the window, star-flecked or a clear aching blue, and at dawn—or was it dusk?—the odor of sweet bay trees wafted into the room. The sun on his white coverlet warmed him; when he wasn't dreaming of knives, he would watch it move slowly across the bed, and imagine the soft golden light was healing him.

His mind drifted. He felt Grace's hand sliding gently out of his and he let it go, too weak to hold on.

"How is he?" A man's voice. Not Ah You; the other one. Henry.

"He's a little stronger, I think. Ah You says the wound is mending well."

"Ah You would know."

Reuben opened his eyes a crack and studied him through his lashes. Up close, Henry wasn't as old as he'd thought, probably not even fifty. He was better-looking, too, if you liked that dapper, debonair style some men fell into in middle age. But he put oil on his mustache, and in Reuben's book that meant he was vain. He didn't like him.

He liked him even less when he took Grace's hand and pulled her off the bed. "You're exhausted," he said in a deep, distinguished voice. "You've had no rest in two nights."

"I nap while I sit here."

"There's nothing for you to do now."

"I know, but—"

"Come to bed, Grace. Ah You will stay with him tonight."

Reuben heard her sigh. "Okay," she said, and he could hear the fatigue in her voice. He opened his eyes to see them leaving. They had their arms around each other's waist.

Come to bed, Grace? His hip throbbed harder, hotter. He tried lying on his left side, but that made it worse. Sometimes Ah You gave him a sip of something nasty-tasting that took the pain away for a while, but he wasn't allowed to have it very often.

Come to bed, Grace?

"Henry's not my husband, we just live together," she'd said. He had a sharp memory of when and where, and why, she'd told him that. At the time, the distinction had reassured him. It didn't any longer.

Outside the window a cricket sang. The eerie hoo-hoo of an owl carried on the night air, softened by the scent of sweet bay. Reuben shut his eyes and dreamt of blades.

"We should talk," Grace said, halting at the bottom of the stairs.

"You should sleep," Henry countered, his hand on the banister.

"You wouldn't be trying to avoid talking to me, would you?"

"Don't be ridiculous." He looked offended. Nevertheless, she suspected the reason he hadn't said a word to her since she'd come home about the house or the mortgage or the tax bill was because the situation had gotten worse, not better.

"Let's sit outside," she suggested peaceably.

He shrugged, and followed her through the

living room to the wide screen doors that opened onto the veranda. "Drink?" he suggested, detouring at the liquor cabinet. She said no, and kept going. He joined her a minute later, brandy glass in hand, and sat beside her on the steps that led down to the garden.

"It's so good to be home." She sighed, drawing in a breath of the perfumed air. She couldn't have put the night smell of Willow Pond into words; she only knew it was sweet, and there was nothing else like it anywhere in the world. How could she give it up? She'd come home a failure, though, and that was something neither she nor Henry, in their optimism or their stupidity, had ever foreseen. "Did you miss me?" she asked, resting her elbows on the step above.

He busied himself lighting his pipe, an affectation he'd acquired fairly recently, and grunted.

She smiled in the dark. She knew he'd missed her. "How's your leg?"

"Nice of you to remember to ask. It's fair," he grumbled.

It was well, as far as she could tell; he wasn't limping or using his cane anymore. She remembered how he'd broken his leg—by falling off the veranda steps on a dark, rainy night last May. He still claimed he wasn't drunk, but he'd been drinking brandy that night, like tonight. "I told Reuben you had a bad heart," she mentioned.

"Ha," he said, puffing smoke. "Why?"

"To explain why we needed money, at first.

And then to explain why you didn't come with me when I was fleecing the dioceses. I thought it sounded better than a broken leg. More dramatic." He made a sound of amused agreement, and she felt them falling back into their old, comfortable camaraderie. She really had missed him.

"What else did you tell Mr. Jones?" he wanted to know.

"Oh, I told him some awful lies."

He nodded approvingly. "Tell me about him. Your letter was, how shall I say, cryptic. Tell me everything that happened, from the time you threw four thousand dollars away—"

"*I* threw—"

"—to the time you got home, and don't leave anything out."

She was familiar with his diversionary tactics. "I'll tell you everything, because I've got nothing to hide. But first you have to tell me: exactly how much do we owe, and when do we owe it?"

Furious puffing. She'd hound him until he told her all of it, though, and he knew it. He took his pipe out of his mouth and confessed. "The bank wouldn't agree to the extension. We've got till the fifteenth of August to come up with the money."

"All of it?" she asked, aghast.

"All. They won't mortgage again, and they won't accept any more partial payments. If we can't pay the whole six thousand by the fifteenth, they say they'll foreclose."

"Oh, no. Oh, no." It was worse than she'd

thought. "What about that man at the other bank, the one you thought might—"

"Don't you think I'd have told you if that had worked?" he flared. "He turned me down flat, and that's the end of it."

He couldn't stand to talk about it. It was even worse for him than her, because he thought it was his fault. In a way, at least technically, he was right: she'd advised him against getting involved in the complicated mineral rights scheme that had taken all their money and plunged them into debt. In particular, she'd warned him against remortgaging the house, which belonged to her, not him. But never, not once, not by so much as a sarcastic word, had she ever thrown that in his face. Oh, how had they come to this? How could they leave Willow Pond? Stupid, shiftless people got evicted, not people like them. They were too clever—weren't they?

"Well? Go ahead, Grace, I'm waiting to hear all about your adventures."

Sighing, she put her elbows on her knees, cupped her chin in her hands, and told him everything. Or almost everything. Henry was amazingly tolerant, and she'd never once known him to be remotely fatherly during their six-year acquaintance. Some things were private, though, so she glossed over the more unsavory particulars of her captivity at Wing's house, and she left out completely what had happened afterward at the Bunyon Arms. When she finished, he was silent for a long time, puffing on his pipe.

She yawned. She was dying for bed. Maybe she ought to sleep in Ah You's room tonight, though, which was across the hall from Reuben's on the first floor. That way she'd be sure to hear him if he called out, whereas she wouldn't in her second-floor bedroom at the other end of the house. Silly, she knew; there was nothing she could do for him if he did call out that Ah You couldn't do much better. Still—

"Tell me about this Wing character again."

"But I've told you—"

"Tell me again. Everything you know about him, every detail. Go ahead, Grace."

She heard that tone in his voice, quiet, exaggeratedly calm, an unmistakable intonation she was probably the only person on earth who recognized. It raised the hairs on the back of her neck. It meant he was plotting something. He had an idea.

She wasn't sleepy anymore. She told Henry everything she knew about Mark Wing.

The mission clock on Reuben's bedside table chimed the half hour, nudging Grace out of a shallow doze. She rubbed the back of her stiff neck and flexed her shoulders, trying to shake off the muzzy fatigue. Except for a cricket outside and the faint rasp of Reuben's breathing, the night was silent. Moving quietly, she got up and tiptoed closer to the bed.

His face was still as pale as the sheet under the dark stubble of his three-day beard. She oughtn't to touch him; his sleep was restless enough these days without risking disturbing him. But she wanted to smooth away that line of pain that was always there between his eyebrows. She put her hand out and stroked him—softly, softly.

Without a warning, scalding tears filled her eyes and streamed down her cheeks. She brushed at them clumsily, feeling idiotic. Reuben wasn't going to die; in fact, Ah You said he'd start getting stronger tomorrow, and in matters like that Ah You never erred. *Relief* was what was making her so teary and emotional, partly. The other part...

She didn't want to think about the other part.

She sank down on the edge of the mattress, careful not to shake the bed. Reuben's dark lashes fluttered once, then stilled. She was longing to touch him. In her mind, she slid her hands under his shoulders and pulled him close, holding him, and imagined him waking up and smiling at her. He'd call her Gus, say something to make her laugh. Just thinking about it made the damn tears start up again.

Ridiculous. She got out her handkerchief and blotted her face, calling herself a noodlehead. A *tired* noodlehead. She'd had about six hours' sleep in two nights, and even less the night before that at the Bunyon Arms. Weariness was the culprit, the only explanation for why it was hardly possible to look at Reuben or even *think* about him without the dismal certainty closing in on her that, as soon as he got strong again, he would go away.

Hadn't he as good as told her so the night they'd shared their life goals? His dream was to keep moving, keep on circling the globe until he'd seen everything, and after that he wanted to loll around on a big cattle ranch like Edward Cordoba's. Needless to say, a bankrupt female bunco artist with no prospects didn't figure in his plans. Well, what had she expected? That he would fall in love with her? Marry her, settle down, and become a pillar of the community? Sometimes her secret, old-fashioned, absurdly conventional hopes embarrassed her so much she wanted to pull a blanket over her head. Reuben might want her, might even feel a moderate fondness for her from time to time, but lukewarm sentiments like those couldn't turn him into a different kind of man.

She touched light fingertips to his wrist, which was resting on his stomach. Anyway, she didn't want him any different. She liked him exactly the way he was—smart and funny, good-natured, resourceful, and extremely brave so long as there weren't any knives around. She loved his slipperiness, the way his devious mind worked. Except for Henry, she'd never met anyone as deceitful and untrustworthy.

Just then he turned his hand over and curled his fingers around hers. "Hey, Gus," he said in a gruff whisper.

Startled, she cleared her throat and gave her wet cheeks a swipe with her free hand. "I didn't mean to wake you. Try to go back to sleep."

"Don't go."

"It's late, you need to rest."

"Aw, Gus, just for a minute."

"No, you really—"

"I'm dying of thirst. Can I have some water, please?"

"Oh. Sure." She reached for the pitcher and refilled his empty glass. He struggled up onto his elbows; she slipped her arm behind his neck to help him and brought the glass to his lips. Holding him like this, even for a few seconds, was such a sweet, guilty delight. She let his upper arm press against the side of her breast, fighting the need to bury her face in his hair. Or blow in his ear.

When he finished drinking, he looked up at her; for once the pained furrow between his brows was gone, and the expression in his light brown eyes was clear and hopeful. He was so close, she could've dipped her head two inches and kissed him. With more willpower than she knew she had, she lowered him gently to the pillow and straightened her back.

"Did Ah You give you your medicine tonight?" she asked, all business.

"Yeah. It tasted like buffalo dung tea."

"It probably was." He looked horrified. "Kidding," she assured him—although nothing Ah You put in his medicinal concoctions surprised her anymore. "How do you feel?"

"Better when you're here."

She went all soft inside, like a crock of butter left out in the sun. She felt a big, stupid smile spreading across her face. "That's nice."

"But you look tired."

The smile turned rueful. She'd seen what she looked like, in the mirror over his bureau: like a bag of dirty laundry somebody had flung down the basement steps and left to mildew. She made a move to get up, but Reuben reached over and pulled one of her hands out of her lap and held onto it. She stared down at his long, bony fingers and his clean white nails, comforted by the strength of his grasp. How she loved his hands. "I wish I'd shot Tom Fun sooner," she murmured in a rush. "I'm so sorry you got hurt. It just—kills me."

"I'm okay now, Gracie."

"But if I'd pulled the trigger sooner, you wouldn't be lying here. If I'd just—"

"You saved my life. I'd be dead if it wasn't for you." He brought her hand to his pale lips and closed his eyes while he kissed it.

She held her breath, inexpressibly moved. "Reuben," she whispered. "Oh, Reuben, I wish—"

At a noise behind her, she twisted around.

"Here you are. My God, Grace, it's almost three o'clock in the morning."

Henry's voice sounded too loud after the soft, intimate words she and Reuben had exchanged. She dropped his hand and stood up, smoothing her skirts. "I'm coming to bed right now."

"Good." Henry came over and put his arm around her shoulders. Barefooted, he wore his plaid velveteen dressing gown over his yellow nightshirt.

She rested her temple on his shoulder tiredly. "I guess you two never met formally. Reuben, this is my friend, Henry. Henry Russell. And Henry, this is Reuben Jones."

The two men looked at each other; after an odd moment they nodded, but neither made any move to shake hands. She listened to the rather awkward silence in dismay. Of all the men in her life—not that there were that many—these were the two she wanted to like each other. They didn't seem to be getting off to a good start.

"Well," Henry said, ending the peculiar pause. "Grace is exhausted, so we'll say good night to you, Mr. Jones."

"Good night," she echoed obediently. "Ah You's across the hall if you want anything. Are you okay? Do you need to—"

"Yeah, I'm fine," Reuben snarled, pushing his fingers into his wild hair, making it stand on end. "What I'd really like is a little peace and quiet. Could you please turn out this light?" Grimacing, he twisted his body toward the wall, away from them, and slammed the extra pillow against the side of his head.

Grace frowned down at him, mystified, while Henry went to extinguish the lamp on the bedside table. They went out of the room quietly. "Night," she said again, softly, in the doorway. Reuben must not have heard; he didn't answer.

After that, everything got worse.

With Ah You taking care of him, Reuben's hatchet wound healed quickly, and within a week he was out of bed and hobbling around the house, using a hickory stick for a cane. Grace was relieved, of course, but sometimes she had to wonder if all the medicines, poultices, and exercises Ah You prescribed for him were causing some kind of reaction, an adverse effect on his mental state. It was an understatement to say that she and Reuben had been through a lot together during their brief acquaintance; but even during the worst, the direst, the most *inappropriate* times, she'd never known him to be anything except jocular and lighthearted. So his surly, glowering, ungracious behavior now that he was practically all well was a mystery she couldn't fathom, even though she pondered it about a hundred times a day. In fact, the healthier he got, the worse she felt.

All she could think was that he didn't like her anymore. Simple as that. Or else he couldn't, he wouldn't, treat her so coldly. But why didn't he like her? Hadn't he just told her she'd saved his life? What had she done to make him reconsider and withdraw his affection? Only two possible explanations came to mind: one, that she'd already slept with him, so he'd lost interest in her; two, that he couldn't use her in any more money-making schemes, so he'd lost interest in her.

And he wasn't even consistent! If he was going to treat her like a leper, the least he could do was keep it up full-time. But he seemed to enjoy torturing her, because sometimes he *forgot* to be nasty to her. Then she'd forget she was angry and hurt, and pretty soon they would be talking and laughing, teasing each other and carrying on like old times. Then, *bang,* the wall would drop back down between them, for absolutely no reason she could see, and he would go back to treating her like some girl he barely knew and didn't much care for.

As a result, she was losing her mind. She didn't sleep, she was irritable, forgetful, out of sorts, she couldn't think straight. Considering how impossible she'd already decided he was as a candidate for a steady lover or, God forbid, a husband, she should be *glad* he was apparently finished with her. After all, he'd taken the hard part—giving him up—out of her hands. But she wasn't glad. When she wasn't crying because of him, she was thinking up ways to kill him. He was driving her insane.

And if she'd ever entertained any hopes of him and Henry becoming friends, he put them to rest the first day he got out of bed. She'd been sitting in the living room, sewing new buttons on Henry's plaid night robe. Reuben came limping in with his stick and stopped short when he saw her, obviously startled, and actually looking as if he might turn around and limp out. *Couldn't he even sit in the same room with her anymore?* She wanted to jump up and yell that at him, but she subdued the impulse

309

and made herself inquire casually, almost sweetly, "Won't you come in and keep me company for a while? It's good to see you up and around. I hope that means you're feeling better." She kept talking, giving him no opportunity to refuse her invitation, until finally he came all the way in and plopped down in the chair across from hers. Determinedly chatty, she kept up a pretense of normalcy by not allowing any silences to fall, while Reuben alternated between gazing vacantly out the window and staring with an extremely odd, fixed concentration directly at her.

If she had any spine at all, she'd simply blurt out the questions flailing around inside her head: *Why don't you like me anymore? What's happening between us? Why do you want to hurt me this way?* But her relentless chatter finally coaxed a few words out of him, and then a few more, and then an actual *smile*—and she was filled with such relief, such foolish, pathetic happiness because he was speaking to her again, that she wouldn't have risked spoiling that rare moment for anything.

Then Henry came, and it was spoiled anyway.

"Ich bin Herr Doktor Heinrich Zollenkleimer, und ich bin selling dis here Miraculessen Goldwasser."

He stood in the hall doorway, holding up a muddy-looking glass jar. Bushy gray sidewhiskers—fake—sprouted from his cheeks, and a matching wig had slipped down over one eyebrow. The sofa cushion he'd stuffed under his vest made him look more deformed than portly, but the silver pince-nez stuck on the end of his nose added a nice doctorly touch.

Accustomed to his impromptu disguises, Grace didn't even blink. "Needs work," she said critically. "What's in the bottle?"

"Water." He crossed the room and sat beside her on the sofa. "And a few gold filings— see 'em?" He held the bottle up to the light. "The whole thing's worth at least five dollars."

"Mm-hm. And what are you selling it for?"

"I was thinking an even fifty. It's *concentrated,* don't you know. Comes with a brochure. The customer adds a tablespoon to a gallon of water, freezes it in little blocks—*et voilà*— he's got solid gold bricks worth a fortune." Grace's tickled laugh made him stiffen his neck, offended. "What's wrong with it?"

"That's the worst idea you've ever had!"

Even Reuben was chuckling. "What happens when the bricks melt?"

"But that's the best part," Henry insisted. "Along with the fifty-dollar bottle of Gold-wasser, we sell a certificate promising that the Zollenkleimer Institute—no, Foundation; that's better—the Zollenkleimer Foundation will maintain all the gold bricks in pristine frozen condition for perpetuity, or until the purchaser instructs otherwise. And in addition, the Foundation will undertake to perform any fiduciary transfers which the purchaser authorizes, with no loss of integrity to the financial instrument."

"Come again?" Grace inquired. "No loss of—"

"Integrity to the financial instrument."

The light dawned slowly. "We guarantee the bricks won't thaw?"

"Right."

She couldn't help it: she threw back her head and roared with laughter. A second later Reuben doubled up, guffawing and smacking his knee. Henry glared at them for as long as he could, but pretty soon their hilarity was too much for him. Grudgingly at first, then heartily, he laughed with them.

To Grace, the sound was sweeter than music, and Reuben's mirthful, unguarded face made her heart sing. Still chuckling, she snatched off Henry's wig and ruffled his hair affectionately. He grinned, sheepishly, then put his arm around her and squeezed. "Rascal," he muttered fondly.

She smiled across at Reuben. "Tell Reuben about the time you sold fake silkworms to the farmers with government subsidies."

"Now, that was a good one. I dug up grubs for two days, put 'em in egg cartons, and stenciled the American flag on..." He trailed off, realizing he was talking to nobody. Reuben had hoisted himself out of the chair and was hobbling toward the terrace doors.

"Reuben?" Grace called after him anxiously. "Are you all right? Is anyth—"

Without stopping, he turned his head and snapped, "I need some fresh air." The contempt in his face froze her in her chair.

"Well," Henry said faintly when he was gone. "Moody fellow, isn't he?"

She got up, mumbling something about lunch, and raced from the room. If she was going to burst into tears, she was damn well going to do it in private.

Three days went by, during which she made an effort to keep out of Reuben's way, but without much success. Avoiding him in her own house was like trying to pretend a fly wasn't crawling across her nose. There were too many places where they both were expected to be, together, at the same time. Like the dining room, three times a day unless she skipped breakfast. Or the veranda, after breakfast, where she liked to sit and sun herself, and *he* liked to do his exercises.

On the third day, lurking in the morning-dark shadows of the parlor, she saw him through the open terrace doors, swaying and bending in the bright sun. He was still stiff on his right leg, but getting smoother and more graceful every day. With a sinking feeling, she realized that in spite of everything she was dying to see him, and damn the consequences. Besides, avoiding him was a coward's way out. Who knew—maybe today he'd be nice to her. If not...by God, she'd make him as miserable as he was making her. Patting her hair at the back, smoothing down her skirts, she sailed out onto the porch.

"Oh," she said, feigning surprise, "I didn't

know you were here. Don't let me disturb you, just go on with what you were doing."

For one lovely, unwary moment, he smiled. Delighted, she started to smile back, but then he remembered himself—remembered he was a bastard—and his face shut down; it was exactly as if he'd seen a friend in the distance, gone closer, and realized it was nobody he knew after all.

Crestfallen, hating herself for it, Grace went to sit on the low stone wall, positioning herself so she could watch Reuben while she appeared to be looking out over the garden. Presently he went back to staring at the clay pot of pink geraniums on the top step, which she concluded must be his "subject" today. Ah You said you should focus your mind on something quiet and pleasing while you did the tai-chi-ch'uan, so your brain as well as your muscles could flow into a state of relaxation. Reuben closed his eyes and slowly turned his torso to the left, clenching his left hand at his waist while pushing his right hand out in front. Then the reverse, twisting slowly to the right, inhaling on the push-out, exhaling on the draw-back. The movement looked like "Thrusting Hands into Mount Hua" to her; either that or "An Immortal Pushes Over a Stone Tablet." He was wearing the linen shirt and brown cord trousers she'd gone into town to get for him over the weekend—now they'd *both* bought each other new clothes— and it was an illicit thrill to admire the way he looked in them openly instead of covertly for once, at least as long as he kept his eyes closed.

He was tall and strong, but not brawny or muscle-bound, and his strength was more wiry than brute. The tight new corduroys clung to his hips and his long, strong legs in a way that made it difficult to take her eyes off him. She watched his bare toes on the wooden porch floor as he slowly twisted and thrust, swayed and bent. The white shirt billowed loosely out of his unbelted trousers, drawing her eye to his flat belly and the neat line of buttons down his fly. He pivoted, and she feasted her eyes on his wide shoulders and handsome back, the high, hard curves of his buttocks. Sex was a paradox, she philosophized randily; having seen a man naked, she'd have thought a lady would be less interested in his body, her curiosity having been satisfied. Apparently it was just the opposite. Then too, she wasn't much of a lady.

The direction of her thoughts irritated her. "What's that," she asked for a distraction, " 'Grasp the Bird's Tail'?"

"Grace, you wound me. This is 'Wave Hands Like Clouds.' "

"Don't stop," she said quickly. "I'm sorry I disturbed you."

"No, I was finished."

"Oh." She felt disappointed; she'd been hoping he'd do "A Skilled Craftsman Uses His Drill."

She was afraid he would leave, but just then Ah You appeared, holding a tray with one cup and a small pot on it. Grace declined when he asked if she wanted some too, while he poured hot, steaming liquid into the cup.

"What is it?" Reuben asked suspiciously, peering.

"Tea, boss." Ah You addressed all white men as "boss"; it was simply a word, like "sir," and it might or might not connote respect, depending on his opinion of the person he was talking to.

"What kind of tea?"

"Tangerine and jujube. Make you gain weight. Also good for liver and muscle."

He took a cautious sip. "Mmm," he judged. "Not bad."

"Also phlegm and flatulence," Ah You added, and started waving a feather duster around the veranda furniture.

Reuben frowned down into his cup. "You mean it's good *for* phlegm and flatulence, or it's good for getting rid of them?"

Ah You put his finger on the side of his nose, thinking. "Question too tricky," he decided, tapping his skull with the finger. "Simple mind not understand."

Grace snorted.

To her amazement, Reuben sat down beside her on the railing. She could smell sun-warmed linen and clean sweat, and if she leaned closer, she could smell pine soap and bay rum—she'd bought them for him in town, too. Sometimes the intimacy of the things she knew about Reuben Jones scared her.

"So," said Ah You, still dusting. "You two meet Godfather in Fah-lan-sze-ko, hah?"

Reuben looked at her sharply, then at Ah You. "How do you know that?"

"He knows everything," Grace answered for him, unsurprised. "Have you been talking to Henry?" she asked the houseboy.

He gave a high, exaggerated shrug of his skinny shoulders.

"He's been talking to Henry," she confirmed positively. "What do you know about Wing, Ah You? Tell us whatever you told Henry."

"Don't know much," he said deprecatingly.

"We heard he's in exile for trying to overthrow the Manchus about twelve years ago," she prodded, to get him going. Why it hadn't once occurred to her to ask Ah You about Mark Wing was an embarrassing mystery; she guessed she'd had her mind on other things.

"Mark Wing not exile," he corrected, "he escape. Belong to White Lotus, ancient sect in Forbidden City—Peking. He try with friends to kill Kuang Hsu, Emperor. All caught but him, he run away. All executed, set on fire, turn into celestial lamps."

"Lovely. And now he lives in Chinatown."

"Just so. Very rich man, very bad. Rich from opium and whores and thieving. He say he go home with tong army someday, kill Emperor for good."

"Well, I for one," said Grace, "hope he goes soon."

"He never go. Too sick from smoke, too corrupt from money. All talk, no go. He try to be white man once, wear wool suit, hard shoes, cut hair. White men laugh, ha ha, big joke, make him crazy. Now he stay home, crazy crazy."

You don't know the half, she thought. Then again, he probably did.

"How do you know all this?" asked Reuben.

Ah You spread his hands. "How does deer in forest find green grass in winter? How does ant build city? How does wood thrush know storm is coming?"

Reuben stared at him, flummoxed.

The houseboy took the teacup out of his hand, humming approval when he saw it was empty. "Lunch today, make you turnip dumpling. Good comfort for internal organs." When he bowed, his long queue slipped over the shoulder of his red flannel shirt. He backed up, still bowing, then turned and padded into the house in silent cloth slippers.

Reuben said, "I can't figure him out," shifting on the railing to ease his hip.

"He doesn't want you to figure him out."

"You know what he said this morning? I couldn't find my handkerchief, I'd mislaid it, and he said, 'Look in nightshirt.' Sure enough, there it was in the pocket. 'How'd you know it was there?' I asked. Guess what he said."

"What?"

" 'Wind sough in pine tree same as willow, but one-eyed wolf still sleep soundly.' What the hell does that *mean*?"

"Nothing, I'm sure," Grace answered, laughing. "He loves to make up profound sayings that turn out to be gibberish. He drives Henry insane." Reuben smiled; that pleased him. "He likes you, though," she added.

"Who, Henry or—"

"Ah You. He didn't trust you at first, but now he does."

"How can you tell?"

"I can tell." He'd said so the night he'd given her a lecture on the necessity of male and female mating calls in song sparrows; the species would die out, he maintained, if either bird was too shy or too proud to let the other know it was interested in mating—all this in the halting Pidgin English he affected, of course, to make the moral sound more mystical and profound. But the message wasn't very subtle this time; he hadn't couched it in enough gibberish: he thought Grace had something important to say to Reuben, but she was too scared to say it. Which was absolutely ridiculous. She had *nothing* to say to him. If anybody had anything to say to anybody, it was Reuben who ought to be saying it to *her*.

"Where did Ah You come from, Grace?" he asked.

Why was he being so talkative? "I'm not really sure. He's been with Henry for years. I know he's got a lot of cousins in San Francisco, and I know he worked on the Pacific Railroad back in the seventies, but that's about all. He never talks about himself."

"He's very protective of you."

She nodded. Sometimes Ah You was down-

319

right maternal. She got up from the railing, surprised to see how high the sun had risen. "It's getting late—"

"Don't go yet."

She stilled, staring down at the hand Reuben had put over hers. A breathless moment passed, and then he let go. Her heart finally stopped hammering; she was able to look up at him with a pretense of calm. What she saw in his eyes only confused her more, though: it looked almost like tenderness. But how could it be? She licked her lips and asked as carelessly as she could, "Did you want to say something to me?"

His features seemed to sharpen; something significant happened behind his eyes, but for the life of her she couldn't put a name to it. In the end he said, "I—just wanted to ask you why it's failing."

"What?"

"The farm, why the farm is failing. It looks so fertile."

She followed his troubled gaze across the border of acacias and pepper trees to the sloping wheat fields in the distance, fallow this year, gently rising toward the unkempt orchard and the wild, uncultivated uplands beyond. "It's not Henry's fault," she said defensively.

He swung away from her. "I didn't say it was."

"It's just that he's not a farmer. I'm not either, I guess, although I haven't tried very hard to be one. I wish now I *had* tried," she said bitterly, "instead of getting involved in schemes."

He whirled back around, shocked. "You sound like a reforming character!"

"No, I'm not," she denied automatically. The very idea. "I'm *not*. All I know is, we're going to lose everything in a month unless we come up with...some money."

"How much money?"

She hesitated only a second, then confessed. "Five thousand, eight hundred dollars." Odd, considering what a scoundrel he was, that she felt relatively safe telling Reuben the details of her finances. She guessed it was only her heart she didn't trust him with.

He whistled.

"Henry had a scheme that took all our savings, and it fell through."

"What kind of scheme?"

"Fake mineral rights. It was complicated, I never really understood it. Anyway, now there's nothing left. This spring we had to let our last two farmhands go."

"What are you going to do?"

She looked away. "I don't know." The old depression threatened, but she rallied. "Henry will think of something. Whenever things look really bleak, that's when he comes up with his best schemes." She smiled determinedly. "It never fails. Henry always—"

"Shut up."

She blinked. "What?"

"Just *shut* the hell up."

She bristled like an angry cat. "What on earth is the—"

"What the hell kind of a woman are you?"

She began to sputter, completely bewildered. "What's *wrong* with you? Have you gone crazy?"

"Don't you have any conscience? Hell, of course you don't, what am I saying? But—Jesus Christ, Grace, doesn't *anything* mean anything to you?"

She hauled back to punch him, but he grabbed her loose, harmless fist and flung it sideways. With the most pained, most tortured look on his face, he jerked her to him in a steely, unbreakable embrace and kissed her. His body was hard and angry, his hands almost violent, until the moment when he sensed her perfect willingness. Then his mouth softened and his kiss turned unbearably gentle. He still had her arms pinned down, so all she could hold onto was his hips. A thought skittered through her addled brain—*This makes no sense whatsoever*—but she didn't let it distract her. All that mattered right now was Reuben's mouth, and his restless hands, and the lean, hard feel of his body against hers. Starving, weak with wanting, she took what he could give her, and gave him everything she had.

Even though she'd been half expecting it, she still gasped when he let her go, suddenly and not very gently, holding onto her arms but pushing her away from him. "What are you doing to me?" he had the gall to ask.

"What am *I*—"

"What kind of man do you think I am,

Grace?" He shook her—*shook* her—and demanded, "Do you think I'll *settle* for this?"

Gnashing her teeth, trying to strain out of his grip, she made an anguished sound in the back of her throat. Then the damn tears started, turning his face into a blur.

Immediately his hands softened. "Ah, Gus," he whispered, "don't do that."

Gus? He could call her *Gus* after what he'd done? The name nobody ever called her but him, the name that called to mind all the—the *sweetness* between them before he'd betrayed it because—because—she had no idea why!

"Don't call me that," she cried, and his arms fell away. "Don't ever call me that again or you'll be sorry." His face turned into a rigid mask; he made a grating sound that was supposed to be derisive laughter. No point in trying to hit him again; he was expecting it. "I don't understand you," she threw at him— her final insult. She backed away to the garden path, spun around, and ran.

15

Misery loves company, but company does not reciprocate.

          —Addison Mizner

Reuben stood planted in the middle of the sunny terrace, staring around with angry, jaundiced eyes at the weather-stained furniture and the great tubs of flowers and herbs. In his mind, he seized the nearest chair and smashed it against the stone railing, upsetting a giant pot of begonias. Clay shattered; black dirt scattered everywhere. He imagined grabbing another chair and battering it against the table until nothing was left but a stump of wood in his hand. He picked up the table next (an impossibility; it must weigh two hundred pounds) and heaved it through the closed glass doors to the living room. Crash! Glass everywhere, a million fragments glittering in the sunshine.

A miniature lemon tree sat in a tub on the terrace steps. He saw himself yanking it out by the roots, tramping inside, and smearing the ball of muddy dirt into the carpet with his bare feet. No, not his bare feet—there was broken glass everywhere. With his boots. Back outside, he dropped into one of the two remaining chairs and plunked his muddy boots down in the other. He was exhausted.

Imaginary mayhem was a trick he'd used to cope with frustration for years; since childhood, really. It always helped. It helped now—he didn't want to wring Grace's neck quite as much—but he wasn't cured. What he needed was a drink.

The house was dim and cool; the thick, glass-free carpet felt pleasant on his bare feet. A library table against the left-hand wall of the living room served as a liquor cabinet; he'd seen Henry mix himself plenty of drinks from it, but this would be the first alcohol that he, Reuben, had drunk since before his injury—Ah You's orders. Whiskey, rye, sherry, gin—aha, bourbon. He found a glass and poured himself a generous three fingers, ignoring the pitcher of water.

"Good God, man, it's ten o'clock in the morning! Pour me one, will you? No good to drink alone."

Reuben whirled, spilling bourbon on the floor. Henry sat with his feet up behind a cluttered desk in the far corner of the room, a pen in his hand, engaging grin on his handsome face. No disguise today; he wore a collarless pink shirt with the sleeves rolled up, navy striped trousers, and tartan plaid braces. Reuben peered at him for a long time, debating whether to make him a drink or challenge him to a duel. If he challenged him to a duel, he might choose swords. Splashing bourbon into another glass, Reuben marched over and smacked it down on Henry's desk.

"Thanks." Henry lifted his glass for a little

toast, but Reuben ignored the gesture and swallowed down a big slug of liquor, setting his throat on fire. When his eyes stopped watering, he saw a crafty look come over Henry's features. "Want to see something?"

He shrugged.

Henry took his feet off the desk, unlocked the kneehole drawer, removed a square tin box, and opened it. It was full of money.

Reuben went closer, sat down on the edge of the desk. "Well, now," he said cautiously.

Henry cackled. "Nice, huh? All tens. Four hundred of 'em. Here, have a feel."

Surprised, he took the bundle of bills Henry handed him. "Very nice," he said perfunctorily, and was about to hand it back when something about the heft of the bundle arrested him. Too light. He peeled off the top tenner and held it up to the window. A reluctant smile twitched at his lips. "Not enough cotton," he judged, squinting. "The inking's good, though. Nice seal work, nice corners. Who did it?"

Henry took the money back, a little peeved. "Fellow named Smith."

"Ah, Smith."

"It's not bad, though, for a first effort." He sounded defensive.

"Not bad at all. Grace know about this?" Reuben asked casually.

"Hell, no, and she'd kill me if she found out. This isn't her sort of thing. No, not her sort of thing at all."

"Why not?" he asked, but he hated hearing

Henry talk about Grace; hated the intimacy of the things Henry knew about her and he didn't.

"Too risky. Plus she's against anything that might involve the government. I try to tell her that's un-American, but she won't listen. Cigar? Why don't you sit down in a chair?"

Reuben hesitated, then took the proffered stogie. What was going on? Henry acted as if he wanted to be friends. Out of the question. Under different circumstances, maybe. Possibly. He wasn't all bad, after all; in fact, he had a few undeniably good qualities. Funny how, up to a point, Reuben felt most comfortable with people he couldn't trust. He knew where he stood with them, and they didn't excite any unrealistic expectations. Then again, he'd been attracted to Grace in the beginning for that very reason—that he couldn't trust her—and look where that had gotten him. Life was getting too damn complicated.

Two hours and four shots of bourbon later, life seemed a lot simpler. Take Henry, for example. True, he'd stolen Reuben's girl—sort of; actually, Reuben had stolen her from him before he'd stolen her back—but still, once you got to know him, Henry was a helluva fellow. He'd been employed in Reuben's line of work for better than thirty years, and he knew everything. He was a master, and Reuben, by contrast, was a journeyman apprentice, a mere acolyte. It was fascinating to sit, figuratively speaking, at the master's feet and listen to his rich confidence lore, stories of brilliant bunco successes interspersed with his philosophy on greed, gullibility, and the art of flimflammery. In a vague way, Reuben had always known that his life's work was an art, but somehow Henry raised it even higher than that to something mysterious and sublime, something...metaphysical. Then again, maybe it was the bourbon.

At noon, Reuben declined a sixth shot and suggested they have lunch. He'd been about equally hoping and dreading that Grace would join them; when she didn't, he couldn't decide if he was sorry or relieved. After the meal, the men returned to the living room, where Henry told Ah You they were out of bourbon and Reuben asked for a cup of coffee.

"You play cards?" Henry asked innocently.

He might be nursing a sleepy afternoon hangover, but Reuben wasn't so far gone that he couldn't recognize that tone of voice. Hadn't he used it often enough himself on a hundred greenhorn sheep? "Oh, a little," he answered, nonchalant.

The battle was on.

Henry's game was "Flinch," a form of liar's poker for two that Reuben knew by the name of "Bull's-eye." Same game, same exhilarating opportunities to cheat. Hand after hand they played to a draw, until Reuben's eyes started to cross. "How long have you known Grace?" he heard himself ask during a lull.

"Six years? Seven years? Something like that." Henry lit a cigar and blew smoke at the ceiling. The only sign that he'd drunk a pint and a half of liquor in three hours was a slight glassiness of the eyes; otherwise, he was unimpaired.

"So she was—?"

"Sixteen. And already pretty as a picture."

"But just a child," Reuben pointed out, scowling.

"Oh, I doubt if Grace was ever much of a child. Not the way she was raised."

"How was she raised?"

"Badly." Henry scowled back at him. "I hate to think what would've happened to her if I hadn't come along."

Reuben fired up his own cigar. "Don't you think you're a little old for her?" he asked bluntly.

"Old for her? Certainly not. We complement each other—my wisdom and her freshness. My experience, her nerve. My—"

"Got it." He slid lower, till the edge of the chair cut into his backbone. "You dealing or what?"

The afternoon wore on, with Reuben unable to summon the energy to get up and do something useful. Like what? The only useful thing he could think of would be to pack up and get out. He'd been here too long already. But this time he'd spent with Henry had accomplished one thing, at least: when he said goodbye to Grace, he'd say it without anger. Only sadness and regret. It wasn't her fault she was devoted to Henry. If there was blame anywhere, Reuben deserved it, for mistaking her open, affectionate nature for something deeper than friendship.

Then too, that extraordinary night at the Bunyon Arms had disoriented him, clouded his judgment. Grace had a free, clean, generous sexuality you didn't find in many women, but to read more into it than what it was only guaranteed misunderstanding. Out of the whole sorry mess, he could think of only one consolation: that he'd never said anything to her about how he felt. Anything of a personal nature, that was. So he could leave her with his pride intact. Bloody cold comfort.

"Hey, Grace, come and join us," Henry called out unexpectedly, causing Reuben to fluff a shuffle. "Where've you been all day?"

She stopped in the doorway, looking trapped; obviously she'd intended to sneak past unseen. "Around." Even from here, Reuben could tell she'd been crying. His chest tightened like a fist.

"Well, come on in," Henry boomed. "Come on, you weren't doing anything."

"I was going to help Ah You with dinner," she temporized.

"He doesn't need any help. Come on, we've never tried this game with a third."

She was about to refuse. Reuben saw it coming, and stood up. "Won't you join us?" he said formally, pulling out the chair between his and Henry's. "We'd both like it if you would."

She stared at him for a long, tense minute, scrutinizing his face, clearly trying to figure out what kind of mood he was in this time. *Don't worry*, he wished he could tell her, *you're safe;* her tragic, red-rimmed eyes had taken the last of the fight out of him. But he'd never intended to hurt her. Even at his angriest, he'd never intended that.

Grace continued to hang back, wondering what to do. Henry was beginning to look puzzled, and she had no wish to draw his attention to her problems with Reuben. Reuben looked...oh, who the hell knew how Reuben looked? *Sad,* she'd have said, if that weren't so outlandish. As if he'd lost something, and had no hope of getting it back.

"Grace?" he said quietly. Hopefully.

Disconcerted, she gave a careless shrug and came in.

The game was Flinch, and it took only a couple of hands to figure out that both men were cheating. The mood between them surprised her: she'd thought they didn't like each other, but here they were, chuckling at each other's jokes, interrupting each other's sentences. Once she'd hoped they could be friends, but it didn't matter much anymore. Now their jocularity just made her feel cold inside.

"Flinch," Reuben crowed, two tricks into the third hand.

Henry reached for his discard. "You crimped that deuce," he said admiringly, holding it up to the light.

Determined to join in, to sound lighthearted if it killed her, Grace heaved a humorous sigh. "I'd get a new deck, except it wouldn't make any difference. You two would have it defaced in ten minutes."

Henry looked flattered. "Look who's talking," he said proudly. "I taught her everything she knows."

"That's so?" Reuben said neutrally.

"Absolutely. You've seen her in action—isn't she something?"

"She's something." He started to smile at her, but she glanced away.

Henry tapped her wrist. "Did you tell him about the time you convinced half of San Francisco you were Andrew Carnegie's daughter?"

"No."

"We cleaned up on that one," Henry gloated. "She got loans so big you wouldn't believe it, on promissory notes with forged signatures. Offered the gulls twenty percent interest, see, and repaid the borrowings early to make sure they came back for more. She—"

"Flinch," she said loudly, plunking her cards down. "Tell him about the train you invented." She made herself look at Reuben directly. "It could do a mile a minute, and it ran on water."

Henry raked in the cards and started to shuffle. "Ah, that was a sweet one," he reminisced. "I called it the Silver Pronto. The shares went like hotcakes at ten bucks a pop. I had diagrams, photographs—I told 'em it had a 'vibratory generator with a hydro-pneumatic-pulsating vacue machine.' "

He and Reuben chortled, and Grace sat back, glad when the conversation shifted to swindles in general, not ones she'd participated in in particular. She listened with one ear while Henry bragged about his rash youth, when he'd sold fake death warrants for Salem witches to hobby collectors, bogus lottery tickets, nonexistent real estate, fake jewelry, phony stocks and bonds, windfall inheritances contingent on a small preliminary fee. The conversation turned philosophical, with the two men arguing over which human frailty benefited the confidence artist more, greed or vanity. "Every man I've ever swindled had larceny in his heart," Henry declared, "and the easiest sheep of all is the one who thinks he's helping you fleece somebody else."

"That's the truth," Reuben agreed heartily.

"People don't like to be fooled, but they dearly love to fool themselves. They don't even hear you when you start your patter. They go into a dream."

Reuben said, "That's it, that's right," in perfect understanding.

"And they dream of all the money they're going to make and how they're going to spend it, and they've signed on the dotted line before they come out of the dream."

"Right, exactly right."

She stopped listening, because the light brown hairs on Reuben's forearm had her complete attention. Nobody she knew slouched the way he did. He sat low on his long spine, dusty bare feet propped on the fourth chair,

333

sipping warm beer in his shirtsleeves. His cheroot had gone out, but he kept it clamped in his strong white teeth. There was something so neat and clean about him, and she thought it was partly the way his hair grew out at his temples and the back of his neck, some vigorous, youthful strength in his profile. The set of his shoulders excited her, and the way he held his cards near his chest, the arrogant curl of his nostrils when he was bluffing...

"Your *play*," Henry repeated.

She flushed, and drew a card.

Ah You poked his head in the door. "Missy Waters come in buggy, boss."

"Lucille?" Henry's face lit up. He threw his hand in and shoved back in his chair. "Well, this is a surprise!" he exclaimed, and hurried out into the hall.

Out of habit, Reuben checked Henry's cards. "Pair of jacks," he informed her. "Who's Missy Waters?"

"Mrs. Lucille Waters," Grace said tightly. "An old friend of the family." The day had started off badly; why shouldn't it go completely to hell?

Reuben was looking at her. She busied herself with shuffling the cards. She was a grown woman, too old by now and surely too mature to still be jealous of Lucille Waters just because she was perfect. But Henry was the only family Grace had, and for six years she'd lived in fear and dread that the beautiful, accomplished Lucille would take him away from her.

"She's a widow, she lives in town," she explained for Reuben's benefit, keeping her eyes on the cards. "She and Henry...keep company. She won't marry him till he gives up all his confidence games, and he won't marry her because he's not ready to go straight. It's a standoff." She looked up to see Reuben's arrested face slowly break into a smile, and then a delighted grin. "What?" she said. He looked as if he'd just won the lottery.

"You mean Henry—you and Henry—you—" Before he could get out whatever he was trying to say, Lucille and Henry swept into the room, arm in arm, beaming with goodwill. Grace stood up and greeted Lucille as civilly as she could, responding politely to the questions about her month-long stay with her "cousins in Santa Barbara" (the story Henry had cooked up to explain her absence while she was out soliciting for the Blessed Sisters of Hope). But it was no use: Lucille always made her feel like a surly child. Every time she came to visit, Grace saw herself regressing to her worst, her most immature Grace-ness, eventually retreating into total, puerile silence. It was nothing Lucille did on purpose; she was unfailingly kind and gracious, and patient even when Grace was rude to her, although she hadn't been openly rude in years.

It was just that she was so damn perfect. Watching her shake hands with Reuben, Grace noted sulkily how attractive she was, with her deep, stately bosom, the thick chestnut hair that was finally—thank *God*—starting to streak with gray, her handsome, smooth-skinned face, always alive with charm and intelligence. "Grace, you're looking so beautiful," she exclaimed, with every evidence of sincerity, taking the easy chair and reaching for the glass of sherry Ah You offered her, like a queen accepting her crown.

Grace ought to like her. How childish to hold back affection from such a paragon. But no matter how she tried, she couldn't seem to see Lucille as anything but a threat. Reuben would go away soon, she could feel it; Willow Pond, the only home she'd ever known, was as good as gone, forfeited to the creditors. She wanted Henry to be happy, to have his heart's desire, but—but—what would she have left if he abandoned her, too?

Dinner was an ordeal. Besides everything else, something was the matter with Reuben. "I have to talk to you," he muttered urgently, following her out of the living room when she excused herself to go help Ah You. All she needed was another traumatic encounter with him tonight. "No," she said tightly, "absolutely not," and pushed past him, leaving him stranded. At the table, he stared at her in the oddest way, not saying much, but laughing uproariously at anything anyone said that was even remotely funny. Was he drunk? He hardly touched his wine, or his food for that matter. His eyes had a strange, excited glitter; he looked wound up, ready to explode. He made her nervous.

Somehow she got through the meal without snapping anybody's head off. But she sagged with relief when Lucille said she couldn't stay for coffee, she had to get home before dark. They said good-bye in the hall, and Henry went outside with her to her pony gig. Grace turned away, and walked straight into Reuben.

"Can we talk now?"

"No!" She slid past him; he started to follow. Luckily Ah You came through just then with an armload of dishes. She snatched a stack of plates out of his hands—"Here, let me help you"—and sailed down the hall ahead of him, heading for the kitchen.

She stayed there as long as she could, cleaning and washing, lavishing muscular energy on the grease-spattered stove. Ah You watched her in wise, knowing silence, which didn't improve her mood. When he finally spoke, to say, "Lady redwing who wake up to find new wife in nest should never—"

"Don't start!" she cried imperiously. "Not one word!"

He made her a low bow full of mock deference, and handed her the coffee tray to take up to Henry and Reuben; they were in the parlor, he told her, reading the afternoon newspaper Missy Waters had graciously thought to bring with her.

That proved to be only half true. Henry was reading, but Reuben was pacing. He looked like a big cat in a zoo, caged and restless, ready to leap over the fence. She handed him his coffee charily, afraid to get too near.

"Want to go for a walk with me, Grace?" he asked, smiling tensely.

"No." What now? Was it a *campaign* to drive her mad?

"Why don't you, Grace?" Henry asked without looking up. "Do you good. There's going to be a full moon, it's a nice—"

"Because I don't want to!"

He lifted his head, startled by her tone.

"I'm—it's—I've got a headache," she said lamely. "Excuse me, I still have chores." Without looking at either of them, she escaped again and went back downstairs, to scrub the pot she'd just told Ah You to soak overnight.

She couldn't believe it when Reuben followed her. She thought the footsteps on the stairs were Ah You's until a low, tentative voice said, "Hi," from the doorway, and she whipped around, hands dripping soapsuds, and saw Reuben. "Oh, God," she groaned, and took two steps sideways.

"Wait, Grace. You're not scared of me, are you?"

That did it. Knees locked, back braced against the spice cabinet, she prepared for battle. "Scared of you? Scared of *you*? You miserable— There's only one thing I want from you, Reuben Jones, and that's for you to go away and leave me alone!"

He came closer.

"Don't! Don't, I can't stand this anymore. No, don't you *dare* touch me—"

"Grace—"

"Stop it, I mean it. If you think you can sweet-talk me, kiss me, and then turn around and tell me I've got no conscience—"

338

"That was before—"

"I've got a conscience! It's telling me to stay away from maniacs like you."

"*Listen.* Would you be quiet and listen to me for one minute?"

"No, I won't. You're not the man I thought you were—"

"I know I've been—"

"—and I can't stand how you treat me, Reuben. It's not fair and I don't deserve it. I've never been anything but straight with you—"

"Gus—"

"Don't call me that! If you're finished with me because you've—you've had your fun with me, or you can't *use* me anymore to—"

"Shit!"

"—get *rich* somehow, the decent thing to do would be to just go away, not hang around thinking up new ways to torment me." She snatched the handkerchief he handed her and batted at her eyes. "Why are you touching me?"

"Shhh."

"I never cry," she snuffled, heartbroken. "If you'd go away, I wouldn't have to."

"Are you through yet?" He had her in a loose, perversely comforting embrace, softly rubbing her shoulders.

She heaved a wavery sigh. "I suppose."

"You mean I can talk now?"

She glared at him through wet lashes. "Who's stopping you?"

He opened his mouth to speak, but then he closed it. All of a sudden he looked uncertain, not urgent. "There's a reason why I've been a little difficult these—"

"Difficult?"

"Why I've been a bit of a...a bit of a..."

"Prick?" She made a face and put her hand over her lips. "Wash my mouth out with soap," she muttered bitterly.

"Why I've been somewhat out of sorts—"

"Out of—"

"Okay! Okay! Why I've been a complete horse's ass since I got here!"

She scowled up at him, satisfied. "Well, that's a start. Let's hear the reason."

"The fact is I've been...I was, um..."

"Yes?"

He muttered something that sounded like "jels."

"Pardon me? You were what?" His lean cheeks went faintly bronze; he couldn't meet her eyes. "Jealous?" she guessed, incredulous.

"Yeah."

"Jealous?"

"I *said* jealous."

"Of what?"

"Of Henry. You and Henry."

She stared at him, unable to speak. Then a laugh bubbled up, a helpless, giddy giggle that made him blush even harder. She pressed her hand to her heart, which was thumping wildly. "You were jealous of Henry? Of me and Henry? Oh, *Reuben.*"

He grimaced. "Well, hell, Grace, you told me he was your husband, and then you said he was your lover—"

"I did not, I *never* said he was my lover!"

"The hell you didn't. You said you lived with him—"

"I do live with him! He's my uncle."

"Your uncle!"

"Well, not really my uncle, not technically—"

"Hah!"

"Hah! What does that mean?"

His frowning face suddenly cleared. "Nothing. It doesn't mean a damn thing." He scooped her up and hugged her, laughing, and she could feel the same gladness and relief in him that were streaming through her.

"You were jealous," she whispered, awed, running a line of soft kisses across his lips from cheek to cheek. "You must be crazy about me."

"I must be crazy." He looked serious. She thought of taking offense, but then he caught her up again and covered her mouth with a rough, passionate, unconsidered kiss. Her mind flew off; lighter than air, her body almost followed, but Reuben's strong arms anchored her. Jealous, she thought dizzily; oh, God, he'd been jealous. Hands down, it was the nicest thing that had ever happened to her.

"Lord, you smell good," he told her, nuzzling behind her ear. "I missed you like hell, Gus."

Her heart skipped two consecutive beats. "I missed you. It was awful, Reuben, not knowing why you were so angry with me."

"I'm sorry. I couldn't see straight. All I

knew was that I wasn't going to share you with some old man."

"Henry's not old." She laughed at his expression. "And now you don't have to share me with anybody." *Because I'm all yours.* But she didn't say that out loud.

She loved the rough texture of his shirt under her hands, but she wanted more: she wanted bare skin. Frustrated, she found his mouth and kissed him deeply, and they held each other's face with the same fierce, possessive tenderness. Another admission, a joyful, searing truth was on the tip of her tongue— but caution, or maybe cowardice, kept her from saying it. Anyway, she forgot it when Reuben wrapped his arms around her and lifted her up, pivoted, and set her down on top of the kitchen table.

She felt her own cheeks redden; her eyes went wide with excitement. He was watching her while he put his big hands on her knees and pulled her thighs apart. She gasped, and he stepped into the V of her legs. "Holy saints," she breathed. "Oh, my, my. Reuben, what you do to me." She had her eyes closed and she was humming with pleasure, her feet hooked around his calves, running her hands up and down his ribs. But the humming broke off when she felt him pulling her skirts up over her knees. "Uh-oh. Wait now. No, we can't do this, absolutely not. Are you crazy?"

"Yeah. Simple as that, I am completely crazy. Look at your legs, Gus. Holy—what is it?"

"Saints—Reuben, we're in the *kitchen*."

"So?" His hopeful smile turned her muscles to jelly. "Think of all the time we've been wasting," he coaxed.

"Yeah, but we can't—"

"Why not?"

She forgot.

He pressed closer, sliding his hands up the sides of her thighs, above her stockings, until he had her petticoats up to her waist. A lot of feeble, insincere arguments for why this wasn't a good idea came and went through what remained of her mind, but when Reuben kissed her they all skulked away, whipped, their tails between their legs. He caressed her with his magic hands, and crooned to her, "It's all right, Gracie, it's all right," and they were really going to do it, "it's all right, Gracie," and her fingers were fumbling at the buttons on his trousers—

And then Henry called them.

"Grace? Reuben? Where the devil are you?"

Luckily they were kissing; otherwise Henry might've heard her scream.

"Come to my room tonight," Reuben commanded, holding her still when she tried to jump down off the table.

"Oh, God. I want to—but I can't!"

"Yes, you can."

"No, I can't. Not in the house. I don't know why, I just can't, I can't." Never mind that she'd just been about to make use of the kitchen table. She had her wits back now.

"Grace?" Henry hollered. "You down in the kitchen?"

"Tomorrow," she blurted. "I know a place outside—it's not too far." A terrible thought struck. "You can walk, can't you?"

He sent her a look that made her laugh. "If not, I'll crawl."

"I'll carry you."

"*Tomorrow*, Grace," he promised grimly.

Footsteps on the stairs.

He picked her up and set her on the floor. They kissed, both red-faced and shiny-eyed. "Tomorrow," she repeated, breathless. "I can hardly—"

"Here you are. Didn't you hear me?"

They made ambiguous noises.

"Look, I've found it!" he exclaimed, shaking the newspaper at them.

"What?"

"The hook, what we've been looking for! It's right here on the front page."

Grace took the paper from him, and she and Reuben read the headline he thumped with his finger. "Nineteen Years after Enactment," it said, "Burlingame Treaty Finally Enforced." They looked up, uncomprehending.

"Here," he said emphatically, whacking the paper a good one.

" 'Under the treaty's provisions,' " Grace read aloud from the third paragraph, " 'it is now unlawful for any Chinese resident of the United States or American resident of China to import opium into this country.' " She skimmed the rest in silence, still mystified. The new law, which was really an old law that had never been implemented, prohibited the importation of smoking opium—that containing less than nine percent morphine—altogether, and limited the import of other kinds of opium to American pharmaceutical companies and other legitimate medical concerns.

"Don't you get it?" cried Henry. "Wing's supply is cut off. If he wants to stay in business, he's going to need some help from the white devils."

Understanding dawned. "Medical white devils," Grace realized. "A doctor!"

Reuben's smile stretched wide as a mile. "And I know just the man."

16

Truth is ever incoherent, and when the big hearts strike together, the concussion is a little stunning.

—Herman Melville

"I can't believe you forgot our date."

"Hm?" sounded from a far-off corner of the wine cellar.

"What in the world are you doing?" Grace hung her lantern on a hook in the wooden post holding up the crossbeam overhead, and hugged her arms. It was chilly down here after the hot noon sun. She took off her floppy straw hat and moved toward the glow of the oil lamp Reuben was holding at head height while he peered into nooks and crevices. "What are you doing?" she repeated when he didn't pay any attention to her.

"Ah You told me about this," he answered finally, gesturing around the dusty, echoing cellar. "Do you know what you've got here?"

She glanced around. "Old wine-making stuff?" He made a face. "Well, isn't it?"

"Yeah, but that's such a... I mean, what a... *Look* at this."

She went closer, in case she was missing something. "A stack of old casks?" she guessed, more tentatively.

"Four-foot white oak puncheons coopered in Germany," he informed her, with poorly disguised amazement at her ignorance. "And this is a basket press, one of the biggest I've ever seen, and these are pupitres for holding the bottles at an angle. And it's all just—*sitting* here, molding and rusting and mildewing."

"Well, I told you Willow Pond was a vineyard before it was a farm," she reminded him.

"When did it stop being a vineyard?"

"When my stepparents bought it. They thought wine-making was a sin."

He muttered something unkind and resumed prowling around the cellar, looking for more treasures. "Look at these walls," he said, smacking his hand against the one in front of him. "Know what they're made of?"

She'd learned her lesson: she didn't guess,

"damp, dirty old stone?" She just shook her head and waited for enlightenment.

"Limestone. A hundred years ago somebody—monks, probably—carved these cellars out of the living rock. The temperature down here doesn't vary all year by more than about two degrees."

She made an impressed sound. "Would you like to see what's left of the vineyard?"

He whirled around so fast his lantern nearly went out. "You mean you've still got *vines*?"

She nodded. "Up on the hillsides, above our part of the valley. Want to see?"

"Yes," he said, with enough subdued fervor to tell her it was an understatement.

"I could be mad at you, you know," she said, catching his hand and leading the way out of the cellar. "You said you'd meet me on the terrace at noon for our, heh-heh, *walk*."

"I didn't forget," he grinned. "How could I? I just got distracted."

"Oh, now I feel better. I guess I'll have to keep you away from old limestone walls if I want your undivided attention."

He grabbed her around the waist and kissed her, holding her a foot off the ground. He let her down slowly, so their bodies slid against each other with maximum contact. By the time her toes touched the grass, she wanted to keep sinking lower and lower, and lie down with him right here behind the hollyhocks. He smiled, reading her mind. "Show me the vines," he ordered, murmuring it against her lips. "I'm dying to see the vines."

"You're a very peculiar person, Jones."

"Show me the vines."

So she took him to see the scraggly, wasted remains of the hilly wine fields, where the old grapevines ran wild through thimbleberries and manzanita and thorny chaparral. He called them "Mission-Monica" vines, and swore some more when she told him there had been others, on the flatter fields below, but her stepfather had plowed them under to plant wheat. She couldn't understand his dismay, his near-violent disappointment over the fate of the vineyard; he seemed to take the whole thing personally. "What difference does it make?" she dared to ask. "The soil here is terrible—look at it. Nothing much could grow in these foothills, Reuben. Even the valley is too dry for wheat most years—"

" 'Bacchus loves the hillsides,' " she thought he said, squatting in the weeds and sniffing at the two dead ends of a dried-up vine he'd broken in half.

"What?"

"That's Virgil. You're right about the soil, Grace, it isn't very fertile. But it's got exactly the right minerals for grapes. The best vines in the world grow on flinty hillsides just like this."

"But—"

"And these Mission vines make lousy wine, good for slugging down at Mass and that's about it. But they're strong and sturdy and they never get sick. If you grafted these hardy Papist vines onto the best European *vinifera*, the Pinots of Burgundy and Champagne or the Cabernets of Bordeaux—my God, you'd have poetry in a bottle."

What was it about listening to Reuben talk about grapes and wine that thrilled her so? His handsome face turned serious, his voice became low and intense. The purity of his obsession excited her in the oddest way, for no logical reason she could think of.

"How do you know so much about wine?" she asked him. "And grapes and soil and everything."

He stood up, slapping the dirt from his hands. "It's just a hobby," he answered rather brusquely. "Every man's got a hobby. Wine's mine."

They walked back down the stony track to the green valley floor holding hands. It was a bright, hot day full of golden sun, the kind of day she'd missed during her week and a half in cold, foggy San Francisco. She asked Reuben if he wanted to see why the farm was called Willow Pond, and took him to the prettiest spot, to her mind, on all of the two hundred acres she owned. It was the dry season, so the creek that fed the little pond was only a rocky trickle meandering through mosses and ferns and clumps of green azalea. But the willows still shadowed the shallow banks and bent over the quiet blue water like graceful mothers tending their children.

"Willows were my favorite trees when I was little," she told Reuben, "because they were the easiest to climb."

"Were you a tomboy?"

"No, not really. I wanted to be, but I wasn't allowed. I wasn't allowed to do much of anything, to tell you the truth. What was it like growing up in the South, on a plantation and everything?"

"Oh, you know. Cotton and tobacco," he said vaguely. "White pillars, black folks singing. Women in crinolines." He put his hands in his pockets and started to walk back across the wildflower meadow. She watched him for a second, then followed.

She slipped her arm through his, and thought of a question he wouldn't mind answering. "Do you really think Doc Slaughter will come in with us?"

"Well, we'll soon find out," he said readily, "but I'm betting he will. It'll be risky for him, but I think he'll like the odds. I've never known Doc to turn his back on a main chance."

"Why didn't you tell me he was a real doctor?" Reuben shrugged, and she thought of what he'd told her and Henry last night—that a coal-stove accident twelve years ago had scarred Doc's face so badly he'd lost all his patients. So he'd turned to his second love, antiques and curios; but he'd turned to alcohol, too, and eventually he'd fallen into the demi-world of fencing and forgery. He still kept his medical diploma on the wall of his shop, for a joke. A sad joke, Grace thought.

"If he does agree to help," she said, "I guess we'll all be going to San Francisco in a few days. I wonder where we'll stay. Henry and

I used to stay at the Palace, but now that he's—"

"Hold it," Reuben cut in, coming to a halt in mid-field. "What are you talking about, Gus? Why do you think *you're* coming?" She looked blank. "Not that I wouldn't love to have you, honey, just you and me at the Palace Hotel—wouldn't it be great? But the thing is, there won't be anything for you to do. And if things get sticky, the farther away you are from Wing—"

He stopped when she laughed at him. "Are you out of your mind? Of course I'm coming! And Henry, and Ah You."

"What?"

"Well, what did you think? That Henry would let you out of his sight while a great money-making scheme, which *he* thought up, was going on? He likes you, Reuben, but frankly, he wouldn't trust you as far as the front gate."

"I'm offended," he said after a startled pause. She shook her head at him. "What about you?" he asked. "How far would you trust me?"

She laughed again. "With my money? Forget the gate. Not past the front steps." He smiled back rather weakly; he couldn't tell if she was serious or not. The hell of it was, she didn't know either.

They started walking again. "If this trick works and you get rich," she mused, "do you still plan to just sit around in your ranchero with your feet up, watching other people do all the work?"

"Sure." But he said it listlessly, she thought. "Why not?"

After a moment, she said with great nonchalance, "With a wife by your side, no doubt."

He seemed to consider it seriously. "Maybe a wife," he conceded. "And definitely kids. I've always liked kids. What'll you do with your money, Grace? After you pay off the bank and the tax man."

"Try to be a farmer, I guess," she said, dejected. "Plant raisin grapes and wheat, maybe try corn again."

"Raisin grapes?" He grimaced. "That's disgusting."

"Well, I don't know anything about wine," she said a little too loudly. "You're the one who knows about wine, Reuben, not me." She was intensely aware of the implications teeming under the surface of this conversation. Because he was a smart man, she could only assume that he was, too. But they didn't look at each other, and a silence ensued, and she thought he was letting the subject drop until he spoke again.

"You're the one who'll get married soon," he said lightly.

"What makes you think so?"

"You're the marrying kind. I see you with a loving husband, a big lumbering sort of fellow, a little simple in the head but with a heart of gold. Doting on you. And a passel of kids running around all over the place."

Her smile faded. "I want to show you something," she murmured. "It's not far."

It was just over the hill, hidden from the house and the fields by a grove of oaks, low-branching and far-spreading, silent and lovely, guarding the tombstones at their feet like faithful soldiers. The weather-stained picket fence around the tiny graveyard was sagging and gap-toothed; it couldn't last much longer. Good: she'd never liked it anyway. Her stepparents had built it long ago, preparing early for the day of salvation. It suited them—straight, sharp, restrictive, confining. They lay within its four sides now, at peace for eternity. But another soul rested here too, and for her Grace wanted space and freedom and no boundaries. The fence couldn't rot soon enough.

Reuben's hard arm came up around her shoulders, as if he sensed her sadness. "These are my stepparents' graves," she told him. "Claude and Marie Russell."

"Russell," he repeated, squinting at the dates chiseled into the stones. "Not Rousselot."

"It used to be Rousselot; they changed it when they came here from Canada."

The third gravestone was smaller, and as far away from the other two as the small space allowed. Grace knelt in front of it and rearranged the little bouquet of wildflowers, wilted now, that she'd laid here yesterday. *Baby Girl Russell*, the stone read. *March 12, 1881.*

"Who is it?" Reuben asked softly, coming to his knees beside her.

"My baby. She died so soon, before I could name her. But I got to hold her for a minute."

He took her hat off so he could see her face. She reached for his hand and whispered, "Now I can't have any more children. The doctor said so."

"Ah, Gracie." He put his arms around her, even though she wasn't crying. His sadness for her hurt her heart, and comforted her at the same time. "Poor Gracie," he whispered, rubbing her back like a father.

She lifted her head from his shoulder. "Can I tell you about myself, Reuben?"

His stroking hand stilled; he tried to hide it, but she saw the flash of shock in his eyes. "You mean—the truth?"

She nodded, and waited, in complete sympathy with his alarm. The truth was something they hadn't overburdened each other with before.

Finally he took a steadying breath and said, "All right. Yes. You can tell me."

There was a low, semicircular bench around the base of one of the oak trees, a little distance away from the graveyard. They sat there beside each other, not touching, listening to a mockingbird's cheerful gurgling overhead, while Grace readied herself for the extraordinary task of telling Reuben the truth.

"I was born in St. Louis," she began, because telling where you were born seemed like a logical place to start. "I don't know anything about my father, but my mother was French and she was an entertainer. That is—" She stopped, stymied already. This was supposed to be the truth. "She danced and sang, I know

354

that; what else she might've done to make a living, I'm too young—I mean I was too young—to know. Her name was Lili Dushane. Maybe." She tried to laugh. "Can you imagine having a mother named Lili Dushane?" Reuben smiled, and she took heart.

"All my earliest memories are of train rides and hotel rooms and men, and the sound of my mother laughing. The later memories... there's less laughter. More men. Seedier hotel rooms and the smell of gin. When I was ten, a Catholic social-worker lady came to our hotel in Sacramento and talked to my mother for a long time. After she left, Mama cried all night. The next day, the lady came back and explained to me how I was going to go live with a real family, and it would be wonderful—I'd have a daddy and schoolmates, a beautiful house on a farm with animals, and no more moving. And Mama said she'd come and see me so often, I wouldn't even miss her.

"So I came to Willow Pond to live with the Russells, and I never saw my mother again."

Reuben put his fingers on top of hers, on the space of bench between them. She turned her hand over, so they could be palm-to-palm.

"My stepparents were very strict, very religious. For the life of me, I couldn't figure out why they wanted me. They didn't seem to like me, much less love me. I don't think they even liked each other. They were French Canadian Catholics. They kept me out of school because it was an occasion of sin, and my stepmother

355

taught me prayers and the catechism at home. That's just about all the education I've got," she said bitterly. "It's a damn miracle I can even read." It still made her angry.

"All through my adolescence, I saw my mother's abandonment as a trick, something she'd done on purpose because she didn't love me, or just to be mean. But when I got older, I started to be able to—to conceive of the *possibility* that something had happened to her, that she'd died, or gotten too sick from drink and excess to be able to act responsibly. Now I really think that's what must've happened, and I've forgiven her. But when I was growing up, all I knew was that she'd thrown me away and never looked back. So I rebelled against my stepparents. We fought constantly. I made it my life's work to do everything they didn't want me to do."

"And then along came Joe," Reuben guessed.

She smiled. He'd put his elbow on the back of the bench and twisted around to watch her while she talked. He looked fascinated. "Along came Joe," she agreed. "I thought he was so good-looking. But he could've looked like Quasimodo and it wouldn't have mattered, because he had one quality that was absolutely irresistible to me: he was forbidden.

"And we really did love each other. Those two months we had together were the happiest days of my life. We'd meet everywhere, as often as we could, we couldn't keep our—" She trailed off. "Well. Anyway. It was sweet and innocent, and I thought it was beautiful."

"Did he really fall off the rose trellis and break his neck?"

"Yes, he did. I know—it's so crazy, it sounds like something I'd make up, but it really happened that way. After he died, and the truth came out, my stepfather locked me in my room. They passed meals to me through a crack in the door, and they even boarded up my window so I couldn't climb out. It went on for weeks. Literally, *weeks*. And all that time, I was living for just one thing: to see the look on their faces when they let me out and I told them I was pregnant."

She stood up, and looked out past the picket fence and the graves to the low hills rising in the sunny distance. "Well, it was nice while it lasted, but that little victory was over very quickly. Guess where they sent me."

Reuben's face was a study. "Don't tell me a convent."

"You guessed. Yes, a convent! In the Sierras. I couldn't believe it, either. And 'Blessed Sisters of Misery' would've been a good name for those nuns, believe me. They treated me just like the sinner they thought I was, so much for Christian charity. They kept telling me I'd have to give up the baby as soon as it was born—which, of course, only made me even more determined to keep it. Somehow. When I was seven months pregnant—"

"You were sixteen?"

"Sixteen. When I was seven months gone, the Mother Superior came to tell me my stepparents had died. On a pilgrimage to Los

Angeles, to see a little Mexican girl who had the stigmata and who claimed she'd been visited by the Blessed Virgin."

"Hmm, this has a familiar ring."

"The steamboat they were on blew up, and every pilgrim on board was either killed or drowned."

"Well, at least they all went to heaven." He winked at her.

"A few days later Henry showed up."

"At the convent?"

"Yes. He was my stepfather's black-sheep brother—so you see, Reuben, he is sort of an uncle. His name was hardly ever mentioned at home; all I knew was that he was a terrible sinner. Naturally I took to him immediately."

"Naturally."

"He got me out of the convent and brought me back to Willow Pond, which I'd inherited. We became best friends. He was kind, funny, affectionate, and best of all, *normal*. I don't know what I'd have done without him when the baby died."

She caught a fleeting look of skepticism on Reuben's face before he could hide it. "Oh, I know what you're thinking. That he was using me, at least for free room and board, and then anything else he could think of."

"No, no, I—"

"It's all right, the thought's occurred to me too by now. But even if it was true then, it's not anymore. That's all in the past, completely irrelevant."

He stood up and came to her. "I've seen him with you, Grace. You don't have to convince me that Henry loves you."

She wound her arms around him and squeezed. They stood together quietly, not talking, just holding each other. In that moment she knew she loved him, and that she probably couldn't have him. But she had him now. So she would make the most of it.

She smiled up at him, blinking away a secret tear. "Come on, I want to show you a special place." He groaned piteously. "No, it's the last place, and I promise you'll like it."

It wasn't far, and when they reached the spot, she could tell by his face that he liked it. "This was my church," she announced, spreading her arms. "My chapel in the woods." All it was was a little clearing in the trees on the side of the mountain that bordered the western fields. Only a clearing, but the soft, grassy slope was flecked with mock-heather and violets, and overhead the tall pines and buckeyes and fluttering maple trees made a perfect lace canopy, as lovely as any cathedral ceiling. "I called it the Church of the Damned Sinner. I was the only member of the congregation. Also the priest."

Reuben laughed. "I love it. But just tell me one thing, Gus—that you never came here with Joe."

"Never. Only with you." They stared at each other until he reached for her, but she slipped out of his hands and sat down on the green grass. "I haven't finished telling you my life story." She tugged on his trouser cuff until he dropped down beside her, sighing philosophically. "Where was I?"

"Henry," he answered, moving closer and rearranging a loose strand of hair behind her ear. "How long did it take you to figure out he had another occupation besides farming?"

"Not long. But he didn't try very hard to hide it. And after the shock wore off, I was delighted. Well, it was illicit, illegal, probably even sinful—I was all for it! Before I turned eighteen, I became his confederate."

"What else did you do besides impersonate Andrew Carnegie's daughter?"

She closed her eyes; he'd started to kiss the back of her neck. "My favorite was when we pretended to be French aristocrats, father and daughter, in this country for a visit. In two weeks, we convinced the richest families in Sacramento to invest in the 'Comte de Villefort's' new wine-making process, which he'd recently perfected at his château in the Loire." Reuben chuckled; his breath tickled her ear and made her shiver. And he was running his fingers along her backbone, slowly, up and down. "The hardest part was keeping a straight face when Henry would try to speak French. *I* can speak French—my stepparents spoke it at home—but he can't; he left Quebec when he was a boy and forgot everything. So he'd make words up, just gibberish that sort of sounded French—worse than his German—and everybody believed it. Thank God we never met any real Frenchmen."

Now he was doing something to the front of her dress. Unbuttoning it, if she wasn't mistaken. She didn't think the story of her life had his complete attention anymore. "But then you fell on hard times," he prodded, hurrying it along.

"Then we fell on hard times. It started when they banished him from San Francisco."

"Who did?"

"Businessmen, city-father types. They didn't like it when the silver mine he'd tricked them into investing in turned out to be nonexistent. But they were too embarrassed to prosecute, so they just banished him." Her pulse was jumping, her mind starting to cloud at the edges.

"How could they 'banish' him?"

"They just did. They threatened him. They're like the Croakers, only they work in city hall." Reuben's fingers began to play a game with the sensitive skin in the hollow between her breasts. "So anyway," she resumed, eyes squeezed shut so she could concentrate, "that's when things started to go downhill. He wasn't allowed into the big action in the city anymore, so his schemes became more and more small-time. I knew we'd hit bottom when I caught him planning to bilk the life savings out of consumptive invalids in a sanatorium in Santa Barbara. Well, I mean, you have to draw the line somewhere. That's when I decided to take matters into my own hands. I became Sister Mary Augustine."

"And a beautiful nun you were. Especially

after you got out of the habit." In one smooth move, he had her flat on her back, with him on top.

"Reuben, wait—" He'd grown more hands, and they were all diligently going about their one job, which was to get her out of her clothes. "Wait, Reuben," she said again, as ineffectively as the first time. "Stop! We can't do this."

"Why not?"

"Because it's your turn!"

Now he was using his teeth as well as his hands to get out the knot he'd made in the ties of her chemise. He lifted his head. "My churn to what?" He frowned, a lace sticking out of his mouth like a noodle.

"I want to hear about you—*your* life! The truth, Reuben. It's only fair."

He spat the lace out and sat back, incredulous. "Wait a second. Are you making it a condition?"

She thought about it. "Yes," she said boldly.

His lip curled in a sexy snarl. "I don't like conditions." Before she could stop him, he took her by the shoulders and pushed her gently back to the ground. While he kissed her, he moved his bent knee across her legs, a maneuver that held her down and dragged her skirts up around her thighs at the same time.

Everything changed. His life story could wait. She let him know, with her pliant lips and her eager tongue, that she was willing—so he'd untrap her clenched fists between them and let her touch him. When he did, she slipped her hands across the bunched muscles of his back and down inside the waist of his trousers, searching for skin. She found it, and used her nails on his hard buttocks to make him growl. The brilliant blue of the sky through the tree leaves dazzled her eyes; she closed them, and a raspy cricket opera assailed her ears. The soft, bruised grass under her body smelled wild and sweet—like Reuben. They kissed some more, and then she sat up, shaky fingers untangling the fine mess he'd made of her laces. She got everything untied and shrugged her shift over her shoulders half a second before he pressed her down again and fastened his mouth on her left breast.

"Ah, ahh—" She clenched her teeth to keep from yelling, while the fiery nerve path from her nipple to her vitals sparked like a lit fuse. Opening her legs, she let him press the place where he was hardest of all against her. She put her heels on the backs of his knees and arched up. "Reuben," she cried, "Reuben—"

The delicious scraping pain of his whiskers on her chest stopped all of a sudden. He made a terrible groaning noise, full of ruined hopes and frustration. "Okay, okay," he said nasally, his nose still mashed between her breasts. "Goddamn it to hell, I'll tell you."

Now she did yell. "What? What?" Fresh air hit her where his nose had been. "I'll kill you! Reuben? Don't stop *now*—"

He was sitting up with his head in his hands, scrubbing his scalp with his fingers. "You want to know the truth about me? Okay, I'll give it to you."

"Oh, no," she wailed. "Now?"

"Now. But cover yourself up, Gus. Jeesus Christ."

"Cover myself up," she muttered, teeth bared, sitting up and sticking her hands into the two tawdry-looking halves of her chemise. "Who got me this way?" she asked in a high quaver, shaking inside like aspen leaves.

"Do you want to hear this or not?"

She flopped back down and crossed her arms over her middle. "I'm all ears. Hit me."

17

When in doubt, tell the truth.

—Mark Twain

"First of all, my name isn't Reuben Jones." Grace covered her eyes with her hands and moaned. "I changed my mind, I don't want to hear this."

"Too late. You asked for it."

"Just tell me you're not married and you don't have six children."

"Will you be serious?"

"I'm deadly serious. All right, all right. Tell me your real name."

He brought one knee up and wound his arms around it, staring down at the different impressions the heel of his shoe could make in the soft grass.

"I'm waiting," said Grace. She still had her hands over her eyes.

He plucked three pieces of clover and plaited them together, admiring the tightness of the weave. He watched a bumblebee on a head of clover nearby, gorging itself.

"Still waiting."

It shouldn't be this hard; it wasn't as if he were a pederast or something. "I'm—" He had to clear his throat; it felt rusty, as if he'd been on a desert island for twenty years and Grace was the first person he'd talked to. "I wasn't born in Virginia and my father wasn't a Confederate colonel named Beauregard. He was a tenant farmer in the Ukraine named Morris. That's where I was born. My name is Jonah Rubinsky. I'm Jewish."

He hadn't expected laughter. "You're *Jewish?*" she chortled, sitting up to stare at him, her face full of equal parts amazement and amusement.

"Half Jewish," he corrected. "My mother was a gypsy."

Her laughter broke off. "Damn it, Reuben! That's not fair, you said you'd tell the truth!"

"This *is* the truth. Will you keep quiet and listen? I was conceived one night in a tent, after my mother told my father his fortune. He only saw her once more after that, the day she brought him his new infant son and gave him to him. Gave *me* to him."

"I thought gypsies *stole* children," she said suspiciously.

"She was dying. She told him she didn't want her son to be a gypsy and die young."

Her face softened. "What was her name?"

"Bella. Isabella, maybe, I don't know. My father never even knew her last name. I grew up in Kalus—that's a small town in Podolia Gubornia. My grandfather, Aaron Rubinsky, leased vineyard lands from a Polish high *mache*—man of substance—and sold the grapes to a vintner in Letichev. We weren't rich, but we were better off than most of the Christian peasants in the village. I was a normal kid, I was—happy. My favorite pastime was following my grandfather around in the fields, watching him work. He had huge hands, but he was as dainty with a grafting knife as a surgeon."

He lay down on one elbow, and Grace moved closer and stretched out beside him. "So that's how you know so much about grapes," she said softly.

"That's how."

"And you had a happy childhood—and then what happened?"

"Then...my grandfather died. He had a heart attack in the fields one day, and died that night in his bed. I loved him very much. I still miss him.

"My father tried to keep up the family business, but he was no good as a vineyardist, and pretty soon he couldn't pay the rent on the fields. Rather than join the czar's army, he decided to emigrate to America. The first thing he did when he got here was marry a pious widow named Leah Smilowitz. The second thing he did was choke on a fish bone and die." Grace reached out with a gentle touch on his shoulder, but he didn't need comforting. He could barely remember his father, a quiet, remote man who had always seemed more bewildered than pleased with his son's existence.

"So there I was," he resumed, "seven years old, stuck in a cold-water tenement on Division Street with a maniac."

"Is that in New York?"

"Manhattan, yeah, the Lower East Side. From the first day, it was war. Leah was Orthodox. Do you know what that means?"

"Sort of. She—"

"It means the *halakah* ruled her life. Eat a piece of bacon, and you were delivered up to the devil. She thought Satan lived in the pages of the *Ladies' Home Journal*."

"The *Ladies' Home Journal*?"

"Also in Maxwell House coffee, in chewing gum, in a bed made with two sheets instead of one. It killed her that she couldn't afford to send me to the Jewish school. I went to the public school until the day she heard me singing 'The Battle Hymn of the Republic.' 'The glory of the coming of the Lord' was too much for her—she yanked me out of school and taught me nothing but prayers at home for a year, until the social worker found out and made her send me back to the fourth grade."

"We have something in common," Grace

exclaimed, delighted. "We both had religious stepparents who kept us out of school!"

"I know." He grinned. "And we both made a career of spiting them. I just started earlier than you."

"What did you do?"

"I was eight when I found out I had this amazing ability to make people believe anything I said. Partly it was my face, which at that age looked as innocent as yours—almost—but mostly it was the stories I could tell."

"What kind of stories?"

"Oh, terrible tales of tragedy and loss, stories of abuse, orphaning, parental neglect, alcoholism—to total strangers, Grace, who'd listen and then give me money! The notes I'd forge to explain my absences from school were masterpieces, if I say so myself. In sixth grade, I invented this disease that was so complicated and debilitating it kept me out of class for four months."

Grace looked awed. He took her hand and rolled over onto his back. "My early vices were pretty harmless. All I wanted to do was go to the ice cream parlor—a terrible sin, mind you—and consort with the goyim, who wore porkpie hats instead of yarmulkes. Later, I took up with more dangerous companions. One of them taught me the art of thimblerigging."

"Uh-oh."

"Exactly—the beginning of the end of my innocence. I'd skip school and play it all day on Second Avenue, then gamble my winnings at the all-night crap games under the street lamps.

"By thirteen, I could see my future didn't lie in New York City. I wasn't interested in pushing a cart or working in a sweatshop. I'd look around at the German Jews—'uptown Jews,' we called them—and I'd despise them because they were trying so hard to hide their Jewishness. When I'd hear about a Rothstein who changed his name to Ralston, I'd sneer along with the other Russian Jews. But at the same time, I desperately wanted to be an American. I had three goals in life: to get out of the ghetto, to make money, and to sleep with blonde, blue-eyed shiksas."

"What's a *shiksa*?"

He grinned. "You are."

"Oh."

"Getting an education might've helped me find a way out, but between my crazy step-mother and my own rebelliousness I let that chance slip away. So I ask you—what was a poor, slick-fingered Jewish boy to do except change his name and head west?"

"Nothing I can think of. How old were you when you left?"

"Fourteen. It took me ten years to make it all the way across the country to California. I've been here for two years."

"What did you do while you were heading west?"

"Tended bar, prospected for silver."

"Were you—"

"Sold real estate. Taught English to immigrants."

"Did you—"

"Gambled on riverboats, punched cows. Clerked in a store. I think that's all. Oh, I was a hotel desk clerk once."

"You left out president of the International Society of Literature, Science, and Art."

He put his finger on her nose. "That was in San Francisco; you asked me what I did on the way."

"Have you ever been married?" she asked, playing with a button on his sleeve, not looking at him.

"Nope."

"In love?"

"Once."

"What happened?"

"She was too good for me, I had to let her go."

She smiled knowingly. "In other words, you chickened out."

"I did her a favor." He took Grace's hand and kissed it, marveling at how alike they were. And how easy it had been, after all, to tell her his life story. He couldn't remember now what he'd been afraid of, except maybe breaking an old, old habit.

She was watching him intently, and it struck him that she had an almost masculine way of listening when he talked—unseductive, unselfconscious. But she was looking anything but masculine with her golden hair tumbling over her bare shoulders, her skin pink and glowing in the leaf-dappled light.

"Is all of that true, Reuben?" she asked carefully. "You wouldn't lie now, would you? The other times it didn't matter, but now..."

"I haven't lied. I couldn't now."

They sat up at the same time and reached for each other. She put her mouth next to his ear and whispered, "Jonah Rubinsky." A shivery tremor passed through him, and not just because her breath tickled. He said, "Grace Russell" into her ear, and felt her shiver in answer. Their arms around each other tightened. This was a closeness he hadn't expected, and in some ways it was better than sex.

What was he saying? He pulled her head back and kissed her until they were both shaking. "Quick," he muttered, "take your clothes off."

"Oh, I want you to do it."

"Okay, but help me, it'll be faster."

"You've got 'em half off already."

They started fumbling with ties and laces and eyelet fasteners. Her simple flowered gown looked so easy, but it turned out to be mined with hidden traps and snares for the overeager, and her underwear was worse. "You do it," he suggested again, and this time, in the interest of speed, she agreed.

"I've been going meshugge," he told her while he watched, "looking at you every day, so prim and proper in your pretty dresses. And cursed with knowing exactly how you look under 'em."

She wriggled out of her drawers and kicked off her last white stocking. "It's your own fault," she retorted, breathless, clumsy-fingered, coming up on her knees beside him. "You shouldn't have been *jealous*."

Oh, what a sight she was. "You love saying that word, don't you?" She practically smacked her lips over it.

"I do," she admitted, "I dearly do. You have on way too many clothes."

He was naked in half a minute. They came together for a hungry kiss, and tumbled to the sweet grass in a tangle of arms and legs, rolling and rolling. She landed on top, and stretched herself over him like a sheet over a mattress, trying to cover every inch. She took his wrists and pulled his arms over his head. "I've got you," she gloated. "You can't move."

"Right, I'm completely helpless. What are you going to do with me?"

"Unspeakable things. Things for which there are no names." She started with one he could name, a deep, stirring kiss, using her tongue and her teeth until he was squirming under her. "No moving," she warned, sliding her stomach in lascivious figure eights across his belly. She put her knees on the ground for leverage, arched up, and offered him her breasts.

"I'm not allowed to move," he reminded her.

"Just this once."

Lifting his head, he slicked his tongue across one of her tasty little nipples, drawing a satisfying groan from her. She lifted up with her hips to capture his stiff cock between her thighs, and began a slow, excruciating squeezing in time with the soft suction of his mouth on her breast. Raw, rough passion clawed inside him; he forced his hands to be gentler on her, afraid he'd leave bruises. But it was time for a new game; at this rate, they wouldn't last two more minutes.

Breaking her halfhearted hold on his wrists, he took her by the waist and pulled her up till she was straddling his middle. "I know something you like," he said, running his hands along the insides of her thighs, following the lines of the taut tendons into her pubic hair. She was warm and wet; he watched her face, heavy with desire, teeth clamped over her bottom lip, while his fingers slipped and slid and his palm cupped her. She said, "Oh, mmm," when he asked her if she liked it, and she threw her head back and wailed when he put his fingers inside her. Her exuberant, uncomplicated response laid to rest a fear he hadn't even realized he was harboring—that she wouldn't like this half as much without Wing's drug in her system.

Thinking of the Godfather could still make his blood boil. Hot, leftover anger prompted him to ask, "Would you really have done this with Wing if I hadn't gotten you out of there?" As soon as he said it, he was sorry.

She leaned over him, arms braced, letting her hair caress his face. "Maybe." She bent lower and whispered against his mouth, "But I'd have imagined the whole time that he was you."

Laughing, he gathered her up and rolled over again. She folded her legs around him and he came into her, slow and easy, as natural as breathing. She held him tight, pressing her lips to his cheeks, his eyes. "I never thanked you for not laughing at me that night. You saved me, Reuben. What would I have done without you?"

"If you really don't know, Gus, I'll tell you sometime. But not now."

"No, I mean it. You *saved* me."

"The pleasure was mine."

"And you were so gallant."

"That's me. Now—"

"If you hadn't—"

"Listen, *ziskeit,* I hate to tell you, but we're only doing this once this time. So if you want me to get it right, you should keep quiet and let me concentrate." She smiled, and he slipped his hands into her hair to anchor her. The fresh smell of the grass they'd flattened beneath them mingled with the scent of sunshine in Grace's hair, filling his head, making him dizzy. Nobody kissed the way she did, wide, wet, luscious kisses that jolted into him like electrical currents, obliterating everything except the soft feel and the sweet taste of her mouth.

"I'm not worried," she said, pulling away to bite his chin. "About you getting it right. See, I know what was in the tea you drank this morning."

He blinked down at her. "Chinese wolfberries."

"And something else."

"What?"

Her eyes twinkled. "You won't believe me."

"What?"

"Boiled bull's balls."

What could he do but laugh? "You're right, I don't believe you. You made it up."

"No, I didn't! Ah You says it's good for virility. Henry swears by it."

Ridiculous, absurd, completely a product of his imagination—and yet—a definite, extra-powerful surge of energy came to him just then from *somewhere*. He used it to good purpose, regaining Grace's complete attention.

"I *love* this," she gasped into the air over his shoulder. "Not just this—I mean you and me, everything—all of it—"

"Me, too—shut up—"

"Okay."

But a little later she turned her head aside to mutter tragically, "Oh, God, Reuben, I don't want to fall in love with you!"

Amazed, he saw a tear shining at the corner of her eye. "Would it hurt so much?" He made his voice casual, brushing the tear away with his lips.

"The end. I might as well kill myself." He laughed uncertainly. "What would you do if you fell in love with me?"

The question took him off guard; he said the first thing that came into his head: "Run like hell."

She sighed, her soft breath fanning his face. She kissed him as gently as anyone had ever kissed him, and whispered, "Then I hope you never do."

He hated this conversation; he wished they'd never started it. He arched up over her and sucked her breast into his mouth almost roughly, while the rhythm of their bodies quickened. She clutched at handfuls of earth on either side, writhing under him and making those soft, incredible sounds he remembered from before. He could make her lose her mind, he exulted, reveling in the illusion of control—until she slipped one hand beneath her own straining thigh, and took hold of his testicles.

His breath whistled through his teeth. He slowed his strokes, but the power in him mounted higher. "Mmm," she hummed, caressing him softly, her eyes closed, while he swelled in her hand. He lifted her, wanting her deeper, harder. She yelled; he stopped. But he'd misunderstood; she wanted exactly what he wanted, and she told him so with her urgent hips and her heels pressing against his calves. She cried out all at once, shifting under him until her body made a long, undulating bridge, supported by the flat of her feet and the back of her head. When she climaxed, her strong, rhythmic contractions tightened around him—fast at first, slowing gradually, and he had time to think that a woman was a wondrous thing, God's finest creation, and this one was the most wondrous of all.

He let go. Pulsing into her without reserve,

he let it be what it was, a free, abandoned, frighteningly natural act of love. What it had in common with the only other time they'd done this was that he wanted it again, immediately. She was like Wing's drug, he mused as he sank down, joyful and fatalistic, on her breast. Grace was addictive.

"What does *ziskeit* mean?" she murmured a few minutes later against his hair.

"Mmmm. Hard to translate."

"Try."

"Sweet one. Sweetheart."

She sighed dreamily.

He wanted to tell her something important, something timely. What was it? It flirted at the corners of his mind, dancing away each time he closed in on it. He let it go, too lazy and contented to catch it, and hazily relieved when it was gone.

When she could move, she kissed his damp temple and ran her fingers through his hair. "Ah, Reuben." He took it as a tribute and accepted it humbly, whispering, "Ah, Gracie," in the same spirit. But then she said, "What am I going to do without you?" as if she didn't expect an answer. He didn't have one, so he didn't reply.

The sun had begun to slide toward the mountains by the time they started for home. Home? Just a figure of speech, Reuben told himself; it was what you called wherever you'd been living for a while. You could call a hotel home if you were speaking figuratively. They didn't hurry, and they stopped often along the way to kiss, or just to hold each other. Grace had a lovely soft blowsiness about her, her skin still flushed, her mouth blurry from kissing. Neither of them had much to say, but the silence wasn't awkward. He guessed talking about certain things—feelings, stuff like that—wasn't any easier for her than it was for him.

They were still a hundred yards from the house when they spied Henry on the front porch. He saw them at the same moment and bounded down the steps, hollering for them to come on, hurry up, he had news. Before they reached him, Reuben thought to say quickly, "Come to my room tonight, Gracie. Hurry—say yes!"

He'd have dropped her hand, for Henry's benefit, but she held on. "Yes," she said immediately, smiling up at him sweetly.

"*Ziskeit,*" he whispered.

Henry was waving a yellow piece of paper. "Telegram!" he shouted, jogging toward them. "He's in! Doc Slaughter says he'll do it!"

"Hot damn!"

"But only for half the gross," Henry added, without as much enthusiasm. "That's his price."

"That's okay with me," Reuben told him. "He's the one taking most of the chances."

"And if everything works out the way it's supposed to," Grace pointed out, "there'll be plenty for everybody. I say we accept his terms."

Henry nodded grudgingly. "He says he'll start looking for the two rental properties right away, and he expects to meet us in San Francisco by the day after tomorrow."

"So soon," Grace breathed.

"Are you strong enough for it?" Henry asked Reuben.

He didn't look at Grace and she didn't look at him. "I believe so," he said gravely.

Inside the house, Henry said they should drink a toast to celebrate the start of their venture. They clinked glasses of whiskey and drank. "I still say *I* should be the doctor," Henry said peevishly. "I did it once before, years ago. I can't call to mind now exactly why, but I remember I was damn good at it. What do we need an outsider for?"

Reuben smiled down into his drink, warmed by the notion that Henry considered him an insider. "We need Doc because he *is* a doctor," he said reasonably. "Wing's smart; he's bound to investigate the setup before he agrees to anything."

"Besides," Grace chimed in, "you haven't seen him, Henry, you don't know how perfect he is. He looks like an M.D. you could corrupt, because that's exactly what he *is*."

"Hmpf," grumped Henry, not consoled. "Who the hell am I, then?"

"You're the mastermind," she said diplomatically. "You're taking a big enough risk as it is just by showing your face in the city. If anybody recognizes you, we're dead."

Ah You poked his head in the door. To

announce dinner, Reuben thought, but instead he rubbed his spidery hands together and said, "I go, too—I be messenger! Right, boss?"

Henry flopped down in his chair, taking the bottle with him. "That ties it," he groused. "Now *everybody's* got a job but me."

18

The cunning of the fox is as murderous as the violence of the wolf, and we ought to guard equally against both.
　　　　　　　　　　　　　—Thomas Paine

"Perfect."

Reuben stood on the cracked sidewalk, looking across Balance Street at a small, shabby, two-story office building with a shiny new sign. "J. Hayes, M.D.," read the shingle, "The Painless Doctor." The building sat between a grog shop and a Salvation Army meeting hall.

"Perfect," he reiterated. "How did you get it set up so fast?"

Doc Slaughter stepped on the half-inch butt of his last cigarette and felt in his pocket for a new one. "I had all my old equipment, never threw it away. It only took a couple of hours to move everything in." He pointed up at a dirty second-floor window. "I slept upstairs last night."

"How was it?"

"Noisy."

Reuben grunted. It was a rough neighborhood. "Have you gotten any patients yet?" he asked, half joking.

"Not yet."

"What'll you do if one walks in?"

Doc gave him one of his day-old cadaver looks. "Treat him."

They strolled up to Pacific Street and turned left. It was a typical summer day in the city, chilly, nasty, and damp. Everything had a vague but grim familiarity to Reuben, who was pretty sure he'd gotten lost in the fog with Grace on these same seedy streets not very long ago. Doc asked him if he wanted to see the empty warehouse he'd leased on the Embarcadero; Reuben said it wasn't necessary, and asked how much the rent was.

"Twenty dollars a month. I had to take it for six months, minimum, and they wanted forty dollars up front."

"Crooks," Reuben said automatically. "I can't stand throwing money away for nothing."

"But it's necessary. Wing has to believe we've got a legitimate place to store his drugs, however temporarily. Without that, he's not going to hand over thousands of dollars to us, no matter how impressive he finds my papers."

Reuben had already seen Doc's papers.

Masterpieces, as usual; the doctor was a true artist. "And as soon as he hands over the money, we disappear."

"Sounds simple," Doc agreed cautiously. "But what if he hands it over in the form of a check?"

"He won't. He knows he can't be connected to the transaction in any way. You'll open a bank account, and he'll hand over cash to purchase the stuff. He'll want *you* to write a check to the supplier in Turkey, or wherever the opium comes from."

"Mm."

"But instead, you'll fade away into the wide white-devil world, never to be seen again."

Doc's dour face brightened. "With half the gross," he said cheerfully.

The Claymont Hotel wasn't the Palace, but it was clean and quiet, and Grace thought it had a sleek, dark, European atmosphere that added class. She walked into Henry's room, which connected to hers, and started with the same mild shock she felt whenever she came upon him suddenly. She just couldn't get over it. All he'd done was shave off his mustache and the hair on top of his head, and put on horn-rimmed spectacles. But the transformation was astonishing. "You look like an intelligent newborn baby," she told him this time; this morning it had been "a sexy monk who illuminates manuscripts."

He preened at the praise, looking up at her

from the book he was reading beside the window. "I don't know why I didn't think of this a long time ago. Think of the opportunities we've been wasting."

She sat down on the end of his bed. "It's not that good," she said dampeningly, "so don't start getting ideas. I'd recognize you after a long second glance, and so would anyone else who knew you well. Is Reuben back?" she asked before he could start arguing.

"Not yet. He should be—aha." They both turned at the sound of a key in the lock. The door opened and Reuben strode in.

Not being allowed to do what she wanted to do—rush over, throw her arms around him, and kiss him—added an illicit thrill to an affair that was already so intensely exciting to her she could hardly stand it. Not that her reticence was fooling anybody; she suspected Henry knew everything, and Ah You undoubtedly knew even more. But hiding her passion for Reuben in public seemed like the respectable thing to do.

That was just a guess, of course, respectability being a somewhat shadowy and irrelevant concept in the life she'd led up to now. More than once lately she'd caught herself thinking of Lucille Waters, and wondering how she managed to project her elegant, ladylike image so flawlessly even though she'd been sleeping with Henry, Grace knew for a fact, for years. It must be something you were born with—or not. Did she herself have that quality? She didn't know. She worried that even if she did have it, she'd throw it away if Reuben wanted her to. She'd stand on her head if he wanted her to.

"Hi," he said casually, but the hot, private look he sent her made her toes curl. "Ah You's not back yet?"

"Not yet," said Henry, throwing his book aside and getting up. "How did it go with the doctor?"

"Fine, everything's set on his end. You should see the office; it's unbelievably seedy, a real work of art. He's got the warehouse, too, and all the paperwork's done. There's nothing to do now but wait."

Grace stood up, walked to the window, and came back.

"She's been doing that all morning," Henry confided in a stage whisper.

"Why?"

Their nonchalance bewildered her. "Because *somebody's* got to worry about all the things that might go wrong!" she burst out. "You two— oh, what's the use." She threw up her hands and resumed pacing.

"I wish you'd relax," Henry said, maddeningly patient. "This Wing character's no different from any pigeon we've ever plucked. Greed motivates him, and it'll blind him, same as it blinds all of 'em, to the flaws in the scheme. If there are any, which there aren't."

"Besides," Reuben added, "we'll distract him from the dubious here and now by giving him a vision of the future. Which we paint as so rosy and full of profit, he won't see the one-time dodge going on right under his nose. Think of it as a mental thimble trick, Gus."

"That's it." Henry nodded approvingly.

Their confidence didn't reassure her, it only alarmed her. "What if you're both wrong? What if he cheats us as easily as he did the last time? What if he kills us?"

"First of all," Reuben argued, with a touch of Henry's irritating patience, "there is no 'us.' Doc and I talk to him; you and Henry stay right here. You in particular, Grace, don't go anywhere near him."

"Right," said Henry.

"It won't work."

"Why not?"

"Because he'll want me in on it. I told you, he's got a yen for me."

"Well, he'll have to get over it." Reuben sounded casual, but she knew it was an act; he'd have said more if they'd been alone, but he hid his steely hatred of Wing from Henry to protect her. Sometimes she wondered what Henry would do if he knew the whole truth about what had happened that night at Wing's house.

"What keeps him from killing *you*?" she persisted.

Reuben grinned. "My lightning-quick wits."

She couldn't smile back. She couldn't stop thinking of the way he'd looked lying in the Chinatown alley, white-faced and bleeding. "I don't like it. I don't like it. Besides everything else, even if we get the money and get away, who's to say he won't find us someday and then kill us? You say he won't leave Chinatown, but how can you be sure? He had his hatchet men rob an armed stagecoach in broad daylight, he—"

"That was an aberration," Reuben insisted. "The man's got a screw loose when it comes to death, Grace—he *had* to have those funeral sculptures."

"Well, now he has to have me." She turned her back on him, embarrassed by her distress. She wasn't a worrier by nature, but memories of Wing's depravity kept gnawing at her peace of mind, robbing her of the ability to see anything amusing or entertaining about this swindle. She had never let Reuben see how frightened she was, though, and she hated herself for starting now.

"Hey, Gracie," he said softly, coming up behind her. He caressed the back of her neck, and she dropped her head. "It's going to work perfectly. Trust me, honey, we're going to live happily ever after."

She dredged up a nod and a smile. "I know. I'm fine, really." But along with everything else, she was nearly sick from the fear that his idea of happily ever after had nothing in common with hers.

Another knock sounded at the door. When Henry opened it, Ah You came in, carrying a bundle of clean laundry—his entrée into the conservative Claymont Hotel's private guest rooms.

"Did you see him?" Henry demanded before

he could get the door closed. "Did they let you in? Did anybody follow you?"

"Nobody follow. I see number one lieutenant, Tom Fun."

"Buddy Tom!" Reuben said jovially. "How's his butt?"

Grace didn't laugh. "What did he say?"

"He say Kai Yee meet you tomorrow night at Red Duck Tavern on Clay Street."

Reuben let out a whoop and smacked a grinning Henry on the shoulder.

"And more good news. I go home the long way, visit my cousin who unload the big ships in Gum San Ta Foy harbor. Big clipper ship in the Bay today, come last week, call *Star of India*. Cargo in a warehouse now, but owner not allowed to take because of new raw." He shook himself. "New law. Guess who is owner, and what is cargo he not allowed to take."

"Great Scot," said Henry.

"Jesus, Mary, and Joseph," sighed Grace.

"It's a miracle," breathed Reuben. "He's stuck! He'll think we're his saviors, he'll pay us anything we ask!"

"Is the cargo paid for yet," Grace asked, "or only on order?"

"Don't know."

"Can you find that out? And also how much it's worth?"

"It may be so."

"A celebration," Henry decided, opening his nightstand drawer and removing a pint bottle.

Ah You cleared his throat uncomfortably.

"That good news. Now bad." Henry turned around, bottle in hand; Reuben's smile faded. "Kai Yee say Missy Grace have to come to meeting, too, or no deal."

She sank down in Henry's chair. "I told you," she whispered, stricken. "I knew it."

Gray dawn crept past the edges of the window, pearling the dark shapes of bureau and chairs and coffin-shaped wardrobe. Grace sat up slowly, careful not to wake Reuben. He lay beside her in the big bed on his stomach, one leg drawn up, arms outflung as if he'd dropped there from a height, exhausted. Which he had, pretty much. She touched her fingertips to his forearm, gently riffling the soft brown hairs. His face in the dimness was pale but distinct, his profile clear-cut against the blue-white of the pillow. His long, hard body at rest fascinated her—so foreign, so *other*, and yet she could reach out and touch him, bring him to life with a caress if she chose to. *Who are you?* she wondered in silence, resisting the urge to wake him up, make him...more real.

Yawning, she looked around his hotel room, reflecting on how little it had in common with the room they'd shared at the Bunyon Arms. No torn paper shades at the Claymont: discreet draperies covered the old-fashioned casement window, and the bed was wide, soft, and voluptuous; instead of a gritty wood floor, a thick woolen carpet stretched from wall to wall. But in a year, ten years, fifty if she lived that long, it was the sordid details of the Bunyon Arms, she knew for a certainty, that would still be etched like acid in her memory. Even now she couldn't think of that unforgettable night with Reuben without a moment when her heart stopped beating, overcome with memories of passion, and acute embarrassment, and finally a simple, aching sweetness.

She had never exposed herself to anyone to such an intense degree before—physically, of course, but even more, emotionally. It was as though she'd taken off her skin along with her clothes, and shown Reuben her raw nerves, her stark-naked neediness. And he'd saved her. How easily the situation could have turned ugly, or foolish, or degrading. But he'd made it all right; perfect, in fact. Was that when she'd begun to fall in love with him? Maybe. Oh, but last night...last night she'd taken the real plunge, and landed at the bottom in a hopeless, helpless heap. She was a goner.

Who knew lovemaking could be like that? It never had been for her, not even with Reuben. The fire had still been there, but they'd banked it for long, slow hours, touching each other with a different sensibility. Tenderness—that's what it was, so unbearably sweet sometimes that she'd wept. The hot desire they knew best hadn't come until the end, but then it had burned them to ashes. And every kiss, every soft, murmured word, had added a link to the thick chain that bound her to him.

Reuben, Reuben, Reuben. She leaned close, aiming her thoughts directly at his left temple.

Why can't you fall in love with me, too? Weren't we made for each other?

In bed he told her she was beautiful, she drove him wild, he was dying, he was crazy for her—but never a word about love. If she could trust only her senses, she might believe he loved her anyway, because of the way he touched her. Before last night she'd never dreamed there could be gentleness and generosity like that between two people, never imagined such sweetness could exist without embarrassment, without the sheepish need to make it into a bit of a joke. But it still wasn't love, not for him. Reuben had strong passions and an affectionate nature; he thought of her as his friend and he liked sleeping with her, but he wasn't in love with her.

He wanted to see the world and live on a ranchero, drinking champagne with his feet up. He wanted children.

Her throat swelled; the old familiar ache throbbed in her chest. She wanted him to be happy, truly she did, but oh, if only he could love her! Was it because he didn't trust her? She didn't trust him either, but that hadn't stopped her. One of her worst daydreams was that she ran away with him after bilking Wing out of thousands of dollars, and one morning, in Caracas or Paris or Timbuktu, she woke up to find him gone, and all the money with him.

"Would you do that?" she wondered, leaning close to whisper in his ear. "Would you?" No answer.

Sighing, she kissed him for the last time, and slipped out of bed. Faint sounds from outside the window said the world was waking up. Time to steal back across the hall to her own room. She found her nightgown in a trampled ball on the floor; while she put it on, she thought of all the lovely things Reuben had said to her last night when he'd taken it off. And before that, the look on his face when he'd answered her shy tap at his door—so glad, so…joyful. Rubbing her arms, she tiptoed back to the bed. The temptation to wake him rose again, stronger than before—but no; he was sleeping so soundly. It would be wrong.

If only she could stop time right here, right now in this dim, neither-nor hour between night and day. So far, they hadn't spoken a word to each other about the future, or what would happen between them once their business with Wing was finished. It was easy to imagine Reuben giving her one of his killer grins and saying, "Well, Gus, it's been fun." A good-bye kiss, a sexy, teasing squeeze. And he'd walk away. Oh, it was too easy to imagine that scene.

They might not have a future, but they still had a present.

"Reuben," she murmured. No response; he slept on like a dead man. What a shame to wake him. She leaned over and kissed him on the lips, trailing her fingers down to the small of his back. His eyebrows twitched. She rubbed her mouth softly across his lips, taking tiny nips, feeling his warm breath on her cheek. His breathing changed; she felt the subtle shift to wakefulness under her hand as she stroked the silky smooth skin of his back.

"Gus," he mumbled, opening one eye.

"I'm sorry," she lied, voice contrite, "I didn't mean to wake you. I just wanted to kiss you good-bye."

"What time is it? You don't have to go yet."

"I should."

"What time is it?"

"Still early, but—"

"Don't go. Stay a little longer."

She pretended to consider while he pulled on her elbow and made her sit down beside him. He took her hand and pressed it to his chest, palm down, right over his heart; his soft, sleepy smile was irresistible.

"Well, okay," she conceded, with a sigh that said this was against her better judgment. She put her arms around him. "But just for a minute."

"A minute?"

For a man who'd been asleep thirty seconds ago, he moved fast; she was naked, in his arms, and under the covers before she could say *boo how doy*. "Or so." She grinned up at him, already breathless.

The Red Duck was a big, dark, nondescript alehouse on the eastern outskirts of Chinatown—neutral territory, since its clientele ran roughly fifty-fifty, Caucasian to Chinese. Grace had no doubt that she and Reuben had raced by it any number of times the night they'd spent fleeing from the Godfather's hatchet men. The prospect of seeing Wing again disturbed and demoralized her, but she'd spent the last day and a half hiding her nervousness out of a fear that if he fully understood it, Reuben might cancel everything, and it was much too late for that. Sitting beside him at a scarred, gin-soaked table in a dark corner of the Red Duck, she took furtive opportunities to touch him, just her shoulder against his or a soft hand on his wrist, to keep up her courage.

Across the table, Doc Slaughter signaled the waiter for another rum, which he was drinking with a beer chaser. Reuben sipped a weak whiskey and water. Grace had elected to have nothing, figuring she'd need all her wits when Wing arrived; but as the minutes stretched and her nerves tightened, she began to regret that decision.

"He's here," Doc said quietly. With an effort, she didn't spin around; she forced her shoulders to relax, and loosened the grip she had on the edge of the table. "He's got three bodyguards," Doc continued. "One's coming over."

With dismay but no surprise, she looked up at Tom Fun, the Godfather's Chief Swordsman. He bowed. His ugly, pockmarked face was completely expressionless, so it must've been his hooded eyes that radiated the hostility.

"Hey, Tom," Reuben said amiably. "Care to sit down? Oh—sorry, I forgot."

The hatchet man's sallow complexion pinkened and his scar turned crimson. "Who is this man?" he said through his teeth. "You were told to come alone. Kai Yee will not sit with a stranger."

"Well, you tell him this gentleman is Dr. Hayes, and he's an integral part of the business opportunity we've come to discuss."

Tom Fun bared his eyeteeth and made scary flexing movements with his right hand. Grace's grip on Reuben's elbow tightened in a warning, but the Chief Swordsman turned away without a word and walked, stiff-legged, back to his master.

"Reuben," she hissed, "he's going to cut your ears off if you don't stop teasing him!"

"I can't help it, the guy rubs me the wrong way."

A moment later, Wing glided up. He stood beside the table quietly, expectantly, as if waiting for them to stand up and bow. Nobody moved. Grace could hardly look at him, so suave in his sober brown coat and tan trousers, his long white hair tied back tonight with a silk ribbon. His languid elegance was obscene to her now. She remembered too well the silky soft touch of his hands on her bare skin, and the stench of his breath. The gurgling sound of opium cooking at the end of a long pipe. She shuddered.

He took the chair at the end of the table, on her right. "Thiss is an unexpected pleasure," he said very softly. "It seems such a long time since lasst we met."

As usual, he looked only at her. His avidity made her skin crawl. Rather than cower, she lifted her chin and stared straight back at him. She couldn't prevent the flare of her nostrils, though, or the slight curl of her lip. "Really? It seems like only yesterday to me." She loathed his smile; there was nothing behind it but corruption. How had she ever, even for a second, found him good-looking?

Reuben shifted against her; she could feel the tension in him, and the restless, hair-trigger anger.

Finally Wing looked at him. "Your messenger spoke of a bissness proposition," he said neutrally. "Since I am a bissy man, p'raps you will come to the point directly."

Reuben folded his arms. "Well, that's Western of you," he drawled, insulting him on purpose. "Okay, I'll be direct. We do have a business proposition. I won't say we weren't a little peeved with you after our last encounter, but—"

"Peeved?"

"Yeah, you know, pissed off. You did steal our tiger, after all—"

"*My* tiger."

"—and you took a few liberties with my sister that weren't very sporting. Not what we *fan kwei* would call gentlemanly, you know what I mean?"

Wing kept his lips pursed and didn't answer.

"But in spite of that, we're willing to let bygones be bygones, in a spirit of cooperation and forgiveness. Why? Because that's the

American way, and also because if we work together we can all get rich."

The Godfather spread his hands. "But I am already rich."

"Right, but you won't be for much longer. Not without the help of some entrepreneurial white devils."

Grace could feel Wing's enmity like heat from an iron; if anything, he hated Reuben even more than Tom Fun did. He turned a jade ring around on his pinky finger and said calmly, "In what way can you be of service to me?"

"You've got the question backwards," said Reuben. "Ever heard of the Burlingame treaty?"

Wing lowered his eyes, but not before something flickered in their obsidian depths. Grace felt a premonitory flutter of triumph, and beat it back superstitiously; it was way too early to celebrate. "Perhaps," he said softly.

"Good, that saves time. Then you know as well as I do that your days as an opium boss in Chinatown are over unless you find a middleman to take delivery of the stuff for you. A Caucasian middleman."

Unexpectedly, the Godfather laughed. "You are absurd, Mr. Smith, as well as a thief and a scoundrel. The customs officials would never permit you to import opium. Under your country's new law, it can only be sold to drug and medical-supply companies."

"That's true. Are you personally acquainted with the heads of any drug and pharmaceutical companies?"

Wing stared back stonily. "It is a problem on which I am currently working."

"Well, that's good, but listen, Mark: it's a problem on which we've already worked. Where are my manners? Mark Wing—alias the Godfather, alias Mother, alias Ah Mah, alias who knows what all—meet Jonathan Hayes. That's Dr. Jonathan Hayes, M.D."

The two men eyed each other without moving or speaking.

"So much for manners." Reuben took a sip of his drink.

"Am I to understand that you represent a drug company, Dr. Haiss?" Wing asked finally. He was interested, Grace could tell, but not willing to show it. This was a poker game, and everybody was bluffing.

"Not exactly." Doc's bass voice rumbled up from his scrawny chest as if from inside a deep, dark cave. He reached into his coat, and Wing tensed slightly until Doc brought out a packet of folded papers. "But with these, I could convince the agents of the San Francisco Customs House that I do."

Wing's long-fingered hands opened the papers, his fingertips touching only the corners as he studied them—an annoying affectation, Grace decided. One of the forms, she knew, was a certificate of incorporation, which, along with a couple of other miscellaneous documents, validated the lawful existence of Hayes Pharmaceutical Company. There was also a Customs Service drug import license, beautifully forged, and a so-far unexecuted sales agreement between Mark Wing and Hayes Pharmaceuticals for the purchase of twenty-five thousand, four hundred sixty-six pounds of opium at a price of ninety thousand, two hundred dollars.

Wing's eyes narrowed when he came to the sales agreement. "You have been very thorough," he noted. It was clear their thoroughness didn't please him. He must find it galling to learn that—thanks to Ah You's cousin—they *knew* he had ninety thousand dollars' worth of opium sitting in a harbor warehouse, utterly useless to him unless he accepted their offer.

Long minutes passed. At last Wing looked up and asked in a monotone, "How much do you want?"

"Half," Reuben stipulated.

Wing blew a little puff of air through his nose in derision. "This is a pointless conversation." But he didn't get up.

"Half for us is better than nothing for you. Of course, if you're not interested, I'm sure any number of others would be. The leader of the Hip Sing tong, for example. Or Mr. Low Yet of the Chee Kong."

Wing stiffened, then sneered. "I do not need your help, Mr. Smith. There are other ways to obtain the product I need for my business."

"You mean smuggle it in?"

"There are many who do. To avoid the tariff."

"True, but why take the risk? With us you

can do it legally. Well"—he smiled—"almost legally. The customs people only care about collecting their duties; after the stuff is in, taxed, and warehoused, they don't pay any attention to what the purchaser does with it. That keeps you out of the circle, see? You're invisible. But if you smuggled it in and got caught, they'd deport you. Last I heard, that wouldn't be such a good deal for you. What was it?" He scratched his head, trying to remember. "Something about a celestial lamp?"

Wing's flat nostrils flared, but he waved his hand dismissively. "Do not try to frighten me, Mr. Smith. You only make yourself foolish."

Reuben had told her, as usual, to keep quiet and let him do the talking, but Grace was tired of sitting there like a bump on a log. "It might be helpful to look at the situation in a broader context, Mr. Wing," she said politely, even though the sight of his face, softening with sudden tenderness as he turned toward her, made her feel sick. "I can see years of prof-itability ahead if we all try to think of this as only a first step in a long and mutually satis-fying business arrangement." In other words, don't look at my hand, look at my face while I palm this card.

"How so?" he asked mellifluously.

"Well, I'm sure I don't have to tell you that in this country we don't always live up to our democratic ideals, especially in the way we treat people who weren't born here. Or whose skin isn't the same color as ours."

"No, Miss Ssmith," he said, eerily quiet, "you don't have to tell me that."

"And that puts you, as a shrewd and dynamic entrepreneur, at an unfair disadvantage. You've succeeded brilliantly in the carefully defined area where society has allowed you full expression of your talents—but why should you have to stop there? It's unfair and it ought to be illegal, but the sad fact is, if you want to extend your empire beyond the narrow boundaries of Chinatown, you'll need representatives to act on your behalf."

She folded her hands. "So we're proposing a partnership. Think of it as a corporation in which you're the majority stockholder. We're your surrogates in the places where you can't go. The trade we're offering is your financial backing for our skin color and expertise, and the first transaction will be a test of our skill and good faith."

"You intrigue me, Miss Ssmith." It was the truth: he was practically drooling on her. She had to look away. "Forgive me," he said, turning to Doc, "but are you really a doctor?"

"Of course. I've been a doctor for twenty-two years."

"Do you have a medical specialty?"

"No, I'm a generalist."

"Ah, a generalist. Where do you practice?"

Doc gave him his crummy Balance Street address.

Wing's lips thinned derisively. "Then you do have a sspecialty," he corrected. "In knife wounds and abortions."

Doc didn't reply. His hands shook ever so slightly as he downed another rum shooter. The grotesque scar on the left side of his face was shadowed but still visible. She knew him to be a fastidious man, but he'd nicked himself shaving this morning, and he'd put on yesterday's shirt—two small touches that were all the more convincing because of their subtlety.

"So," said Reuben, breaking the nasty silence. "Here's what we have in mind. You've got a few tons of opium stashed in a warehouse that all of a sudden you can't touch. If you want to stay in business, you need to sell it to somebody who looks legitimate, and who'll sell it back to you as soon as nobody's looking. That's us. So what you do is deposit ninety thousand dollars into the special account Doc Hayes here is going to open. In cash—it'll have to be in cash; you can't have any traceable connection to it, to protect yourself." Grace kept her eyes lowered, knowing this was the one absolutely vital element in the plan, and that to look up might betray her anxiety. "Doc writes a promissory note on the account made out to you," Reuben continued. "You sign the sales agreement, and he takes it to the customs office along with the note when he goes to pay duty and take delivery of what's now Hayes Pharmaceuticals' shipment of medical supplies. They'll think you sold it to him. It's delivered, all nice and legal, to the Hayes warehouse— Where's that warehouse again, Doc?"

"Second Street, a block from the China Basin."

"Right. After a suitable length of time—say an hour or so, ha-ha—you get your people to transfer the stuff to wherever it is you store it in Chinatown. And for this swift, untraceable service, all we're asking is half the wholesale cost of the merchandise. Forty-five thousand, up front and in cash."

Grace's folded hands tightened on the table. *Wherever it is you store it in Chinatown.* For the first time since that awful night in Wing's house, she thought of the wooden chests she'd seen the workmen shoving around in his basement. He stored his opium right in his own house! She couldn't wait to tell Reuben. "Preposterous," Wing whispered, but she had a feeling he was stalling for time, weighing the pros and cons in his mind.

"Not really. We're running the major risk, plus we've got expenses—those papers weren't free, and neither was the warehouse on Second Street. We've already done all the work; all you have to do is reach into your pocket. Besides, there's three of us. That's a measly fifteen thousand each."

Measly, thought Grace. Her heart was hammering.

"What is to prevent Dr. Haiss from taking the money and absconding with it? And you with him?"

Good question, she applauded.

"Nothing. Except practicality. We're not stupid; you'll have to rely on our intelligence

402

to figure out that we can get much richer with you than without you."

"Rely on your greed, in other words?"

"Now you're catching on."

The Godfather pressed his fingertips together; it was impossible to tell from his face what he was thinking. Finally he looked up. "It has been a pleasure meeting you, Dr. Haiss."

In the startled pause, Doc looked at Reuben, who nodded. Doc finished his beer chaser, shoved his chair back, got up, and walked out. Immediately Wing lifted his hand, and one of his henchmen hurried over to the table. Wing gave him a quiet order in Chinese; the henchman bowed and left.

He'd been told to follow Doc, Grace assumed. They'd figured Wing would want to investigate Doc's background and credibility. She only hoped that following him was all the henchman planned to do, and that Doc would stay in character on Balance Street while he did it.

"Well?" prodded Reuben, drumming his fingers to indicate he was getting impatient. "That's our offer. What's your answer?"

This was the moment. Trying not to squirm, Grace looked expectantly at Wing. The widening smile on his suave face wasn't reassuring.

"My answer is no."

She sensed rather than felt the tension draining out of Reuben's body. "No?" he repeated, struggling with disbelief.

"No. No, I'm afraid not. You see, I would

have to have something else besides your word, Mr. Smith, to insure your good faith."

Hope surged back. "Such as?"

"I would have to have…" His voice mellowed; he said it like a prayer. "I would have to have…Augustine."

19

Men, like musical instruments,
seem made to be played upon.
                              —C. N. Bovee

Reuben laughed.

Grace held up one weak finger. When the waiter came, she said, "Whiskey, no water," in a numb voice.

"Is it so very shocking?" the Godfather asked her gently, leaning in. "My deep regard cannot have esscaped you, Augustine."

"Deep regard? That's what you call drugging and stripping her, and then making her smoke dope? Listen, you perverted son of a—"

Grace put her hand over Reuben's clenched fist and squeezed it. "Now, Algernon, don't lose your temper. We've said we were willing to let bygones be bygones." He looked incredulous, and she sent him a message with her eyes

that said, *Let's hear what he's got in mind.*
One of Henry's maxims was, "If you cut off
a sucker's rope supply, he won't be able to hang
himself."

Enchanted, Wing leaned closer. She leaned
back. He got a grip on himself and turned businesslike again. "The situation is simple. You
want much money from me in exchange for
nothing—"

"Not nothing," Reuben started to inter-
ject, but Wing waved him to silence.

"It is customary in your country as well as
in mine for the party asking for money to
offer something in return. Collateral, you
call it."

"And you want Gus as *collateral*?"

"Why not? All I know of you, Mr. Smith, is
that you are a charlatan who once tried to steal
from me. Of your sister, I know a little more.
I know that she, too, is a thief, but this does
not matter to me. What matters is that she is
my desstiny."

Reuben slouched against the wall. "Oh,
well, why didn't you say so?" He jerked a
cigar out of his pocket, lit it, and blew smoke
at the ceiling.

"It is true. She is the golden one, for whom
my life and my loins were fated."

"Your what?"

"It will be, Mr. Smith," he said serenely. "It
is the way of the Tao."

"It is, huh? Well, tell me this, Mark: what
would you do with my sister if you had her?"
He was taking her silent advice, doling rope

out to the sucker, but Grace didn't care much for the question.

Wing turned his black eyes on her, and his look was so full of smug, fiendish proprietariness that she shivered. But even he seemed to appreciate the indelicacy of a full disclosure of his unwholesome plans, because he merely said, "I would enjoy her."

"Yeah, but under what circumstances? Would you set her up as a concubine? Sell her into white slavery? Visit her occasionally in a downtown hotel? What exactly are your intentions?"

Wing brought his fist down on the table with a thundering smack, making them jump. "You insult me, sir," he said, red-faced, "and you insult and degrade my bride-to-be. Augustine would not be my slave or my misstress, she would be my wife!"

They stared at him.

"My helpmeet, my beloved, the mother of my sons." He rubbed his hands together eagerly. "Strong sons, many, many strong sons, who would say prayers, perform sacrifices, make obeisance. The journey to Nirvana would be unimpeded. Yesss."

Grace sent Reuben a look, and his expression confirmed her opinion. What they had here was a certifiable fruitcake.

The horrible tenderness came over him again. "Augustine, my dearest, I would give thee everything—everything. My empress, my queen, no one in my household would be above thee. Rich clothing, priceless jewels, servants at your beck and—"

"Money?"

Wing paused with his mouth open.

"Money?" she repeated more sharply.

"Yes, yes, money, as well as—"

"How much?"

"As much as you want! And all the—"

"In an account of my own? My name on it and nobody else's?" She wanted to see how far he would go.

After a little hesitation, he said, "Yes, all right."

"A hundred thousand dollars," she said recklessly. "In a private account."

He grinned from ear to ear, enjoying himself, anticipating a happy ending. "Of course," he agreed readily.

"Hold on a second," Reuben put in, playing along. "What about me?"

Wing's grin disappeared. "What about you?"

"What about our deal?"

"If Augustine consents to be my bride, then you and I and the doctor will form a partnership, Mr. Smith. Soon, p'raps tomorrow, Dr. Haiss will pay a visit to the customs office and arrange for the transfer of the merchandise to the warehouse you have been so eager to secure. My Chief Swordsman will, of course, accompany him at all times, first to the bank and then to the customs house. There will never be an opportunity for the doctor to be alone with my money; therefore, thoughts of absconding with it would be futile and, I musst tell you, very, very dangerous."

Grace dropped her head. Well, that was that. It was over. In the back of her mind she'd known all along he was too smart for this trick, that he'd never hand over a fortune in cash to an untrustworthy stranger, then deliberately turn his back long enough for the stranger to get away. A "mental thimble trick," indeed. How could they have been so stupid?

"Where does my cut come in?" Reuben asked dejectedly. He knew it was over, too.

"You and Dr. Haiss will be paid ten percent of the wholesale cost of the goods, and not until they have been safely delivered into my cusstody."

"Nine thousand dollars? The hell you say." He was arguing by rote now; he had no intention, she knew—she assumed; she *hoped*—of actually going into the opium business with the Godfather. "We want five percent of the retail," he snapped, "and that's not negotiable. Assuming you mark the stuff up about five hundred percent, that comes to roughly twenty-seven thousand bucks."

Wing looked ready to explode. "Very well," he grated, "I agree to your extortionist terms. You have much audacity, Mr. Smith. You bring nothing to this enterprice except a drunken abortionist. You risk nothing, you offer no investment capital of your own, yet you truly believe twenty-seven thousand dollars is just compensation—"

"You've got it wrong, Mark, I am giving something up. What do you call Gus here? My only sister, my helpmeet, my—"

"And you would sell her to me for money," Wing cut in, "like a slave!"

"You'd buy her like one."

"You are a filthy swine. Augustine is worth a hundred of you!"

"Oh, yeah? You're lower than a snake's belly. Gus wouldn't spit on you if you were on fire."

The argument degenerated into name-calling; Grace wondered when they'd challenge each other to see who could pee farther. An idea had begun to germinate in the back of her mind; she stopped listening to the bickering so the idea could grow. It was a lovely, outrageous idea that made the original opium deal seem like a bucket-shop bunco. An idea Henry would be proud of.

Touching Wing was repellent to her. She made herself do it anyway, a fingertip on his bony wrist, and he closed his mouth in the middle of calling Reuben a pig-catcher demon. Reuben retaliated by labeling him a *shmuck*, whatever that was; she had to silence him with a pinch on his forearm. "Excuse me, gentlemen. Excuse me, may I say something?"

The Godfather crossed his hands over his heart and bowed from the waist. "Of coursss," he whispered.

"What?" Reuben said rudely, rubbing his arm.

She turned her back on him and batted her eyelashes at Wing. "You haven't heard my answer yet—assuming what you said before was a marriage proposal?"

"Most sincerely. Most fervently!"

She put her hand in her lap before he could reach for it. "In that case, I accept."

"What?" Reuben screeched.

"I'm tired of rackets, Algie, I want to settle down. It's been fun, but this fast life is wearing thin. I deserve better, and Mark here is making me an offer I'd be silly to refuse." The silent opening and closing of Reuben's mouth reminded her of a carp. She slid her hand over to his thigh and pressed it, hoping he'd get the message: *shut up and trust me.* "I want it all this time, though, not just a piece of it. Here's the deal, Mark, and it's all or nothing. I want a hundred thousand up front, in an account with my name on it."

"I have agreed to this," he said joyfully.

"And I want a Catholic ceremony."

"Ah. Well. This is difficult." He looked sad.

She looked shocked. "But this is America—you weren't going to ask me to give up my religion, were you?"

"Nooo," he said uncertainly. "No, of course not."

"Okay, then. And I want a big church wedding, lots of flowers, bridesmaids and attendants, the whole—"

"Ah, my dear," he said gently, shaking his head, "already it is time for a compromice. I will agree to a Catholic ceremony—but in my home, not in a church—if you will agree to a traditional Chinese wedding immediately afterward."

Even better. It was hard not to conceal her

elation. "But I've always wanted a church wedding," she wheedled, for effect.

"I'm so sorry. That I cannot allow."

She pushed her bottom lip out. "Oh, all right. But can it be a big wedding?"

He looked ready to cry. "I am afraid not. No guests at all, my dear, because of the circumstances. But"—he brightened—"afterward, I have no objection to a large, festive reception. Would you like that?"

Reuben snorted in disgust.

"We'll see," she pouted. *Holy saints, it was perfect, perfect, perfect.* She could feel Reuben's nerves jumping; he was biting back a hundred curses and questions while he struggled to take her wordless, one-handed advice.

"So," said Wing, all business again. "Let us conclude our terms. An account will be opened for you, my dear, in the amount you specified earlier"—he was too delicate to mention the actual vulgar figure—"but it will not be in the name of Augustine Smith."

"But—"

"It will be in the name of Mrs. Mark Wing."

She sat back, exhaling silently. This son of a bitch wasn't stupid—but she already knew that. No matter; it made things harder, but not impossible.

"As soon as the goods are transferred into my cusstody, you and I will exchange sacred vows, my darling. After the ceremony, Mr. Smith, you and Dr. Haiss will be paid your exorbitant commission. Assuming all goes well, we'll continue to do business, but I'm afraid

I must insist that you and Augustine not meet again."

"But—but she's my sister!"

"Ah, well," Grace sighed philosophically. "A woman's first duty is to her husband."

"And one last little thing." Wing's casual tone alerted her to more danger. "Thanks to your excellent advance planning, these business matters can probably be concluded within two or three days—by Friday, shall we say?" They nodded warily. "Such a short time. For its duration, I feel the need to secure another small piece of collateral. Call it insurance."

"What now?" Reuben asked, suspicious.

Wing smiled. Grace was beginning to dread his smiles. "You."

"No." It came out of her mouth involuntarily; a reflex.

"Me?" said Reuben.

"You will come with me when I leave in a few moments, and remain an honored guest in my home until the wedding. After the ceremony, you'll take your leave, a richer and p'raps even a wiser man."

"Why?" Grace demanded, hard-eyed, letting her guard fall. "You're holding all the cards already, why do you need him?"

"Insurance," he repeated. "A gesture of good faith. Please don't take it amiss, but I do not trust your brother, dearest Augustine. I want him where I can see him, until it's too late for him to attempt any of his foolish tricks. Well?" he said to Reuben. "Do you agree?"

"I'd like to speak to Gus alone."

Wing narrowed his eyes evilly. Obviously the idea rankled. Grace didn't think for a second he really believed Reuben was her brother. His urbanity deserted him for a moment, and she caught a quick, unnerving glimpse of his madness. "Very well," he whispered. "For a minute. Be quick." He stood up and walked over to the door, where Tom Fun and the other hatchet man were still waiting.

"Grace, what in the—"

"Shh, we haven't got much time! I don't want you to go with him, but I don't know what to say to get you out of it!"

"What the hell are you doing? What's this about a wedding? Why did you—"

"Reuben, shut *up*," she hissed. "And quit looking like a disgruntled lover. Try to look brotherly."

"To hell with that, just tell me the plan."

"I haven't got a plan."

"You—"

"Not a *whole* plan. Trust me." She sat back, smiling for Wing's benefit. "Don't worry, though, it's all going to work out."

"I'm worried."

"Listen to me, Henry used to *do* a priest, it was one of his specialties. He'll 'marry' Romeo and me, and then..."

"And then what? He wants you in his *house*, Gus. Even if it's not a real marriage, how are you going to get out? And when does the charade end, before or after the honeymoon?"

"I'm working on that."

"Oh, great."

"Well, what do you want from me? I just thought it up five minutes ago! Don't worry," she repeated more calmly, "Henry will think of something."

"Wing's not going to hand over the drug money until *after* the ceremony," he reminded her, "and you can't touch your hundred thousand dollar dowry until you're Mrs. Wing. And after that, I'm supposed to just walk away and never see you again."

"Would you care?" she couldn't resist asking.

"Shit," he muttered, suddenly fascinated by the wet rings his glass made on the table.

"Well." She eked out a grim smile. "That's not quite the answer I was hoping for."

"Yes, I'd care." He kept his eyes on the glass rings. He opened his mouth and closed it. "I'd care," he repeated.

She guessed that was all she was going to get out of him. "Good," she said softly, and blushed, chagrined because of the words she'd secretly been longing for him to say.

Wing came back, and sat down without being asked.

Reuben said, "Okay. I'll play hostage at your house till Friday."

"On one condition," Grace specified, trying to sound casual. "You have to promise not to hurt him. If he's got black eyes or he's bleeding from a hatchet wound when I get there for the wedding, the deal's off. Agreed?"

Wing bowed again. "Just so. Not a hair on

his head will be harmed." Her hand was resting on the table. He snatched it up before she could react, and kissed it.

"This is so sudden," she managed weakly.

They stood up.

"Until Friday," Wing said lovingly. "My man will see to a conveyance for you. Where do you live?"

"I'm not telling you, and I'll see to my own conveyance. If you send messages to me in care of the Lombard Street Western Union, I'll get them."

"Augustine—you don't trust me?"

She didn't answer. She tried hard to bury her revulsion and look at him speculatively, as she might look at any man who purported to offer wealth and security for life in exchange for her so-called favors.

It worked. He smiled his spooky smile at her before saying, "Mr. Ssmith? Shall we go?"

She couldn't read Reuben's expression. All at once the whole scheme struck her as insane and perverted. She lost her nerve.

Maybe he saw it, maybe not; but to cut off her inarticulate protest, Reuben abruptly grabbed her by the shoulders, jerked her to him, and kissed her on the mouth. Their teeth clashed; the kiss was painful, not pleasurable. But she got to feel his body against hers and hold onto the hard muscles in his arms, and for that too-brief moment he was solid and real, and she was immeasurably comforted.

Then he let her go, grinning his cocky grin.

"So long, Gus, it's been fun. See you in church," he said with a wink.

Wing looked murderous. Ignoring the danger, Reuben put a loose, heavy arm around his shoulders, turning him. "So, Mark, what's to do at your house? You don't play poker, do you? Is your cook any good? I'm starved, by the way. Say, do you know any nice girls? I'm really..."

The rest was lost as the door to the Red Duck closed behind them.

20

In olden times, sacrifices were made at the altar—a custom which is still continued.
—Helen Rowland

The Godfather's idea of hospitality was to keep Reuben locked in his room, feed him well, and send him a whore every night. He welcomed the whores; at least they talked to him and kept him apprised of world events (the world consisting of two connecting buildings on Jackson Street), but for the rest, he might as well have been in solitary confinement. He hated it, and complained loudly and often, for all the good it did him, to the impassive hatchet son on the other side of the door. With cold, contemptuous courtesy, the guard would listen to his complaints, bow, close the door in his face, and relock it. Reuben might've pressed the issue harder if not for the unsheathed bowie knife in the guard's belt.

What he hated most about his imprisonment was all the time it gave him to contemplate how completely and spectacularly he'd botched this swindle. Manfully resisting the temptation to shuffle all the blame onto Henry, whose brainchild it had been, he had hours to own up to the truth that he'd behaved exactly like one of his own victims by letting greed cloud his judgment. "A mental thimble trick," he'd called it. "He won't see the one-time dodge going on right under his nose." How embarrassing. A clearer case of wishful thinking motivated by avarice and revenge he'd never seen.

On the third night of his captivity, a Thursday night, he sat up in bed and stubbed out his second-to-last cheroot. His room was large and lush, with a peculiar mix of Oriental and Occidental furnishings—venetian blinds on the windows and a dragon frieze below the plaster cornice; a homey hooked rug on the floor and painted storks and water lilies on the ceiling. Books and magazines were plentiful, but he was sick of reading. The clock on the mantel struck midnight. The house was finally quiet.

Out of the debacle, he could discern only one good thing, that Grace was out of it and at least temporarily free of Wing's clutches.

But she was coming back, because she had some half-baked plan that would save the day if it worked and get them all killed if it didn't. But what the hell *was* the plan? The wedding was definitely on; he knew that much because Wing had paid a visit to his opulent prison cell this evening to tell him the opium transfer had gone off without a hitch this afternoon, and the blessed nuptials would commence tomorrow in the courtyard, weather permitting, at eleven A.M.

For two days, from his third-floor window, Reuben had had a good view of the preparations going on below, the cleaning, sweeping, and whitewashing, the extravagant decorating with potted trees, banks of flowers, hanging lanterns, tinsel, streamers, wreaths, and on and on. The colorful spectacle depressed the hell out of him. Henry was going to be the priest, and Wing had relented enough to allow one wedding guest: Doc Slaughter. What Reuben couldn't figure out was the mechanics of the getaway, the "outlet," in bunco lingo, after the ceremony was over. How were they going to escape with their skins still on, much less a hundred thousand dollars in their pockets? Granted he'd done a lousy amateur's job of helping to plot the first scheme; it still drove him crazy that he had to cool his heels while Grace and Henry and Doc plotted the second one.

Lying in his arms that last night at the Claymore, Grace had made a shame-faced confession. The other thing she had against the scheme was that even if it succeeded, all

Wing would lose was money, which he could easily afford. It wasn't very Christian of her, but she couldn't help it: she wanted something bad to happen to him.

At the time, he'd sympathized with the sentiment, but not enough to consider altering the plan they'd set in motion to accommodate it. But something had happened since then to change his mind.

The prostitute Wing had sent him tonight and last night was Toy Gun, the plain-faced little girl Reuben had terrorized with the derringer in the House of Celestial Peace and Fulfillment. Tonight, over a peculiar card game she'd taught him called foo-foo, she'd told him about her life in the brothel—not much, since she was still shy and distrustful, but enough to chill him. Her poor but reasonably happy childhood had been cut off abruptly at the age of fourteen when her parents had sold her to slavers in Hong Kong for two hundred dollars. But she'd sold on the barracoon for two thousand, she bragged with pathetic pride, and she'd been one of Kai Yee's singsong girls ever since. How did she like her new life? he'd asked, and she'd shrugged her small shoulders. Was she ever mistreated? Oh, no. No one beat her? Oh, no. No? Well, sometimes, but only when she was bad. When was that? Oh, when she was lazy, when she didn't please a customer, when she wasn't respectful enough to her masters. Did Kai Yee ever beat her? She wouldn't answer that; she'd paled and hidden her face, but not before he'd seen the stark fear in her eyes. She was tiny, demure, hardly bigger than a child; the thought of someone raising a hand against her—or a belt, or a whip—made him feel sick.

Would she leave if she could? he'd asked her. The adult stoicism in her little-girl face was heartbreaking. "Never go." But if she *could*? "Never get away. Never." She told him the story of Quee Ho, a sixteen-year-old singsong girl who had tried to run away from the house last year. Wing's highbinders found her and beat her to death—accidentally, thereby bringing down the Godfather's wrath on their own heads for destroying valuable property. Toy Gun knew other stories, of girls in other brothels who'd had their feet cut off for trying to escape, or their tongues cut out for telling lies. She'd never heard of anyone who'd successfully gotten away. "Never leave," she repeated stolidly. "Never."

Tonight, when it was time for her to go— Wing's generosity didn't extend to letting a working girl stay with a non-paying customer for longer than a few hours—she'd begged Reuben not to tell anyone that she hadn't "pleased" him, that all they'd done was play cards. Why, he asked, because she'd be punished for it? She wouldn't answer. "Don't tell, okay?" she repeated, anxious. He gave her all the money he had, which wasn't much, and said okay.

He was in sympathy with Grace now. He very much wanted something bad to happen to the Godfather.

He started again on his familiar pacing route—bed to window, window to door, door to bed. It reminded him of Grace pacing in the hotel room the day before the meeting at the Red Duck, glaring at him and Henry, saying, "Well, *somebody's* got to worry about all the things that might go wrong!" The shoe was on the other foot tonight. She had a plan by now—she'd better have a plan—but what if Wing saw through it as easily as he had the last one? What if he didn't believe Henry was a priest? What if he called the wedding off, forcibly evicted everybody but Grace, and had his way with her? He was already more than a little deranged; what if he went completely around the bend, killed everybody but Grace, and had his way with her?

Reuben stopped at the window in mid-circuit. No fog tonight. The courtyard below was dark and quiet, and empty except for the hatchet man on duty at the street door; from here it looked like his old pal, In Re. Only a few windows in the brothel were still lit, and whatever was going on behind them was going on silently. In the dark stillness, Reuben accidentally let his guard down. Just for a second he saw clearly the lurid picture his mind had been battling for two days—the picture of the Godfather bending over Grace on a bed. He saw his silk robes and white, slithery hair; smelled the sweet reek of opium; heard the soft slide of sallow skin over white. If Wing got his hands on her again, she'd be scared, no matter how many drugs the bastard gave her, how much dope he made her smoke.

Snarling, Reuben picked up a ceramic vase—priceless, he hoped—and flung it at the door, where it smashed to bits with a loud, satisfying crash. Immediately the key turned in the lock and the door swung open. Reuben charged the shocked guard, who took one look at his face, jumped back, slammed the door, and locked it as fast as he could. Reuben kicked at the door until his toes ached, then limped back to the bed and set a match to his last cigar.

Wing was a fiend, and he would put his hands on Grace over Reuben's dead body. His *dead body*. It was terrifying to realize that finally, at last, there was someone in the world he cared about more than himself. It seemed impossible; he'd have denied it, laughed at it, if the circumstances hadn't gotten so dire that the truth was staring him in the face. But there it was. And even though it was terrifying, it was also exhilarating; wonderful, really, in a horrible kind of way. He lay on his back and blew two perfect smoke rings, wishing Grace was lying beside him so he could tell her the news. Painful, intense longing gripped him; he needed her now, right now, not just to touch her but to tell her what he was thinking.

But would he? If he did, it would be for the first time ever. Why was it so hard to say out loud the things he was feeling? Why couldn't he even imagine himself saying to her, "Grace,

I'm in love with you"? To say to her straight out, "I love your toughness, and how smart you are, the way you make me laugh. I never knew a woman with so much courage and guts. You're so damn beautiful, sometimes it hurts to look at you, and when we make love I feel like I've got a soul. A *soul*, Gus"—How could he say those words to her? Even thinking them, lying here *thinking* them, was making his face turn red, he could feel it.

The last night at Willow Pond, before they'd all packed up and come to San Francisco, Ah You had given him a piece of advice. They'd met under somewhat awkward circumstances—in the dark hallway at dawn, as Reuben was sneaking back to his room from Grace's. Ah You had looked like a convict in a black and white striped nightshirt.

"You know story about two stars, Mira and Hamel?" he'd asked without preamble. Used to his roundabout-parable style by now, Reuben had simply said no and waited. "They live in sky, Mira a fisherwoman, Hamel a cowboy. Fall in love, all happy, till Hamel quit doing cowboy duties and make God of Sky mad. God of Sky make Hamel mute for punishment." Reuben yawned without covering his mouth, hoping to speed things along. "Now along come handsome fisherman name Didra, fall in love with Mira. All day, Didra say love words to Mira while poor Hamel watch, can't talk. Mira give Didra big carp for present, go off together, love-love. Too late, Hamel make big scratch in sky with horseshoe, write, I

LOVE MIRA. Too late—Mira already go. Too late. Sad, sad."

The main thing that had bothered Reuben about Ah You's tale was its lack of subtlety. He'd never known the pesky Chinaman to be so damn literal with his unsolicited hogwash. The other thing that had bothered him was how the hell Ah You could know so much about his private business, stuff he didn't even know himself, or not for certain.

Well, he knew his own mind now. He could even wonder now *why* it came as such a big surprise to realize that he loved Grace. Hadn't he broken a thirteen-year moratorium on truth for her sake? Nobody in the world except Grace knew he was a Ukrainian Jew from lower Manhattan—not that there was any shame in that; it just wasn't the sort of thing that got a man very far here in the land of the free. He guessed it was ironic that he'd given his poor, inexperienced heart to a woman who was arguably even more untrustworthy than he was, and unquestionably as big a liar. But there you were again. Hearts went where they would, and his was solidly in the hands of a larcenous, yellow-haired angel.

He'd never get a wink of sleep tonight, he thought as he extinguished his cheroot and blew out the candle stub by the bed. This was a night for worrying. He owed Grace that much, considering all the worrying she'd done and all the times he'd told her to relax, everything would be fine. "Trust me. We're going to live happily ever after." What insufferable arrogance. He'd make partial amends by staying awake tonight and worrying. It was the least he could do.

A good intention. But he was asleep before the clock struck one, dreaming of a happy ending.

"Lovely day for a wedding," Doc Slaughter opined, hands in the pockets of his sober blue morning coat, gazing across the fragrant, flower-bedecked courtyard. The black-robed *boo how doy* standing around in whispering clusters looked like crows in an exotic garden. *Armed* crows: everybody sported one or more pointed, sharp-edged implements of destruction in his belt. Doc himself resembled a stork, Reuben thought; he'd never seen him in formal clothes before, but his long, gaunt frame took to them perfectly. Maybe even more than a stork, he looked like a prosperous undertaker.

Reuben was in black himself—he hoped not prophetically—and felt grateful to Doc for thinking to bring him some clean wedding duds. Wing hadn't thought of it, and the clothes Reuben had been wearing since Tuesday had gotten a trifle ripe.

"I think the prostitutes are a nice touch," he said to Doc, who nodded and glanced up at the singsong girls, gaping down at them from every window in the whorehouse. Reuben tried to spy Toy Gun among them, but couldn't find her.

Behind him, Tom Fun cleared his throat. Reuben glanced back, and the hatchet man sent him an evil glare, ostentatiously fingering the ivory handle of his sword. If not for his ubiquitous presence, Reuben could've asked Doc what the hell was going on, what exactly the plan was. But Tom made sure they were never more than two or three feet away, so there was no opportunity.

"He looks radiant, doesn't he?" Reuben said to the hatchet man, shrugging a shoulder in Wing's direction. Tom Fun bared his teeth—predictably; it was so easy to get his goat, it wasn't even fun anymore. But Reuben's observation was the literal truth: the Godfather positively glowed with excitement and anticipation. His wedding attire was sober in the extreme, and Western to a fault. He wore a gray tweed frock coat and plain trousers, a dark waistcoat, high-collared white shirt, and a butterfly bow tie. He was saving himself, finery-wise, for the Chinese wedding following the Catholic ceremony, when he would don a bright orange Ming robe with a multicolored girdle and silver scimitar. (Reuben knew this from Toy Gun, who had gladly passed on all the wedding gossip she knew.) Right now the bridegroom looked stereotypically nervous; he was pacing, in fact, to and fro in front of a newly erected temple to Nu Wo, goddess of creation.

Reuben checked his watch: eleven-ten. The bride was late. For that matter, so was the priest. Beside the temple, a little band was tuning up.

426

Reuben had heard them practicing on their cymbals, gongs, and drums yesterday. He hoped to God they wouldn't start playing their unbelievably awful racket now; his nerves were shot already.

He couldn't hear the knock, but the hatchet man on duty at the courtyard door leading to the street swung the big door open to admit a new arrival.

Reuben stared, blinked, and stared some more. If he hadn't been expecting Henry, he'd never have recognized the balding, portly, red-nosed, patently Irish clergyman who bustled bowleggedly into the yard, staring around in a vaguely scandalized way at the milling hatchet men, the joss house, the tuning instrumentalists in the corner.

"Father O'Brien," Wing exclaimed animatedly, coming toward him with outstretched hands.

Henry kept his disapproving air throughout the murmured greetings and introductions. Ignoring Tom Fun, Reuben went closer. Father O'Brien wore a black cassock and a white clerical collar; he carried a prayer book and a small black case with a handle. "Most irregular," he was blustering to Wing, and something about having to waive the banns. He had a watch fob attached to the breast of his cassock; he made a show of checking the watch, and Reuben clearly heard him say, "Sure, and where's the bride? I've got a major funeral across town at noon, I can't be stayin' here a second past eleven-tharty." Wing said nervous, placating things, and checked his own watch.

Tom Fun put a warning hand on his shoulder, but Reuben shrugged it off and strode up to Father O'Brien. "Pleased to meet you, Father," he said, shaking hands. "I'm Algernon Smith, Augustine's brother."

"Lovely garl," Henry muttered distractedly, and looked at his watch again.

This time Reuben heard the knock at the door, an irresolute two whacks followed by a plucky, stout-hearted four. Everybody turned toward the sound, and In Re opened up. And there stood Grace in the portal, splendid in a wedding gown of virginal white satin, complete with train and eye-popping decolletage, and a floppy leghorn hat trimmed with orange blossoms. She carried more flowers in a bouquet in one hand and a saucy white parasol in the other. The Godfather's delighted smile faltered, and Reuben recalled gleefully that in China white was the color of bad luck. Wing pulled himself together quickly, though, and hurried to greet his bride.

As soon as he touched her, just his hand on her hand, Reuben moved toward them, careless of the growling noise Tom Fun made behind him. Grace's gaze skittered over his, the blue eyes glittering with nerves. She looked so beautiful he couldn't stand it. "Sis," he greeted her, but Wing kept him from touching her by pulling her to his side and anchoring her there with a steely arm around her waist.

"Hello, Algie," she said, smiling tensely. "How are you?"

It wasn't a casual question; she wanted to know if anybody had been using him for sword practice. "I'm fine," he said adamantly, and the relief in her eyes made him miss a couple of heartbeats.

"Weel, now," said Henry, rubbing his hands together in a priestly way, "are we after bein' ready, then? You want to stand here by this—this *shrine*, is that it?" He opened his black case and began taking out vestments, a long white nightshirtlike garment that Reuben thought was called a surplice, and a shiny green scarf affair that went around his neck and hung down to his knees. Where had he gotten this stuff? Even Reuben felt slightly shocked to think he might've robbed a *church*.

In a low voice Reuben could barely hear, Grace murmured to her smitten bridegroom, "Before we start, isn't there a little bit of business we need to address?"

"All taken care of, my darling," he answered tenderly, bending over her.

She sent him a luminous, devastating smile that would've reblinded a blind man. "It's not that I don't trust you," she purred, sexy and good-humored, "but would you mind if I took a tiny peek at the bankbook?"

Enslaved, he reached into his inner coat pocket and withdrew a slim, leather-bound passbook. Grace opened it and glanced inside. She was much too accomplished to let even a trace of greedy satisfaction cross her features; simple pleasure was another thing, though, and she let that emotion radiate through another dazzling smile. "Lovely," she murmured, and opened the dainty white reticule dangling from her wrist.

Her hypnotized lover reacted immediately. With the speed of a striking cobra, his hand shot out and grasped her wrist. "Not yet," he whispered, showing his teeth. "Not quite yet."

The flush on her cheeks could mean either anger or pain. Not knowing which, Reuben stood still, tense and impotent, while Wing extracted the bankbook from her white-fingered grip and slid it back inside his pocket. The incident was over in seconds. Afterward, a cloud seemed to have drifted across the sky, darkening the courtyard and turning the banks of crimson poppies to blood-red. The black-garbed hatchet sons looked more sinister to him than they had a minute ago, and even the monotonous plinking of the orchestra sounded menacing.

Father O'Brien took up a position in front of the creation goddess and cleared his throat loudly, signaling the start of the ceremony. "Who'll be givin' this woman to this man in holy matrimony?" he boomed, skipping the preliminaries and getting down to business. Since this was undoubtedly Wing's first Catholic wedding, Reuben thought Henry could probably recite the baptism ceremony, or the one for extreme unction, and the Godfather wouldn't know the difference.

"I am," said Doc, taking Grace's hand. There was a minor scrambling for places;

Wing looked confused until Henry took him by the arm and planted him directly in front of him. Reuben started forward, thinking he'd stand for best man, but Tom Fun loomed up out of nowhere, sword and all, blocking his way. Reuben moved to the side without a murmur.

The ceremony didn't last long. Henry made a perfunctory speech about sanctity and fidelity, and then got down to it. Even knowing it was a farce, Reuben hated it. Grace's soft-voiced responses set his teeth on edge and caused an odd, stifling sensation in his throat that felt uncomfortably close to panic. He wanted it over soon, *now*—but when it was, and Wing leaned down for the bridal kiss, the profound unthinkableness of letting him touch her rose like bile in his mouth and he came close to violence. Doc's bony hand on his sleeve snapped him back to reality. Repelled, he watched Grace accept the Godfather's kiss with perfect composure, betraying no distaste, and for once her professionalism didn't charm him.

Father O'Brien cleared his throat again, cutting the tender moment short. "Lovely, just lovely. I've got the marriage certificate," he announced, pulling it out of his black case. "If you and the two witnesses would be kind enough to take a moment to sign, I'll leave you to yer celebratin' and be on my way."

There was a long table covered with refreshments along the wall by the door. The wedding party trooped over and used the table to sign the marriage certificate. Doc and Tom Fun were the witnesses. Left unguarded, Reuben trailed after them, on pins and needles to know what was going to happen now. When the signing was over, Henry gave Wing a hearty, bone-numbing smack on the back, cried, "Congratulations!" and proceeded to wring his hand in a painful-looking shake, all the while turning him in an arc away from the table. If he hadn't been waiting for something like it, Reuben would never have noticed Doc's swift, silent capture of the marriage certificate and its smooth slide into his derby hat.

For all his previous hurry, Henry took off his wedding vestments very slowly, and folded and put them away with great deliberation. He checked his watch again and glanced apprehensively at the door. "Is there no wedding toast, then?" he asked jovially. "I'm thinkin' I've just got time for a quick one." His about-face wasn't hard to swallow; he looked like the kind of priest who enjoyed his toddy. Why was he stalling? What hadn't happened that was supposed to happen?

Wing took the priest's elbow and moved him across the courtyard. "We have another ceremony now, as you know. Afterward, we will celebrate. P'raps you can return then and join us?" The invitation was barely courteous; Wing's steady progress toward the door said he wanted Father O'Brien gone.

"God bless you, then, and grant you a long and happy life together," Henry oozed at the

432

door. "And may your children spring up around you like grapevines."

"Thank you, Father." Grace had the same drawn and anxious look around the eyes as Henry. She embraced him, pressing against his padded belly. He hugged her back, hard and quick; the look he sent Reuben over her shoulder was full of veiled alarm. Helpless, Reuben watched him turn. In Re opened the door for him, and a second later he was gone.

"Dr. Haiss," said Wing dismissively. "Until we meet again."

"Right," muttered Doc, taking the hint. He turned to Grace. "Congratulations again."

As if on an impulse, she embraced him. Reuben heard her say, "Thank you," then murmur something else he couldn't hear.

"See you," Doc said to Reuben, shaking hands, and in the barest whisper from the side of his mouth, he added, "Stall." Then he was gone, too.

Stall?

"And now, Mr. Ssmith, I believe you and I have some unfinished bissness." Reuben went rigid when Wing's hand went to his pocket, and he only relaxed a fraction when the Godfather didn't pull out a dagger or a straight razor, but a long brown envelope. The payoff?

Opening the envelope, he blinked down at a two-inch-thick wad of greenbacks. More money than he'd ever made, stolen, or swindled in his whole life. They might as well have been pages from a book on agrarian reform, though, for all the excitement they aroused in him. Right now they were just another way to stall. "You don't mind if I count 'em, do you, Mark?" Leaving the bills where they were and without waiting for Wing's answer, he squinted down into the envelope and proceeded to count them one by one, or pretend to, as slowly as he could. Twenty-seven thousand on the nose. "I think you're a hundred short. Let me double check."

Wing uttered a vile-sounding word in Chinese, pulled a wallet from his pocket, extracted two fifties, and almost threw them at Reuben. "We bid you good day," he said pointedly.

"I'd like to say good-bye to my sister alone," he blurted, reaching for Grace's hand. It was ice-cold.

"I'm afraid not." Wing glanced back at Tom Fun.

"Why not?"

Tom Fun came around his master, bristling with animosity, obviously relishing the prospect of throwing Reuben out on his rear end.

"Hold it—*hold* it! The least you can do is let me kiss the bride." He tried a sickly smile. Whatever happened, he wasn't walking out of here without Grace.

"It's all right," she said evenly, with a calmness belied by the fear sparking behind her eyes. "Isn't it, Mark? After all, he is my brother." Wing couldn't seem to speak, and Grace took the initiative by lifting her arms and gliding past him toward Reuben.

They embraced. His ardor knocked her

floppy hat sideways, and for a moment her face was shielded. She took the opportunity to mumble in his ear, "How come there's never a cop around when you need one?"

"Gus, what the hell?" he whispered urgently. She straightened her hat, one-handed, and kissed him on the mouth. It wasn't the least bit sisterly. He barely heard the vicious hiss of Wing's curses, because the warm, solid reality of Grace in his arms crowded everything else out of his senses. But he retained enough presence of mind to drop his hand and grope her left thigh, the one turned away from the Godfather, in hopes of feeling the hard shape of a little derringer under her wedding gown. Not this time.

"Take your hands off my wife, do you hear? Otherwice I will kill you."

No more time. He grasped her hand, which was slick with sweat, like his. "Let's go," he muttered. Spinning, pulling her with him, he made a dash for the courtyard door. The knob turned under his hand and the heavy door opened. In Re, who had been facing the street, pivoted in surprise. He looked a little like Santa Claus, Reuben remembered thinking once; but he reached under his black pajamas and came up with a big, shiny meat cleaver, and then he looked more like the world's most intense butcher.

"Uh-oh," said Grace.

They whirled back around. Tom Fun whipped his sword out of his belt, grinning, and made a bombastic whirring noise with it over his head. Wing barked out something in Chinese. Reuben felt the prick of In Re's cleaver between his shoulder blades, nudging him forward. Tom Fun moved nearer in front. Reuben and Grace were in the middle: a hatchet sandwich. The muttering and yelling on all sides grew louder as the other highbinders closed in. Wing held out his hand. "Come, my dear," he said seriously.

Then Reuben felt a rougher shove from behind. Grace stumbled; he caught at her and they both turned around, expecting an attack. "Hallelujah," Reuben prayed in an awed whisper. "It's the cavalry."

Almost. A phalanx of blue-coated policemen funneled into the courtyard, wearing helmets and wielding pistols and wooden billies. Like spooked prairie dogs, the whores in the windows ducked out of sight, and a weird quiet blanketed the concrete courtyard. Grace came into Reuben's arms with a soft cry, and he held her tight, whispering, "Baby, baby," not sure which of them was trembling harder. He'd never been so glad to see a policeman in his life, and damn the consequences.

The lead police officer gave an unintelligible order that sounded like "Soich douse," and two officers trotted across the courtyard and into Wing's house. The police were outnumbered by about five to one, but when the leader ordered everybody to drop their weapons and put their hands up, the hatchet men obeyed. All except Wing, who was paralyzed. He wasn't even mad yet, he was just—paralyzed.

"Youse!" bawled the lead cop, whose back was to Reuben. "Is your name Mark Wing?" The Godfather came out of his trance enough to nod. "Den I got a soich warrant for youse. Dis is it." He handed him a folded paper, which Wing mechanically unfolded and tried to read.

Reuben pulled back far enough to look at Grace, who was grinning like the Cheshire cat.

"I'm Captain Gallant, see, I'm wit' a special task force dat's charged wit' cleanin' up vice and rootin' out illegal drug importers, get it? We had a tip about youse, and we're crackin' down now."

Reuben dropped his forehead on Grace's shoulder and let the laughter bubble up, smothering it in her veil. *"Captain Gallant?"* he wheezed, afraid to look at her. She was trying to make her snorts and snickers sound like sobs of relief, which only made them both laugh harder.

"We found it, Captain!"

The two "policemen" who'd disappeared into the house lumbered out, hunched over a heavy wooden chest. They set it down at Lincoln Croaker's feet. "It's opium, sir," said one; if Reuben wasn't mistaken, it was Winkie. "Dere's half a ton o' the stuff down in the basement."

Captain Gallant drew himself up and said something he'd probably wanted to say all his life. "You're under arrest."

Wing finally came out of his stupor. "For what?"

"Violations of the Narcotics Act."

"If there isn't such a thing," whispered Grace, "there ought to be."

"We've had youse under surveillance for mont's, Wing. Get the resta the stuff outa there, boys, and hurry it up. We're confiscatin' it for evidence, see? You'll have t' come wit us downtown." He turned around. Reuben couldn't get over how official he looked in his uniform and helmet. His shiny buttons winked in the sunshine, dazzling the eye; even his posture was authoritative, and his raspy voice carried like a rusty bell in the courtyard. Who would've thought it? Lincoln had missed his calling.

"An' who might you be?" he demanded, smacking his wooden club against his palm.

"Algernon Smith, at your service," Reuben said respectfully. "And this is my sister, the new Mrs. Wing. She can go, can't she?"

He stroked his mustache, which hardly looked pasted on at all. "I don't see why not. We got nuttin' on no *Mrs.* Wing, so she's—"

Wing lunged like a springing tiger, clawed fingers straining for Grace's throat. Reuben only had time to pivot, so Wing's snarling, flat-out onslaught landed on him, not her. But they were both slammed against the wall with torpedo force, and Reuben felt rabid fingers clutch and close around his neck. Through blurring eyes, he took note that Wing had his teeth sunk into the unpadded shoulder of his coat, and he was shaking him like a badger while he strangled him. Grace screamed.

A bony *whack* sounded loud and clear, and

instantly the pressure was off. Reuben gasped for air, while Wing slid to his knees and toppled over on his back. Above him, Lincoln shook his head in deep disappointment, twirling his billy. "Tsk-tsk-tsk," he mourned. "Now I gotta add assault to the charges. An' resistin' arrest. Cuff 'im, Sergeant."

Grace pulled Reuben, who was still clutching his throat and choking, away from the body. "He *bit* you, she marveled, checking his torn sleeve.

"It didn't go through," he grated hoarsely. "He only got a mouthful of coat."

"Now dere's just one more little thing." Turning his back on all the gawking, emasculated-looking hatchet men, Lincoln lifted his beetle brows expectantly.

"Pay him," Grace muttered when Reuben looked blank.

"Ah, of course," he said agreeably, as understanding dawned. "And what was the, ah, arrangement?"

"All of it."

He looked at her in disbelief. *"All of it?"*

"Shhh. Pay him, Reuben, and let's get out of here."

Lincoln gave his palm a few more smacks with his club, waiting.

Deeply disgusted, Reuben pulled the bulging envelope out of his pocket and handed it over. "Of course we'll be happy to cooperate," he said loudly. "Here's my card if you want to get in touch with me, Captain."

"Yeah, I'll do dat."

"Oh, one last thing." Grace dropped Reuben's hand and left him to walk back over to Wing's prostrate body. He had his eyes open, but they weren't focusing on much. Not until she bent over him, leaning into his line of vision, and plucked the little leather bankbook out of his breast pocket. "That's mine, I believe," she murmured, securing it in her reticule. "Bye, Mark. I'll come and visit you sometime in prison." Wing mouthed, quite distinctly, a blunt Anglo-Saxon curse. Grace gasped prettily. "All right, then, I won't," she huffed, and flounced away. "Come on, Algie, let's go home."

"Yes, Augustine."

But at the door, a thought struck him. "Wait here for two seconds," he told Grace, and walked over to where Lincoln was supervising the burgeoning pile of opium chests in the center of the yard. "Do something for me," he said quietly.

"I ain't done enough already?"

"You've done splendidly, and been well paid for it."

He couldn't argue with that. "So now what?"

"That's a whorehouse," Reuben said, dipping his chin at the House of Celestial Peace and Fulfillment. "There's a girl in it named Toy Gun. I want you to get her out and take her to the Presbyterian Mission on China Street. She'll be scared to death, she might even claim she doesn't want to go. But she does. Take her there, and don't let her out of your sight till she's safe. Will you do it?"

Lincoln twirled his fake mustache while he looked at Reuben curiously. He didn't leer and he didn't make any lewd remarks; he just said, "Yeah, sure. Consider it done."

"Thanks." He felt like shaking hands, but decided it wouldn't look right. "See you around," he said instead, although he considered it unlikely.

"Yeah," Lincoln rasped in his sandpaper voice. "See you around."

Out on Jackson Street, Grace grabbed Reuben's hand and pulled on it. "Hurry, there's a hansom cab waiting for us right—"

He scooped her up and twirled her around in a jubilant circle, cutting off her startled laugh with a kiss. "We did it!" he crowed. "*You* did it," he amended out of fairness. Over her shoulder, he saw a covered patrol wagon and four horses standing beside the curb. Part of the Croakers's constabulary force, he surmised. "Where are they really taking Wing?" he asked, setting her on her feet but not letting go of her.

She grinned that sly grin that always unhinged him. "To the Embarcadero. The captain of the *Silver Pearl* was persuaded to take on a last-minute passenger for his Canton run."

All he could do was shake his head.

"Hurry, Reuben," she urged, pulling on his arm. "We have to meet Doc at the Colonial Bank on Montgomery Street at twelve-thirty."

"How come?" He came along amiably, thinking they looked pretty spiffy together, she in white and he in black.

"Because he's got the marriage license."

"Of course."

"Plus he's waiting to get paid."

"How does he know to go to that particular bank?"

"Because I—"

"You whispered it to him when he kissed you good-bye," he guessed, enchanted.

She dropped her eyes modestly. "Hurry," she remembered, pulling on him again. "After the bank, we've got a one o'clock ferry to catch."

"Where are we going?"

She looked amazed at his dullness. "Home, of course! Where else?"

21

Would you hurt a woman worst, aim at her affections.

—Lew Wallace

"It's empty!" Reuben whispered in Grace's ear.

She started; she'd been staring out at the Sonoma hills gliding past the train window, her head filled with a hundred and one thoughts, and she hadn't heard him come back. He'd only left a minute ago. "What's empty?"

"The smoking car!" He glanced over the back of her seat, where Henry was snoring in his chair, having drunk a little too much champagne on the ferry boat to Vallejo. "Come on, Gus," he urged, reaching for her hand. "Let's go."

"To the smoking car? Why—" She stopped. She knew why, and if she hadn't known, his face would've told her: he wanted to be alone with her. Smiling like a child's drawing of the sun, she picked up her purse and her wedding bouquet and went with him.

The smoking car smelled like a smoking car, but the couchlike seats, facing each other across low tables, were more comfortable than the regular parlor-car chairs. But the main attraction of this particular smoking car was that nobody was in it. Grace sat down primly on the bench seat opposite Reuben's, and watched him reach into his pocket for a cheroot. "Nasty habit," she remarked, admiring his dexterous, long-fingered hands and the white flash of his teeth when he stuck the cigar in his mouth. He'd taken off his tie; he looked like a cross between a pirate and a riverboat gambler in his handsome black wedding suit. A Jewish riverboat gambler. She remembered the first time they'd met, on the Monterey stage, and how easily she'd swallowed the story that he was a blind Spanish ranchero with an Oxford education. She wasn't a gullible person; she saw through most buncos because she'd perpetrated so many herself. But Reuben had rooked her like the greenest gull on the

443

wire, and all she could do was admire him for it. Truly he was a prince among thieves.

Her mouth dropped open when he set a match to a rolled-up dollar bill and used the bill to light his cigar. "How unbelievably tacky," she reproved him, while a smile twitched at the sides of her mouth.

He grinned and uncrossed his long, handsome legs. "Come over here and sit on my lap."

The grin and the gleam of his teeth clamped around the cheroot did something profound to the muscles of her stomach. She clucked her tongue. "I've never seen this vulgar, boorish side to you before. This is a real awakening."

He patted his lap. "Come on."

"I will not. Somebody might come." His brown eyes twinkled with humor and innuendo, and she heard her words in a different light. She blushed.

He patted his lap again. "Come on over here and give me a kiss. And bring your money with you."

The rakish tilt of his cigar got to her. If only he wasn't so damn cute. She made disgusted sounds, staring out the window. Then she got up, with a defeated sigh, and went to sit beside him.

He was quick. While she was lowering her behind to the seat, he seized her around the waist and forced her to detour, dragging her onto his lap. She put up a halfhearted fight, even said, "Reuben—damn it—" before she subsided, relaxing against his chest and clasping her hands around his far shoulder.

"Did you bring your money?"

She smiled that smile that always got to him, and batted her eyelashes. "I did, but do you know what? I can't remember where I put it."

"I'll help you find it," he said silkily. "Do you think you left it somewhere on your person?"

"Definitely." She closed her eyes as he began to stroke her up and down her spine, up and over her shoulders and down her arms. Her hands came unclasped and dropped in her lap, useless. "Do you like my wedding dress?" she breathed, letting him nibble on her jaw while he squeezed her knee with one hand and caressed the side of her breast with the other.

"Mmm." His breath on her skin was another caress. "Virginal white—a piquant touch."

"The groom didn't seem to care for it. Are you still looking?"

"Looking? Oh, yeah." He dipped his head.

She smiled, letting her lips tickle his hairline. A cloudy thought drifted across her lighthearted mood—that this lovely, funny moment would be perfect if they both weren't in disguise, if by some miracle their wedding finery were the real thing... But this was no time for wistfulness. She held her breath when he flattened his palm across her chest, an inch above the low shirred bodice of her gown. "You're getting warmer...warmer..." He dipped a long middle finger inside her dress and slewed it between her breasts. Her feet flexed; she drew her breath in through her teeth. "You're getting very warm."

"You're telling me."

"And I'm burning up. Oh, God, Reuben." She squeezed her eyes shut. "I think you should find it soon!"

"But you've hidden it so well."

The finger was sliding back and forth across the swell of her bosom, coming closer to her nipples with each slow pass. She couldn't help kissing his temple, his intent eyebrow. She hoped he never found the money.

He turned his head, and she pushed her hands into his dark hair, pressing a long, ardent kiss to his lips. Their tongues met. Her soft sigh changed to a groan when she felt the cool, slow, papery slide between her breasts. *Damn.* He'd found it.

The sight of all that virgin money, crisp green bill after crisp green bill, went a long way toward restoring her composure. "Look at it," they took turns saying, voices pitched to identical marveling tones. They passed the thick wad back and forth, riffling it like playing cards, smelling it, reveling in the heaviness of it. "Have you ever? I mean, *look* at it."

But finally they put it all back in its sedate brown envelope, more because they feared somebody would come in than because the charm of handling it had worn off. Reuben started to slide the envelope into his inside coat pocket.

"Oh, no, you don't." She caught his wrist, amazed at his brazenness.

446

"Honey," he exclaimed, all wide-eyed inno-cence, "I just didn't want you to be uncom-fortable."

"Oh, Reuben, how *thoughtful*. But I'm not the least bit uncomfortable."

He could do hurt and reproach better than anyone she knew. "Does this mean you don't trust me?" He even put his hand over his heart.

She had to laugh at him. But then a sober, practical thought occurred to her. "I sup-pose we could divvy it up now," she said dully. "Your share and ours—mine and Henry's." And then what? Would he leave her? She couldn't bear the thought, literally couldn't stand it.

He didn't look any more enthusiastic than she felt. "Okay, but not here," he decided. "Let's wait till we get home."

"Home" on his lips sounded so sweet, she had to kiss him again. She wasn't so addled as to give him the money back, though. "We'll put it right here in my little white pocketbook," she suggested. "That way we can both keep an eye on it."

"Good idea." But his eyes were on her mouth, and a second later his thumb was too, brushing her lips softly, opening them. "God, Gus, I missed the hell out of you. Do you know how long it's been since we've been alone together?"

"Three nights," she answered with alacrity, "and two and a half days."

That made a lovely smile curve his lips. "Yeah. Three long, lonely nights."

"Was Wing mean to you? Did anybody hurt you?"

"Nah. They just made sure I had plenty of time alone to think about you."

"I thought about you, too." She felt shy, and couldn't go on. She wasn't any good at this sort of thing. The *talking* part of lovemaking.

He lifted her chin with his fingers so she had to look at him. She suspected his eyes mirrored hers, cloudy with the same hard-to-say feelings and confusions. Luckily they thought of the solution at the same moment, and came together with a soft, almost bashful tenderness that set up a sweet aching in her heart. "Reuben." She could say that, so she said it over and over, while his mouth pressed against hers and his fingertips caressed her face.

When he tensed and pulled away, she knew they'd been discovered. She wasn't sure if she was relieved or appalled that it was Henry who stood swaying in the open doorway, holding a bottle of champagne in one hand and three empty glasses in the other. "I see you had a different kind of celebration in mind," he remarked dryly, taking the seat opposite. Grace unwound her arms from Reuben's neck, her heart pounding; he helped set her on her feet, and she hurriedly sat down next to him. "Where did you get that bottle?" she asked, going on the offensive to cover her embarrassment. "You're not allowed to have booze in here."

"What kind is it?" Reuben asked—typically. "Let's see the label."

"I tipped the dining-car waiter to let me take it with me. Then I tipped the porter to look the other way." The cork hit the ceiling with a celebratory pop.

"You're a regular tipping fool," Grace mumbled. "Reuben just lit a cigar with a dollar bill."

"Say, I like your style." Henry grinned, passing him a glass, and one to her. "To ostentatious display."

"Ostentatious display," Reuben seconded, clinking glasses.

Grace shook her head at them. "The only good thing about that toast is that if you can still say it, you know you're not drunk yet." She took a sip of her wine. "Mmm. Youthful, but not callow. Fun-loving; a hint of mischievousness that intrigues but never overwhelms. A certain—"

"Oh, knock it off," Reuben grumbled. "Champagne is the wine of the future," he said seriously, holding his glass up to the window and peering at it. "The country's on a roll. As the economy prospers, more and more Americans are going to celebrate with champagne. Mark my words."

Henry held up his glass and offered another toast. "To the future."

"To the future," they echoed solemnly, and drank.

Ah You, who had gone home on an earlier train, greeted them in the yard with open arms and an anxious face. "It worked?" he demanded before they could get out, dancing around their hired carriage like a sprite. "Nobody get hurt?"

Grace stepped down to the ground and gave him an impulsive hug. Hugging Ah You always felt like hugging a child. "It worked! We're rich!" she exclaimed—softly, so the driver couldn't hear. "It's all here"—she patted her purse—"and we got away clean. Everything went perfectly."

"Ho, excellent!" he cried, clapping his tiny hands. "Come in, we celebrate. I make special dinner already."

The men carried the luggage into the house while Grace paid the coachman. Extravagant tipping must be contagious, she thought, surprising him with an extra dollar. In the house, she decided to change out of her wedding gown before joining the party that had already started in the parlor. She put on a pretty pink-and-green-flowered frock Reuben had never seen before, and tied her hair up with a ribbon.

The sun was sinking behind the western hills, throwing long shadows and shafts of golden light across the polished living-room floor. She stood in the doorway for a moment, unobserved, watching the three men in her life as they talked and laughed and congratulated themselves on their nerve and intelligence. Reuben looked up and saw her before the others; the private pleasure in his eyes warmed her to her bones. She smiled, and for a second everything else blurred and receded; they might have been alone in the universe for all she knew, or cared. There was no one but him, and he was everything to her. If he left her now, what would she do?

"Grace!" exclaimed Henry, breaking the little spell. "Come in and drink more champagne! We've decided to get drunk."

"Drunker, you mean." She took the glass he handed her. The bubbles tickled her nose. "I do love this stuff," she told Reuben, and he toasted her approvingly.

Henry plopped down in a chair. "Well, where's the money? Show me the money, I want to look at it."

"It's in the hall, in my purse. I'll get it." She set her drink on the mantel, but Ah You said, "I get," and danced out ahead of her. Reuben leaned in the doorway to the terrace, watching her. She wanted to celebrate with her family, but right now, even more, she wanted Reuben all to herself. Not being able to touch him, to go to him and put her arms around his waist and her lips on his throat...it was a hardship. The sadness that had tried to waylay her on the train nudged at her battered heart again; once more she shunted it aside—but it was harder this time. *Buck up,* she commanded. If this was going to be a bittersweet moment, she meant to focus on the sweetness, and save the bitterness for later.

Ah You came back. "Here, Missy," he said, handing her the pocketbook.

Even before she opened it, she knew something was wrong; it felt too light, it wasn't thick enough. "It's not in here." Handkerchief, comb, change purse, fountain pen, scraps of paper, ticket stubs—she sifted through it all twice, three times, unable to believe her eyes. "It's not here."

Henry laughed; he was used to her jokes. She raised her head, and when he saw her face he stopped laughing. "What," he said slowly, "are you talking about?"

Reuben had gone still as a statue, the red sun behind him obscuring the expression on his face. She waited for him to explain it, or to break up and tell her the joke was on her. He didn't move or speak, and when she couldn't stand it any longer, she said, "What did you do with it?" and tossed the purse on the sofa.

"What did I do with it?" he repeated, and she thought that if his voice were shards of ice, she'd be impaled by a hundred slivered pieces. "That's not very funny, Gus. Where's the money?"

She watched him, stunned. "You stole it. Oh, Reuben, no."

"Goddamn son of a bitch." Henry got up slowly, trying to believe it. "I *knew* we shouldn't've trusted him." He couldn't stop shaking his head. "Goddamn son of a bitch."

"Thirty-three thousand isn't enough for you?" Grace said wonderingly. "You had to take our share, too?"

"When did you grab it," he snapped back, "when you went to change clothes? That means it's still in your room."

"How could you?" She was struggling against the need to burst into tears. "How could you betray us? How could you betray *me*?"

"Oh, that's good, Grace, that's really good. But I know you, don't forget. I already know that the guiltier you are, the better you get." He came toward her out of the shadows; she could see his face clearly now, and the anger in it made her blanch. When he threw his drink in the fireplace, she jolted. "But you won't get away with it, because your luck just ran out."

He got as far as the door to the hall when Henry yelled, "Hold it!" Reuben whirled, and Grace was as shocked as he was to see Henry beside the bookshelf, waving a pistol. "Where'd you put it, Jones? Just tell us where, and then you can get the hell out of here!"

Reuben looked back and forth between them in amazement, and just for a moment she thought he looked innocent—*really* innocent. Then she remembered how good he was, and her heart hardened. "Are you going to shoot me?" he asked, astonished. "Go ahead, then, do it! Keep the money, and to hell with both of you!"

Grace pressed her hands over her eyes. "Put it away, Henry," she muttered hopelessly. "For God's sake." To Reuben she said, "It's not even loaded."

Henry cursed, dropped into his chair, and reached for the champagne.

Reuben pierced her with one last look, spun on his heel, and walked out.

Ah You had been cowering in the corner.

"Maybe money get lost?" he suggested, wringing his hands. "Fall out on way home, get lost?"

She shook her head, listening intently. Reuben hadn't walked out the front door, he'd turned right and started up the staircase. He was going to her room. Without answering, she hurried past Ah You and followed.

He'd opened her traveling case and emptied all her clothes out on the bed. "Stop it," she said, fighting to get the words out past the lump in her throat. He glanced up briefly, then went back to ransacking her belongings. She came closer. She made a club with her two hands and smacked him on the back between the shoulder blades. "Stop it!"

He whirled. She didn't flinch when he lifted his hands, but she was still surprised when he only took her by the upper arms and gave her a soft shake. The hurt in his beautiful eyes made her want to hold him—made her want to sock him in the jaw. "Why'd you do it, Gus?" His voice sounded raw and exhausted. "Want to hear something funny? I was going to give it to you anyway. Then I was going to ask you to let me stay and help you turn Willow Pond into a vineyard."

How had her hands gotten spread out across his chest? "Stop lying," she said miserably, "I can't stand it. I was going to give you my share, Reuben, and beg you to stay. Damn you." She locked her fingers at the back of his neck. "I wanted you to marry me. You could've had me *and* the money, you bastard."

His arms came around her. He bent his head and pressed his lips to her temple. "What made you do it?" he asked tenderly. "Habit? It's okay, don't cry. It's in your blood, you can't help yourself. I forgive you."

"You snake, you lying snake in the grass." She found his mouth and kissed him passionately. "Stay with me," she said in a broken voice. "Don't go."

He backed her up against the wall. "We'll get separate bank accounts."

"Strongboxes."

"Safes with separate combinations."

She shuddered, and let him slide his knee between her thighs. "We'll hire lawyers," she managed. "Accountants to audit each other every year."

"Marry me, Gus. I can't live without you, you damn thief."

"Yes," she sighed into his mouth. "I will. But stop lying. I love you, Reuben, I don't care anymore."

"You stop. You can have everything, I'm telling you, all of it."

"Do you love me?"

"I love you. Keep the money, all I want is—"

A deafening shot and the smash of glass made them jump apart. Henry stood in the doorway, bottle in one hand, a smoking gun in the other. "Now it's loaded!" Taking aim, he shot another hole in the window.

"Henry!" Grace started for him, but Reuben grabbed her shoulder and pulled her back, trying to shield her.

"Where is it, Jones?" Henry hollered, drunk and wild-eyed, waving the gun in the air. "This's gone far enough!"

Another shot. Plaster sifted down from the ceiling. Grace let out a yelp and fought Reuben's frantic hands, struggling to get in front of him before Henry could fire off another shot. "Stop it, have you gone crazy?" she shrieked at him. Bang! Another bullet ripped a hole in the rug.

Ah You darted through the door. Henry took aim at the ceiling again, but before he could squeeze the trigger, Ah You danced under his guard and snatched the gun out of his hand. Henry roared out his fury, but stayed planted where he was, swaying, while Ah You scampered to the window and flipped the pistol out between the broken panes.

Grace sagged; Reuben held her so tight her spine cracked.

Henry stumbled to the bed and sat down hard. "Shit," he said mournfully.

Ah You grinned nervously and cleared his throat. Everybody looked at him. "So," he said, fidgeting. "You now okay, you two? You say love words and get mellied? *Married?*"

Grace blushed, but felt better about it when she saw the same pink stain on Reuben's cheeks. They said, "Yes," shyly, in unison.

Henry's mouth dropped open and he toppled over on his back, struck dumb.

Ah You laughed with delight. "Ho, good, good, then everything okay now. You be happy, make good wine, make babies."

Reuben gave her a squeeze. She kissed him and laid her head on his shoulder.

"So." Ah You reached into his baggy trouser pocket. "Hew is money. Good joke, huh? I borrow for a short time so clouds in mind go away, clear sky show tluth. *Truth*. Good to love each other even without money, yes?"

They started toward him menacingly, but he pranced backward, nimble and uncatchable. "We talk latew," he suggested, dropped the envelope on Grace's dresser, and escaped. They heard his light, staccato footsteps on the stairs.

Dazed, Reuben picked up the envelope and checked the contents. Grace reached for it, but he held on. "You thought I robbed you," he said accusingly.

"You thought I robbed you," she echoed, deeply offended. She pulled harder, but he wouldn't let go. They engaged in a brief tug-of-war.

"I'll take that." Henry loomed between them and plucked the money from their hands. "You're both too incompetent to trust with it." And he walked out the door.

"Wait, now—"

"Where are you going to put it?"

They got stuck in the doorway for a second, trying to get ahead of each other.

"I'll come with you—"

"Henry, wait, let me help—"

They trotted down the stairs after him, stepping on each other's heels.

Epilogue

All things come round to him who will but wait.
> —Henry Wadsworth Longfellow

May was Reuben's favorite month. The vineyard was at its loveliest then, the vines on the hillsides crowded with the heavy young emerald-green grapes. The air smelled so sweet you could get drunk just breathing it, and the sunshine felt like a clean, pure blessing. This morning the mountains had been shrouded in a sea fog before the sun broke through. Such a light—such beauty. Reuben thought that if he could make one perfect wine, it would taste like this green valley.

He left the two new workmen clearing chaparral from the unplanted acreage on the southern hillsides, and started along the dusty path toward the house. René had said to come at noon, when the new cuvée would be ready for sampling. It was good; they already knew that from a dozen previous tastings. René said it was very good, but Reuben was afraid to say how good he thought it was. This was the final sampling, the formal one, when he and his wine master would decide whether or not the last seven years had been worth all the blood and tears.

He rounded a turn in the track and saw his house at the bottom of the hill. The rose trees almost covered it up in May, with their big, absurdly fragrant blossoms, every color in the rainbow.

"Blood and tears" was an exaggeration. There had been no blood to speak of and very few tears in the seven years he'd lived in this house, with Grace for his wife and Henry and Lucille for his in-laws. The '89 harvest had been a disappointment, but mostly because, in his enthusiasm, he'd overplanted; and half of the cru in '90 hadn't met anyone's expectations, but at least they'd learned something—the Pinot Noir grape didn't do well on Willow Pond soil, at least not that year. Those were setbacks, and they'd been hard to take. But if that was the worst hand life could deal him, Reuben counted himself one lucky zhlob.

Grace's garden came into view as he topped the last rise before the long descent. He shaded his eyes with his hand, searching for her among the fig and orange trees, the golden poppies and deep blue lupines, before he remembered she'd gone into town today with Ah You. But she'd said she'd be back before lunch. Even if the tasting didn't go as well as he hoped, he had good news for her. The state viticultural commissioners had asked him to represent his district on their board next year. She'd laugh, he knew; he hadn't gotten over it himself: he, Reuben Jones/Jonah

Rubinsky, Jewish Ukrainian immigrant and reformed confidence hustler, invited to advise his respectable vineyardist neighbors on wine production, taxation, and marketing strategies. Life got stranger and more wonderful every day.

She wasn't back yet—the carriage was gone and the two chestnut bays he'd given her for her last birthday weren't in their stalls. He saw a flutter of blue from the veranda; Lucille waved to him, calling across the yard, "Henry's in the cellar with René; they're waiting for you!"

He waved back, and veered away toward the flagstone path that led past the house to the wine cellar. He'd won ten dollars from Grace when Lucille had married Henry; she'd given him three-to-one odds, and then she'd had the nerve to claim he'd misunderstood the terms of the wager. She tried to pull that all the time; he had to watch her like a hawk. But she'd been so sure Henry wouldn't give up drinking— Lucille's newest stipulation. Reuben had had a hunch, though; he'd caught Henry watching him and Grace together with poorly hidden envy once too often, and he'd just known Henry was a goner. Now they all rattled along together like family in the sprawling old house, with Ah You to look after them. Sometimes he wondered, a little fearfully, how his life could get any sweeter.

He ducked his head to descend the low-ceilinged stone steps, enjoying the sudden shock of cold and dark after the hot noonday glare. Claude Reynaud, his chief *remueur,* tipped his leather cap and went back to turning, one at a time, the twenty thousand magnum bottles lying nose-down in racks that spread sixty feet out into the lantern-lit dimness. "Much breakage today?" Reuben asked him automatically.

His eyes gleamed behind the wire-mesh mask he wore for protection from bursting bottles. "The usual," he answered, "four, five every hundred."

Claude's job drove Henry crazy. Why couldn't they just shoot carbon dioxide into the big wine vats like everybody else did except Paul Masson, he asked about three times a day, and save two and a half years of in-the-bottle fermentation? Think of the time and money they could save! Who'd know the difference? Who would care? Excuse him, but weren't they in this business to make money?

Reuben had stopped wasting his breath. If Henry didn't get it, he didn't get it; telling him the bubble wasn't married to the wine if you injected it artificially, trying to explain the difference between effervescence and indigestion— that only made him crazier. They'd come to a prickly understanding over the years: Reuben made the wine, without interference from anyone but his wine master; and Henry ran the business, without interference from anyone but Grace.

And Henry did his job beautifully. They'd all gone to France twice in the last five years, once to Epernay and once to Reims, and both times Henry had driven hard, shrewd bargains on the finest equipment money could buy: basket presses whose delicate pressure allowed only the free-run juice, special first-corking and *dégorgement* apparatus, pupitres as elegant as artists' palettes. He showed equally sound judgment in managing their taxes and selecting investments to build up their capital. For the first time in his life he was legitimate, and he was basking in it. Grace laughed at him and told him he was getting stuffy. He denied it, but lately Reuben had noticed he affected a dry, almost bankerly air. And he was putting more wax on his mustache than ever.

"Here he is," Henry told René, and the two men got up from the desk in the cramped, lamp-lit office to greet him. "We've been waiting," Henry grumbled, always impatient, and Reuben thought again that he was, unfortunately, temperamentally unsuited for the waiting game that fine winemaking demanded. He himself, on the other hand—who'd have thought?—was born for it.

René already had two bottles, checks against each other, cooling in a bucket of ice. In his taciturn way, the heavyset Frenchman was almost as nervous as Reuben. They'd met five years ago in Epernay, where René Morrel had been an assistant to a wine master at one of the small, fine, ancient châteaus near Avize. They'd made promises to each other before Reuben had extended, and René had accepted, the invitation to come to California and make beautiful Sonoma Valley wines. In a way, the little ceremony about to begin in the dim limestone cave-office represented the fulfill-ment—or not—of those promises.

René prized off the metal clamp and gently uncorked the first magnum. The smoky, whis-pery pop sounded just right—quietly jubi-lant, Reuben would've described it to Grace, just to get her. René poured two flutes to three-quarters full and handed him one by the stem. Over the rims, they exchanged a brief, solemn stare, and then they went to work.

"The sparkle is good."

"High-class sparkle. And the color's gor-geous."

"The color is good," René amended, always the cautious one. "We go outside later and look." He stuck his nose in his glass.

"Dreamy," Reuben judged, exhaling. His excitement was mounting. The smell of the very best champagne was like no other, and unbe-lievably tempting. This one had that special, superlative bouquet. *It had it.*

"Good," René decided at last.

"More than good?" Reuben probed; René's mastery of English was still basic, and some-times precise adjectives eluded him.

"Yes," he eked out after an interminable pause. "More than good."

Henry looked ready to explode. He didn't say it, but "Will you just drink it?" was written all over his face.

They drank.

The '91 cuvée had been three years in the bot-tle, a blend of a Napa vineyard's Pinot Noir grapes and Willow Pond's own Pinot Meunier and white Chardonnay. This was the first-run juice. The *méthode champenoise* was the only winemaking method Reuben allowed, and the champagne in the bottle from which they were drinking was the product of about two hundred individual handlings. He knew what he thought of it, but he was too scared to say it.

And René couldn't be hurried. Reuben grew as restive as Henry, scouring the Frenchman's face for a clue to his opinion, but the pursed lips and big twitching nose gave nothing away. Just when Reuben thought he'd have to shake him, the master lifted his hooded gaze and gravely pronounced his judgment. "It's good."

"It's good?" Henry queried, disappointed. "That's it?"

"How good?" Reuben asked quietly.

René smiled—something he rarely did, maybe because of the big gap between his front teeth. *"C'est magnifique, mon ami. C'est épatant—formidable. C'est tout."*

Henry did a little dance. "You like it?"

Reuben laughed out loud, overcome with relief. "Yes! Because it's superb—I wish you could taste it. The finesse of the Chardonnay is incredible. The persistence of the taste on the palate—it's *classic,* truly. It's lively, rich—"

"Not too dry or too hard," René put in.

"No, but not cloying—"

"No, never. A big wine, round and full. And soft, but not too soft. Full of life. *C'est joyeux*—a joyful wine, we say."

"I'd like to call it 'Sparkling Sonoma,' " Reuben said boldly. He'd named the cuvée months ago, when he first began to suspect it would be a classic, but he'd kept his hopes to himself.

"Why not?" said René, still smiling. "In my opinion, it could also be called *de luxe*."

He hadn't dared to hope for that. "Willow Pond Sparkling Sonoma, Brut, *de luxe cuvée*," he said lovingly, picturing it written on the bottle.

"You're *sure* you don't want to put a French label on it," Henry tried one last time. "I'm telling you, we could sell it for twice the price."

Reuben rolled his eyes. All of a sudden he had to see Grace. "Henry, bring the other bottle," he said, backing up. "Come up to the house, René, we'll celebrate."

"*Oui*, later," he answered, predictably; he never put pleasure before business. "I must do some things first, then I will come."

"Okay. I'll see you in a little while, and we'll talk about marketing." Impatient, he didn't even wait for Henry, but bolted out the door, across the main keeping room, and charged up the cellar steps.

Ha! The carriage was in front of the house, and Ah You was unloading packages from the back. "Is Grace inside?" Reuben called.

"Inside!" the diminutive houseboy called back. Even from here he looked excited. How could he know about the tasting already? Reuben wondered. He couldn't, of course. "The champagne is good!" he yelled, cupping his mouth. "It's great! René agrees!"

Ah You clapped his spidery hands together and grinned from ear to ear. "Go tell Missy!" he suggested, but Reuben was already sprinting up the front steps.

"Grace!" he hollered in the hall.

"Reuben?"

She was upstairs. He started up, she started down, and they met in the middle. "Grace—great news!"

"Reuben, I have to tell you!"

His wife of seven years was prettier than ever. He'd gotten used to feeling floored by the sight of her when he hadn't seen her in a while—three or four hours, say—but when she came upon him all of a sudden wearing *white*, like now, it was always a double-flooring. He wasn't sure why; something moving and terribly sweet about innocence and goodness, and then something deliciously ironic about chastity and virtue...or maybe it was just the way white made her skin even creamier and her hair look like spun gold... "What?" he asked, coming out of his pleasant trance when he noticed how flushed her face was.

"No, you first."

"Okay." He started back down the steps.

"Oh, no, let's go up," she suggested, plucking at the back of his shirt. He turned around obligingly and followed her up the stairs.

They went to their bedroom, which was Grace's old bedroom, with a wall knocked out years ago to add more space. They had a new bed, too, an oak four-poster with a white tester and quilt, and pillows at the headboard piled halfway to the ceiling. Grace took Reuben's hand and led him to the bed, which was where she wanted to be when she told him her news. Her husband of seven years was handsomer than ever, which didn't seem possible but was the literal truth. She loved the way he looked in his work clothes—the faded blue work shirt and the old gabardine trousers he wore with suspenders—and she liked to tease him by asking, on days when he looked particularly sweaty and filthy, if he was really the same man who used to tell her that all he wanted to do was sip iced champagne on his veranda and watch other people do all the work. She didn't know anybody, René Morrel included, who worked harder than Reuben, or anybody who enjoyed what he did so completely.

She could guess what he wanted to tell her, but she didn't say so. Sitting beside him on the high mattress, brushing a dark, beguiling lock of his hair back from his suntanned forehead, she said, "Okay, what?"

"The '91 is smashing," he said with a proud grin.

She couldn't spoil his news, but pretending to be surprised by it was another thing. "I knew it," she gloated, slipping her arms around his neck. "Haven't I been telling you it would be magnificent?"

"You have," he admitted. "That's exactly what René called it, by the way: *magnifique*."

"Ah, *très bon*." She gave him a smacking kiss

468

on the cheek. His happiness multiplied hers—something else that didn't seem possible, not on this day of days. "Will you take it to the French Club exhibition in June?"

"Hell, yes. We'll blow the hair off their heads, Gus. René says we can call it *de luxe*. I'm naming it Sparkling Sonoma," he said reverently.

"Sparkling Sonoma," she repeated, with suitable awe.

"We'll stay at the Palace Hotel when we go, and dress up and put on the dog, go to the opera every night if we can stand it—"

"The Palace?"

"Why not? We're going to be rich, Gus, I can feel it. The luxury market's been waiting all its life for this wine."

"I'm already rich."

He didn't hear. "René wants to go back to Cramant and Avize this summer and bring back more cuttings. He says the Pinot Noir might do better higher up, and I've been thinking we could try Pinot Blanc for part of the '98 cru, but not unless Cutler sells us those thirty-seven acres on the mountain." He jumped up, too excited to sit. "I'll go get you a glass. You won't believe—Oh." He grinned, sheepish. "I forgot. You have news, too."

"Well, compared to yours, it's hardly anything."

"Okay, then, I'll—"

"Reuben! I was kidding; come back and sit down. This is—this is—*news*."

He sat.

She faced him, shiny-eyed and flushed, and unable to stop smiling. "I went to see Dr. Burke while I was in town."

He frowned. "Why?"

"Because I've been feeling funny."

He took her hands, his elation gone. "Gracie, what's wrong? You didn't say a word; I didn't know you were sick—"

"I'm not sick," she interrupted, beaming. "Oh, Reuben. We're pregnant."

He didn't move; he was in open-mouthed shock. "But we can't be," he finally got out.

"I know! But we are!"

"How?"

"The usual way, I guess." She giggled. "Dr. Burke says it's one of those things."

"One of those things," he echoed, wide-eyed.

"He started talking about Graafian follicles and egg viability and blastocysts—but then he just admitted he really can't explain it. I said it was a miracle, and he said that was as good an explanation as any." For no reason she could think of, she started to cry.

Reuben wrapped her up in his arms. He was still dumbfounded, still trying to believe it. "A baby," he said, trying the word out.

"A baby," she sniffled.

"Ours. Oh, Christ, Gus. Our own little baby."

They rocked each other until she pulled away. "Are you crying, too?" she asked, astonished.

"Hell, no."

"Yes, you are." She pressed her wet cheek

against his and whispered, "Thank you for giving me a baby. I love you, Reuben."

"I love you, Grace. Let's lie down," he whispered.

They kissed, and fell back on the bed, and touched each other with gentle hands. It could've gone either way then; they could've kept laughing and crying and caressing each other, or they could've pulled themselves together and made love. A moment passed, and Grace felt things beginning to move in the latter direction—when the sound of footsteps coming down the hall told her they were about to have company. She tried to sit up, but Reuben wouldn't let her—he hadn't heard a thing—until Henry coughed, Lucille tittered, and Ah You sighed, all of them huddling in the doorway like sheep trying to get into the fold.

"Hello, there," Reuben greeted them, with a noticeable lack of enthusiasm.

"I thought you were coming right back down," Henry complained, bustling in, oblivious to nuance.

"Are we interrupting?" Lucille trilled good-humoredly. "We thought we'd have a toast."

Grace acknowledged her half-wink with a grin. This sort of thing happened fairly often, and if it wasn't Lucille accidentally walking in on her and Reuben, it was Grace accidentally walking in on Lucille and Henry. They were all newlyweds here, or at least they felt like it.

Ah You carried a tray with a magnum of champagne and four glasses. He set it on the edge of the bed, opened the wine expertly, and began to pour.

Reconciled to the interruption, Reuben brightened. "We've got something even better than this to toast," he announced, reaching for one of the bubbling glasses. "God, will you look at that *color*?"

"No, let's drink to the wine first," Grace said quickly, touching his arm. It seemed only fair; they had the rest of their lives to celebrate their miraculous new child, but Reuben's champagne victory was necessarily fleeting. She would be gracious, secure in her glorious motherhood, and let him go first.

"Sure?" he said softly, skimming his fingers up the back of her neck. "Ah You knows already, doesn't he?"

She nodded. Ah You knew everything at all times. "No, I want to toast the wine first. Then we'll tell."

"Okay." He touched his lips to the side of her mouth, then faced his family and held up his glass. "A toast to Willow Pond."

"To all of us," Lucille put in.

"To rolling in dough," Henry amended crassly, lifting his shot glass of orange juice.

"To Sparkling Sonoma," Grace offered.

Ah You was a teetotaler, but today he was making an exception. Holding up his bubbling flute, he cried, *"Mazel tov!"*